The IVORY DUCHESS

DELIA PARR

St. Martin's Paperbacks

THE IVORY DUCHESS

Copyright © 1997 by Mary Lechleidner.

ISBN: 0-312-96213-4

Printed in the United States of America

St. Martin's Paperbacks edition / June 1997

10 9 8 7 6 5 4 3 2 1

Dedicated to my sisters
Patricia, Susan, Carol, and Joanne
and my brother, John,
but most especially to our sister
Kate,
one of God's precious angels
who watches over us all.

Prologue

As far as Kate was concerned, the instrument encased in gleaming mahogany was the most ingenious torture device ever invented.

Seated squarely beneath the menacing shadow of her guardian, she continued her rehearsal on the grand piano—for the sixth grueling hour. Spasms twisted the muscles in her neck and back. Numbness tickled at her arms and legs. Needles of pain pricked her fingers, yet she persevered, clinging to her resolve to silently endure . . . until this day's torment ended and yet another began as she prepared for her well-publicized debut on the London stage as the Ivory Duchess.

Dazed with exhaustion after a year-long Continental tour, she blinked back tears as her hands moved by rote over the keyboard. The ivory and onyx keys blurred into a gray cloud that swirled and blended with the cold mist of misery that chilled her heart.

Struggling to find release in the mystical realm of her favorite sonata, she began the first movement of Beethoven's *Hammerklavier* Sonata Number Twenty-Nine. Instead of comfort or peace, however, the pure and lyrical melody unleashed a deluge of resentment for the pianoforte that churned through her spirit.

The pianoforte.

It had seduced her, transporting her to a world of beauty and delight only to betray her, transforming the gift of her natural talent into a curse that now darkened every day of her life. Drudgery laced each hour of rehearsal. Dread preceded each performance. Shame, inspired by the mystery and scandal that surrounded her stage persona, sentenced her to a life without truth or honor, even though the elaborate costume of veils held in place by her trademark cameo brooch hid her face and form from the audience.

A knot tightened in her chest. Had her love for the music that had flowed from deep within her heart to the keys of the pianoforte also been destroyed?

Distracted by the depth of her disillusionment, her fingers stumbled over a series of difficult chords. Discordant notes crashed together, and she faltered as panic sent tremors racing to the tips of her fingers.

''Stop!''

Kate jerked and her hands froze in midair. Her heart thudded in her chest, and fear sucked the air out of her lungs as ominous silence swallowed the last echo of her guardian's command.

A zealous taskmaster, Simon pounded his fist on the piano. His eyes blazing with contempt, he leaned toward her. Imposingly tall and darkly handsome, he had always intimidated her with his strict and forbidding nature. After he had arranged her first concert tour last year, his explosive temper had turned her practice sessions into a series of nightmares.

Instinctively shrinking back into a subordinate posture, she lowered her head and dropped her hands to her lap. Resisting the powerful urge to massage some feeling back into her hands or to offer an excuse for the mental lapse that had caused her poor rehearsal, she braced for her guardian's wrath.

Simon tipped her face up and held one finger under her chin to force her to meet his angry gaze. "Begin again," he growled.

Gulping down the lump in her throat, Kate nodded once as a single tear trickled down each cheek.

"And this time, don't paw the keyboard! Use a little finesse! This is the London stage waiting for you. London! Do you intend to convince them the only talent the Ivory Duchess possesses is between the sheets?"

He hissed and dropped his hold on her. Her cheeks flaming, Kate tensed as the sound of rustling skirts broke through the thumping of her heartbeat.

Simon's wife, Helen, rose from her window seat and approached them carrying a bowl of sugarplums. Fashionably slender with striking red hair, she moved quickly to her husband's side and patted his arm. She placed the crystal bowl on top of the grand piano and frowned at Kate. "Sit up straight," she murmured. "Wipe away your tears."

"I'm sorry," Kate whispered, wondering why Helen had decided to speak up instead of maintaining her usual ambivalence during rehearsals. Squaring her shoulders, Kate brushed her cheeks dry with shaking hands and took a deep breath. She swallowed yet another lump in her throat, too weary to consider how much longer her rehearsal would be prolonged if she dared to ask for a brief respite. Desperation, however, overrode past experience. "May I . . . may I please rest? Just . . . just for a little while?"

"Rest? After a rehearsal that rivals the worst I've ever heard?" Simon took a step away from his wife and his eyes narrowed to slits of black disdain. "I'm not moved by your tears or your apology or your . . . your lazy nature. Despite your experience on the stage, you still lack self-discipline and can't resist the urge to daydream—which has been blatantly obvious for the past three days.''

"Concentrate on the music," Helen suggested, softly offering criticism more constructive than her husband. "Remember everything Monsieur LeBlanc taught you. It's not enough to play flawlessly. You have to *move* your audience with your performance, not bore them—''

"Or insult them with mediocrity." Simon glanced down at his wife and took a deep breath before looking at Kate. "Do you understand what we're saying?"

His gentled tone echoed frustration instead of anger, and Kate gulped hard, praying his outburst had truly been spent. "Y-yes. Yes, of course. I'm . . . I'm sorry."

"Start the sonata over. If you manage to finish without making a mistake, you may help yourself to a sugarplum," Helen offered with surprising generosity. She looped her arm with her husband's. "Simon and I will be in the next room." She tipped her head back and smiled up at her husband. "I have something to show you," she whispered, cajoling a reluctant smile from her husband.

They turned their backs to Kate and walked from the room. When the door slammed shut and the outside lock clicked into place, she trembled with relief. The sweet scent of the sugarplums caught on a breeze from the open window and drifted down to her. Stomach growling, she refused to succumb to temptation and add disobedience to the long list of complaints already filed against her today.

Buoyed, instead, by this unexpected reprieve from Simon and Helen's suffocating presence, Kate arched her back and stretched her limbs. With her hands poised above the keyboard, she took several deep breaths and stared at the magnificent grand piano before her. Longing, pure and sweet, filled her heart. Was it too late to stem her growing aversion for this instrument, find a way to immerse herself in her music, and escape the loneliness that etched her existence?

Tears welled in her eyes as she struggled to reach deep within her own heart, searching for a place that Helen and Simon had not destroyed. There had to be one small corner where she might rediscover the joy she had once had as a child when she still had her beloved grandmother, her pianoforte . . . and her dreams.

Determined, she furrowed her brow, harnessing all her energy into intense concentration. Deliberately composed to test and explore the dynamic potential of the pianoforte, the sonata had a mystical and spiritual quality she longed to claim, if only to soothe her troubled spirit. She closed her eyes as she lowered her hands to the keyboard to heighten the power of her senses. The keys felt cool beneath her fingers as she began to play the strong, deep opening chords. Tentative at first, rich, vibrant notes soon filled the room, tempting her, daring her to open her heart and allow the beauty and joy that had eluded her under Simon's guardianship these past six years to reenter.

Gradually, like small beams of shimmering sunlight struggling to break through an overcast sky, the notes became playful and coalesced into vivid, sonorous music that dissipated the agony of her discontent and began to heal the hurts of the past. Joy, dazzling in its intensity, beckoned to her and offered her the gift of precious freedom from the shame and grief that had consumed her for far too long.

As the spirited allegro in the third movement gentled to an aching, flowing melody, a spark of hope flickered in her spirit. Fueled by her newfound peace, hope flared into brilliant flames that reduced her despair to ashes and warmed every corner of her heart with a glowing vision of a future very different from the one Simon and Helen had planned for Kate.

Miraculously, one word seemed to whisper through the mellifluous music that filled the room: *escape.*

Escape?

Heart pounding and breathless with impossible wonder, she dared to consider the idea that she could actually defy Simon and Helen and live a respectable life of her own choosing.

Escape.

The idea was so frightening, her eyes blinked open. Glancing at the locked door, she shook her head. She had little hope of running away now. Not with her London debut only nights away. Always diligent, Simon and Helen had become fanatical, locking her in her room at night and making sure she never left a room unattended.

She was only seventeen. She had no one to help her. No one beyond the walls of this estate even knew she still existed. She had no coins and nowhere to go if she did.

Escape.

The word echoed with every beat of her heart, and her mind began to race with excitement that refused to be intimidated by the very real obstacles that made escape seem incredible. Impossible. Or was it?

She shook her head again, knowing there was virtually no chance she could escape unless she won the battle that warred in her own soul. She urged the sonata toward a stunning conclusion, vowing that one day she *would* escape, but only after she had found a way to make peace with her only helpmate: her piano.

Only time—and the depth of her own courage—would prove whether or not the piano was truly her nemesis or a faithful guide that would one day lead her back into a world where mistakes might be forgiven and dreams once lost could be redeemed.

Chapter 1

Had the young woman become lost or stranded?

More curious than alarmed, Maggie Gresham held aside the heavy curtain on the front parlor window and studied the young woman pacing around a trunk at the end of the walkway that led to their front door. Unexpected visitors were as rare as company, but travelers almost never stopped along the roadway that ran in front of the cottage she shared with her older sister, Dolly. Of average height, the slender girl carried herself with uncommon grace. The brim of her straw bonnet hid her features, but she appeared to be young and clearly troubled.

Maggie glanced at the door, but quickly dismissed the urge to go outside alone to speak to a stranger. Dolly would certainly disapprove, and Maggie did not want to interrupt her sister who had just sat down for her morning session at the pianoforte.

When the girl paused and looked directly down the length of the walkway, Maggie instantly dropped the curtain back into place. By the time she had stilled her racing heartbeat and silenced her scolding conscience long enough to chance another peek, the girl had taken a seat on the trunk. Her cape and bonnet lay beside her, and bright sunlight danced in dark brown hair neatly pulled into a knot at the nape of her neck.

Intrigued, Maggie watched as the girl turned and pulled a letter of some sort out of her cape pocket. Her brows furrowed as she read the letter, sighed, and bowed her head. The minutes dragged interminably, and Maggie wondered if the girl would ever leave her perch on the trunk. In the very next heartbeat, she stood up, brushed the wrinkles from her cape, wiped the road dust from her shoes, and smoothed her hair. After donning her cape and bonnet, she squared her shoulders, turned, and started walking—directly toward the cottage.

Startled, Maggie dropped the curtains back into place again and stepped back away from the window. She turned and glanced nervously at her sister who was in the music room seated at the pianoforte with her back to the parlor. Totally immersed in her playing, she was oblivious to her surroundings. What would it hurt to step outside and help the poor child? Certain she could have the young woman on her way without Dolly ever knowing a thing, Maggie tiptoed her way to the front door, her steps covered by the melodious music that filled the cottage. She paused at the door, trying to decide what she would tell Dolly on the odd chance her sister discovered she had gone outside alone to speak with a stranger.

Kate took determined steps down the walkway and slipped her hand into her pocket to wrap her fingers around the letter that had inspired her desperate flight to this humble dwelling. Since Simon and Helen routinely confiscated any correspondence directed to the Ivory Duchess, the fact a new maid had given her several letters from admirers, including this one, convinced her the maid was truly an angel in disguise—an angel sent to help her to escape.

A small twinge of guilt tugged at her conscience. When Simon had found out Kate had several letters given to her

by the maid, he had fired her immediately and forced Kate
to turn the forbidden letters over to him. Returning all of
them except this one had been risky, but he had never suspected she would have had the courage to defy him.

Her heart began to pound with anticipation as visions of
her hopes and dreams danced from her mind's eye to swell
within her heart.

Sanctuary.

Would she find sanctuary here in this rural, pristine setting? Would she be able to begin her new life here, far
from the decadent world of the stage she had abandoned?

When she reached the front door of the cottage, sunshine
splayed on her shoulders and warmed the chill that raced
up her spine. Taking a deep breath, she raised her hand to
knock on the door, but her arm froze in midair as the first
notes of Mozart's Sonata Number Sixteen in B Flat Major
filtered gently into the natural stillness that surrounded the
cottage.

She lowered her arm to her side, reluctant to interrupt
the pianist. The pounding of her heart eased into a softer
cadence as she closed her eyes and listened intently to the
melody. Of modest talent, the player nevertheless demonstrated competence far beyond the student level. The intan-
gible yet unmistakable essence of love for the pianoforte
laced each movement of the sonata and echoed the very
same joy that Kate had discovered so many years ago and
worked so hard to rediscover and reclaim for herself.

Immersed in a reverie induced by the powerful sonata,
her eyes blinked open with surprise when the door swung
open, and she flinched. A slightly built woman with crystal
blue eyes and silver-frosted brown hair put one finger to
her lips and stepped outside, closing the door behind her.

"I saw you coming down the path," she said softly. "Is
there something I can do to help you?"

Kate's heart began to race. "I hope so. I've come to see

Miss Dahlia Gresham. The driver said this was her cottage.''

The woman's smile was warm, but the expression in her eyes was guarded. "We don't often have visitors."

Kate swallowed hard. "I have a letter Miss Gresham sent to the . . . to the Ivory Duchess several weeks ago." The infamy of her stage persona was strong enough to trip her heartbeat and sully the beauty of her surroundings. A heated blush crept up her neck and across her cheeks as she took the short missive out of her pocket and handed it to the woman.

Shaking her head, the woman frowned. "Dolly is busy right now, but maybe I can help you. My eyesight isn't what is used to be. Why don't you read the letter to me, dear?''

"Yes. Of course." Kate gulped hard. She had hoped to be able to speak to Dahlia Gresham directly, but the woman who greeted Kate seemed to be kind and very interested in helping her. She started to read the letter aloud, although every word had been branded into her memory.

I read newspaper accounts of your recent benefit performance at the Westfield Conservatory in New York—a noble endeavor that should help to silence your critics. Your generosity is exceeded only by your talent which one day will be rewarded with the respect you deserve.

Although my sister and I were unable to attend your recent tour in Philadelphia, my sister and I were privileged to enjoy your performance there last year. I feel we share a mutual love for the pianoforte, and I pray you will forgive my boldness for burdening you with a request for your assistance.

"Oh, yes!" the woman interrupted, her eyes sparkling. "What a wonderful performance! We don't get to the city

often, but Dolly insisted . . . Oh, dear. I'm sorry," she said
softly. "I didn't mean to interrupt you. Please go on."

Kate nodded, growing hopeful when she realized the
woman must be the sister mentioned in the letter. Without
any time to reflect further, she read the part of the letter
that was ever so critical for her future.

> *Torn between duty to my beloved sister and my
> students, circumstances nevertheless dictate my im-
> mediate retirement as a teacher of the pianoforte. To
> my great distress, I have been unable to find a suit-
> able replacement. Responsibility weighs heavy on my
> heart, and I am deeply troubled to think my students
> will be denied the opportunity to continue their in-
> struction.*
>
>   *If you know of a young woman in need of a proper
> home and willing to share her talent and devotion to
> the pianoforte with my students, I would be forever
> in your debt if you would send her to me that I might
> interview her for the position. To that end I have
> included directions to my home. I would, of course,
> be honored to come to Philadelphia to discuss this
> with you first before you finish your tour and present
> letters of reference at that time.*
>   *Respectfully,*
>   *Miss Dahlia Gresham*

She let out a sigh and looked up at the woman. "Do you
think your sister might be able to see me? I'm very interested in the position."

Eyes twinkling, the woman smiled. "You hold onto your
letter and come with me." She took Kate by the hand and
led her into the cottage. They walked through a modestly
appointed sitting room and an archway that led to a small
music room. With her back to the parlor, a well-rounded

woman with white hair fashioned into a chignon continued to play on a handsome square pianoforte encased in gleaming rosewood, totally oblivious to anything beyond her music.

Smiling, the woman settled Kate into a cushioned, high-backed chair just inside the room before taking her own seat in an identical chair to Kate's right. After folding her hands, the woman settled back and closed her eyes as she swayed rhythmically from side to side.

Intrigued by the woman's curious behavior, Kate ventured a quick study of the room. Tall, narrow windows flanked a brick fireplace on the outside wall and flooded the room with natural sunlight. A metronome, standing silently on duty for students, rested on one side of the pianoforte. A mahogany sideboard held a stack of music books and a sturdy coatrack stood sentry in the far corner.

Walls painted a pale shade of blue matched the background of the floral design in the area rug in the center of the room, and Dahlia Gresham's poignant interpretation of the sonata resonated as softly as a breeze that rustled the delicate first petals of spring flowers. When Kate recognized the opening notes of the final movement, she struggled to keep her heartbeat from racing.

With little time left for reflection, she mentally compared the information in the letter with what she had observed in her brief time inside the cottage. Something was awry, yet she was hard-pressed to determine exactly what it was that tugged at her consciousness. She slipped her hand into her cape pocket and clutched the letter with her fingers. The music room had clearly been arranged to accommodate student instruction so it did not appear that Dahlia had misrepresented her intentions in the letter. Kate glanced at the woman seated next to her. Dahlia had cited duty to her sister as the reason for her forced retirement, yet the woman sitting next to Kate was the very image of health.

Had Dahlia made a deliberate misstatement about the reason for her retirement? If she had, what else in the letter might be untrue? Was there actually a position available, or had Dahlia used that possibility as a ruse, hoping for a chance to meet the Ivory Duchess?

When the last echo of the end notes faded, the woman who had welcomed Kate into the cottage sat up and winked at Kate. "I have a surprise for you, Dolly," she announced with a broad smile.

Kate held her breath, hoping that Dahlia would be as welcoming as her sister.

"Surprise? It's a bit early in the day for surprises," Dolly quipped as she began to play a new piece without turning around.

The woman next to Kate frowned. "Aren't you curious? Just a tad?"

Halting midmeasure, Dolly turned around slowly in her seat. "Maggie, you know how much I enjoy my music. Can't it wait until—" With upraised brows, Dolly sucked in her breath. Her gaze met and briefly locked with Kate's before settling on the other woman. "What's going on, Maggie?"

Giggling like a schoolgirl, Maggie clapped her hands together, apparently undaunted by the stern look on Dolly's face. "I knew you'd be surprised! You were so intent on your music, you never heard us come in."

"And just who—"

"Why, she's your replacement, of course. The Ivory Duchess sent her to us. Isn't that right, Miss . . . Miss . . . Oh, dear. I . . . I didn't even get your name," she stammered as she glanced hesitantly at Kate.

"Danaher. Kathryn Danaher," she replied quickly to ease the woman's distress. A faint blush warmed her cheeks. "My . . . my gram called me Kate," she offered spontaneously. With her fingers trembling, she smoothed out the creases in the letter, rose, and handed it to Dolly. "I apologize for interrupting. You play quite beautifully," she offered, aware that all of Dolly's attention was riveted on the letter.

A glimmer of recognition flashed through Dolly's eyes as she pursed her lips. "Are you truly here to interview for the position?"

Swallowing hard, Kate took a deep breath. "Yes, I am. That is . . . if the position hasn't been filled—"

"Of course it hasn't been filled," Maggie interjected. She came to stand alongside Kate and smiled.

Dolly pursed her lips and shook her head. "Perhaps you should tell me why you answered a knock at the door without me."

Although Dolly's reprimand was gentle, Kate still felt a surge of guilt for causing a misunderstanding between the two sisters. Dolly's suggestion, however, that Maggie was not capable of answering the door without assistance gave some credence to the concern expressed in the letter, although Kate was still at a loss to explain what exactly might be so wrong with Maggie that Dolly would be forced to retire.

Maggie, however, simply laughed softly. "I didn't answer her knock. Just before you started to play, I noticed Miss Danaher—Kate—pacing around a trunk at the end of the walkway. Since we don't take students as boarders, I thought she might be stranded or lost. She looked to be a proper young woman. Stopped to freshen her hair and wipe her shoes before she came to the door. Didn't you, Kate?"

Kate felt the blood drain from her face. Maggie had been observing her? "Well, yes. I did want to—"

"I know how you feel about being interrupted when you sit down to play in the morning," Maggie continued, ignoring Kate, "so I went to the door before she had a chance to knock and there she was—listening to you play. She had such rapture on her face. When she read me the letter you had sent to the Ivory Duchess, I just knew she was the kind of young woman you were hoping the Ivory Duchess would send. That's when I ushered the girl inside. Isn't that right, Kate?''

Already feeling like Maggie's ally, Kate nodded her agreement. ''When I heard you begin to play, I was reluctant to distract you by knocking. Mozart's sonatas are difficult pieces. You play with such emotion. I enjoyed listening to you. Please don't be upset with your sister on my account. I . . . I should have insisted on waiting outside until you were finished your practice.''

Dolly shook her head. ''Magnolia, one of these days your curious soul will be your undoing. And mine. But I should think there's no harm done.'' She looked directly at Kate. ''How did you find your way to our cottage?''

Her daring escape from the hotel in Philadelphia where she had been staying with Simon and Helen to travel to this humble dwelling had not been easy, but living in a run-down boarding-house along the riverfront had nearly shattered her nerves. During those first precious days of freedom, she had been consumed with fear and so obsessed with making sure Simon and Helen did not find her she had abandoned her real name and adopted Danaher as an alias. Just last night at midnight, she had slipped aboard the last ferry from Philadelphia to Camden and huddled against the railing, praying that no one had followed her. She pushed the dark memories of her flight aside and ventured a smile. ''Oh, I took the ferry from the city and then traveled by coach.''

Maggie clucked and shook her head. ''Was the trip tiresome?''

Kate trembled and pressed against the back of the chair. Too frightened to leave her garret room, except for a single meal each day, Kate had spent every day in a constant state of fear. The sound of every male voice and every footstep had sent her heartbeat racing into a panicked rhythm until she realized it was not Simon or someone he had hired to find her. With nightmares robbing her of sleep, and her days filled with anxiety, she functioned on sheer determination to live life on her own terms. "No. Not very tiresome," she answered, trying to keep her voice steady.

"I don't travel much anymore, but if memory serves me right, you could probably stand some refreshment," Maggie suggested. She took Kate's cape and bonnet and hung them on the coatrack. "You two get acquainted while I brew a fresh pot of tea." She patted Kate's arm before leaving through a door that apparently led to the kitchen.

Still clutching the letter, Dolly got to her feet and nodded toward the two, now-empty chairs. "Perhaps you can tell me how you came to be recommended by the Ivory Duchess. I was hoping to discuss this with her myself before she sent anyone, however . . ."

Moistening her lips, Kate took her seat again and waited for Dolly to join her before attempting an answer that would soften Dolly's obvious disappointment. "I . . . I met her only once. Briefly. At an audition in Philadelphia for . . . for a position as a pianist to stand by in case she became ill and was unable to perform."

A frown creased Dolly's lips. "Then you weren't a student at one of the conservatories where the Ivory Duchess performed benefits?"

"No," she replied, concerned that if she named a conservatory, her lie would quickly unravel when she could not produce a letter of reference.

"But you have worked with the Ivory Duchess. You know her."

"Not exactly," Kate murmured. "I wasn't hired for the position at the theater because frankly, I just wasn't skilled enough to be a concert pianist, but after the audition, the

Ivory Duchess spoke to me. She said I played with great promise and suggested I enroll at a conservatory for further training. When I explained my circumstances, which precluded such an expense, she gave me the letter you sent to her several weeks ago and suggested I contact you."

"I should have thought the Duchess at the least would have written a letter of reference."

Kate's heart began to pound. Dolly kept her gaze steady and almost accusatory, and Kate tried not to panic. "The Duchess had to leave unexpectedly. She did ask me to express her regret that she had not had time to personally respond to your letter."

Dolly's cheeks flushed a light shade of pink. "I wasn't sure she would even consider my request, but I was hoping to speak to her . . . well, it's not important now."

Kate smiled. "Have you only recently decided to retire?"

"Our lifelong companion, Anne, died in February. Now that she's gone . . ." As though unwilling to continue revealing details she considered beyond Kate's concern, Dolly stiffened her spine. "Even if the Ivory Duchess did refer you for the position, I wonder about your parents. Do they approve of your leaving home?"

The question quickened Kate's pulse. It had not occurred to her that Dahlia Gresham would be interested in knowing about Kate's parents. "My parents died when I was very young. I was raised by my grandmother." She lowered her gaze for a moment as tears welled in her eyes. "Gram passed on several years ago."

She blinked back her tears and met Dolly's gaze as her mind raced to invent a suitable explanation for her interest in the position. "Last year I came to Philadelphia hoping to be married, only to discover that the man who had stolen my heart was already married. With no funds left to return home, I needed to find a way to support myself. I found work as a day maid, but when I saw the announcement for the audition at the theater, I simply had to respond.''

''Then at least you can supply references from your employer.''

''I'm sorry. No. I left rather . . . rather abruptly.'' Kate deliberately eased her voice into a whisper hoping Dolly would not press her further about her background.

Relieved when Dolly's questions led to a discussion of Kate's training on the pianoforte, Kate could hear the rattle of dishes as Maggie worked in the adjoining room to ready their tea. Then the noises stopped. Dolly grew distracted and frequently checked the doorway with concern etching her expression. After several minutes passed, Kate was not surprised when Dolly politely excused herself to check on her sister.

When neither sister returned and there were no sounds coming from the kitchen, Kate grew curious. She went to the doorway and peered into a homey kitchen. A teapot sat on a tray with three delicate china cups in the center of a lace-covered table. A tea kettle on the cookstove hissed a shaky flow of steam into the air, but with her back to the room, Maggie stood still and silent looking out of a window above the sink.

Dolly was standing next to Maggie with her arms around her sister's shoulders, and Kate watched her turn Maggie away from the window.

Kate saw the change that had taken place in Maggie and nearly gasped out loud. Her eyes were glazed, and she stared into space. Dreamy-eyed and serene, she apparently had slipped away into another world, and any doubt that Dolly had to retire to care for her sister quickly melted away because it appeared that Maggie Gresham might be daft.

''Maggie, dear. It's time for our tea,'' Dolly murmured,

adding other soothing words that Kate could not make out.

With a start, Maggie's eyes filled with confusion. Her lips quivered, and she began to weep. "I did it again. Didn't I?"

"It's all right. It was just a little spell. There's no harm done. You're fine now," Dolly reassured her.

"No harm done," Maggie repeated in a ragged whisper that tugged at Kate's heartstrings. "This time."

Fascinated, Kate watched as Dolly led Maggie away from the window and into a seat at the table.

The letter. Understanding rushed into Kate's mind with the sudden fury of a squall. If Dolly had not checked on her sister, the kitchen could easily have caught on fire. No wonder Dolly had been unable to find a young woman to replace her as a teacher of the pianoforte! Only someone like Kate, who had more to fear from the world she had left behind than from the unsettling prospect of living with a brain-sick woman who was dangerous to others as well as to herself, would even consider accepting the position Dolly had described in the letter.

Sanctuary.

In the space of a single heartbeat, Kate knew that her first impressions of the humble cottage in the woods had been far more prophetic than she could have imagined.

Kate was not the only one who had sought sanctuary here. If that knowledge left her shaken, knowing that she had no place else in the world to go left her feeling as vulnerable as the woman weeping in her sister's protective embrace.

And more determined than ever to stay.

As though sensing Kate's intrusive presence, Dolly looked up and stared at Kate, her eyes hard with censure.

Acting decisively and on pure instinct, Kate entered the kitchen and set a fresh kettle of water to boil. Turning to face both women, she caught a glimpse of the garden just outside the kitchen window and smiled gently. ''Perhaps you can describe the duties of the position in more detail while we share a cup of tea, and then I'll play for you.''

Chapter 2

This was the first audition Kate was tempted to deliberately fail.

Hands poised above the keyboard, Kate briefly closed her eyes, slowly winning the struggle to regain control of her runaway heartbeat. Her legs trembled beneath her skirts, and she pressed her feet against the solid planes of the floor to still them. She could not, however, harness the dissonant concerns about the position as Dolly's replacement that crashed through her mind with a power Beethoven would have envied. She lowered her hands and wiped them on her skirts.

Over a cup of tea, Dolly and Maggie had both calmed Kate's concerns about Maggie's spells. An affliction that had obviously destined a secluded life for Maggie, the spells had increased in both occurrence and severity as Maggie had aged. Imagining how cruel people could be when faced with a mental disorder that might conjure up charges of witchcraft or worse against an innocent victim like Maggie sent chills down Kate's spine, and her admiration for Dolly for protecting her sister grew into deep respect. As someone who was also vulnerable to public disdain, Kate offered genuine sympathy and understanding which quickly eased the spinsters' concerns about Kate's discovery of the secret they had kept hidden from everyone else.

She considered deliberately failing the audition because the very idea of replacing Dolly as an instructor of the pianoforte unleashed apprehensions that threw Kate into a maze of confusion.

Miss Dolly, as Kate had been instructed to address Dahlia Gresham, was not a typical teacher of the pianoforte. Kate had expected a position where she would receive students in Dolly and Maggie's home. In rural Delaware Township, however, there were simply not enough students to guarantee even a modest living—a reality that in hindsight, Kate should have noticed when she arrived. While Dolly did in fact have several students who lived close enough to come for instruction, she had managed to support her sister and herself by instructing students who lived within a thirty-mile radius of the cottage in a very unique manner.

Two weeks out of every month, Dolly traveled the roadways that connected a number of small settlements and sprawling homesteads in southern New Jersey. Like an itinerant circuit preacher of earlier days who spread the good news of the Gospel, Dolly shared her love for the increasingly popular pianoforte. By exchanging room and board with some students and their families, Dolly was able to teach other nearby students and charged such modest fees that nearly every man who could afford to purchase even a used pianoforte was able to provide his wife or children with Dolly's instruction.

Thoroughly convinced her talent was meant to be shared, Dolly accepted payment in kind as well as hard coin. Only the increasing severity of Maggie's spells, which made it dangerous for her to be left alone, forced Dolly into retirement.

Kate took several small breaths of air and repositioned her hands above the keyboard. As unique as the position Dolly held might be, it was also far too dangerous for Kate to consider for herself. Constant traveling and meeting so many new families opened up too many opportunities for Simon and Helen to learn of her whereabouts. It was dangerous and far too risky.

Yet what other choice did Kate have?

Instinctively, she pressed one arm against her side to reassure herself that the trademark brooch she had worn when performing as the Ivory Duchess was still safely pinned to her chemise. A stunning cameo surrounded by clusters of diamonds set in a platinum filigree frame, the brooch was extremely valuable in its own right. As the Ivory Duchess' famous brooch it was invaluable.

Guilt dug its claws into Kate's conscience.

She had stolen the brooch when she made her escape, but only as a desperate act of self-preservation. Simon could not report her disappearance to local authorities without risking a scandal that every newspaper from Boston to Charleston would exploit to increase their own circulation. He could, however, hire an investigator—provided he had the funds to do so, and Kate took the brooch to ensure he did not.

In spite of her good intentions to one day return the brooch, she wondered now if she should pawn it or try to sell it. Then she would not need a position at all. With the funds she received, she could flee to Europe and disappear forever.

Not a viable choice—even if she could silence her own rigid sense of right and wrong.

She simply could not take the risk. Any jeweler of note on either side of the Atlantic would recognize the Ivory Duchess' brooch. Even if the jeweler accepted Kate as the rightful owner, once the brooch was pawned or sold, the most novice of investigators would then be able to trace her movements.

Which meant she had no choice at all.

She had to win this audition and play convincingly so that one day in the future when Simon and Helen presented no danger to Kate, she could return the brooch.

With her conscience silenced, she turned sideways on the piano bench and glanced at Dolly and Maggie who had taken their seats in the side-by-side chairs. "Is there a selection you prefer?"

Dolly nodded approvingly, and Kate knew she had been right to allow Dolly the opportunity to control the audition.

Beaming, Maggie spoke up before her sister had the chance to utter a word. "I love Beethoven's *Für Elise*. The Ivory Duchess opens her performances with it." She cocked her head toward her sister. "I would love to hear Kate play that, too, wouldn't you?"

"An excellent idea. For the first selection," Dolly agreed, deferring to her sister but clearly preserving her authority. "When properly played, Beethoven's music is balm for the soul. Mozart, on the other hand, presents a great test of skill for the fingers. Especially for students."

Confident that she could play Beethoven and Mozart to Dolly's satisfaction, Kate turned back to the keyboard with nary another word. She straightened her back and rested her right foot lightly on a pedal. Although Simon had been quite adamant about using *Für Elise* as the opening selection for each performance, it was also one of Gram's favorite pieces. Playing it now for Dolly and Maggie would evoke loving memories of Gram instead of her performances as the Ivory Duchess, and Kate realized that Maggie had that same guileless innocence that had made Gram such an extraordinary and loving woman.

"For you, Gram," she whispered and began to play the first measures with great restraint. Unlike other performances in auditions Simon had arranged for her, however, in this performance Kate had to be very careful not to display more than a modest talent for the pianoforte. She furrowed her brow and concentrated hard, holding back on the cascading notes, yet occasionally giving free rein to her emotions as she played. She stumbled once, deliberately, in an effort to appear to be more of a novice than she really was.

Given the state of her nerves, it was not all that difficult.

She had barely finished when Dolly requested a sonata written by Liszt. Works by Schumann and Wagner followed. Kate hesitated only briefly between selections and stopped just once to sip a glass of water. After enduring Simon's brutal practice regimen and auditions before petulant theater owners, Kate found this audition to be no less intense, and never far from her mind was the deeply troubling worry that she might not be playing well enough to prove worthy of the position she needed so desperately.

Or was she playing too well?

So well she might cast suspicion on her true identity since Dolly and Maggie had attended the Ivory Duchess' performance in Philadelphia last year? With her back to both women, Kate had no idea how they were reacting to her performance, and only her stoicism kept her from a swoon.

"Thank you, Kate," Dolly finally remarked, officially ending the audition.

Kate smiled when she heard the clapping of hands. *Dear, sweet Maggie.* She had already stolen Kate's heart.

Tired but not exhausted after an hour of nonstop playing, Kate flexed shoulders aching with tension. Her pulse pounded in her temples, and she rose to face the Gresham sisters praying to find approval in their expressions.

Maggie did not disappoint her. She dabbed her eyes with a handkerchief and gave Kate a tremulous smile. "Lovely, my dear. Just as lovely as the Ivory Duchess. Don't you find it hard to imagine that the sordid rumors about her could be true? How could she possibly play like an angel on stage and afterwards entertain men—''

''Hush,'' Dolly snapped. Her lips stretched taut, and her eyes narrowed. ''Kate's performance was quite adequate,'' she pronounced. ''A bit more than adequate, perhaps.''

Silence whispered its eerie presence, and gooseflesh wrinkled Kate's flesh. Had she played too well and given Dolly cause to guess the truth—that Kate was really the Ivory Duchess? Feeling more than touched by paranoia, she took a deep breath to clear her thoughts. More than likely, she reasoned, Dolly was just facing the prospect of her own retirement with dismay now that she had found a suitable replacement—assuming she was willing to offer Kate the position.

She held very still, nearly too afraid to breathe while she waited for Dolly to say more. Anything. Something. Still, Dolly offered nothing more.

Pale and drawn, she finally rose, ignored Kate, and addressed her sister. ''Please show Kate to her room and help her to unpack. I have a blistering headache and need to take to my bed before I can discuss Kate assuming the position. On a trial basis.'' Without a single word to Kate, Dolly walked primly from the room.

Startled by Dolly's rebuff, Kate lowered her gaze. When Maggie remained silent for several minutes, Kate ventured a glance at Maggie hoping for a smile of support. She took one look at the elderly woman and sucked in her breath. With a peaceful, faraway look in her eyes, Maggie had quickly slipped away to that distant place where others could not follow.

Kate stood there, alone, with only her hopes and dreams—and her beloved pianoforte—for comfort.

Nagging fear gripped her heart. She had just received permission to stay, and only time would reveal whether she truly had found sanctuary here or she had fallen victim to her own imagination.

Three weeks later, Kate returned from completing her first circuit. The position was all that Kate had dared to hope it would be. And more. So much more that she was convinced she had truly found the sanctuary she needed. She gave Dolly and Maggie a complete accounting of her time which included a number of well-wishes for Dolly. Parcels of fresh fruit and vegetables lined the counter next to the kitchen sink. Letters and notes from some of Dolly's former students or their parents lay stacked on the table next to a small burlap purse stuffed with coins.

And callouses covered Kate's hands.

Seated at the kitchen table with the Gresham sisters, Kate sat back and soaked her pitiful hands in a bowl filled with glycerine and rosewater.

"I thought Dolly lent you her gloves," Maggie clucked as she added warm water to the bowl.

"Two pair," Dolly sniffed, peering over her reading glasses and pausing long enough from reading the notes Kate had brought from several students who wanted to let Dolly know how pleased they had been with her replacement. She effectively condemned Kate with no more than a scowl.

Sighing, Kate could not help comparing the spinsters' reactions to those Simon and Helen would have had if Kate had been careless enough to clip a fingernail too short, let alone have a palm full of callouses. It was like comparing exploding fireworks with gentle fireflies. She leaned back in her chair, feeling secure, if not a tad foolish. "The weather was so warm, I decided I didn't need to wear the gloves." She stifled a giggle when Dolly and Maggie exchanged horrified glances. "I know better now. At least the blisters healed well."

"Blisters? Merciful heavens, child, what kind of impression—"

"Leave her be, Dolly. Kate has natural talent and will make a fine teacher. I know she made a good impression even without reading all those notes your students sent back to you. After all is said and done, experience teaches the best lessons, and now she knows better than to drive the road cart without gloves. Don't you, Kate?"

Groaning inwardly at the host of lessons she had learned while on the circuit, Kate managed to give Maggie half a smile. For someone who had spent the last ten years secluded from all but Simon and Helen, she had fared well on the circuit. Remarkably well. It was her experience performing on stage that had given her the wherewithal to assume her new role, but it was the warm reception she had received in nearly every household that convinced her she had been blessed with the kind of life that she wanted so desperately: a respectable life.

Without scandal.

Without disgrace.

She would never have been able to see her dreams fulfilled without Dolly's short note of introduction which allowed Kate to be accepted as a proper young woman of modest means who pursued a respectable profession as an instructor of the pianoforte.

Still, her first foray into society had not been without several frightening adventures—not the least of which was learning to handle one stubborn mule named Precious.

Dolly finished reading the last note, removed her reading spectacles, and retied the stack of papers with a bit of twine. "It appears you've made a good impression. The students were pleased with your instruction."

Kate's brows lifted. "Even Mrs. Bennett?"

Maggie giggled. "I find that highly doubtful. Nothing pleases that woman. Just ask her husband. Or Dolly. Penelope Bennett could find fault with the Ivory Duchess herself. Why, if she had the slightest inkling we have a connection to the Ivory Duchess—''

"Well, she doesn't," Dolly fumed. "Gossip is the handmaiden of evil and rather beneath you, Magnolia."

Taken aback by Dolly's strong tone of voice, Kate was also surprised at how quickly Dolly had snapped at Maggie's harmless tendency to gossip. Before Kate had started off on the circuit, they had all agreed it was best not to mention how she had been referred for the position, but there was no danger discussing this amongst themselves as far as she was concerned.

Obviously, Dolly disagreed. She turned her attention to Kate, ignoring her sister. "You didn't mention the Ivory Duchess to Mrs. Bennett or anyone else, did you, Kate?"

Chills raced up Kate's spine. "Of course not. I thought . . . I mean, when anyone asked, I told them I had been referred to you by a former student." She paused and decided to be absolutely honest. "Several students did wonder if I had been to see the Ivory Duchess when she performed in Philadelphia, but I . . . I said that I hadn't. They seemed disappointed, but relished sharing the latest gossip about her."

"The Mullan girls, I presume?"

Kate nodded.

"And just exactly what did you tell Patti and Susan when they started to gossip?"

"Why, just that it was time to start the lesson."

Nodding approvingly, Dolly let out a sigh. "The girls are very difficult at times, and their interest in the Ivory Duchess should not be encouraged. They are too infatuated with the theater as it is." She paused. "As for the others, unfortunately, not everyone shares our admiration for the Duchess or her gift for the pianoforte. Scandalmongers. The whole lot of them. Why, it's a disgrace—''

"Hush now. You're getting all atwitter," Maggie crooned, seemingly recovered from her sister's reprimand. "And poor Kate is exhausted." She patted Kate's arm. "Why don't you settle in for a nap before dinner? Then Dolly and I will share some news with you."

"News?" Kate's heart began to race, and she looked expectantly at Dolly.

Stern-faced, Dolly shook her head. "Magnolia, the next time I make you promise to keep a secret, remind me not to bother." She turned to Kate. "I wanted to wait until you had rested, but my dear sister has probably tickled your imagination just enough to keep you awake with curiosity." She straightened in her chair and hardened her expression. "I know you must be disappointed at the meager funds you earn on circuit."

"Not really. I—"

"We agreed that you would keep half of what you earn in addition to receiving room and board while I'll continue to instruct local students as I have in the past. But there's one new student who would like to receive instruction at home. Since I already have a fair number of students, I thought perhaps you might be interested in conducting some lessons during the weeks you're not traveling. It's not terribly far, but you'll have to take the road cart."

"It's a great opportunity. And perfectly proper since Mrs. Spade will be working about and you won't be all alone in the house," Maggie chimed, her eyes twinkling. "Nelda Spade is the housekeeper, and she referred the student to Dolly."

Confused, Kate sat up straight and started to dry her hands. Nearly all of her students had been well-mannered young women, and although she had found several to be trying, she could not imagine needing someone else in the house during the lesson. "I'd be very interested in earning a little extra," she ventured, hoping not to appear ungrateful for her earnings on the circuit, as meager as they had turned out to be.

Freedom, the most precious gift of her position, had no price that could be matched in coin.

Dolly smiled. "I sent Mr. Massey a note suggesting you would be able to begin tomorrow. Is that too soon?"

"No," Kate lied, despite having had every intention of spending the day resting. She did not want to disappoint Dolly or appear to be lazy, but the truth of the matter was she found the prospect of having a man for a student more than a little disturbing, particularly since he was new to the area. Traveling the circuit had been difficult enough, but at least she had known all the families and students had been part of Dolly's circuit before she arrived.

A chill raced up her spine. Was it possible she had taken the brooch to make sure Simon would not have the funds to hire someone to find her, only in vain? Was Mr. Massey someone Simon had hired to find her? Would she have to run away again?

Unable to voice her real concerns, she ventured a safer question to find out more about him. "Has Mr. . . . Mr. Massey ever had instruction on the pianoforte?"

Dolly shook her head. "No. According to the note he sent, he's taken a country seat along the Delaware for the summer to escape the heat in the city. Apparently, he's intrigued by a grand piano in the drawing room. His references are in order, or I wouldn't even consider allowing you to provide instruction in his home."

"And Nelda Spade even sent along her own note," Maggie added.

Dolly's cheeks actually turned pink. "A tawdry letter full of gossip which I consigned to the fireplace as soon as I read it."

Maggie grinned. "Not before I had a chance to read it, too."

"Unfortunately." Dolly sighed and glanced at Kate. "Be careful when you talk to Mrs. Spade. She's an inveterate gossip."

Maggie leaned around her sister to get Kate's attention. "Nelda Spade's sister lives in Philadelphia, and she told Nelda all about him after he leased the property. Seems he takes off and disappears from time to time. Her sister wanted to reassure Nelda the man was well-established in the city and quite well-connected, even if he lives a bit more adventurously than most men which probably accounts for the interest he invites."

Dolly shifted in her seat, halfheartedly blocking Maggie who simply stood up. "He's a jeweler from Philadelphia," she continued. "Massey's Jewelry Emporium. Quite the finest in the city."

"Just how do you know that?" Dolly sniffed. "Another bit of Nelda Spade's gossip?"

"No. They advertise in *The West Jerseyman*. Says so right in their ad."

Instinctively, Kate pressed her arm against her side, and the brooch dug into her flesh. "A jeweler? He's accustomed to working with his hands, I suppose. How often will he expect me?"

"Every day when you're home. Since he'll only be at the country seat for the summer, the weather should be clear for driving. Unless you think it would be too taxing . . ."

Tempted by the image of a filled purse, Kate shook her head. "Not at all," she murmured, hoping the man had not attended one of her recent performances in Philadelphia, but knowing that if he had, he would certainly not recognize her. Excusing herself to take her rest, she chided herself for allowing her fear of discovery to make her suspicious of a man who wanted nothing more than a refreshing sojourn in the country and a few lessons on the pianoforte to fill his days.

Chapter 3

In the dawning rays of a new morning, Philip Massey stood just outside wide glassed doors on the second floor balcony of the country seat he had leased for the summer. Inhaling the heavy, blossom-scented air, he admired the flowering pear and apple orchards that surrounded the house. Like a medieval lord surveying his manor, he scanned the wide expanse of the Delaware River that flowed along the property's western boundary and provided a distant view of the city of Philadelphia.

And the invisible chains that bound him to his past.

Fully satisfied with the expanse of his new domain, he walked back inside and glanced around the double-roomed chamber. Royal burgundy stenciling, which mirrored the design in the Oriental carpet beneath his feet, bordered cream-colored walls. To his left, a crocheted coverlet and lace-trimmed pillows adorned a massive four-poster bed. To his right, a dressing screen decorated with an elaborate mural and an upholstered chaise lounge were positioned on either side of a tiled fireplace.

Whistling softly, he turned away and left the bedroom. He made his way down the hall past the other six chambers and descended the stairs. He went straight to the first floor drawing room where a grand piano gleamed in the early morning light that poured through floor to ceiling windows.

Polished to perfection, the carved rosewood case on the grand piano mirrored the furnishings in the room: a narrow, tufted settee, a woman's writing desk, a small sideboard with a silver tea service. The misty blue and green decor was intimate and elegant, but not overstated—a perfect setting for the daily lessons he anticipated with the instructor he had secured.

Using his reputation as an adventurer who often disappeared for months at a time on buying trips for his Uncle Harold who owned a jewelry emporium, Philip looked forward to an entire summer away from the heat and crowds in the city.

And the memories.

Not that he intended to completely stop working at his craft for the next several months. He entered the drawing room which had been rearranged to accommodate a worktable sitting in front of triple windows to catch the best morning light. The thick carpet muffled his footsteps as he walked over to the table and ran his fingers over his lapidary tools. His mind, however, was not focused on the few jewels he would cut and set into fashionable pieces over the next several months—jewels stored in the bulky safe that stood in the corner.

Satisfied that all was in order, he decided to indulge himself with a brisk morning ride before the housekeeper rose and prepared a full country breakfast and her husband started his day's work on the estate. As resident caretakers for the owner who had returned to England to settle an inheritance, the Spades expressed no interest in his daily routine beyond seeing his basic needs were met.

A bit overbearing and pretentious now that they were employed by a man soon to carry one of the lesser English titles, Abner and Nelda Spade treated Philip like a usurping commoner. He was reluctant to assert greater control over them for fear he might invoke their hostility or worse, their curiosity, which would distract him from expending all of his energy on his true purpose for coming here: to find and return the priceless brooch stolen from Simon Morrell by the Ivory Duchess.

A bitter taste soured his mouth.

Also returning the renowned performer to continue her concert tour appealed to him as much as chewing on a raw fish, but he had no other choice—if he wanted to be free at last from the scandal that had cost him his reputation and his freedom.

Glancing at his pocket watch, he decided to start work on the piece he had coerced Eldridge Bradford into ordering for his wife while waiting for the unsuspecting pianoforte instructor to arrive later this morning.

"Let the game begin," he whispered out loud, vowing that this time, the game would end very differently, and to his own advantage.

Once and for all, he would bury the past and begin to live life. On his own terms. With his head held high. All thanks to one spoiled little Duchess who had made it so easy to find her that he had the luxury of using his own name and of prolonging the game long enough to suit his own needs.

And long enough to make sure that when the game was over, she would know that she had been beaten by a master of the game: Omega.

Kate tightened her hold on the reins as Precious maneuvered around a sharp curve in the road. While the mule still balked occasionally at Kate's handling, they had reached a tentative truce, although Kate had been sure to pack several carrots—just in case Precious changed her mind. Comfortable at the reins, Kate let her thoughts wander to the note

Philip Massey had sent to Dolly requesting instruction on the pianoforte. Challenged by the opportunity to increase her earnings, Kate was anxious to rebuild the nest egg for her retirement that Simon and Helen had squandered, although she was still skittish about teaching a man to play the pianoforte.

Kate continued down Sorrel Horse Road, and after passing the small settlement of Jordantown, which consisted of a small general store and perhaps a dozen small homesteads, she increased her guard. Several miles later when she saw the landmark described in the note, she held her breath. A large boulder marked the entrance to the country seat, and she tugged on the reins with her right hand.

Seemingly agreeable, Precious turned onto a bumpy dirt path. At the top of a small rise in the distance, Kate saw the back of a large, two-story brick residence, and her eyes widened with disbelief. Compared to most of the frame farmhouses in the area, this home resembled an English country estate, and a surge of nostalgia swept through her spirit.

Memories of Gram filled her heart, and her eyes misted. It was in a home like this that Gram had raised her, although the orphaned granddaughter of the housekeeper hardly lived a leisured life. Kate had grown up with hard work as her constant companion, and she was wise enough now to be grateful instead of resentful. Resentment had fueled her impetuous nature as a child—which had led her straight into Simon's snare.

Accepting the past as lessons well-learned, she focused on the challenges of the present. Reluctant to make an embarrassing entrance, should Precious decide to reassert her independence, Kate concentrated on her driving and kept a firm hold on the reins. She passed a small caretaker's cottage and several outbuildings, all in excellent repair. Approaching the front of the house, she passed beneath the shadow of large shade trees surrounded by well-tended gardens with tender young tulips in full rainbow bloom.

Precious apparently viewed something in the gardens as a tempting midmorning treat. Kate tensed and felt the muscles in her arm strain as she refused to give the mule enough slack to get any closer. Precious ground to a halt, dangerously close to the gardens, but Kate held firm although her heart began to pound when the mule started braying. Kate clicked the reins and dug in her heels.

"Not now," she whispered as she looked up at the front of the house. The sun glared off the sharp, steepled roof, and despite the wide-brimmed bonnet she wore, she still had to use one hand to shade her eyes to get a better, close-up view. Wisps of bright yellow forsythia peeked around the sides of the redbrick house. A front porch held an assortment of chairs that all faced the river. A second floor balcony ran across the entire front facade, gently shadowing the first floor porch.

Grand in scale and design, the house had a quiet elegance that appealed to her, and she was more than a little disappointed she would not be staying here for longer than an hour each day.

She brought the road cart to a halt and climbed out, quickly looping the reins in place. As she bent forward to get the small valise that held sheet music and other teaching aids, she heard the front door open. Footsteps crossed the porch, but before she could look up, a man's voice rang out.

"Miss Danaher?"

Kate put a smile on her face. The moment she raised her eyes, however, her lips froze in place and time stood still—as though the earth had temporarily suspended her gentle rotation in the universe. She blinked twice, unable to reconcile the gentleman standing on the porch with her mental image of Philip Massey.

Since he was spending the summer in the country to escape the heat in the city and pursuing the study of the pianoforte as a way of amusing himself, she had assumed he was an older man. The man who approached her, however, was her senior by no more than a few years.

Dressed in fawn-colored trousers and a cream-colored shirt, the man carried himself with energy and purpose. He was not remarkably handsome, but he was definitely not unattractive. Of average height and lean, but muscular build, he had an aura of understated masculinity and self-confidence. As he descended the steps and escaped the shadow of the porch, shards of sunlight caught in the tea brown hair that fell to his collar, and his dark eyes twinkled with a zest for life she found most appealing. And most unsettling.

With limited experience with men, other than Simon, she felt her pulse pounding in her temples with the hope she had jumped to the wrong conclusion about his identity. "M-Mr.-M-Massey?" she stammered, tightening her one-hand hold on the valise.

As he approached the road cart, he flashed a smile that would melt a mountain range of snow. "And you are Miss Danaher, I assume?"

She nodded, unable to speak as hope beat a hasty retreat into wishful thinking. Her heart thudded in her chest, and she was convinced he thought her an idiot or a brazen hussy for staring at him so openly.

He smiled again as he reached from the other side of the road cart to take the valise she clutched with all her might. Nearly half a foot taller, he had a presence at once powerful, but nonthreatening.

He placed his hand on top of hers, and she trembled as disturbing sensations raced up her arm. Unable to move, and incapable of drawing more than shallow breaths of air, she stared at his hand. Beautifully formed, long tapered fingers trapped her own, and she felt the man's strength as well as his gentleness—even through the fabric of her gloves. His nails were neatly trimmed, and his flesh devoid of callouses or stains. He had the hand of an artisan, or more perfectly, a concert pianist, sculpted by nature's design to grace the keyboard with power and masculine elegance. For the first time, vanity fueled regret for the state of her own hands, and she was glad that her gloves covered the unsightly callouses.

"I'm so glad you were able to come. Allow me to carry this inside for you," he urged with more than a hint of amusement in his deep voice. "I'll have Abner take care of the mule for you."

She withdrew her hand as a hot blush crept up her neck and burned her cheeks. "Please don't bother anyone. She's used to staying hitched to the cart."

"Then shall we go inside?" Philip took charge of her valise and turned toward the house without waiting for her to respond.

She gulped hard and nodded, her gaze focused on the muscles that strained beneath his shirt. Simon had intimidated her with his powerful build, unusual height, and dark, handsome looks. He had used his physical size, abrasive nature, and dominating personality to control her and to frighten her into obeying him.

It had taken all of her courage to escape from him, but spending time alone with Philip Massey would require more than courage. When he was near, he made her heart skip a beat. His gaze sent warm, delicious shivers down her spine. His smile brought a warm blush to her cheeks and made her body tingle with the unfamiliar flush of physical attraction.

Gathering her skirts with one hand, she held her breath as she made her way around the road cart, up the steps, and across the porch. As she preceded him through the door and stepped over the threshold, a sudden flash of intuition warned her that her earlier, whimsical desire to spend more than an hour in the house had been a mistake.

She was already counting the minutes until she could take her leave.

Chapter 4

Philip had expected to encounter a sophisticated woman of the world, as striking as an exquisitely faceted jewel. To his amazement, he found himself in the company of an uncut gemstone. Kathryn Danaher was a rather average woman who hid all semblance of worldliness beneath a prim and unsophisticated exterior.

The idea of trimming away her facade sent excitement racing through his veins.

Blinking, he waited for his vision to adapt to the dimmer light in the foyer. Kathryn was chatting softly as she turned her gloves and bonnet over to Nelda. The housekeeper, who was frowning her displeasure at interrupting her gardening to play lady's maid, remained aloof.

Disconcerted that his preconceived image of the piano instructor had been so wrong, he studied her intently and tried to resolve the disparity between her public image, what Simon had led him to expect and what he now beheld with his own eyes.

There were no blond ringlets that fell to her shoulders as she had apparently decided not to use the wig she had worn on stage. Ebony hair that dipped in waves over her ears to be pinned into a small knot at the nape of her neck was not quite the shade Simon had described. Although slender in a form-fitting bodice of pale yellow that matched unfashionable trim skirts, she was taller than he remembered from when he had watched her performance from a balcony box long before he had accepted this assignment.

Either Simon had deliberately downplayed her ability to change her appearance or Philip had underestimated her. As a performer and entertainer, the Ivory Duchess would be able to design a number of convincing disguises, but he was quite ready to admit he had been unprepared for the image she had created for herself as much as her new name and identity. Why the woman had taken a plebeian position as an instructor of the pianoforte instead of pawning or selling the cameo brooch and slipping back across the Atlantic still had him perplexed. At the moment, however, he was still intrigued by her plain and unsophisticated image.

Perhaps he had been misled by the extraordinary costume she had worn on stage that had kept her identity hidden from audiences around the globe. In several clandestine meetings where neither Philip nor Morrell had gotten a glimpse of one another to protect Philip's real identity, Morrell had been frustratingly vague about her background and only provided the name Kathryn Baxter as one she might use. When pressed, he had thrown Omega's reputation right back at Philip and pointed out that at the sum Morrell was paying to get the Ivory Duchess back, he expected Omega to be able to find her with no clues at all about her background.

Newspapers Philip had studied to learn more about her had carried any number of tales written by adoring fans who allegedly had managed to catch a glimpse of her face. Although all of the accounts regaled her beauty, none of them had ever been the same, which only fueled more interest in the mysterious and elusive Ivory Duchess.

According to one rumor, she was an English woman who

had been debauched and quickly abandoned by a cruel duke of a husband and left to depend on her modest talent for the pianoforte to support herself. Another piece of gossip labeled her an Austrian coquette whose sexual appetites and amoral heart had shocked her aged spouse into a fatal stroke. Shortly after returning from a honeymoon, the poor man had found her abed with the stableboy and a kitchen maid. Widowed with no child-heir, the former duchess had been quickly exiled by the next of kin.

Similar rumors that varied only by region had fueled public fascination with the talented performer whose virginal veils either mocked vicious gossip or represented a total transformation of her wicked soul. Audiences filled theaters around the globe, hoping for a glimpse of her face and a firsthand look at the one common element in all the rumors: her trademark cameo brooch.

Purportedly given to her by either her late or former husband or one of her many lovers, the brooch was reputedly an heirloom, and the only clue to her real identity that Simon was willing to reveal with any precise details.

Philip tensed as Nelda took her leave and the piano instructor started to turn toward him. He knew more than the truth of her real identity. He knew the full extent of her flawed character. Morrell had stated that the woman had come to him and traded her brooch for the experience he had as a manager of a number of gifted performers. Exceeding even his own modest expectations, he had turned an unknown, penniless, and modestly talented woman into an international celebrity.

Granted, Morrell did not have the flair that P. T. Barnum used to promote Jenny Lind when she toured the world several years earlier. By the same token, Jenny Lind, who had perhaps the sweetest voice ever to grace the stage, was a woman of impeccable character while the Ivory Duchess had a rather sullied background which only worsened when she chose to disappear last month at the zenith of her second American tour, stealing the priceless brooch in the process. What kind of woman would turn on the man who had dedicated all of his energies to help her?

A traitorous, self-centered, spoiled prima donna with pretensions grand enough to be listed as the eighth wonder of the world!

Didn't his own sins of the past rank as vile?

Shaking his head, he refused to consider how much alike he and the Ivory Duchess might be. "Not anymore," he whispered half-aloud. He had changed, while she simply switched cloaks, and he took prideful pleasure just knowing that he was probably the first person, other than her devoted manager and his wife, who realized that he was seeing the unadorned face and form of the Ivory Duchess.

Although he had to bow to her talent for creating a convincing disguise, he was every bit as talented in subterfuge as she was which gave him unequaled advantage over her.

When she faced him fully, he sucked in his breath, helpless to avoid a reaction as instinctive as breathing normally. When he had stood across from her with the road cart between them, her full-brimmed bonnet had cast a shadow on her face, but now there was nothing but filtered sunlight. He gazed at her now with surprise.

On an otherwise unremarkable, but pleasant face, dark, high-arched brows accented heavy-lashed hazel eyes that sparkled with the most amazing combination of colors he had ever seen. Fern green. Sea blue. Splinters of gold. A touch of amber. Each color outshining the other and glistening with an innocence that was beguiling.

No wonder she had never appeared in public without her veils. Her eyes were distinctive enough to undermine any disguise she might have attempted, with the singular exception, perhaps, of playing a widow with a heavy black veil of mourning weeds that would cover her face.

He had always been able to discern a person's true character by reading the only physical features that could not be altered: the human eyes. They were the windows to the heart and mirrors of the soul, yet this woman had somehow managed to defy nature itself and conceal her true character.

With every beat of his heart, he knew he had met his match, and it seemed totally apropos that his final assignment as Omega would be the most challenging.

Omega.

Philip Massey.

Both identities suited him well.

For all outward appearances, Philip Massey was only a jeweler, albeit a master of his trade. To a desperate few, he was known as Omega—a jewel expert for-hire who traced and restored stolen jewelry to its rightful owners. He was the last resort for some. For those who preferred discretion over the public humiliation and scandal typically unleashed when local authorities got involved or the press reported details most old- and new-money elites preferred to keep private, he was the first.

He cleared the lump in his throat to speak to her, but before he could utter a single hoarse word, she had paused and turned toward the entrance to the drawing room. As though mesmerized, she entered the room and glided out of his view. Perplexed, the moment he entered the room, he took one look at her as she stared at the grand piano and prided himself for his uncanny ability to pierce the most ingenious disguise and cut to the essence of a person's true character in more than just one way.

Intuitively, he had known that even if Kathryn Danaher had reservations about providing the instruction on the pianoforte he had requested, the Ivory Duchess would not be able to resist the masterpiece of all pianofortes that he had acquired for this assignment.

Congratulating himself for having snared her interest, he sat her valise on the floor and walked to the far side of the piano as she ran trembling fingers over the mother-of-pearl and onyx keyboard. "Beautiful, isn't it?"

She blinked and snapped out of her reverie with a blush that stained her cheeks. "What? Oh, I'm so sorry," she murmured as she glanced up at him. "How rude of me—"

"Not at all. Your fascination is quite understandable." Chuckling, he joined her and stood in front of the instrument, his legs brushing against a hooked seat cover on the bench that was carved as ornately as the legs on the grand piano. "They say that Boardman and Gray's pianoforte with the Dolce Campana attachment is the finest instrument of its kind in the world. I believe Jenny Lind insisted on one for her tour several years ago."

"The Swedish Nightingale," she whispered.

"With the voice of an angel."

She smiled, and in spite of himself, he felt a warm tingle rush through his body.

"Boardman and Gray's pianofortes are coveted by the wealthiest of kings."

And a duchess?

He was tempted to put his thought into words, but checked the impulse. He had the entire summer to find out where the Ivory Duchess alias Kathryn Danaher had hidden the stolen brooch, and since he had quickly traced her short flight from Philadelphia to southern New Jersey, finding the brooch was a given.

No reason to hurry the inevitable, he reasoned, as he admired the blush on her cheeks.

"Play for me," he urged, stepping back from the bench.

Her eyes widened, and she twisted her hands together. "I . . . I couldn't possibly take advantage of our short time together. Perhaps it's best if we . . . if we begin your instruction.''

He noted her emphasis on *short* and felt his pulse begin to race as she moved to stand along the side of the grand piano.

"Miss Dolly told me you wrote that you've never had instruction on the pianoforte.''

He crossed his arms and grinned. "Never.''

She took a deep breath and set her features into a prim expression. "Then we shall start with the most elementary of the basics. Will you take a seat on the bench, Mr. Massey?''

"Philip. Please call me Philip,'' he remarked as he assumed a casual position on the bench. "May I call you Kathryn?''

Her lips stretched taut. "I believe it's customary and a sign of respect to use formal titles with your instructor, and for the instructor to act professionally by doing the same,'' she declined, her voice tremulous. "If you prefer a social call, perhaps I might suggest—''

"I'm sorry. I meant no disrespect.'' He cleared his throat. "As you were saying, Miss Danaher . . .''

With her sharp release of breath, her breasts teased the fabric of her bodice. A delightful little morsel, he noted. Such a shame she has a cold, thieving heart.

The greater the challenge, the sweeter the victory.

She studied him briefly and shook her head. "Sit tall and erect with both feet flat on the floor. Place your hands directly above—''

"Like this?'' Shifting into a rigid, formal posture, with his feet set properly, he held his hands stiff and parallel to the keyboard.

She moistened her lips. "Your posture is better, but your hands are too stiff and too high. If you would bend your wrists and spread your fingers a bit . . .''

Raising his elbows, he let his wrists go slack and curled his hands so his fingertips brushed the tops of the ebony keys and his thumbs rested on mother-of-pearl. "Better?"

"Not quite."

"Then like this," he suggested as he rested the bottom of his palms on the thin wooden ledge at the tip of the keys.

"No," she advised and chewed on her bottom lip.

Frowning, he threw his hands in the air. "Am I a dolt or just not meant to pursue this whim?"

She blushed again. "No. Not at all."

"Then perhaps you'd best show me." He started to rise when she swept around the side of the piano and waved him back into his seat.

Bending close, she took hold of his left arm, bent his elbow, and held it in place with one hand while she positioned his hand with the other before repeating her ministrations on his right side. A sweet floral scent hung in the air even as she stepped away from him. Temporarily distracted, he almost missed noting the feel of the rough skin on her hands that had brushed the back of his. Calluses from driving? Odd, since she had worn gloves. He wondered if she had worn the gloves to cover her callouses and had been reluctant to place his hands into position out of embarrassment for the sorry state of her hands.

Vanity.

Not an unexpected vice for a spoiled celebrity like the Ivory Duchess, yet the young woman who called herself Kathryn Danaher and stood beside him seemed far too unsophisticated to have the scandalous past and aura of mystery that had spiraled her to international fame.

Just a clever act that was part of her new role, he decided, and who better to see through her charade than Omega—the supreme master of disguises himself?

"That's perfect," she murmured as he held his hands

exactly as she had poised them. "Your right thumb is resting on center C . . ."

As she recited a variety of names for the keys beneath his fingertips, he studied the sound of her voice and tried to evaluate her diction. While she obviously had received elocution lessons in an effort to mystify her stage persona, he found it nearly impossible to identify a regional accent although she spoke with some hint of European ancestry. English, perhaps. Or possibly French?

Footsteps entering the room distracted him, and he looked over his shoulder to see Nelda standing in the doorway with a tray.

"I've brought some light refreshment," she announced and placed the tray containing a pitcher of peppermint tea and a plate of hot buttered scones on the sideboard. "Unless you need something else, I'll just be getting back to my garden."

"No. You might as well—"

"Merciful heavens! The beast is in the flower bed!" With a startled gasp, Nelda charged to the front window, pushed aside the sheer drapes and opened the window just enough to poke her head outside. "Be gone, you wicked pest! How dare you . . . Argghh!" She pulled herself back inside, put both hands on her hips, and glared at the paling pianoforte instructor. "One good whack of my broom will pitch that meddling mule of yours into the river if you don't do something to get him out of my garden!"

The tone of Nelda's voice clearly implied she considered herself to be Kathryn's equal. He let the servant get away with behavior now that he never would have tolerated in any other situation just to see how the Ivory Duchess would react.

Before Philip drew his next breath, Kathryn swept past him in a blur of yellow that reminded him of melted butter. Shrugging his shoulders when Nelda tossed a glare at him, he followed Kathryn out the door, in no hurry to find her wailing in a fit of tears or crumpled to the ground in a dead faint.

Neither tactic would save her now . . . or later, when he delivered to Simon Morrell the most precious gem of all: the Ivory Duchess herself.

Kate took one look at the devastation and was half tempted to push Precious into the river herself. Like paint left to dry on an artist's palette, crushed tulips littered the once-beautiful flower bed. Decapitated stalks of green, their blossoms destroyed or devoured, lay bent and broken beneath one wheel of the cart in a path of destruction that only ended at the mule's head.

She literally heard every coin she had hoped to earn from Philip Massey roll down a steep path into an abyss of what might-have-been.

"There must be some way to salvage this disaster," she mumbled as she raced to the mule, grabbed her halter, and tugged. "No," she shouted. "No, Precious. Stop that. Right now!" She dug in her heels and pulled up with all her might. "Mules . . . don't . . . eat . . . flowers. They . . . just . . . don't." She huffed out her words and tightened her hold until the mule finally acquiesced and lifted her head. After chomping down a tender bud, she blew air out of her nostrils and brayed, spraying the front of Kate's skirts with spittle.

Now beyond frustration and embarrassment, Kate took one look at her soiled gown and stained shoes and surrendered to shattered nerves. What started out as a fit of giggles burst into laughter that sent tears streaming down her cheeks. Finding humor at the most frustrating times had gotten her into trouble as a child more times than she cared to remember. She thought that Simon's strict tutelage had erased this unforgivable, childish habit, but only a month into her freedom, she sadly discovered otherwise.

Nelda's voice rang out. "You . . . you find this amusing?"

Kate snapped her head to the side, only to find Nelda perched on the bottom step shaking a broom in front of her. Kate caught a glimpse of Philip Massey out of the corner of her eye. He was lounging against the frame of the front door with his arms crossed in front of his chest. He made no effort to intervene and obviously intended to let her fend for herself.

Groaning, Kate immediately sobered. "My goodness, no. I-I . . ." Working quickly, she grabbed a carrot out of a canvas bag stored beneath the seat in the road cart and lured Precious out of the garden and back onto the gravel drive that led across the front of the yard. "I'm so sorry. So truly sorry," she offered to Nelda to make amends as she wiped the last remnant of tears from her cheeks.

"That's as clear as dirty dish water," Nelda spewed. "Just who do you think is going to repair my garden?" She lowered her broom and waved toward the mangled plants with one hand before she clapped it against her chest as though mortally wounded. "My flowers. My precious . . . precious flowers. Ruined. Just . . . just . . . ruined."

At the sound of her name, the mule brayed and stomped her foot.

Kate bit on her lower lip and patted the mule's nose. She bent forward and whispered into her ear, "Hush, you silly animal. Haven't you gotten us both into enough trouble?" Looking over at Nelda while untangling the reins, Kate looped them back into place and set the brake. She had no difficulty looking apologetic because she was the one who had forgotten to brake the road cart after being swirled into a nervous tizzy with one glimpse of Philip Massey. "Please accept my apologies. I wasn't laughing at what happened to your garden, and it's not really the mule's fault. It's all mine. I forgot to set the brake on the road cart."

Nellie sniffed her displeasure. "Apologies might be enough for some folk, but they sure as sin won't replant my garden."

When Philip eased from the door frame and walked across the porch to glance down at the garden, her heart skipped a beat, reminding her it was impossible to be near him without losing her concentration as quickly as a strong wind could hustle clouds across a sky.

Or a mule could turn a garden into a feed lot.

"I'll take care of the garden," she offered as guilt filled her conscience. She unbuttoned the cuffs of her sleeves and rolled them to her elbow. "If you would be kind enough to secure my gloves—"

"You'll need more than gloves to salvage anything from this carnage," he teased as he shook his head with amusement twinkling in his eyes. Before Kate could recover from the shock of his humorous reaction or ponder how nonchalantly he left her to her own devices to undo the damage or placate the housekeeper, he turned and disappeared back into the house without saying another word.

"Somebody better do something about my garden," Nelda snapped. She shouldered the broomstick and marched up the steps, pausing long enough to snort her disapproval at Kate before stomping back into the house.

Left alone with only confusion and a pesky mule for company, Kate muttered to herself as she bent down and started collecting bruised petals and other plant debris without bothering to get her gloves. She made a pile in a corner of the garden wishing she had a shovel so she could mix the ruined plants with the soil. At least the debris would make for good compost.

Surveying the garden, she realized it was too late to plant new bulbs and expect them to bloom this season, but Miss Maggie had a whole patch of irises that needed to be thinned. Kate decided immediately to ask if she could transplant some of the irises . . . just to make amends.

Amends.

The word echoed through her trembling heart.

She worked her way through the garden wondering if there was anything she could do to make amends for this disastrous morning. The key to her chagrin lay in taming the shrewish housekeeper. If Nelda could be placated, Kate might stand a chance of convincing Philip Massey that he should continue his lessons

Without fearing she would send his housekeeper into a tizzy or destroying yet another part of his estate.

Chapter 5

~~~~

The following morning, Philip twisted the gemstick to
let the burnished garnet on the end catch the bright
rays of sunlight that bathed his worktable with late May
warmth. Peering through a jeweler's eyepiece pressed
against his eye, he studied the jewel to make sure he had
missed no imperfections that would render the semiprecious
stone less than flawless. Eldridge Bradford was one of his
uncle's most valued and finicky clients, and nothing less
than perfect would ever adorn his wife's graceful neck.

A tight band of memories wrapped around his heart and
strangled any satisfaction his skill as a jeweler gave him
this morning. He lowered the eyepiece, laid down the gemstick, and rose from his seat to stretch the aching muscles
in his back and neck.

After disappearing yesterday to spend the entire afternoon sailing a small skiff on the river leaving Kathryn alone
to begin repairing the garden, he had returned at dark. After
devouring a late supper he had ordered sent to his room,
he suffered a fitful sleep and rose well before dawn to work
on the necklace Bradford had ordered for his wife. Centered
in a strand of matching pearls, a garnet framed in diamonds
would lie in the hollow at the base of Cynthia's throat.

The very place where so many years ago Philip had pressed his lips against her soft flesh and felt the gentle beat of her heart trip with excitement when he had courted her and asked her to be his wife.

"Fickle woman," he muttered as he carefully removed the garnet from the gemstick and wiped the faceted jewel with a cloth. After wrapping the garnet in a blanket of gold velvet, he placed it into the safe along with beastly memories of Cynthia's ultimate rejection he had thought long tamed.

"Tamed, but not redeemed. Not quite yet," he murmured. He forced his thoughts to focus on the woman who had singlehandedly destroyed the front garden and alienated the housekeeper.

Or did credit properly belong to the mule?

Chuckling to himself, he cleaned his tools and removed his leather work apron. He had hoped to use the bullish Nelda to intimidate Kathryn and shake the charade that covered up her imperious nature. He never dreamed the opportunity would come so quickly! Or so comically.

Finished restoring order to his worktable, he reached into his pocket and took out the note Kathryn had left for him which Nelda had placed on his supper tray. He tilted the torn scrap of paper to let sunlight splash on the short, effusive message.

> *Pray, forgive me for shattering the peaceful atmosphere of your home. I sincerely regret the damage to the garden and hope to make amends. If you would be gracious enough to allow me to continue with your instruction on the pianoforte, I would be humbly indebted to your kindness.*
> *Miss K. Danaher*

He shook his head. "It's not my good graces you need to beg, Duchess." He refolded the letter and wondered how long Nelda would begrudge the pianoforte instructor's presence in the home she ruled with an iron fist and will of steel.

Until the blasted garden was repaired.

Considering that might take a few days—at best—he could use that time to his own advantage. While Kathryn worried about whether or not he would want to risk havoc if he resumed his lessons, he would have the time he needed to think about why this odd position traveling the countryside appealed to her.

While he was entertaining himself with that aspect of his assignment, he had to remain focused on his primary task: to plan how he was going to search the cottage she shared with the Gresham spinsters to find the cameo brooch.

He had to locate the cottage first and decided to make that the order for the day. He could get directions from Abner and needed to think of a good reason why he wanted to know where Kathryn lived. Spending a few hours away from the house would also spare him the chore of sharing Nelda's company, a thought that only reinforced his desire to get out of the house.

One quick glance at his crumpled shirt and trousers led him to rub his hand against the stubble on his jawline. He immediately turned, unlocked the door, and left the first floor workroom to seek his room and freshen his appearance, but voices coming from the kitchen diverted his attention.

And piqued his curiosity.

Changing direction, he turned away from the stairs and made his way past the dining room and study. He pushed open the swinging door to the kitchen, surveyed the room, and stared openmouthed at the two women chatting at the table.

His entrance had the same effect as the arrival of a swarm of bees at a picnic. At least for the woman who looked up, bolted to her feet, and gripped the back of her chair. "M-Mr. M-Massey," Kathryn stammered.

Was it guilt that pulled the plug on her rosy complexion? Or embarrassment? He was too surprised to see her to be able to tell. "Miss Danaher?"

Nelda hissed. "You might try considering your appearance before you barge your way into my kitchen, Mr. Massey. Kate and I are just getting better acquainted."

Kate. The name fit her much better than Kathryn. It was younger. Less sophisticated. More innocent.

He would have to call her Kathryn or risk falling for her ruse.

He clamped his jaw together. "What about the garden?"

Nelda got up and started to clear the table. "Finished and set to right. I'll be getting your breakfast ready now that you're finally up." She narrowed her gaze. "Not that you look like you've been to bed, or did you sleep fully clothed?"

Inwardly seething at the housekeeper's insolence, he waited a few moments until he could trust his voice.

Blushing, Kathryn walked toward him. "Why don't I show you the garden while Mrs. Spade fixes something for you to eat?"

Purposely ignoring the housekeeper, he nodded and followed Kathryn out to the front porch and down the steps. He took a long, lingering look at the garden. In a bed of freshly turned soil, tight-budded irises set in straight rows filled the garden where the tulips had once bloomed. Smaller plants hugged the entire perimeter, and he recognized several as marjoram and dill, herbs that had enticed the mule. The garden had been totally restored.

In less than a day?

Her soft laughter filled the air, and she smiled at him as though she could read his thoughts. "Miss Maggie was so sweet. She even helped me to dig up the irises and insisted on replacing some of the herbs Precious munched to the roots.''

"How did you ever—''

"Mr. Spade was kind enough to bring a wagon to the cottage. We just loaded up the plants and brought them all here in one trip.''

Exhaling softly, he shook his head. "You must have worked—''

"Into early twilight,'' she gushed. "Mrs. Spade put a lot of work into her garden, and I didn't want her to worry that I wouldn't keep my word to restore it. Even though the owners won't be back until fall, I-I felt an obligation to repair the garden immediately. Especially since you've leased the property. You're entitled to have it exactly as you found it. Or nearly so.''

She sounded so sincere, Philip almost believed her. The skirts of her blue muslin gown brushed against his legs and her scent . . . her very feminine scent ignited his pride in his appearance. Chafing at the sorry state of his clothing and his unshaven beard, he frowned and stepped away from her. "It looks fine,'' he said quietly, unsettled by how powerfully she affected him. He started back up the steps and paused when her voice rang out sweetly.

"Did you have a moment to read my note?''

He reached into his pocket, pulled out the scrap of paper, and held it out so she would be able to see it. He counted to five and slowly turned around to face her. "I need a few days to complete a piece of jewelry I'm working on. Perhaps by Wednesday I'll have time to resume taking lessons.''

Her eyes lit with a kaleidoscope of pleasure. "Wednesday.''

"Perhaps,'' he retorted, taking satisfaction with the cloud of disappointment that dulled her expressive eyes. "I'll send Abner with a note when I'm able to resume taking instruction.'' Without waiting for her to offer a reply, he made his way up the rest of the steps, walked across the shadowed porch, and entered the house.

A chill shivered through his body. As he mounted the staircase to the second floor, intending to shave and change his clothes, he admitted to a growing respect for the Ivory Duchess.

She was far more skilled as an actress than he had been led to believe. In the course of a single day, she had alienated, then won the blessing of the housekeeper from Hades. She had pierced through the practiced veneer he wore as Omega to touch his heart with her unselfishness and genuine concern for others, and she had sent a wave of desire crashing through his body that had totally surprised him.

Before he reached the top of the stairs, however, he had already dismissed the question of how she had managed to do that. He was more intrigued with a greater and more challenging question: Why?

''Exile should always be this sweet,'' Kate mused. Still on her knees, she plucked a strawberry from a small plant and plopped it into her mouth, savoring the sweet flavor of summer.

Just in front of her, Maggie sighed. ''You haven't been exiled, but I'd like to find a way to ban that mule from my garden. When she got out of the barn yesterday, she almost trampled my strawberries before Dolly got that animal back where she belonged.'' She moved a woven basket full of red-ripe berries out of her way and stood up. ''You just had a rough beginning. I'm sure Mr. Massey will be understanding.''

Kate took her cue from Maggie and got to her feet. She brushed the dirt from the full apron that protected her skirts and wiped her hands. Frowning, she stared at her pink-stained fingers and the dirt caught beneath several of her fingernails. "Are you sure the stains will wear off in a day or so? If you're right and Mr. Massey decides—"

"Don't you worry yourself. On either account. By tomorrow, the stains will be gone." Maggie turned and winked at her with a grin on her wrinkled face. "Of course, if you'd worn gloves . . ."

Kate wrinkled her nose. "I detest gloves. I can't *feel* anything when I wear them."

Laughing, Maggie worked her way down the double row of wild strawberry plants she had transplanted and cultivated in her garden. "Spoken like a true daughter of the earth. Just don't blame me when Dolly gets a glimpse of your hands. She never did understand how good it feels to touch rich, damp earth or rain-kissed leaves. And the berries . . . They actually tickle!"

Finding herself growing as close to Maggie as she had been to her own Gram, Kate smiled. "Have I thanked you properly for sharing your irises and herbs with Mrs. Spade?"

"'Course you have. Your manners are never lacking." She handed the basket of fruit to Kate. "Let's sit a bit on the portico. You can take the stems and leaves off the berries while I catch my breath."

Kate was as anxious to help Maggie as she was to keep her mind occupied. Conflicting images of Philip Massey had been dueling with the worry that she had lost a wonderful opportunity to earn a small nest egg. While she felt safe and secure in her new home, she still worried that Simon might find her. Without a small purse of funds set aside for an emergency, she would not be able to escape him a second time.

She took a seat on the bench next to Maggie and set the basket on the ground. Thick grapevines covered the portico's overhead trellis, and the shade they provided was refreshingly cool on warm afternoons. She began to destem the fruit that would be cooked into preserves or jelly that very night.

Maggie's hand clasped Kate's. "Listen. Hear the mockingbird?"

More than a few birds chattered overhead, and even though Kate could not tell the difference between the robin's song or the blackbird's call, she held very still and listened. Shaking her head, she sighed. "It's hopeless. They all sound alike."

"Nonsense. Each bird's song is as unique as the sound made by each of the keys on the pianoforte." As Maggie tried to identify and explain the difference in the varying sounds created by different birds, Kate's mind wandered back to her last visit with Philip Massey despite her hopes that she could keep busy enough to forget the whole disastrous affair.

To complicate matters even more, she could not forget the alarming physical reactions to Philip Massey she had experienced whenever he was near. Even when performing the simplest task, she was reminded of him.

Yesterday, when she was taking down the laundry, her hands had brushed against a cream-colored pillowcase. Perhaps it was the color, almost identical to the shirt Philip had worn, that quickened her pulse. This morning she had been sipping an innocent cup of tea that was the precise color of his hair when she felt her chest constrict with longing to see him again.

And just now picking strawberries, when the leaves brushed against her hands, she did not even have to close her eyes to remember how it felt when he had taken the valise from her and his hands touched hers, sending delightful shivers racing up her arm.

Tempted to close her eyes and try to recall his face to memory in precise detail, she caught the sound of Maggie's voice and stole a side-glance at her.

Maggie paused and eyed her with suspicion. "You don't really care about the birds, do you?"

Kate blushed and quickly lowered her gaze. "I'm sorry. Maybe another time would be better. I'm trying to decide what to do if Mr. Massey decides he doesn't want piano-forte instruction after all."

"Whatever gave you the idea I might change my mind?"

The sound of his voice startled Kate onto her feet. The basket of strawberries tumbled from her lap, and fresh fruit went flying through the air. Mortified at her clumsiness, she dropped to her knees and tried to regather the scattered fruit. When she finally looked up, she found him standing next to Dolly at the far end of the portico near the kitchen door.

Dressed formally in a chestnut brown waistcoat and trousers, he was every bit as dashing as the first time she had seen him. He also had that wolfish glint in his eyes she remembered only too well.

Miss Dolly, on the other hand, glared at Kate. "As you can see, we have a visitor. Perhaps we should wait inside until you freshen your . . . your apron."

When Dolly finally broke her piercing gaze, Kate's heart began to pound. She got to her feet, turned to hand the basket of berries to Maggie, and froze in place. Maggie had suffered another spell, and Dolly would be furious if Philip Massey witnessed it.

"Come along, Miss Danaher. Don't dawdle. Mr. Massey doesn't have all day to wait on you."

Fear gripped Kate so hard she could scarcely breathe. Stepping closer to shield Maggie from view, she placed one hand on top of Maggie's and squeezed gently. "Miss Maggie? Please, Miss Maggie. Come back to me," she whispered, trying not to let Philip or Dolly overhear her.

Maggie did not respond. Her eyes remained unfocused,

or were they focused on something ordinary mortals could not see?

"Miss Maggie?" she repeated a bit louder.

"Don't frighten her."

Philip Massey's voice was gentle but firm, and he edged Kate aside. In the next heartbeat, he took a seat on the bench and placed a strong, supporting arm around Maggie's shoulders. Ever so gently, he pulled the elderly woman closer to him. "Now, Miss Gresham, see if you can't let go of your pleasant dream and find your way back home," he crooned as he slowly rubbed the back of her hands.

Before Kate drew two shaky breaths of air, Maggie blinked her eyes and stared up at Philip. Kate chewed her bottom lip. Would Miss Maggie dissolve into tears once she realized she had had a rather severe spell and Philip Massey—a virtual stranger—had seen it happen? Or did she have the presence of mind to try to pass off the spell as a silly or innocent bout of woolgathering?

Maggie blinked her eyes again and smiled. "Why, you must be Philip Massey. And you're every bit as charming as our Kate said you were, although I sense a bit more of the rogue in you, young man, than she did."

· Anything lighter than a feather would have knocked Kate off her feet, and at that singular moment, she hoped she would fall into a very deep hole and that some kind soul would immediately fill it in.

With concrete.

And if they didn't, she would simply keel over and die of shame. If someone had never done that before, she would gladly volunteer to be the first victim.

After she strangled sweet, loving, gentle Miss Maggie.

And after she forced Philip Massey to swallow every peal of laughter that bubbled out of his throat and filled the air.

Chapter 6

Pure and simple, the woman was a sorceress with magical powers that defied rhyme and reason.

Philip could find no other explanation for Kathryn's ability to charm her way past Nelda Spade and into the home and hearts of the Gresham sisters.

Well, at least one of the spinsters.

From his place on the sofa in the parlor where he sat next to the now fully recovered Maggie, he glanced at her older sister as the women discussed the merits of strawberry preserves versus jelly. Taking advantage of this opportunity to study the women, he observed Dolly. Reserved and reticent, she sat in an opposite Queen Anne chair like an imperial monarch at court trying to discover which one of her subjects carried the sin of betrayal in his heart.

Vigilant and guarded during the course of the tea Maggie had insisted upon to thank him for his kindness during her spell, Dolly had regarded him with suspicion, but it was her aloof scrutiny of Kathryn that had caught and held his attention.

Assessing Dolly's demeanor as nothing less than appropriate, given Maggie's fragile state, he did not find fault with her role as Maggie's protector. He immediately found himself cast as her ally, and his aversion for the woman who called herself Kathryn Danaher grew stronger. Like other masters of chicanery, the Ivory Duchess had a remarkable genius. A skilled predator who singled out the weakest in a herd of prey, she identified the most vulnerable part of a person's character and used it to shape the nature of her ploys. He had seen her do it twice now, first with Nelda and then with Maggie Gresham, and he recognized her skills because he had used them himself as Omega, much to his own discredit.

Even Simon Morrell had admitted in a choked and broken voice that the Ivory Duchess had used his dream of orchestrating a virtual unknown to the pinnacle of international fame and fortune to her own selfish advantage. After squandering all of the profits on her costumes and costly accommodations, she had stolen the cameo brooch and left Morrell with a mound of debts, a concert tour pointless without her, and a shattered dream.

Given Morrell's claim that there were no funds to steal and the woman's apparent unwillingness to part with her cameo brooch, the position here was probably her only option which probably explained its appeal. Faced with proving herself to the two sisters, she intuitively knew it would be easier to win Maggie's approval than Dolly's. He also assumed that just as she had charmed Nelda, Maggie, and Morrell, the Ivory Duchess would use her beguiling manner and wholesome appearance to earn the acceptance of the families on the circuit.

With growing respect for her adaptability, he looked at her. Fresh-scrubbed with a clean apron, she was seated now to his right on a rocking chair. She clutched a cup and saucer on her lap in a futile attempt to conceal her berry-stained hands. For a woman who had earned fame as a pianist, he found it oddly amusing to see her hands take the brunt of her new role.

The sound of Dolly's voice ended a momentary lapse in the conversation. "While I'm anxious to convey to you the same sentiments of gratitude offered by my sister, I do expect your word as a gentleman that you will not discuss my sister's condition with anyone."

Putting into words what he had read in her posture and expression earlier only reinforced his perceptions of her as Maggie's protector and guardian. With renewed confidence in his ability to judge a person's character or motives, he nodded. "My word is gladly pledged."

"I would appreciate your complete . . . complete . . ."

"Discretion," he prompted, finding it curious she was unable to provide the right word. Obviously gently bred and well-educated, despite the modest circumstances that marked her declining years, she must have found his presence far more intrusive and unsettling than he had thought.

"Precisely the word I was searching for," she said quietly as the creases in her forehead relaxed. "I'm relieved that you are sensitive to the dangers of gossip and idle conversation which invariably distort the truth and can destroy a person's reputation."

Only too well.

He moistened his dry throat with a sip of tea before he could reply. "Considering that I arrived at your home unannounced and violated the sanctity of your privacy, I owe you an apology. I should have been more courteous and sent a note requesting—"

"There's been no harm done," Maggie gushed. With her hands fluttering in her lap, she smiled up at him.

"Please put your fears to rest," he continued. "I've got no desire to fan the flames of gossip or scandal against you. I've been singed myself on more than one occasion."

If he had been lying, he would have been the first to curse himself a scoundrel. The harsh cries of condemnation and angry shouts vowing revenge against him had dimmed with the passage of time, yet for a brief moment, they roared through his mind.

Humiliation and shame, real enough to sink their claws into his heart again, were not part of his ruse. Pain sliced through his chest. He could scarcely breathe. "I would never say or do anything that would hurt you," he whispered, vowing that Maggie would never suffer from wagging tongues that condemned her for her strange malady.

She would be an innocent victim.

He had been guilty as charged.

"Is it true you've sailed with pirates while searching for gems?" Maggie asked, looking up at him with her eyes shimmering with fascination.

He heard the rocking chair creak and noticed that Kathryn had leaned forward and braced her feet to keep the rocking chair still.

Dolly bolted forward in her seat. "Magnolia! How could you stoop to repeating such gabble?"

He chuckled softly, amazed by the difference between the two sisters. "At least Miss Maggie doesn't try to skirt around her curiosity. I find that rather refreshing," he added, although he had no intention of diluting the air of mystery that surrounded his reputation by answering Maggie's question. "I admit I have an occupation that requires a great deal of travel to exotic locations where I've had a number of adventures that have been exaggerated, but trying to defend myself against gossipmongers only adds credence to their endless prattle."

"A noble and proper attitude," Dolly quipped as she cast a disapproving glance at her sister, "but gossip is best avoided in the first place which is precisely why I am so concerned for my sister."

"I couldn't agree with you more," he said quietly. After spending the past seven years trying to reimburse the investors he had lured into a failed land scheme, he was close to redeeming himself from the scandal that had cost him his reputation as a man of integrity and forced him to assume a secret identity as Omega. Only one promissory note to Eldridge Bradford remained unpaid, and this assignment for Morrell provided the opportunity Philip had been waiting for to satisfy his final debt of honor and sever the last link in the chain that bound him to his past.

Omega would simply vanish as quickly as he had been invented, and Philip would finally be a whole man, free to shape a future for himself although he doubted he would ever be able to resume a normal life. He had been Omega for so long, and he had become so good at subterfuge, he wondered if he would ever be content simply being a jeweler again. The challenge of matching wits with opponents, the thrill of winning against the odds, had become too ingrained to give up easily.

He narrowed his gaze and looked at Kathryn as she sipped her tea. She was no sorceress with magical powers. She was only a woman without a conscience or a soul. She may have been a renowned performer who held audiences in rapture, but to him, she was nothing more than the means to an end, thus an adversary to be outwitted by someone like him whose own character had once been as dastardly as hers was right now.

While a frown of disappointment teased the corners of Maggie's mouth, Kathryn's facial expression remained dispassionate. Only her eyes, glowing like flawless emeralds and sapphires resting in a bed of dazzling sunlight, gave any hint she was curious to know about his past—an interest so genuine and nonjudgmental it melted through defenses that had never been broached by anyone.

Until now.

The instinct for self-preservation flared quickly and erected a new wall between himself and the Ivory Duchess—a wall that would have to be impenetrable if he expected to emerge victorious in the game they waged with one another.

He lowered his gaze, centering his thoughts on the cameo brooch that logic dictated would be hidden somewhere in the cottage. A rush of excitement raced through his body as he anticipated finding the brooch. "I suppose you've told the Misses Gresham what happened when you came for my first lesson," he asked in an attempt to draw her into a conversation she had thus far avoided.

She had the presence of mind to blush. "I felt so badly when your garden was destroyed. I'm so sorry—"

"You don't need to apologize again. As a matter of fact, I came here today to extend my regrets for not helping you—"

"I never expected you to do that," she offered as her lips very slowly shaped a smile that reminded him of the way a bud opened to the warmth of the sun and blossomed into a beautiful flower. "I certainly couldn't have made a poorer impression if I tried."

He chuckled. "I thought Mrs. Spade might toss us both into the river after she made sure the mule—I think you called her Precious?—had either sunk to the bottom or gotten carried downstream by the current to Philadelphia."

Dolly glared at Kathryn. "She didn't lay a hand to Precious, did she?"

Sobering immediately, Kathryn shook her head. "I assured you just yesterday that I wouldn't let that happen. It was all my fault, after all—"

"A totally unintentional and honest mistake," Maggie protested. "Why don't you tell us about your plans for the summer, Mr. Massey. We don't have the entertainments you enjoy in the city."

Chuckling, he shook his head. "After all you've apparently heard about me, I'm afraid I'll disappoint you."

"Really?" she asked, her eyes twinkling.

He grinned. "Actually, I was looking forward to the peace and quiet, but it's harder to adjust to than I'd thought it would be. Maybe it's just that I'm accustomed to keeping later hours or I've grown used to the noise in the city, but I'm finding it hard to fall asleep out here in the country. I don't suppose you've ever heard anyone complain that it's just too quiet to sleep, have you? I'm having a devil of a time."

"I'm not exactly the right person to ask about that," she responded. "I've never had a problem sleeping, and now that I'm getting along in years, I tend to nod off as soon as I sit down after supper. So does my sister, but she'd never admit it."

Dolly stiffened her back, and her lips twisted a bit as though she were about to offer a retort and thought better of it.

"Maybe I just need to keep busier during the day," he suggested. Anxious to begin sparring again with Kathryn, he rose to his feet. "I'd like to resume my lessons. May I expect you tomorrow?"

Chapter 7

Preserves had won out over jelly.

Cleanly washed glass jars lined the counter. Pieces of white paper, cut into circles slightly larger than the mouth of the jars, lay soaking in brandy. The day's bounty of strawberries simmered gently on the cookstove and filled the kitchen with a heavy, sweet aroma.

Wearing a thick cotton mitt to protect her hand, Kate stirred the bubbling mixture of sugar and fruit and hummed to the melody Dolly played on the pianoforte in the next room. Maggie sat at the kitchen table pouring through a tattered copy of Mrs. Child's *The American Frugal Housewife*. Squinting, she bent closer to the book, shook her head, and turned the page.

The music stopped abruptly and Dolly entered the kitchen. She sniffed the air and smiled. "It smells good, Kate." She glanced at her sister and frowned. "Will you please borrow my reading spectacles?"

"Certainly not. I can see perfectly well, thank you," Maggie insisted. She held her place by laying her finger on the page and looked up at her sister. "Why did you stop playing?"

"Because I wanted to check on things in the kitchen."

"Well, Kate and I are getting along quite fine. The preserves are nearly done, and I'm just keeping busy reading—"

"Trying to read—"

"I don't need your spectacles. I'm too young—"

"Your eyes are—"

"My eyes are only fifty-four. Yours are nigh close to sixty. When my eyes are sixty, I'll think about using spectacles. Now if you don't mind, I'd like to get back to my book."

Giggling, Kate put a cotton mitt on her other hand and moved the kettle from the cookstove to a trivet next to the glass jars on the counter. "Miss Maggie is trying to find a remedy for Mr. Massey's insomnia."

Dolly shook her head as she walked over to her sister. "In that cheap little book? Really, Maggie."

Maggie sighed, closed the book and pointed to the cover. "Mrs. Child did not write drivel, and she's quite unconcerned so many people label her work as a 'cheap little book.' She even says so in her introduction. Thousands of hardworking people depend on her for advice. See? It's the twelfth edition."

Dolly leaned over her sister's shoulders and glanced at the book. "I'm surprised you can read it at all. Heaven help poor Mr. Massey. If you do find some ridiculous home remedy, which I highly doubt he needs, you're likely to misread the ingredients."

Kate would have found it hard to believe herself, but she had seen him early in the morning after the garden debacle, and it was obvious the man had scarcely gotten any sleep the night before.

Ignoring her sister's barb, Maggie reopened the book and sighed. "Heaven helps those who help themselves. Since he asked for my help to get a good night's sleep, I'm going to try Mrs. Child."

Dolly turned away and walked over to the counter to stand next to Kate who was ladling preserves into the jars. "I'm relieved to see you're wearing the mitts to protect your hands."

"I didn't want to burn my fingers, but it's a little awkward."

"Here. Let me help you." She took the mitt from Kate's hand that was trying to steady one of the jars. "You ladle the fruit, and I'll hold the jar."

With another pair of hands to help her, Kate made quick work of filling the jars. When the kettle was empty and the last jar filled, Dolly excused herself after securing a whispered promise that Kate would not take to her bed until Maggie had turned in for the night.

With Maggie absorbed in her book, Kate was left alone with her own thoughts for the first time since Philip had cajoled her into returning to his home tomorrow morning to resume his lessons. Impressed by his self-assurance, she envied his ability to remain detached from prattle about his occupation and travels, particularly since she would find herself vulnerable to malicious gossip should anyone discover her real identity.

Dismayed by the web of deceit that still etched her life and her inability to be as strong as Philip and rise above scandal about her that was ill-deserved and blatantly founded in mistruth, she set back to finish working on the preserves. Lifting a white paper circle out of its brandy bath, she laid it on top of the fruit in one of the jars.

As she pressed the final circle of paper into place on top of the last jar, she realized that she had not escaped from her past. She had used a bevy of lies to seal it away, just like the brandy-soaked paper shut the air from the fruit. Not all the seals were perfect. The preserves would have to be checked periodically for mold and replaced, but eventually the seals would be broken and the fruit eaten.

And sooner or later, her lies would be discovered and her past revealed.

Shaken, she wiped the outside of the jars with a damp cloth and put them on the windowsill to cool. Wasn't it time to set aside her burning fear of Simon? Was it fair to deceive Miss Dolly and Miss Maggie when all they had shown her was kindness?

She brushed back the damp tendrils of hair that had fallen forward and stared out the window over the sink at the dark that blanketed the garden. Not a star twinkled overhead. A thick cloud cover hid the moon, and she knew that her future would be as bleak and lifeless as the darkened night unless she found the courage to shine the light of truth on her past, to find the courage to face it, and to be strong and secure enough to ignore scandalmongers who would question her innocence.

Trembling, she realized she had no one better to guide her way through the maze that led from the past to the present and into the future than Philip Massey. If she was a ship adrift in an angry sea, he was a beacon of light shimmering from a distant shore to guide her past dangerous shoals and rocky reefs.

There was so much she could learn from him, and the anticipation of meeting with him for his lesson tomorrow sent her pulse racing and her mind reeling. Once again, the pianoforte would play a pivotal role in her life, and her love for this instrument deepened. She would have to proceed slowly, but she was determined to find a way to gradually lower the barrier of formality between herself and Mr. Massey she had insisted upon. If they became friends, she might be able to learn how to truly claim a respectable life for herself.

Perhaps the greatest paradox of all would be that if she was successful, he would become her instructor and she would be his student when to all outward appearances, their roles were quite reversed.

"Bless the heavens!"

Maggie's outburst startled Kate. She swirled around and pressed her hand to her throat. "Miss Maggie, are you all right?"

Grinning so hard her pale skin wrinkled like thin parchment over her cheeks, Maggie poked her finger at a page in the book. "I knew I'd find it here."

Sighing with relief, Kate walked over to Maggie. "You've found a home remedy for Mr. Massey?"

"Right here. See? Thoroughwort tea. I need to get it ready for him so you can take it with you tomorrow."

Kate peered over Maggie's shoulder and read the passage marked with the tip of Maggie's finger. She furrowed her brow and let her gaze wander to the lines just above the ones Maggie indicated. "I think you mean motherwort tea. It says that 'people troubled with wakefulness, find it helpful.' Thoroughwort tea is used for indigestion. Here. Just below," she murmured as she pointed to the text.

Maggie's lips twisted nervously, and she squinted a bit harder as she lowered her face closer to the book. "Dreadful type is so small. You're sure it says motherwort and not thoroughwort?"

"I'm sure."

"I think my eyes are just a little weary after searching through the book for so long," she mumbled as she rubbed her eyes with the heel of her hand.

"You're probably right," Kate said reassuringly as she sat down to peruse the tiny publication. She found an index at the back. "Oh, there's an index. You could have saved a lot of time—"

"I couldn't use the index," Maggie whispered. She looked up at Kate and glanced around the kitchen as though making sure her sister had not returned. "That type is even smaller."

Kate feigned a stern look. "Why, Miss Maggie, I think you might need reading spectacles."

Maggie shrugged her thin shoulders and smiled. "I believe I might. Just don't tell Dolly. I don't want her to think she's right all the time. It's not good for her character."

"Drizzle was almost nice. I even tolerated steady rain. But a downpour?"

While muttering to herself, the heavens unleashed a heavy deluge that left Kate gasping for breath. Chilled beyond shivering, she huddled beneath the oilcloth cape that had kept her warm and dry. Pellets of cold rain turned slanted in the downpour, and she cringed as the road cart made slow progress.

Despite Dolly's warnings that the weather would worsen before it cleared, Kate had insisted on keeping her appointment with Philip Massey. Precious apparently had no qualms about the weather and plodded steadily over gravel-slick roadbeds and muddy lanes. Maggie, of course, had been very pleased that Kate was not going to cancel her outing and made sure she had a canister of motherwort and a detailed note for Philip in her valise.

More than half-tempted to turn around and return home as the storm worsened, Kate was even more reluctant to admit Dolly had been right: This was no day to be on the road!

When Kate caught sight of the boulder marking the entrance to the country seat just ahead, she nearly whooped for joy. She restrained herself and started to giggle. She would probably drown if she opened her mouth wide enough to cry out her frustration.

A deafening rumble of thunder overhead startled her, and Precious started to balk at her task, braying as she slowed her pace. The rain grew even heavier, and when Kate turned off the main road and started up the lane to the house, she would not have been surprised to see an ark on the property being readied for immediate boarding.

A clopping sound from behind her broke through the rhythmic downpour, but before she could even venture a guess as to who might be out riding, Philip cantered up beside the road cart.

"Mr. Massey!"

He grinned and tipped an imaginary hat as rain plastered his face. He slowed his horse. "Miss Danaher. Don't tell me you braved the elements despite Miss Gresham's arguments otherwise."

"Which one?" she shouted above the din of the rain and struggled with the reins to keep Precious somewhere close to the middle of the muddy stream that moments ago had been a passable lane.

He laughed. "Miss Dolly, of course."

Surprised at his accurate perception of Miss Dolly as the more controlling of the two women, she stole a glance at him. He immediately held her spellbound. Sheer masculine energy emanated from his whole being. His face glowed with a joy for life and a magnetism that was at once frightening and intense—so much so that she could scarcely breathe.

As he laughed, a flash of white teeth piqued her interest in his lips, and she wondered what it would be like to be kissed by a man.

Especially a man like Philip Massey.

Horrified by the impropriety of her thoughts, she lowered her gaze. She took one look at his slick, rain-soaked body and groaned. She had leaped from the frying pan into the fire, a rather absurd thought considering only a magician could light a fire in this downpour.

Only a saint would have been able to look away.

For a lean man, he was built remarkably well. Sinewy muscles in his arms and legs appeared rock solid beneath a drenched shirt and trousers that clung to his skin so provocatively there was little she could do to stop the instant attraction that triggered an attack of gooseflesh on her entire body. She shivered, and he immediately took notice.

"Follow me to the barn. We'll get your mule safely settled inside with a bit of grain and then get you in front of a fire." He urged his mount forward and practically disappeared in blinding sheets of rain.

Bogged down with the road cart, she proceeded more slowly than Philip, and by the time she got to the barn, he had dismounted and managed to open one side of the double doors. In a burst of energy, Precious picked up speed and made straightaway for the inside of the barn.

One minute Kate was literally drenched with heavy rain; the next, she was inside the barn. Rain pounded at the roof, but it no longer pummeled her body. The smell of sweet, dry hay filled the air along with the animal scents common to a barn on a working estate.

After Philip led his horse into a stall, he secured the outside door to the barn. In the meantime, Kate had climbed down from the road cart. She shook the rain from the oil-cloth cape, thankful that her skirts were fairly dry. Her slippers were quite another matter, and she squiggled her toes against water-logged leather. A good time set before the fire would dry her shoes, but one touch told her that her bonnet was probably ruined.

While Philip removed the saddle from his horse, she unhitched Precious and put her into a stall. Moments later, the horse and mule, separated by an empty stall, munched on fresh grains. Neither Philip nor Kate had spoken to one another while they settled the animals, but once their work was done, the silence between them grew awkward. A series of thunderclaps and cracks of lightning cut through the steady din of the rain.

"We'd best get to the house," he suggested.

She joined him at the door to the barn. When he eased the door open, she took one look outside and groaned. Gusts of wind blew walls of rain so thick she could barely see the outline of the house. Puddles had turned into lakes, and a bolt of lightning struck nearby. "It's hopeless," she moaned. "There's no way we can get to the house."

Philip stepped outside and grinned. "Sure there is. Just watch."

Before she could fashion the most limited idea of what he meant, every thought went sailing right out of her head except for one: how to find her breath.

In one rather shocking but fluid motion, he had swept her off her feet. Literally. Her vision blurred for a moment, and only after she lay cradled in his arms did her equilibrium adjust. "Mr. Massey! Whatever do you think—"

"Steady, Miss Danaher. We've a bit of a mad dash ahead of us."

He tightened his hold on her, and she grabbed his shoulders for support as he used one hand to lower the outside bracket on the door.

He readjusted her in his arms and grinned again. "Hold on tight." He turned and started to run, covering the distance between the barn and house in seventeen heartbeats.

Seventeen rapid, very erratic heartbeats.

Even with Kate in his arms, he took the stairs two at a time, managed to open the door, and carried her into some kind of storage room adjoining the kitchen, slamming the door shut with the heel of his foot.

Her heart pounding, she looked around the room. Filled with an odd assortment of outer wear, boots, gardening tools, and sundry equipment that needed mending or repair, the unplastered room served as a catchall, particularly designed and located to keep the dirt that would be tracked into the house to a minimum.

She caught her breath and wondered if he would drop her to her feet as quickly as he had scooped her off them. Instead of releasing her, his arms tightened. When his chest pressed harder against her breasts, she felt the same strange and alarming stirrings that had filled her with wonder when he had touched her hand the first day they met. This time the tingling was even stronger and raced straight to the very essence of her femininity.

She snapped her head back and found him gazing at her with such smoldering interest she was helpless to fight against him. His deep brown eyes held her gaze, and his breath fanned her lips until they were dry and aching. A drop of water fell from his rain-slicked hair onto her lips and trickled in a slow, sensual path down her chin.

Overwhelmed by an outrageous craving to be kissed and to have his lips trace the path taken by the droplet of water, she caught her breath. When he dipped his head toward her, she was unable to stifle the soft moan that escaped from her lips.

An odd look flashed through his eyes, and he tensed as the spark of passion that had ignited disappeared—doused by humor that quickly turned his gaze into sparkling sepia amusement. ''For a woman who insists on proper formality, Miss Danaher, don't you find your behavior today rather ironic, if not thoroughly improper?''

Guilty as charged, she felt her shame burn her cheeks. When he set her down, she swayed on her feet. Every rebuke Simon had ever invoked against her echoed in her mind and crashed with the harsh criticism Monsieur Le-Blanc and other master teachers had lashed at her. Philip's reprimand, however, had been gentle and teasing which encouraged her to speak up in her own defense, something she had never found the courage to do before.

"I didn't invite you to carry me into the house and you gave me very little choice in the matter," she countered. She shook free of the oilcloth cape, hung it on a bare peg, and turned to face him as she removed her gloves to freshen her rumpled skirts.

"Indeed," he murmured as his gaze centered on her bodice and stayed there.

When his eyes widened and smoldered with desire that was unmistakable, she glanced down at her bodice and gasped. Her damp, white lawn bodice clung most shamefully to her breasts, and even though she had worn her finest chemise, her nipples strained against the fabric like small pink buds. Her head pounding with embarrassment, she crossed her arms over her chest and gulped as she tilted her face up to glare at him for being far less a gentleman than she had assumed him to be.

She blinked twice.

To her utter astonishment, she was standing in the room all alone.

Philip Massey was gone.

Chapter 8

⌒◦⌒

Standing barefoot and wearing nothing more than a new pair of trousers, Philip dried his hair with a towel and tossed it onto the floor in his room. Scowling at his reflection in the mirror, he brushed his hair into place. "Fool," he muttered.

He turned away from his image knowing he could not solve his dilemma by indulging in bad temper or self-recrimination. He had to remain calm to have a clear head and remain objective, no easy task when his body still ached with desire and his mind reeled with questions about the Ivory Duchess and his assignment to find the brooch she had stolen and return them both to Simon Morrell.

Unwittingly, he had invited the disaster that now undermined his assignment. Hoping to catch the Ivory Duchess by surprise when he picked her up and carried her into the house, he had been the one caught unaware. True to her accusation, he had held her in his arms longer than propriety dictated proper. When she finally had looked up at him and the brim of that bedraggled bonnet had fallen away from her face, he had been mesmerized by shimmering hazel eyes that were so translucent he could gaze straight into her soul.

Sweet confusion and precious wonder, not lust, had glazed her eyes with a raw, hypnotic passion that took his breath away.

When the raindrop clung to the edge of pale pink lips and then trickled sensuously down her creamy flesh to rest in the curve of her chin, longing for the taste of her on his lips became a thirst that could not be quenched with a single kiss. Or anything less than a lifetime of loving.

Her unbridled innocence reached deep inside of him to tug at his heartstrings and strum the chord of his deepest yearnings. That's when he had let down his guard, and he had almost kissed her. And that's precisely when he knew the reports and rumors she was a well-talented and practiced harlot were more than ludicrous. They were an affront to her true nature.

She had responded to him shyly, genuinely, and with the first wonder of deep physical attraction glowing in her eyes. A woman with as many former husbands or lovers as she reputedly had taken could not feign such innocence. The idea that she had seduced countless men by playing a role to appeal to each man's vulnerability—one that might soothe a broken heart, satisfy a thirst for sexual adventures, or fulfill the lifelong dream of seducing an innocent who would turn out to be a talented courtesan—produced a glaring disparity between what he had seen with his own eyes and experienced with his own body when he had held her in his arms.

Bolting to the privacy of his chambers where he would be able to think through this startling revelation was the only sensible thing he could think to do, but he could not leave her downstairs for very long without inviting the warranted accusation that he was a callous lout for seeing to his own comfort instead of being concerned for her.

"Curse you, Morrell!" He grabbed a shirt from the wardrobe and slipped it over his head, the fabric brushing against lips still aching with the need to kiss her. He laced the opening closed and sucked in his breath. He had not courted a proper woman for nearly seven years for one very good reason: He did not have the right to ask any woman to share his life until he had settled his debts of honor. There was only one debt left unsettled—to Eldridge Bradford—which only served to suggest he had bought Morrell's description of the Ivory Duchess' character and nature as factual substantiation of her reputation because he needed it to be true. He needed the funds completing this assignment would bring.

He especially did *not* need this unexpected complication which might put his success in jeopardy and force him to face the fact that even if he was able to free himself from his past, he might not be able to give up his life as Omega and settle down into a more respectable and normal life.

Not that any woman in polite society would consider him to be a suitable prospect as a husband. Neither would her parents. Not with the gossip, however well-founded, that undermined his reputation for stability by painting him as a man predisposed to adventure and travel that would make it difficult for him to establish roots which would hold him firm to home and family.

Would he ever?

Had he been Omega too long to have a normal life again?

Shoving the answer to that troubling thought aside, he tried to figure out what he was going to do. He slid his feet into a pair of slippers and paced from one side of the room to the other. There was much more to this assignment than he had presumed, and he found himself intrigued by getting to the bottom of it.

Viewing this assignment as nothing more than a gem-stone he had to evaluate as either real or paste, he posed a number of questions about Morrell that needed answers. What motive did Morrell have for lying about the kind of woman the Ivory Duchess actually was? Did he fear that Philip would eventually undermine her public image—one that now seemed deliberately framed? For what purpose?

On the other hand, he had as many questions about the Ivory Duchess. Why did she run away? Was it a ploy on her part to get something from Morrell—something he had denied her and she thought she could gain by disappearing for a while?

He did not have the answers to these questions, but he intended to use every skill at his command to get them. He paced even faster, determined to find an added bonus to today's surprising development. There was only one way to get to the truth: spending time with the Ivory Duchess. If that meant prolonging his search for the cameo brooch while he used his time to get to know her a little better, so be it. He would find the brooch eventually. In the meantime, he had to find a way to keep her from resuming her circuit, which only opened up a whole host of new obstacles.

Dolly, of course, would object to leaving her students without instruction. He also got the sense that Dolly was not thoroughly content in her retirement and would resume the circuit—given the right opportunity. If that were truly the case, why hadn't Dolly simply hired a companion for her sister instead of retiring to do it herself? Companions were far more available than teachers of the pianoforte, but Maggie's fragile state no doubt might make it difficult to find a companion who would be sensitive to Maggie's affliction and immune to gossip.

Nor would it be very wise. Dolly would have had to leave a relatively unknown person with Maggie for weeks at a time, something she could not and would not do. It was easier and far safer, in the end, to find a teacher of the pianoforte who would take over Dolly's circuit so Dolly could stay at home with her sister and be there to monitor the new instructor when she was not on her route.

But how could he keep Kathryn from resuming the circuit? Causing Kathryn some sort of minor physical injury was out of the question, and he felt ashamed of himself for even considering it. Intrigued by the challenge to come up with a way to keep her at home, he decided to go back downstairs and see how Kathryn was faring.

He had not had the time or the inclination to warn her that Nelda and her husband had left at dawn to take the Camden ferry to Philadelphia. Unquestionably, the storm had delayed their return, but none of them had expected Kathryn to brave the weather to come for the day's lesson—an event that turned out to be in his favor.

He had a spring in his step and a heart filled with excitement as he descended the stairs. He and the Ivory Duchess would spend the next several hours together getting to know one another better without anyone else around.

He started to search the entire first floor trying to find her. When he entered the last room, the kitchen, disappointment slowed his heartbeat to a dirge.

The woman was nowhere to be found!

He spied a canister on the table with a note of some sort leaning up against it. Two notes, he realized, the moment he walked over and picked up the papers. One, a short set of instructions from Maggie Gresham, suggested that he try drinking motherwort tea to cure his insomnia. He tossed it onto the table and concentrated on the second note.

Same wide, scrolled handwriting.

Same subservient plea.

Did the woman intend to spend half her life writing notes?

He read the message again:

I'm so very sorry to have inconvenienced you by chancing the weather and appearing for your lesson

*when you obviously did not expect me. I will return
tomorrow at the appointed time for your lesson—
weather permitting.*

Miss K. Danaher

He shook his head, frowned, and glanced out the kitchen
window. It was still raining, although the downpour had
relented to a steady, gentle rain. The barn door was still
open. Was that a bit of oilcloth he saw disappearing into
the barn or just a figment of his wishful imagination? "So
you think you're going to fly back to the safety of the
nest," he commented as he tossed the note back onto the
table.

He charged out of the kitchen, through the storage room,
and out the back door to try to reach her and convince her
to stay. By the time he was halfway to the barn, he was
soaked clear through to his skin.

Again.

Slipping in the mud, he nearly lost his slippers—twice—
and finally gave the blasted things up to the mud. Damn if
this woman wasn't going to drive him to drink something
a lot stronger than motherwort tea!

Barefoot, dripping wet, and growing more furious by the
heartbeat, he took a final jump across a huge puddle and
leaped into the barn. He collided with the wheel of the road
cart and had the air knocked straight from his lungs to a
string of expletives. Pain exploded in his right foot and
turned his anger into seething fury that practically blinded
him.

Taking gulping breaths of air until the pain ebbed to
bearable and his vision cleared, he scanned the barn. One
quick, clear glimpse and his brain slowed to barely functioning when he tried to understand what lay before him.

Carnage?

Not the right word. There was no blood.

Chaos?

Better choice, but not quite right. There was barely any noise. Only the sound of chickens who had flown down from the rafters and pecked at the ground and the mule munching on oats. And barley. And hay. And flax.

Flax!

Limping as fast as he could past sacks of grain that had been knocked over and stomped open, he got to the small bag of flax, shoved the mule's head away, and yanked the sack up and out of the mule's reach. "Stupid critter! How anyone in his right mind tolerates your shenanigans is beyond my comprehension. And my patience!"

A little flax helped horses and mules to shed their winter coats; an overdose could be poisonous. Even deadly. He studied the bag of flax closely and determined that the mule must have just stomped the bag open when he had arrived. Very little, if any, of the flax had actually been eaten. "You're also about the luckiest fool of a mule I ever met," he grumbled. He set the bag of flax on a high shelf, put the mule back into her stall, and latched it closed. Just to be safe, he closed the barred top half of the door and secured it as well.

The emergency over, he bent down to check his aching, mud-covered foot. A large bruise on the top of his instep had already started to swell, but nothing appeared to be broken.

In the midst of saving the mule from herself, he had forgotten what had sent him charging through the rain to the barn in the first place. His heart began to thump in his chest as he scoured the barn with a slow, steady gaze looking for Kathryn. He thought he had seen her going into the barn, but apparently he had been mistaken. Just where was she?

Fast-approaching footsteps caught his attention, and he turned around to see her just entering the barn. Her immediate reaction to the destruction was nearly identical to his: disbelief. Openmouthed, she paled. Her eyes widened until her lashes touched her brows, and she took a step backward. "Wh-what happened?"

He limped toward her. "Fortunately, I managed to get the mule back into her stall before she ate herself to death," he grumbled.

She gasped. "Precious? Precious did all this?"

"She seems to have an insatiable appetite. For disaster," he quipped as he brushed past her and limped out of the barn without giving her a chance to respond.

He was barely inside the house before he considered changing his mind and returning to the barn to help her restore it to order.

He had never seen anyone quite as bedraggled as the woman he had left in the barn. With her stiff oilcloth cape, soggy bonnet, and muddy shoes, she looked pathetic, and the expression on her face when she took a look at the mess in the barn was nothing short of forlorn.

Part of him wanted nothing more than to head straight back to the barn, take her into his arms, and reassure her everything would be all right. The other part—the more cynical—reminded him that the woman had to accept responsibility for that blasted mule's antics. To his absolute consternation, he just could not help feeling sorry for her, which qualified him as the very fool he had seen when he had looked at his image in the mirror.

Fool or not, he would get to the truth about the Ivory Duchess, and nothing would prevent him from completing what he still considered the easiest part of this assignment: finding the cameo brooch.

Chapter 9

Kate stood in the middle of the barn and just stared at the unholy mess that littered the floor. Bales of hay had been knocked over. Half a dozen sacks had been split open and a couple of chickens pecked at the grain that spilled out.

Taking a deep breath for patience, she tried not to find fault with Precious and embraced full responsibility for not remembering how easily the mule rendered a stall door latch worthless. Blaming Dolly for pampering the mule was even more pointless. She also did not want to judge Philip too harshly for scurrying away as fast as he could and leaving the cleanup to her.

She did not even know where to begin to find the energy it would take to put the barn back in order. Her shoes were caked with mud. She was cold and hungry. She was emotionally drained after nearly being kissed by Philip and finding herself rejected in the blink of an eye.

She was tired. Bone tired . . . of Precious and her mischief, of hiding the past, and of just plain being strong!

Her bottom lip began to quiver and tears welled in her eyes. Just once she would like Precious to behave like a normal mule. Just once she would like to slip into another world where everything was quiet and peaceful—like Miss Maggie did.

Just once.

"Ouch!" She jumped back, and the chicken who had pecked at her toes greedily attacked a new pile of grain. When another chicken made a wild, flapping descent from the rafters and nearly landed on her head, she bolted to the clean, empty stall separating the horse from the mule and slammed the bottom half of the door shut.

Precious started braying, and the horse nickered softly.

She ignored the pernicious beast and swirled to the opposite side of the stall to calm the horse. The hem of her oilcloth cape had inadvertently caught in the door, but she noticed it too late. Jerked sideways, she landed in a heap of tangled skirts with a resounding plop onto a pile of straw.

Snap!

Her fall broke the tight rein she had held on her composure, and she dissolved into much-needed and well-deserved tears. They started as slowly as the drizzle that began early that day, but before she knew it, she was crying huge sheets of tears.

She fidgeted her way out of the oilcloth cape, discarded her soggy bonnet and gloves, curled into a ball in the warm straw and just cried her heart out, plain and simple.

Since she seemed to have an endless supply of tears, a bit of time to spend them, and more privacy than she had been privileged to enjoy for years, she had no desire to shortchange herself. If she was going to indulge herself with an old-fashioned cry, she might as well make it a good one.

She cried for Gram. How she missed her still!

She cried for all the years she had spent training with Simon and Helen—years that had nearly destroyed her love for the pianoforte.

She cried for not being strong enough to refuse to be part of Simon's scheme and for perpetrating the shameful and deceptive persona of the Ivory Duchess.

She cried for lying to Miss Dolly, Miss Maggie, and Philip Massey.

And she cried . . . just because if felt so good to cry . . . until her tears were finally spent.

Exhausted and lethargic, she yawned and closed her swollen eyes. Lulled by the gentle patter of rain on the roof and the sweet warm bed of straw beneath her, she slipped ever so gently into a deep sleep where the world of dreams embraced her.

Kate stirred and stretched her limbs. When she reluctantly opened her eyes, she bolted into a sitting position. Momentarily dazed and confused, she shook her head and blinked her eyes until she realized where she was.

And why.

Reality was such a far cry from her dreams she was tempted to curl back up in the straw and glide back into her interrupted dream. Maybe when she woke up the next time, her dream that the barn was all cleaned up might actually be true.

"Wishful thinking won't clean up this barn," she muttered as she stood up and brushed the straw from her gown. Feeling drained, but oddly refreshed, she took a deep breath and blinked when she looked out of the stall into the barn.

She blinked again. The entire mess had been cleaned up!

Stumbling forward, she gripped the top edge of the stall door hard enough to make the wood bite into the palms of her hands. "I must be dreaming," she whispered, half-afraid she might dispel the dream-come-true if she spoke too loudly.

"You're finally awake! How are you feeling?"

Philip's voice startled her, and she looked over to see

him standing in the outside doorway, a silhouette with bright golden sunshine at his back. He stepped inside and smiled as he approached her carrying a tray with several mugs and an assortment of food.

Apparently he had cleaned up the barn while she slept, and his willingness to help her this time, instead of leaving her on her own like he had when Precious had destroyed the front garden, touched her heart. "Tell me this isn't a dream. An incredible, impossible dream," she whispered.

Laughing, he rested the tray on the edge of the door to the stall, but blocked her view of the barn. "It's not a dream."

He was so close her pulse began to race, and she found him even more handsome and appealing than the first time she had seen him. Relieved he could not read her thoughts, she leaned around him and glanced at the barn again. "It's . . . it's all cleaned up!"

He grinned as he lifted up the tray. "I'm glad I managed to get it all done without disturbing you. Are you hungry?"

She nodded, too overwhelmed to find her voice. Aromas too tempting to ignore forced her to take a glance at the tray filled with a plate of thick-sliced, buttered bread, two bowls of soup, two steaming mugs, and utensils. Her stomach growled, and she blushed.

"Good. You're hungry. May I come in?"

With only a heartbeat of hesitation, she unlatched the half door and stepped aside.

Acting like she had just invited him into her home instead of a stall in a barn, he set the tray on a flat place in the straw and fluffed up the straw on either side of the tray to make two "chairs." "Take your pick," he urged and stepped aside as she lowered herself to the closest straw chair.

He took his seat and handed her a spoon and a bowl of soup which she cradled on her lap. "Nelda and her husband went to Philadelphia early this morning. I guess the storm has delayed their return. She made this yesterday, but soup usually tastes better the second day. I hope you like it.''

"It smells delicious. Thank you." She took her first taste and smiled. "It's wonderful."

"Try some bread. It's a bit coarse, but—"

"I think I'd eat buttered paper I'm so hungry," she protested and tried a bit of bread.

They ate in companionable silence and by the time the bowls were empty and the bread long gone, her hunger for the details of why and how he had managed to clean up the barn without waking her up was the only hunger left unfulfilled.

Reluctant to press him with questions and chase away the amiable mood that existed between them, she sipped at her tea and leaned back in the straw. "Thank you. For everything," she murmured.

His smile was as warm as the guilt that glistened in his eyes. "The least I could do was help to clean this up." He shook his head. "I thought for sure I had latched the door to the stall, but obviously I didn't. It's my fault the meddlesome mule got out of her stall."

She lowered her gaze for a moment before she looked up at him again. "No, I . . . I doubt it was your fault. You probably did latch the stall. Precious lets herself out of her stall at home fairly often. Just the other day Miss Maggie found the mule in her garden in the middle of the afternoon."

He started to laugh. "I would never believe a mule could get into so much trouble without seeing it for myself."

"Why didn't you wake me up? I would have helped you," she suggested.

He cocked his head. "Actually, I didn't know you were here. Not at first. With the stall door closed, you had a perfect hideaway. Once I found you, I didn't have the heart to waken you.''

He reached out and took one of her hands. With gentle pressure, he slipped her hand into his. Once again, she was struck by the beauty of his hand. Long, tapered fingers wrapped around her own and unleashed feelings that were dangerously thrilling. When she gazed into his eyes, simmering with hope and flaring with an interest that sent her pulse into an erratic rhythm, her heart started to pound.

Awestruck, she watched as he lifted her hand to his lips and pressed a kiss to her knuckles. Tingling warmth spread from her hands clear down to the tips of her toes.

''You've been crying,'' he whispered.

His touching observation, hoarse with emotion, caressed her heart and tempered all her fears. Philip Masscy was a kind, sensitive, caring man, but after the unsettling episode earlier when he had nearly kissed her only to change his mind, she was too unsure of herself to make any assumptions about his intentions now.

Not until he urged her fingers apart to kiss the palm of her hand, teasing the flesh with the feather-light touch of his lips and scattering all of her reservations.

She closed her eyes and sighed her pleasure as sweet sensations slowly traveled over her flesh . . . until the creak of wagon wheels just outside the barn turned those sensations into panic that raced straight to her heart.

She jerked her hand away and stumbled to her feet to glance outside. ''Nelda and her husband! What are they—''

''They're just getting back from Philadelphia,'' he informed her in a forced whisper. He grabbed the tray, slipped out of the stall, and quickly hid the tray behind the freshly stacked sacks of grain.

''What will they think?'' she wailed as she gripped the edge of the stall.

''I'll start hitching the mule. You get your bonnet and

cape. By the time they notice we're in here alone together, we'll have them thinking you just finished my lesson and I was helping you get ready to start for home.''

She grabbed her cape, plopped her bonnet on her head, and slipped out of the stall. She did not have time to think beyond acting quickly enough to salvage her reputation. She would save worrying about what Philip Massey thought of her until later.

After all the grief that had gone into securing a respectable position for herself as the proper Miss Kathryn Danaher, it would be less than poetic to see it all destroyed because she had forgotten one very basic tenet of her new life: She would never be free to love or be loved by a man. She was a woman tainted by the infamy of her past and held captive by the lies of her present. She was—now and forevermore—the Ivory Duchess.

Chapter 10

A full week had passed since Kate's fateful rainy-day
encounter with Philip Massey. Tomorrow she would
set out again on the circuit.

Not a day too soon.

Today, however, had yet to be spent, and the morning
hours seemed to loom ahead interminably. She had one last
lesson with him, but that had been set back till midafternoon because he had gone to Philadelphia for the morning
to see his uncle and visit an apothecary for another supply
of motherwort. Jubilant that he had found her remedy helpful, Miss Maggie was nevertheless spending the day in bed
nursing a case of the summer sniffles, and Miss Dolly was
in the next room giving a lesson to one of her students,
Abigail Sweet, while the girl's mother observed.

Left to her own devices, Kate decided not to postpone
her packing till evening. She glanced at the pile of garments
sitting on the chair next to the kitchen table and frowned.
Her life as a simple pianoforte instructor had acquired more
wrinkles than the garments waiting to be pressed and
packed for her trip, but the creases in the garments she
would wear for the several weeks would be far easier to
smooth out.

She decided on the mundane task of ironing to pass the morning hours, set the iron to heat on the stove, and cleared the vase of flowers and lace cloth from the kitchen table. After doubling an old blanket in half and laying it on the table, she covered it with a piece of sheeting and smoothed it down. Plucking a garment from the top of the pile, she spread one of her chemises on top of the sheet.

Her fingertips lingered on several holes on the side, and she shook her head. Constantly wearing the cameo brooch pinned to her chemise was taking its toll, but she had no other alternative. She could not feel secure unless she knew the brooch was absolutely safe. Although she was starting to feel comfortable about hiding the brooch in the cottage, she certainly would not leave it behind while she was away.

Deciding there was nothing to be done to prevent the damage to her chemises, she tested the iron with a quick tap of her finger. Satisfied it was hot enough to begin, she started to iron.

From the next room, Dolly's instructions, her voice ever patient and low, kept Kate company as she worked. As practiced as she might be on the pianoforte, she was still new at being an instructor. Being home this morning gave her the added opportunity to listen to Dolly as she conducted her lesson. After a rustle of skirts and another brief discussion, notes rang out from the pianoforte as Abigail played the scale exercise she had allegedly been practicing for a week.

Dull, lifeless, even laconic notes filled the air, and Kate smiled to herself. She did not have to be in the room to see Abigail's facial expression to know that this child had no interest whatsoever in learning to play the pianoforte. Kate recognized the girl's reticence by her lethargic playing and hoped to hear a spark in the sad performance—to no avail.

During a pause in her own work, she stood next to the stove while the iron reheated. She listened intently as the exercise concluded and the child began to play a simple tune she had begun learning only today.

The tune, however, knocked a brick out of a defensive wall Kate had erected in her mind, and the long-forgotten melody from her childhood evoked memories of another little girl who had played that tune just as badly.

Charlotte Ann Ludfallow.

A cherubic-looking child with long dark hair, sparkling blue eyes, and rosy cheeks, she had been Kate's friend and confidante as well as the only daughter of the country gentleman who had employed Gram.

Just when Kate felt herself being drawn back to the past, Abigail mercifully ended her sorry little rendition, and the image of Charlotte Ann started to fade away. Shaken, Kate tested the iron, but it was still too cool to resume her work. While she waited, she could not help overhearing the conversation that ensued between Dolly and Mrs. Sweet or the sound of Abigail's sniffles—a scenario so familiar that it breathed new life into Charlotte Ann's image and swept Kate back over the wall and into the past . . .

"Your daughter is only nine years old. Perhaps she's a bit young for the discipline required to play this selection," Mrs. Harley suggested tactfully.

Mrs. Ludfallow's voice rose an octave in protest. "Charlotte Ann is a sensitive, highly emotional child. The pianoforte is the ideal instrument to allow her to express herself. At fault is your method of instruction."

From behind a settee where she could observe the lesson without being seen, Kate could scarcely breathe. Mrs. Harley was the third pianoforte instructor in as many years, and she prayed Mrs. Ludfallow would not dismiss this instructor, too.

"Charlotte Ann responds much better to praise than criticism," her mother chided.

Kate shoved her hand in her mouth to catch a giggle

*before it erupted and gave her away. Charlotte Ann hated
the pianoforte. Truly hated it! There was not an instructor
in all of the British Empire who could teach her to play
well. Kate, on the other hand, could not recall a single
moment in all of her ten and a half years when she did not
love the pianoforte with all her heart—except for the part
she had given to Gram, of course.*

*To please her parents, Charlotte Ann continued to suffer
through her lessons with Kate hidden where she could
watch. Between lessons, when Charlotte Ann was supposed
to be practicing, Kate would slip into the room and play
the pianoforte while Charlotte Ann kept a watch at the door
for her parents. They were usually too preoccupied with
their own interests to do more than listen to see if Charlotte
Ann was attending to her practice.*

*Mrs. Ludfallow's voice startled Kate and she shrunk
back against the wall. "If you intend to continue at this
position, I should expect you to follow my directions.
Praise. Not criticism. Or I shall find another instructor who
will."*

*Kate's heart began to pound. She held her breath, pray-
ing Mrs. Harley would give in. She had heard Gram talking
to the newly widowed instructor. With three small children
to feed, she needed this position, didn't she?*

*"Perhaps I have been at fault. I've possibly been too . . .
too strident in my methods. Forgive me."*

*Kate's sigh of relief nearly gave her away, but Charlotte
Ann covered the noise Kate had made with several
coughs—just like she usually did. Kate reached out, fumbled, gripped the leg of the settee and held very still. Very,
very still . . .*

Pain. Deep, burning pain tore through her hand, and Kate
instinctively pulled her hand back toward her body. Blinking through her tears, she stared back and forth at the iron
on the stove and her hand until she realized she must have

taken the iron and wrapped her hand around it so the tips of her fingers had gripped the heated surface. Her childhood memory had been so vivid and so real she felt like she must have been in a trance to have been so careless with the iron!

Stumbling blindly away from the stove, she reached the doorway and leaned against the frame for support with her hand cradled in front of her. She stared into the room and sucked in her breath as her confused mind tried to sort between the past and the present. Relief rushed through her body when she saw Dolly, Abigail, and Mrs. Sweet in the room instead of . . .

Red-haired Abigail looked up in surprise and immediately stopped playing. Her mother cast a sharp look at Kate, but Dolly's uplifted brows quickly knitted with concern.

"Whatever is wrong?" she asked as she left Abigail's side and walked over to Kate.

"My hand. I've burned my . . . my hand," Kate whimpered. "I was reheating the iron and the next thing I knew, I had . . ."

Dolly turned her right around, led her to the sink, and pumped water over the tips of her fingers. After filling a deep bowl with cold water, Dolly dipped Kate's hand into the bowl. "There. That should help, but I'm not sure it will prevent blistering. Really, Kate, you must be more careful with your hands."

Sniffling back tears, Kate managed a weak smile. "Next time maybe I should wear gloves."

Her feeble attempt at humor did not bring a smile to Dolly's lips. "You have a responsibility to your students now. How can you expect to give your lesson today or to start the circuit tomorrow if your hand is—"

"It feels better already," Kate argued. "I just need to rest for a bit. Then I'll finish my ironing and be off to see Mr. Massey."

"And if your fingers blister and you can't handle the reins?"

"I'll be fine. Honestly," she insisted as she lifted the bowl and cradled it in the crook of her arm. She excused herself, made a brief apology to Mrs. Sweet and her daughter, and went straight to her room.

She sank down on her bed at the top near the headboard, balanced the bowl on her lap, and used her pillow to cradle her head against the wall above the headboard. The pain gradually eased to a mild throb that seemed to echo the rhythm of her heartbeat. "If I had to go into a trance," she murmured as her eyes started to close, "I wish it would have been a sweet trance like Miss Maggie's."

All told, she was very grateful. At least she had not relived the most painful memory that involved her childhood game with Charlotte Ann: the day her life's path had been forever altered.

Despite sleepless nights and hours of intense self-examination, Philip was close to admitting defeat. He had been unable to find a way to keep the Ivory Duchess from leaving on her circuit tomorrow.

"Not yet," he vowed to himself as he set out a display of intricately cut stones on his worktable. He set down the last stone and surveyed his display. A shimmering green emerald was the most impressive in size, but a cornflower blue sapphire would be sure to catch any woman's attention. A pale pink tourmaline, several outstanding amethysts, and a pair of Hungarian opals were bound to intrigue her, and perfectly matched pearls, like the ones he planned to use for Cynthia's necklace, completed the display.

Collectively, the stones could represent a virtual fortune, depending on whether one was a jeweler or a casual observer.

Uncle Harold had been only mildly reluctant earlier that

morning when Philip suggested he wanted to work on several more pieces in addition to Cynthia's necklace. In the past, when Philip had left the jewelry emporium on an assignment as Omega, he had brought little if any work with him, but his uncle had quickly agreed to Philip's request.

When he saw Kathryn drive up in her road cart with that spoiled, unpredictable mule, he turned away from the worktable and secured the lock on the door when he left the room. By the time he reached the porch, Abner had quite wisely taken charge of the mule and road cart, and Kathryn was halfway up the steps.

Dressed in a pale green linen gown, she looked as young and fragile as a tender stalk on a spring flower. With flushed cheeks and limp skirts, however, she looked wilted, as though suffering in a drought. "I'm sorry to bring you out in the heat of the day," he offered by way of an apology.

"It's rather warm for early June. At least that's what Miss Dolly tells me."

"It's a lot cooler here along the river than farther inland or in the city." He gestured to the porch chairs and a table already set with refreshments. "Why don't we sit outside a moment. Mrs. Spade was worried you might be overheated, and if you don't at least try her raspberry shrub, she'll set me to task for being ungracious."

She eyed the refreshments with such longing, he chuckled. He took her valise and guided her to a chair. "Why don't you remove your bonnet and gloves and relax a moment in the shade? The raspberry shrub is actually quite tasty."

She hesitated and as he poured two tall glasses of the summer drink, he noticed that her attempt to untie the ribbons on her bonnet was a bit awkward. She eventually managed to work them free and remove her bonnet, but her hands were still gloved when she accepted her glass and took a sip.

"Thank you," she offered with a smile. "I don't believe I've ever tasted raspberry shrub before. It's tart and quite refreshing. I must be sure to thank Mrs. Spade, too."

He took a seat in the chair next to her thinking it rather curious she held the glass in her left hand. He could have sworn she was right-handed. "You must be new to the area."

She moistened her lips and dropped her gaze. "I'm originally from the Continent, but I've been in Philadelphia for over a year."

First lie of the day, he mused. He congratulated himself that he had thought her slight accent might be European, unless that was as much of a lie as claiming to have been in Philadelphia for the past year since she had only arrived at the beginning of March for a series of concerts. He was quite relieved she had emerged from the prim cocoon she had hidden in ever since the episode in the barn. He had pushed her too fast that day, but seeing her relaxed demeanor today, he felt more confident in his plan to get to know her better so he could begin to unravel the truth behind her disappearance. At the moment, he was more than curious about why she did not remove her gloves.

"Do women on the Continent typically keep their gloves on when they're having refreshments?"

She dropped her gaze to her hands and shifted nervously in her seat. "No. To be truthful, I . . . I forgot I was wearing them."

Second lie.

He could see it in her eyes the moment she looked up at him.

"I'm very grateful you found them in the barn. I left that day in such a hurry—"

"My pleasure. It would have been a bit awkward to explain. To Abner," he added, noting the way she kept the conversation going without making any attempt to remove her gloves.

She rose abruptly and set her glass on the table. "Perhaps we should start your lesson. I have a long day ahead of me tomorrow, and I need to finish packing."

"Of course." He rose, picked up her valise, and they went directly to the parlor. He took a seat at the piano bench, and she went to her usual position at the side of the grand piano after struggling to open her valise to take out a new instruction book for him.

She was still wearing her gloves.

He demonstrated his skill at the scale exercises he had practiced for the past week, and he was rather pleased with himself.

She praised him and opened the new book. "I think it's time you tried a simple melody. Study it for a moment. Don't worry about the tempo. Just try to pick out the notes."

He frowned. Still terribly inept at reading music, he struggled through the selection. Three times. Shrugging, he shook his head. "Pretty awful, wasn't I?"

She grinned. "Not so awful at all. Try again."

He did. Twice more. He could not believe how hard this was! He could take an uncut stone and turn it into a magnificent jewel, but he could not make the notes on the grand piano sound anything less than pathetic.

"Why don't you show me. That might help," he grumbled, oddly embarrassed and quite certain she had six-year-old students who could do better than he had.

He stood up to give her a place on the bench. She took a step back and seemed to hesitate before she finally sat down. She lifted her hands to the keyboard.

"Your gloves," he quipped. "Shouldn't you remove your gloves?"

She paled so quickly, he thought he might have asked

her to remove her clothes. In the next breath, she caught her lower lip with her teeth and slowly removed one glove. Her left glove. She started to remove the other glove, but no sooner did she have it halfway up her palm than she stopped and lowered her head. "I'm sorry. I . . . I'm not feeling very well," she whispered. "I'm afraid your lesson will have to be over for today. There's no charge, of course. If you'll excuse me . . ."

She started to rise, but acting totally on instinct, he placed his hand on her shoulder to keep her in her seat and sat down beside her. She was trembling, but offered no resistance when he lifted her right hand and gently laid it in his palm. "You've hurt your hand."

She nodded, and a trickle of silent tears ran ever so gracefully and silently down her cheek: "Just my fingers," she managed.

"Why didn't you just tell me? And why on earth did you wear gloves if—"

"I couldn't let anyone know, especially Miss Dolly. I have to start on the circuit tomorrow. If she thinks I can't drive the short distance to your estate, how will she ever think I can . . ."

He wanted to feel some measure of thrill or excitement that she might not be able to go on the circuit and that Dolly might have to take her place, but he took no pleasure in seeing her in pain. He also took no pride in remembering that when the notion of Dolly and Kathryn changing roles first occurred to him, the possibility that an injury of some sort would do the trick was something he had immediately rejected.

Inexplicably, he still felt guilty, as though his thoughts had been grabbed and implemented by some overinspired agent of fate. "Tell me what happened," he murmured and listened closely as she quickly explained her injury as burns on her fingers caused by a hot iron. He frowned. "I suppose they blistered," he ventured.

She nodded.

He wanted to shake her! "And you wore your gloves on top of the blisters? Are you daft or just inclined to self-mutilation?"

She tried to pull her hand away, but he held tight to her wrist. "I put ointment on them first. To protect them," she argued defensively.

"Sooner or later, you'll have to take off your gloves."

She bowed her head. "I know. That's why I need to leave. I want to go home and get to my room. I'll manage on my own."

"You can't go home. What if you can't get the glove off by yourself? Who will you ask for help? Miss Dolly?"

"No. I can do it by myself."

"Sure you can." He helped her to her feet. "I'll help you."

She pulled from him and backed away. "No. I have to leave. I can't let you help me. What if Mrs. Spade sees my hand? She'll tell Miss Dolly."

"Mrs. Spade won't see a thing. I promise you." He took her arm and led her across the hall and unlocked the door to the former sitting room before she could voice another argument. "This is my workroom. Believe it or not, it's the one room in the house I made Mrs. Spade agree not to enter. On penalty of death," he added dramatically, attempting to use humor to persuade her his offer to help her was sincere.

She giggled, obviously aware of how disrespectfully the housekeeper treated him. She looked longingly into the room and sighed. "Are you sure?"

"Absolutely. And I can lock the door from the inside—"

"You can't lock the door. It wouldn't be proper! Mrs.

Spade would never permit me to be alone with you behind a locked door.''

Or in a stall in the barn on a rainy day?

He gritted his teeth. "I won't lock the door.''

"It also has to be left open, which means Mrs. Spade will be able to see what we're doing. So . . .'' She turned away from the door. Reluctantly.

"Trust me,'' he urged in a whisper. "Let me help you. Why must you always try to be so independent? Is it so very difficult to let anyone help you?''

She pressed her lips together, and her eyes dimmed to opaque shades of blue and green that reminded him of a churning sea. If she let him help her, he could judge the extent of her injury for himself. With a little prodding, she might be convinced to delay her departure. Having an extra few days with her was less than he had hoped to gain, and he was not about to let her be so foolish as to risk further damage to her hands by being stubborn and independent.

Why would she disappear in the middle of a concert tour, leaving Simon and numerous theater-owners in awkward and financially precarious positions, yet feel so strongly about her position as a teacher of the pianoforte? He noted this new and troublesome incongruity in her character as Simon had described it and held his breath, waiting to give her time to reconsider.

When she finally nodded and slipped into the room, he let his breath escape in slow relief. "I'll just need to get a few things for you. I'll be back in a moment,'' he said softly before he turned and left her alone in the room before she could change her mind.

Chapter 11

Drawn to the triple window by the compelling view of the river, Kate was halfway across the room before she realized her arrival must have interrupted Philip at his work.

Eyes wide with wonder and disbelief, she stared at the jewels casually left on the worktable. Her heart tripped a beat. The jewels were worth a fortune, and they bore magnificent, shimmering testimony to the gift of his talent for his craft.

Enthralled by the exquisite beauty that lay spread before her like teardrops from a heartbroken rainbow that had been crystallized for eternity, she could not resist the temptation to touch them, to hold something he had created with his extraordinary hands.

Amethysts in shades of purple, reminding her of the violets that grew wild on the Ludfallows' estate, sparkled in the afternoon sun that splashed the worktable. She cradled two in the palm of her left hand, scarcely able to breathe. Only a superb artisan could have turned simple purple crystals into breathtaking beauty. Each stone had been cut with such intricate facets that she could scarcely imagine having the expertise or the patience required to turn a semiprecious gem into a jewel that rivaled the finest diamond for brilliance and clarity.

Only a man who loved his work would have been able to create the beauty she held in her hand. Only a perceptive and sensitive man, one who saw beyond the rough exterior of an uncut stone, would know just the right way to reveal the inner beauty hidden from the rest of the world.

Or how to see beyond a facade of deception to cherish the woman within?

Tears of regret misted her vision for a moment. She could never expect any respectable man to simply dismiss her past or excuse the lies that wrapped around her present. She was rather like an uncut stone lying on a gravel roadway, ignored by hundreds of travelers, until one man—a rare and talented man—might pass by, notice her, and care enough to see if there truly was a woman of any value inside.

Philip Massey was possibly such a man, but it was far too soon in her freedom days to even consider a life beyond her teaching position. Simon could still find her, or worse, send someone she would not know to find her. While she felt safer with each passing day, she had to face the likelihood that she would spend the rest of her life alone, ready to run away at the first sign she may have been followed or identified.

Alone.

The very word made her tremble, and the stones in the palm of her hand began to quiver brilliantly in the sunshine that poured through the windows.

"I'm sorry I took so long."

Startled by Philip's voice, she instinctively closed her fist and spun around. Her cheeks burning, she uncurled her fingers and held out the stones. Before she could offer a stammered apology for tampering with the jewels on the worktable, he flashed a smile.

"I see you found your way to my stones."

"Stones? They're not just stones. Not anymore. They're exquisite jewels," she argued as she awkwardly set the amethysts back on the table. "They must be worth a fortune."

He paused a moment, then smiled. "Actually, they don't belong to me. I'm just setting them for my uncle's clients."

"Aren't you the least bit concerned about leaving them out in plain view?"

With his hands full of items he had procured to help her to remove her glove, he merely shrugged as though he might be a bit embarrassed. "I keep the door locked when I'm not working, and the stones are usually in the safe."

He unloaded the items and put them on the worktable. "Actually, I just brought most of them back with me today. I couldn't resist looking them over and obviously lost track of the time. When you arrived, I just left them here and locked the door."

He glanced at her gloved hand, looked at the jewels on the table, and frowned. "If you're ready to see about that glove, I'd better put these in the safe. Do you mind? If your hand is bothering you . . ."

"No. Please. I'd feel much better knowing they were put away. I've never seen so many beautiful jewels, not up close, but I have read enough about them to know they're quite valuable. In part," she said softly, "because they've been cut so skillfully."

"Really? You've read about gemstones?" he responded, apparently too refined to dwell on the compliment she had just given him. "Most people find the subject rather boring. They'd much rather see the stones than learn about them." He picked up the emerald and placed it into a white velvet drawstring bag.

"I did, too. Find it boring," she explained when he looked at her quizzically. "I didn't understand the concepts that go into selecting a proper cut that was appropriate for different gems.''

"I'm not surprised. That takes years of study. So what did you find fascinating enough to keep you reading past the frontispiece?''

She giggled. "Nothing very important. At least not to someone with your knowledge and skill.''

His brows lifted. "Oh?''

"I liked the myths and legends that surround each of the gems, but I doubt anyone pays them much mind anymore,'' she gushed, feeling very foolish. Simon and Helen had kept her isolated from other people, but they had not been total ogres. On several occasions they had rented a house with a small library and allowed her free access to the books. With little else to fill the hours between her lessons and practice, she had read books on topics that had ranged from history to . . . to gemstones.

"Some people take the myths very seriously,'' he countered. He turned the drawstring bag upside down and let the emerald drop into the palm of his hand. Wonder lit his eyes like golden stars in a chocolate sky. "In ancient times, they used emeralds to cure diseases.'' He chuckled as he put the jewel away. "I suppose that means the only people ever protected from disease were the very wealthy.''

He chose the sapphire to put away next. "Ancient rulers wore these to guarantee their immortality. I wonder if it worked.''

She cocked her head. "You know something of the myths?''

"I have to. Clients can be very difficult at times. A man will come in, order a necklace or earrings as a gift for his wife, and the woman will no sooner open it than it's returned. She won't wear a pair of opal earrings, for example.'' He picked up the twin opals, stared at them oddly, and put them in a blue velvet bag.

"I think they supposedly bring bad fortune to the wearer," she offered, "but to some society, I forget which one, they were sacred and represented the spirit of truth."

He glanced at her, and for a brief moment, their gazes locked. She held very still, scarcely able to breathe, as his gaze seemed to reach deep inside of her and explore her soul. When he looked away, a shiver that ran up her spine made her tremble. Could he truly have seen to the depths of her soul, somehow been given a vision of her past, and discovered her deception?

Shaken, she held silent as he wrapped up the pearls and pink gemstone she could not identify by name. Only the amethysts remained, and when he held them up to the light, all traces of his odd mood had vanished.

His lips eased into a broad smile. "These are my favorite, I think, although I'm hard-pressed to remember if there are any myths attached to them."

"I think they are said to prevent the wearer from becoming poisoned or intoxicated."

He gazed at her tenderly this time, and she grew warm and soft inside as her bones seemed to melt like wax touched to a flame. Her pulse began to pound, and every thought she had was pulled away like shells caught in a strong tide.

All that mattered was the emotion that swelled in her heart whenever he looked at her like she was as treasured as the jewels he held in his hand. Feeling weak and strangely vulnerable to emotions she had no right to feel, she was half tempted to grab the amethysts for protection from the very intoxicating effect this man had on her.

Nelda Spade, however, soon made a charm of any kind totally unnecessary. "I came to see if your lesson was done. Then I had to traipse around the first floor trying to find both of you," she complained.

Kate spun around to find Nelda glowering in the doorway. Obviously Philip had not exaggerated. The woman did not put as much as a toe in the room. For a brief moment, Kate wished there was a gemstone that would protect him from a nasty housekeeper.

In a single fluid movement, he stepped farther back to prevent Nelda from seeing the items on the table he would use to help Kate remove her glove. "Yes. We're finished for today, but Miss Danaher is interested in seeing some of my work. I'll see her out as soon as we're finished. And we'll leave the door open," he added with a quick wink to Kate.

"I should say you will. I won't have that young woman's reputation tarnished. Not in my own good home!" She stomped away muttering to herself.

Laughing softly, he turned to Kate. "I think that's her problem."

"Protecting my reputation?" she asked as he pulled another chair over to the worktable and motioned for her to sit down facing the window.

"She's under the very misguided impression this is her home, not mine." He took the seat next to her and nodded toward the door behind them. "As long as we work at the table with our backs to the room, she'll just assume you're admiring my work. Now let's see that hand."

She laid her right forearm on the table palm upward. The ointment on her fingertips had long dried, acting like an adhesive that glued her fingers to the inside of the glove. Taking off her glove meant the skin covering her blisters would be ripped off, but there seemed to be no other alternative. She could not wear the gloves indefinitely, and if she did, infection would be the least of her worries.

She braced her feet on the floor and took a deep breath, expecting him to simply peel off the glove in one strong motion. When he brandished a small pair of scissors, she cried, "No!"

Scissors poised in midair, he paused. "I'm only going to cut off the gloves here." He pointed to her fingers just below the second knuckle.

"You can't! You'll ruin the gloves! They're not even mine. They belong to Miss Dolly," she argued as she pulled her hand away.

He blinked hard. "How did you expect me to remove the glove? Just rip it off?"

She nodded.

He frowned. "That will only cause more injury to your fingers. Trust me. I'll do my best not to hurt you any more than necessary. And for pity's sake, don't worry about the gloves. I assume you have another pair."

One shaky nod.

"Then use those and you can buy Miss Dolly a new pair to replace this one."

She laid her arm back on the table, resigned to spending her tiny, but growing nest egg on a new pair of gloves for Miss Dolly. "Since you're so persuasive, maybe you can tell Miss Dolly how I just happened to cut the fingers off one of her gloves."

"That's easy," he remarked as he snipped the leather and folded it back toward the tips of her fingers. "Just tell her the truth. That you were too stubborn to admit you should wait a few days for your burns to heal before you started the circuit—"

"I'm not stubborn. I just have a responsibility—"

"Stubborn," he reiterated. "Now soak your fingertips in the bowl of water, and we'll see if we can't get the leather off without ripping any more skin than we have to. Just be stubborn for me now and don't pull your fingers out of the water even though it might sting at first."

She clenched her jaw. "Water shouldn't sting too badly."

"It will if something has been added to it."

"What? What did you add—" She caught her breath. The tips of her fingers felt like they were on fire! Pain flashed, exploded, and then surprisingly, she felt nothing. Nothing at all. Her fingertips were nearly numb. "What on earth did you . . ."

Her voice dropped off as he ignored her, and she watched him peel away the leather from each fingertip and toss each ruined bit of leather aside. The skin on the large blister on each fingertip had broken, but except for one, most of the skin still lay attached to her finger, protecting the raw skin underneath.

Surprisingly, she felt only a gentle throb in each of her fingers, and she leaned back in her chair as he urged the rest of the glove from her hand.

When he finished, he let out a huge breath and studied her face so intently she dropped her gaze. "How are you doing so far?" he murmured as he cradled her hand in his and stroked the palm of her hand with his thumb.

"Better than I thought I'd be. Thank you. Again." She tried to rise, but he put his other hand on her shoulder and urged her to remain seated.

"Not so fast. I still have to clean your burns."

"I can do that when I get home."

"The anesthetic won't last that long," he argued. "Trust me. I've used it often when I've cut my fingers instead of the stone I was working on."

Against her wishes, he rinsed each finger again, spread a sweet-smelling ointment across the blistered flesh, and wrapped a small towel around her hand. "Keep this covered as you drive home to keep out the dirt. Once you're home, let the air hit the blisters for a few days and you should be as good as new. Once Miss Dolly sees how badly—"

"I can't let her see what I've done. I have to learn—"

He threw the scissors into the bowl. "If the circuit is so

almighty important, why doesn't Miss Dolly go and let you stay with her sister?''

Her heart began to pound. "Because . . . because I've only been offered the position on a trial basis . . . until Miss Dolly is satisfied with my performance." She paused to take a deep breath. "I've only completed a single circuit. If I delay this one, I'm only proving I'm too irresponsible to be trusted with the position."

A humorous glint lit his eyes. "You're not irresponsible. Just a bit clumsy when you iron."

She should have resented his remark; instead, she was unable to resist his good-natured humor and his efforts to help her. She laughed. "Clumsy and forgetful. Sometimes I'm my own worst enemy. I'm so worried about doing everything right, I wind up accomplishing quite the opposite."

He joined her in laughter. "Like not remembering to set the brake on the road cart?"

She groaned when a vision of the ruined garden flashed back in her mind to haunt her. "Or forgetting to *tie* the latch on the stall closed."

"Now that caused a real mess," he noted with another round of chuckles. "Seems to me most of your problems concern one very cantankerous mule."

She laughed with him, enjoying a casual exchange of banter until she could not delay starting for home any longer. She took her leave with the understanding that she would return after the circuit to continue his lessons.

As the mule plodded home at a leisurely pace to accommodate her towel-wrapped hand and her attempt to handle the reins with her left hand, she was glad to be leaving on the circuit. And she grew absolutely convinced that Philip was wrong about her problems.

It seemed very clear to her that all of her recent problems did not concern Precious at all. All of her problems concerned one very sweet and gentle man who had already found a special place in her heart: Philip Massey.

She would need at least two weeks away from him to find the strength to accept the fact that until she was able to match his courage, face her past and live with the gossip that might still taint her new life, she had no right to invite him into the rest of her heart.

As the road cart crunched homeward on the gravel road, she realized she was still too new at freedom, too much at risk from Simon, and too inexperienced with men to be ready to make a commitment to any man. And too quick to use new lies to protect her present. She needed a few days for her hands to heal, and lying to Dolly because Kate was afraid to tell the truth was wrong. Hadn't Philip's first suggestion today been to tell Miss Dolly the truth?

She glanced at the roadbed below and knew without any doubt she was still just an uncut stone lying amid the gravel, unworthy of the one man above all others who might be able to set aside her past and accept her—with all of her flaws.

Until she found the courage to admit her mistakes and accept the consequences, and if that meant she lost her position here with Miss Dolly, Kate would do what she had always done in the past: She would find another way to survive.

Chapter 12

When Kate returned home, she heard Dolly beginning a lesson with Carolbeth Hamilton. There was no sign of Maggie, and Kate assumed the younger of the two sisters was still abed nursing her sniffles. Granted a temporary reprieve, Kate slipped into her bedroom.

Situated just off the kitchen, her room at the back of the cottage was kept cool by a stand of shade trees. After the hot drive home, the room provided more than welcome relief from the sun. In sharp contrast to all the other rooms she had ever called her own, this chamber offered something none of the others ever had: privacy.

When she had first arrived, Dolly and Maggie had made it perfectly clear they expected each of their own bedrooms to be sacrosanct, and the only time she had been inside the women's adjoining bedrooms was the day she had helped them to wash the windows. They had also agreed to honor Kate's privacy. For a young woman who had never had her own private corner of the world, Kate treasured the room. It did not matter that the room was sparsely furnished with only a bed, her trunk to hold her clothes, and a hazy mirror on the wall above a rickety table that held a small washbowl and her brush.

A hand-braided rug, just large enough to cushion her feet, lay next to the bed with only a summer weight yellow blanket as a coverlet. Pegs on the wall held her limited number of gowns and bonnets, and they added a splash of color to the whitewashed walls.

The room was plain and sparse even by modest standards, but to Kate, it was a small haven within the sanctuary she had hoped to find at the cottage.

She unwrapped the towel from around her hand and winced when it caught on the finger with the worst blister. She removed her bonnet, hung it on a peg, rinsed her hand in the washbowl, and splashed water on her face.

Refreshed, she waited until Carolbeth had finished her lesson and Dolly had had enough time to put away her instruction books before venturing out of her room.

She took a deep breath for courage, but she had scarcely taken a step into the kitchen when Maggie and Dolly entered the room together.

"You're back," Dolly noted. "I didn't hear you come in."

Maggie sighed. "Of course you didn't. Kate knows not to make any noise that might distract your student when you're giving a lesson."

Kate smiled her fondness for Maggie's support. "You must be feeling better, Miss Maggie."

Dabbing her reddened nose with a lace-trimmed handkerchief, Maggie sniffled. "Quite a bit. Thank you, my dear."

Dolly took her usual seat at the table while her sister removed a shank of cooked ham from the icebox. Taking her cue, Kate set the table and hid her right hand as best she could.

"How was Mr. Massey's lesson?" Dolly asked, typically oblivious to the task of preparing supper.

Kate's heart began to race. "He's progressing slowly, but he promised to practice more."

Maggie giggled as she cut several slices of ham and put them on a platter she placed on the table. "The man can't keep his mind on the pianoforte. He's too busy watching you."

"Your deportment should be professional at all times, Kate," Dolly exhorted like she was issuing a decree.

Blushing, she nodded. "Of course."

"And I certainly hope you don't encourage the man," Dolly added. "You have a responsibility to fulfill to your students. I should be very disappointed if you let the *second* man who pays you any heed fill your head with silly, romantic notions."

Dolly's direct reference to the suitor Kate had allegedly and foolishly followed to Philadelphia did little to ease her guilt for inventing that part of her background, but she was much more concerned that she would be able to convince Dolly of her commitment to her position.

"I've learned my lesson, Miss Dolly. All I want to do is devote my energies to being the very best teacher I can be."

Nodding as gravely as a queen who had just heard the answer she wanted from a lowly subject, Dolly sighed. "It's especially rewarding to know you respect your obligations and have the good sense, as well, to realize that Mr. Massey is not a solid prospect for you or any well-bred young woman."

Maggie nearly dropped the plate of quartered tomatoes she was carrying to the table. "How can you say that? Philip Massey is a good man who toils for an honest living. It certainly won't hurt to have him spend time with Kate. He's only here for the summer. It'll do the girl some good to enjoy a little attention after her experience with that other man. Mr. Massey is a gentleman and—"

"He's a worldly adventurer, not a man of domestic habits, who will break the heart of any decent woman who sets out to change him," Dolly sniffed.

Maggie took her seat at the table and her eyes widened with disbelief. "I'm not sure I can believe my own ears. Aren't you repeating idle gossip?"

"I read that letter from Nelda Spade's sister, too, and I'm only repeating what I read because Kate needs to know that Philip Massey is not the kind of man to settle down. Even if he did, he wouldn't change. Sooner or later, he'd find some excuse to wander off on some new adventure."

"He's a man of good character," Maggie suggested.

Sensing this was the opening she needed, Kate sat down at the table. With her hands on her lap, she swallowed hard. "I've never met anyone like him before. I admire him. Nothing more," she admitted, although she could not even begin to unravel her true feelings about him in her own mind.

Both sisters accepted her statement without further comment, and when they filled their plates and put the serving platter in front of Kate, she knew she had better speak her piece before either one of them noticed her awkward attempts to cut her food. "I've learned a great deal from Mr. Massey, and I have a confession of my own I'd like to make," she blurted.

Maggie continued to chew her food slowly as though Kate had just made a casual remark about the weather. Relieved, Kate looked at Dolly, but the blood drained from her face immediately.

Dolly's normally pale skin turned nearly translucent, and her spine stiffened like someone had just strapped a broomstick to her back or had just pronounced her death sentence!

Thoroughly ashamed of herself for making the woman think Kate might have devastating news and worried the poor woman might have a stroke, Kate acted quickly. She pulled her injured hand from her lap and held it out for Dolly and Maggie to see. "I wasn't truthful about how badly I burned my hand. I tried to hide it from you today by wearing my gloves which only made matters worse. I'm sorry. I . . . I really don't think I'll be able to drive the road cart for a few days. I can't begin the circuit tomorrow."

Having spent nearly all of her courage, she lowered her gaze. "I'm sorry. I know I've let you down, Miss Dolly. I've let your students down, too, and if you can't find it in your heart to forgive me or to believe me when I tell you how much I regret being so clumsy and so irresponsible—"

"Let me see your hand."

Dolly's command, calm and quiet, gave Kate the extra bit of courage to look up as she reached her arm across the table. Out of the corner of her eye, she saw Maggie's sad face, but she saved all her thoughts for Dolly.

Dolly's touch was cool, but gentle as she cradled Kate's hand, and when she shook her head, Kate could almost feel her heart begin to tremble. Would Dolly send her away? Where would she go? How far could she go on the little bit she would have left after she replaced Dolly's gloves . . . if she even had enough to pay for a new pair of driving gloves?

The gloves!

She had almost forgotten to tell Dolly about the gloves. "Mr. Massey tried to help me. He had to cut the glove off my hand, but I promise, I'll replace your gloves as soon as I can," she blurted.

There.

She was done with it!

Oddly enough, instead of feeling afraid now that she had admitted to the truth, she felt almost weightless. She had finally set herself free from the huge boulder of guilt she had carried for the entire day.

She owed Philip a great deal for inspiring her to begin

to redeem her new life, but as quickly as her spirit had soared, it dashed to the ground, struck by the lightning of her past.

It was one thing to divulge a small lapse in judgment to Miss Dolly and Miss Maggie; it was quite another to find the courage to admit that Kate's entire persona was a sham. She would need a lot more time with Philip Massey before she could take that one final leap of faith and admit to being the Ivory Duchess . . . to explain why she had lied . . . to trust . . .

She felt a gentle tug on her hand and looked up to see Dolly with a quizzical expression on her face. She must have been talking to Kate who had drifted into her own thoughts so completely she did not even hear her.

Another trance?

She trembled. "I'm sorry. I didn't mean to ignore you."

Maggie rose from her seat and wrapped her arms around Kate's shoulders. "You poor dear. I told Dolly she was too overbearing. She's got you frightened to death over something we decided almost the day you returned from the circuit. Just because . . . Go on, Dolly, tell her. Can't you see she's worried herself sick?"

Even if Dolly put her out of the cottage without a single coin for all her efforts, Kate knew Maggie had enriched her life with a most treasured gift: her affection. She glanced sideways and gave Maggie a smile.

"I'm very satisfied with your performance and want you to remain in your position as long as you like. I don't suppose it will be the end of the world if you delay the circuit for a few days." Dolly spoke as though she had just issued a royal decree, but to Kate, they were the sweetest words in the world. Her smile broadened, and her heart swelled with blessed joy.

In the next breath, however, Dolly's eyes hardened with censure. "I do expect you to be more careful in the future."

Kate nodded, willing to promise anything to keep her position.

"If you do something wrong or have a problem, you must speak up at once."

"I promise."

"Good." Dolly rose and stood beside her chair. "When you stop in Haddonfield for Patti and Susan's lessons, you may stop to see Mrs. Spencer at her shop. She knows my size. I'd like a pair of calfskin gloves. In dark brown."

She turned and made an exit as dramatic as Kate had ever made from the stage. The image was so real she could almost hear the sound of her fans' applause, but the sound that echoed loudest in Kate's mind at the moment was made by her cheering conscience.

She longed to hear that applause again one day, louder and even sweeter, when she could leap over the hurdles between the past and the present and share her joy and her life with the one man who was unwittingly guiding her and who had nearly stolen her heart in the process: Philip Massey.

Chapter 13

Kate had little energy left. Her patience had also been nearly depleted. After twelve days on the circuit, she faced an afternoon with the Mullan girls which was bound to use up what little patience she had left before she finished the last two lessons on her circuit. Since she had started the circuit late, several students had canceled their lessons, and she was actually longing to spend tonight in her own bed.

The Mullan girls, however, came first, and she had to put aside her excitement and gear herself up for their lessons. Sixteen-year-old twin daughters of a widowed minister in a small settlement just east of Haddonfield, Patti and Susan breathed credence into the popular stereotype of ministers' daughters.

Vain and superficial, they were prone to gossip and enamored with reading dime novels. It was their fascination with the Ivory Duchess which they had mentioned the first time Kate gave them lessons that made her particularly leery of returning today.

Surprisingly, they played the pianoforte like gifted angels. Conducting their actual instruction was a gentle zephyr compared to tolerating the gale force of their high-pitched prattle which required nerves of steel. Kate was still trying to establish her authority with the girls who were close enough in age to her they treated her more like an older sister than their instructor.

While Kate waited for the girls to appear in the sitting room, she unpacked the metronome and set it on the top of the upright piano next to a neat stack of music books. She heard the girls long before they entered the room. Groaning softly, she set her lips in a taut line and tried to imitate Miss Dolly's sternest expression just as a whirlwind of pink skirts and blond curls blew into the room and swirled around her.

"Miss Danaher, tell Patti it's perfectly natural to expect a young man will want to kiss you before you're betrothed. And it's totally proper."

"It's not!" Patti argued. "Not on the *lips*. That's shameful."

Kate shaped her best frown. "Now, girls—"

"Joseph Andrews kissed me twice. On the lips. And it wasn't shameful at all. It was divine! You're just jealous because you haven't been kissed." Susan puffed out her bottom lip and set her chin defiantly.

"That's not true! Matthew Leel kissed me—"

"On the cheek. That's not the same thing at all."

"Girls!" Kate cried, secretly relieved they had not broached the subject of the Ivory Duchess, but astounded they were arguing about kisses. Kisses!

Two pairs of startled blue eyes met her steady gaze. "Your bickering is distressing to me, and discussing such an intimate and personal matter is highly improper for young ladies. If anyone should overhear, your reputations would be ruined. Now I suggest we start with your lesson first, Susan, since you seem more preoccupied today than your sister."

Praying her stern reprimand would defuse the girls' interest in the topic, Kate held absolutely still. Her heart pounding, she scarcely drew a breath and never dropped her gaze.

Patti lowered her head as a blush stained her cheeks. "I beg your pardon, Miss Danaher."

Susan's eyes flashed. "You've been kissed properly, haven't you, Miss Danaher?"

Kate blinked hard. "I don't think—"

"Of course you have," Susan pouted. "At your age, you've probably been kissed properly by at least three or four men and you're certainly not betrothed yet."

Kissed? Very nearly. But just once.

The memory of the kiss she and Philip had almost shared rushed straight to Kate's cheeks and tripped her heartbeat. There had scarcely been a night when she did not lie awake wondering why he had turned away from her when his lips had been so close. So very close. And yet later in the barn . . .

With a shake of her head, she forced the memories aside. "I have no intention of discussing my personal life with you or anyone else," she warned. "A proper young lady would not be so impertinent."

Susan shrugged her shoulders. "Then you haven't been kissed at all."

Stunned by the girl's audacity, Kate could do no more than stare at her. No, she had not been kissed, but at least she thought she had finally figured out why. The only reason Philip had not kissed her was because he had been too afraid she would ultimately reject him. Obviously, gossip about him had cost him any hope that a woman of worth would find him suitable as a marriage partner. Even Miss Dolly had expressed her doubts about his suitability.

"What I haven't got is any time for gossip," Kate admonished, hoping the motherwort tea was still proving to be effective for him. "Shall we start your lesson, or shall I simply tell Rev. Mullan—"

Susan plopped onto the bench, obviously less than anxious to disrupt her father who was upstairs preparing his Sunday sermon. She reached up to set the metronome herself and knocked several music books to the floor. Patti tried to scoop them up from the floor, but in the process, several new books toppled over the edge.

Kate bent down to pick up the books and noticed a clipping from a newspaper that lay on the floor. She assumed it must have slipped out of one of the books. She reached to pick it up and her hand collided with Patti's as they both took hold of the clipping. Their gazes met and held as neither relinquished possession.

"Please, Miss Danaher. May I have my clipping?"

Although curious about the glint of guilt in Patti's eyes, Kate let go of the clipping immediately. "Is it a poem you found appealing? Perhaps you'd share it with me. I love poetry."

The girl glanced from Susan to Kate and shifted from one foot to another. "It's not a poem. It's just something Susan and I wanted to save."

"Don't be such a ninny," Susan ordered. "Let her see it. We've already copied it into our day books."

Patti turned to her sister and frowned. "Miss Danaher said we shouldn't gossip about the Ivory Duchess."

Susan groaned. "Reading about the Duchess isn't gossiping about her."

Kate's heart leaped and pounded in her chest, but she made no move to interrupt as the girls' second argument of the day escalated into another verbal battle. If the newspaper article was about the Ivory Duchess, there was no doubt in her mind that Simon had been unable to find her and had done the unthinkable: He had reported her disappearance to the authorities! Wasn't he afraid to put the new concert tour in jeopardy? If he was trying to enlist popular support in an effort to find her, how much of a description would he give them? How many people were already looking for her?

Light-headed with fear and the desperate need to read the article, she reached out and took it out of Patti's hands.

Patti's mouth dropped open, and Kate smiled as sweetly as she could. "I came here for your lessons, and I intend to teach today. When your lesson is concluded, you may have your clipping." She glanced at Susan who was still sitting at the piano bench and nodded. "Please begin."

The lesson progressed slowly, giving Kate time to grow concerned that the girls might interpret her interest in the article as something other than a distraction to their lessons. It would be mean-spirited to refuse to return the clipping, but it would be more than dangerous to return it to Patti without knowing what news the article contained. Unless Kate read the clipping, she would not know whether it was safe to stay here in southern New Jersey or time for her to disappear.

Again.

Oddly, as she pondered the appearance of the article, her heart filled with another emotion—wonder. Although she still felt ashamed for playing the role of the Ivory Duchess, a role that was the pure fabrication of Simon's moneygrubbing imagination, she did have hope. If there was any redeeming value to the years she had spent as the Ivory Duchess, it was knowing that she had been able to share her love for the pianoforte with the audiences and inspired some young women, like Patti and Susan Mullan, to learn to play the pianoforte because they admired her talent.

Although she would never get the chance to tell these young women how much they meant to her, she could tell Patti and Susan. Suddenly, it seemed much more important to speak what was in her heart than to worry about keeping the clipping. She would simply have to find another way to get the newspaper article. Worry, however, did not lose easily to better sense and it tugged at her heart.

By the time both girls had completed their lessons, Kate was in a quandary severe enough to give her a splitting headache. She recorded the girls' payments in Dolly's record book, sighed, and handed the clipping back to Patti. "I'm sure the Ivory Duchess would be very pleased to know you care enough to write something about her in your day book or to keep a clipping about her."

Patti smiled. "Thank you. I think I like you almost as much as the Duchess."

Before Kate could draw another breath, Patti tucked the clipping into Kate's hand and tugged her sister out of the room.

Torn between the overwhelming urge to read the clipping and afraid of the information it actually contained, she closed her eyes and thought of Philip. What would he do? She listened to the beat of her own heart and knew he would not hesitate to read it.

But she was not Philip, and she did not have the fortitude he had developed. Not yet. If the news in the clipping was devastating, there was nothing she could do to change it. If by some miracle the news was in her favor, this was not the place to celebrate. She could, however, choose the time and place to read it. For now, that was about as much courage as she could garner, but it was a far cry from what she would have done only a month ago, and it was a beginning step toward the rest of her life she was anxious to acknowledge.

She had two more lessons scheduled for this morning and had to stop at Mrs. Spencer's shop in Haddonfield to order Dolly's gloves. Then and only then would she have a moment to herself to read the article before driving home.

The more she thought about waiting, the more the idea

appealed to her. There was a secluded spot along Cooper's Creek she had noticed when she had traveled the circuit for the first time that would be perfect.

Excited by having chosen when and where she would read the clipping, she packed it safely inside her valise and set off for her next lesson.

The moment Kate had waited for had finally come. Nearly hidden from the roadway, she sat along the bank of Cooper's Creek. Several barges carrying farm produce made their way along the water, but the article she carried with her held all of her attention. The late afternoon sun promised a few more hours of daylight and plenty of time for her to be alone as she confronted the first real threat to her freedom.

The river lapped gently against the shoreline, a calm and peaceful rhythm that did not ease the pounding of her heart as she removed her bonnet to enjoy the full warmth of the sun and laid it on the grass beside her. She unfolded the article, and her hands shook as she smoothed the clipping against her skirts. When she glanced at the top, a date, June 15, 1854, was penciled across the margin. That was nearly a week ago!

She heaved a sigh of relief and closed her eyes. If a full week had passed since the article had appeared in the newspaper, then perhaps there was nothing to fear, and she felt brave enough to take another look. Nearly a full column long, the article entitled *An Adopted Daughter* featured a small stencil of a pair of pianofortes on either side of the title. Nearly frantic to know what the intriguing title might mean, she read the article as slowly as she dared.

In seclusion following her most recent American tour, the Ivory Duchess is preparing for the fall concert season. Through her agent, Mr. Simon Morrell, she wishes to publicly thank her many fans for their support and offers heartfelt encouragement to the young women across the country who are discovering the joy of playing the pianoforte.

Overwhelmed by the growing popularity of this remarkable instrument in this fair country, she is pleased to announce her decision to make her permanent home in America.

Information surrounding the precise location where she will reside is as shrouded in mystery as the performer herself or the itinerary for her fall tour. Mr. Morrell promises further details will be announced in August to allow her many admirers to make plans to attend what promises to be the highlight of the fall season.

With the possible exception of Miss Jenny Lind, there has yet to be a woman who has graced the American stage with such elegance. The Ivory Duchess is to be commended for inspiring the daughters of liberty to add their competence on the pianoforte to their list of accomplishments. Clearly there can be no greater blessing than to have the mothers of our future citizens include a love for music as yet another cornerstone in family life which is so critical to the proper formation of good character.

To her detractors, we urge silence! Her many admirers applaud her and welcome the Ivory Duchess as an adopted daughter of liberty.

Blinking back tears, Kate's heart would have burst with gratitude for the kind and effusive words in the article, but all she could focus on was the first paragraph. Simon was far more devious than she had expected, and twice as arrogant as she remembered. To even think she would return to the stage in September was outrageous! He knew perfectly well there would be no fall concert tour because she had escaped and disappeared. To make his statement to the newspaper constituted fraud.

Nothing had changed, she realized. He was still the master manipulator of the press he had always been.

"But I've changed," she whispered, refusing to let her fear of him paralyze her thoughts and send her running blindly to escape his clutches. She closed her eyes briefly and brought Philip Massey's image to her mind as well as his strength, his courage, and his confidence.

She claimed them now for herself.

Using all of her powers of concentration, she tried to analyze Simon's intentions. Clearly he expected her to return to perform, and since he knew she would never do so willingly, she could only reach one conclusion: He had hired someone to find her. Someone who had tried to trace her movements from the moment she had made her daring daytime escape from the Morningstar Hotel, spent a week in hiding at a boardinghouse, fled at midnight on the ferry from Philadelphia to Camden, and made her way to Dolly and Maggie's cottage.

Since the man Simon had hired had not found her yet, there was a very good chance he had lost her trail. He needed a new one, and that's why either he or Simon had planted this article—to frighten her and force her to run again so there would be a fresh trail to follow.

But she was not going to run. She did not have to run. She had found sanctuary here in this rural, peaceful countryside. She had found a home with Dolly and Maggie and a position with students who admired and respected her. And she had found a very special man who had taught her the redeeming power of honesty and courage.

Nearly giddy with relief that the article could not hurt her, she jumped up and spun around, dancing to the music her own joy created in her heart. She danced and danced, swirling until she was breathless . . . and dizzy. She swayed on her feet and braced her legs, closing her eyes until her head stopped spinning and her heart stopped racing.

When she finally felt steady on her feet, she opened her eyes, slipped the article back into her pocket, and turned away from the river. She stooped down to retrieve her bonnet, and caught the glimpse of a shadow on the grass. The shadow of a man who was approaching her.

Still low to the ground, she dropped her hold on the bonnet and clutched one hand to her heart. When she finally looked up and saw the man who now was standing only a few feet away, she gasped.

Chapter 14

~~~~~~

Philip approached her slowly, hoping not to frighten her, and the moment she looked up at him, he stopped and held absolutely still. His heart pounding, he reached out to her. When she took his hand briefly to stand up, she smiled tentatively.

Fear flashed in her eyes, but the glimmer of recognition quickly extinguished that fear. Unadorned desire smoldered and reached out to touch the yearning in his heart that had been aching relentlessly since she had left for the circuit and set off an internal struggle that had robbed him of his sleep and perhaps, he feared, his very sanity.

Riding home from a trip to Haddonfield, his longing to see her again had been so strong, he was certain that the woman dancing by the creek had been created by his own traitorous imagination until he had seen Precious tethered nearby.

With his gaze locked with Kathryn's, he paused, rendered still by his own indecision only briefly before deciding that even the King of All Fools was entitled to one weak moment. He made a conscious decision he knew he was bound to regret later. Much, much later.

He stared at her, knowing he could not alter the will of

the fates that had destined them to be adversaries, but determined to suspend reality long enough to satisfy the deep desires of his heart—desires that had been denied for too long.

He gazed deep into her eyes and held very still as Omega slipped away to await another assignment. Even Philip Massey, with his checkered past and uncertain future, took his leave. For just this moment in suspended time, he was standing there as a man who had needs and desires that could only be met by a woman similarly chained by her own multiple identities on this earth.

He commanded them to leave.

Within a heartbeat, he watched in awe as he saw the prim and proper Kathryn Danaher flee and the imperious Ivory Duchess stomp off to await resurrection later. Only Kate— beautiful in her youth and innocence and tender heart— stood before him.

He held his breath as time continued to stand still, giving two troubled souls a moment to seek comfort and rest with one another as new creations in the universe. She moistened her pale pink lips with the tip of her tongue, and he stepped closer to dip his head and accept the invitation to sample the taste of her sweetness.

The afternoon sun was still hot, and when he touched his lips to hers in a feather-light kiss, he found cool refreshment for his body as well as his soul. He cradled her face with his hands, teasing the hollow of her cheeks with the pads of his thumbs, intrigued by the feel of her satin flesh.

She held her eyes closed and leaned into his hands. His fingers intertwined in her hair where the power of the sun added even more heat to the warm sensations that rippled through his fingers.

More. He wanted more.

He stepped closer still, and when she moved into his arms, his heartbeat quickened. She laid her cheek on his shoulder, and he enfolded her in his embrace as tender emotions surged through his body and the need to protect her grew almost as powerful as the need to kiss her again. And again, until the thirst in his soul could be quenched for all time.

He tilted her face up to the sun and pressed gentle kisses to her closed eyelids. When she trembled, he claimed her lips, teasing them with the tip of his tongue until she gave him yet another invitation to explore and discover even more of the mystery that was Kate.

His face shadowed hers before he closed his eyes and delved into the cool and blessed wonder of their kiss. Deeper. Probing. Searching for the source of her as he shared his own pleasure with a groan that rumbled in his throat.

Soft and warm, her breasts pressed against his chest, and her hands gripped his shoulders. A new surge of desire, centered in his loins, sent shock waves spiraling through his body. Shaken by the powerful urges he could not satisfy with mere kisses, however sweet they might be, he eased from their kiss with one regret: His escape into nonreality had been far too brief.

Breathing hard, he stepped away from her. He could almost feel his two identities as they clamored to reclaim their rightful places: Philip Massey—the idealist—and Omega—the cynic. He watched with fascination as the prim and proper Kathryn Danaher slipped back into place and knew that the Ivory Duchess was hiding once again, just beneath the surface.

The sweep of time, it seemed, had begun again.

A flustered and pale Kathryn put a trembling hand to her lips and lowered her gaze. Chuckling, he pushed a tendril of hair from her cheek. "If I have misstepped propriety's boundaries, please forgive me," he murmured. "I found myself totally enchanted. Do you make it a practice to dance along every creek on your circuit or just this one?''

Her cheeks flamed the color of a brilliant sunset. "I-I . . . of course not,'' she stammered, but her eyes flashed with reprimand. "I thought I had chosen a very secluded place. One that was private. Are you always in the habit of sneaking up on a woman and scaring her half to death and then . . . then taking advantage of her?''

He could not stop a wide, teasing grin. "Only when the woman is quite receptive.''

Berry red cheeks this time, he noted.

"How totally out of character for you, Mr. Massey. I had thought you to be a total gentleman. Obviously, I was mistaken.'' She turned and stooped down to fetch her bonnet.

Intrigued by how quickly she had slipped back into a more formal role, he realized how badly he was performing in his own. He walked up to her back as she stood there, ramrod stiff, at the creek. "I'm sorry. You're absolutely right. Please accept my apology and my promise that I won't let it happen again. I was just so surprised to see you I wasn't thinking clearly. I didn't expect you to return for a few days yet.''

He held his breath until finally, when he thought his lungs would burst, the tense set of her shoulders eased. She turned around as she tied the ribbons on her bonnet. She looked up at him with those damnably gorgeous hazel eyes. They were a bit misty. With unshed tears?

"I accept your apology and offer one of my own.'' She glanced over his shoulder and squinted at the sun. "We've both probably been a bit touched by the heat.''

He nodded.

"It's been a long circuit, and I'm anxious to get home.''

"Do you mind if I ride along with you, or . . . No. Perhaps it might be better if I took a different route.''

Her gazed softened. "Not at all. I'd enjoy the company.

I don't often get someone to talk to while traveling," she offered as they made their way to the road cart.

He took her hand to help her get to her seat and paused to turn it over to find pale new skin on her fingertips. "Your hand looks well."

She smiled. "Thanks to your intervention. I trust you received my note?"

Smiling, he helped her into the seat. "I'm glad you told Miss Dolly and took an extra few days to let those blisters heal. I didn't think you'd be back this early, though, since you had a late start."

"Several students canceled," she explained as he untethered the mule. She caught her bottom lip with her teeth for a moment. "Shall we start your lessons again tomorrow?"

He noted her now-pale cheeks and saw her hands tremble as she put on a pair of gloves that had been lying on the seat before taking the reins he held out to her. Did she think she had tarnished her reputation and jeopardized her chance at continuing his lessons by allowing him the liberty of a few sweet kisses?

He was more than tempted to let her think so, but she was not the only one who had been knocked off-kilter by their chance encounter and spellbinding embraces. When he had kissed her, he had tasted the fulfillment that promised to await him in the arms of a woman who would love him and respect him. Knowing he was probably never going to find such a woman, especially since he was not even sure he could ever give up his life as Omega, made their kisses even more bittersweet.

Growing anxious to find the brooch and bring a quick end to this assignment before he completely lost his focus and dared to dream about how sweet his life could be with a woman like Kate by his side, he attempted to smile. "Tomorrow morning at ten?"

She nodded, a look of pure relief in her eyes, and he had the most uncommon and inexplicable desire to set her mind completely at ease and see the glow of happiness on her face. He tugged on the reins. "Wait here a moment." He jogged back to his mount which he had tethered closer to the roadway, took a small package out of a saddlebag, and ran back to hand it to her. "Since I'm riding along with you, I'd like to . . . well, just open this."

She stared at the package. "What's this?"

"A gift," he said quietly. "Open it."

She stared at the brown paper package for several moments. Eyes wide, she acted like no one had ever given her a present. "I-I can't accept a gift from you," she whispered, although unconcealed longing glistened in her eyes. "It wouldn't be proper."

He chuckled. "Then it's not a gift. Consider it repayment for a debt I owe you." He took the package away from her, opened it, and handed her the present he had gone to Haddonfield to pick up for her, thinking he was several days ahead of her return. "Mrs. Spencer makes the finest in the area, or so Nelda tells me."

She turned the tan leather gloves over and over, her eyes misting, and this time he knew there were tears in her eyes. "They're beautiful. But why did you buy them for me?" She turned her face to him and he saw it in her eyes again—that amazing combination of innocence and wonder that she could release from her pure heart so naturally he caught his breath and found it hard to rein in his desires.

This time he was not fantasizing.

This time he was not facing this woman in a brief moment when time had suspended and erased their mutual pasts.

This time, he was Omega, and he saw through her agent's lies and beyond her reported reputation to behold a very special and unique woman.

At once bewildered and beguiled, he lowered his gaze. "Since I was the one who insisted on cutting your glove, I felt an obligation to replace it."

"But I was the one who foolishly wore the glove. I ordered a new pair for Miss Dolly just today with Mrs. Spencer."

"And since I knew you wouldn't order a decent pair of your own, I took the liberty," he countered. "Now at least try them on."

Without any hesitation at all, she pulled off the cracked old gloves she had used as a spare pair and started to slide her hands into the new gloves. Convinced he could steel himself against her allure, he was unprepared for the evocative thoughts that crackled through his mind like bolts of lightning as she studied her hands.

When she slipped one of her hands into the palm of a new glove, his heart started to pound with the memory of how her hand had felt when he had helped her to stand up. When she eased her fingers into each leather slot and pulled the glove taut, he could feel the pressure of her hands on his shoulders during their kiss. Their second kiss. The kiss that unleashed far more dangerous desires pulsing through his body than the first.

"Perfect fit," he announced, trying not to grit his teeth. "I gave Mrs. Spencer a rather hard time of it, but the gloves fit and that's all that matters. Wear them in good health," he said softly and turned away to get his mount before she could mouth another single word of gratitude or protest.

His mind, however, would not release the image of how she had molded against his body, "Perfect fit," he muttered as he mounted his horse, but knew better than to sustain any kind of hope their lives would ever be entwined beyond the duration of this assignment.

Despite the many questions about the Ivory Duchess he had that remained to be answered, he instinctively knew the guileless nature of this woman. If she had turned her back on the stage and planned to live a more normal life, she deserved a man who would be able to give her deep community roots with a home and a family, not a man so accustomed to intrigue and subterfuge he had difficulty believing he would ever be able to reclaim a normal life for himself.

Reminding himself to stay focused on his assignment long enough to find the cameo brooch, he spurred his horse and rode back to join her. He could not, however, return her to Simon Morrell until he knew exactly why she had chosen to abandon her stage career and why Morrell was so determined to override her decision and force her back.

On the short drive from Cooper's Creek to the cottage, Philip Massey rode alongside her road cart, and Kate found it difficult to keep her mind on the road. Fortunately, Precious knew the route so well she hardly needed much attention, and Kate found the reins slack more often as not as she gave the mule her own head.

"How do the gloves feel?" he asked, breaking a brief lull in the conversation.

"Like pure gold. I can't thank you enough," she said with a smile that came clear from the bottom of her heart. "It was very thoughtful of you."

He smiled back at her. "I'm glad I could brighten your day, although I gather you had an unusually good day as it was."

She frowned, but quickly smiled again. "As a matter of fact, I had one glorious day. Even with the Mullan twins." Her heart started to race, and she was relieved that the girls' argument about kissing had taken place before she had experienced the thrill of her first very proper and thorough kiss! For half a heartbeat, she had feared he would turn away from her the same way he had done the day he had carried her to the house in the pouring rain.

She had seen his vulnerability, his need, and his indecision again today, and when he finally touched her lips with his kiss, her heart and body had rejoiced with a thrill that was far more than physical. He trusted her with his heart. Could she trust him with hers?

She glanced up at him, but he just shook his head and shrugged. "The Mullan girls?"

"Rev. Mullan's daughters. Patti and Susan."

His gaze remained confused.

"They're rather a precocious pair," she explained. "They're also prone to silly gossip, but they have a flair for the pianoforte that more than makes up for it. Once they finally get to their lessons."

He laughed with her. "And what were the girls gossiping about today?"

Kisses. Proper and improper kisses.

She almost blurted out her thought. Horrified, she gulped hard and almost bit her tongue. If she dared to even mention the topic, it would no doubt lead to a discussion of what had magically taken place by the creek when they had kissed. That was one topic she had to avoid until she had the time alone to understand the enchantment of their kisses completely herself—before she talked about it with him.

She slipped her hand into her pocket and wrapped her fingers around the newspaper clipping. Did she dare mention the Ivory Duchess? If she did, would she find him unsympathetic and disinterested, or would this be an opportunity, albeit a limited one, to discuss the Ivory Duchess and test her ability to speak about her in a detached way?

There was no one she trusted nearly as much as Philip Massey, with the possible exception of Miss Maggie, and it was far too risky to discuss the Ivory Duchess with her without invoking Dolly's censure. Borrowing a bit of his courage to add to her own, she ventured into the unchartered waters that might carry her to her future.

"The girls are both quite enamored with the Ivory Duchess," she gushed before she could change her mind.

Dear God, did he tense for a moment at the mention of the Ivory Duchess or was it just a temporary change in his stance as he shifted in the saddle? She nearly sighed with relief when he glanced back at her. His expression was blandly matter-of-fact.

"The pianist?"

"You've heard of her," she said, trying to control the pounding of her heart.

"Most people have," he noted with amusement. "Actually, I attended one of her performances this past spring in Philadelphia."

Two strong fists of panic and fear gripped her throat and nearly strangled her attempts to breathe. Her hands froze around the reins, and her heart pounded in her chest. Dolly and Maggie had seen the Ivory Duchess perform last year. They had not recognized her, but he had seen her only weeks ago. Had her veiled costume truly prevented him from recognizing her, or had he been playing with her all along? She groped for some hint of an answer that would not make her association with him a dreadful, careless mistake.

"Talented lady," he remarked, as casually as if he were discussing any other performer who might have included Philadelphia on a tour. He looked at her, and his eyes filled with concern. "Are you all right?"

She nodded and dared to take a few breaths of air. He looked so sincere and worried about her, she labeled herself foolish for doubting him and blamed her own shame for her past and her guilt for deceiving him for tainting her perceptions of him. "The girls are inspired by her talent for the pianoforte," she offered, trying to discover whether he was one of her detractors or supporters, "but her past is quite scandalous."

His expression softened, and he shook his head. "I'm surprised you find her an objectionable source of inspiration since no one has even been able to identify the Ivory Duchess or prove any of the gossip about her is true. Until that happens, I withhold judgment about the woman, and even if there is some truth to the gossip, I'd be more inclined to wish her well than condemn her. At least she's trying to put the past behind her."

Stung by his gentle reprimand, yet grateful for his defense of her stage persona, she gave him yet another piece of her heart. She lowered her gaze and concentrated on a curve in the road. "Not everyone would agree with you."

"I expected you might."

Her head snapped to the side. "I do, but Miss Dolly is very adamant about stopping gossip, especially among her students. It distracts them from their lessons. The first time I was with the Mullan girls, the very first thing they wanted to know was whether or not I had ever seen the Ivory Duchess perform."

His brows lifted. "Have you?"

She gulped hard. "No. I've . . . I've never had the funds to purchase a ticket." It was the best excuse she could offer and still avoid a direct lie. It pained her conscience not to be able to tell him the truth, but she was not ready to tell him. Not yet.

He eased back in his saddle. "There are probably dozens of pianists who have more skill for the pianoforte, but no one can play with more emotion. Her gift to the audience is unique."

Intrigued, she nodded. "What gift might that be?"

"Love. Simply put, she doesn't play the piano, she caresses it. She doesn't interpret a selection from Beethoven or Mozart—she becomes the music. It's that magical, mystifying love affair she has with the pianoforte that captures the audience and the heart of every little girl fortunate enough to be there.''

Tears welled in her eyes, and she had to take shallow breaths of air. ''No wonder the girls are so enamored with her and dedicate themselves to their lessons.''

''And now you know why I was inspired to take lessons, although I daresay she'd shudder if she ever heard a single one of my miserable attempts,'' he said with a small laugh.

''She's had years of training, I'm sure. She wouldn't laugh,'' she countered.

''Now there's the gracious and tactful instructor I know so well!'' He furrowed his brow. ''As a matter of fact, *The West Jerseyman* recently ran an article about the Ivory Duchess. Did you read it by any chance?''

The article in her pocket suddenly felt like a hot coal. Frantic to avoid any further discussion about the Ivory Duchess, she shrugged her shoulders. ''Not really. I just skimmed through it.''

''Apparently, she's going to settle in the United States permanently which isn't a bad idea,'' he suggested, refusing to let the subject drop despite the disinterest she tried to convey. ''She has a new tour scheduled for the fall, and her agent is reportedly going to provide a list in August of the cities where she'll be appearing. I expect Philadelphia will be included, which means you'll have another opportunity to see her.''

Panic scampered from her brain to her fingertips again, and her hands rattled the reins. ''I-I don't . . . I don't think I'll see her perform.''

He grinned. ''Of course you will because I'm going to take you. Miss Dolly and her sister, too, if you like. Then you can all see what I mean for yourselves.''

''No! I mean . . . Miss Dolly and Miss Maggie saw the Ivory Duchess perform last year—''

"That's even better," he said as he brought his horse to a halt. She looked around and realized they had reached the entrance to the drive that led behind the cottage to the barn.

"I'm not sure—"

"Of course you'll go. We'll discuss it again tomorrow. At ten." He grinned again and took his leave before she could argue with him.

"Tomorrow at ten," she repeated as she urged Precious to take the last few steps home slowly. The odds that Philip Massey and Kathryn Danaher would ever sit in the audience to watch the Ivory Duchess perform had about the same chance of happening as the sun changing places with the moon or having one of the stars slip from the sky to rest in a ring on her finger.

Or finding a way to tell him the truth before she gave him the last little piece of her heart.

Chapter 15

By the time Kate unharnessed Precious and unloaded the road cart, exhaustion had drained all thoughts about her conversation with Philip Massey from her mind. Feeling grimy and overheated, she gladly accepted Maggie's suggestion to bathe before supper.

Emerging from her room with her hair still damp, she found the table set with filled platters and both sisters waiting for her to join them. "I'm sorry I took so long," she murmured as she took her seat across from them at the table. "Thank you for waiting."

She glanced at her plate which was filled with slices of chilled chicken, fresh garden greens, and a mound of corn relish. "This looks delicious."

Dolly nodded as though officially signaling the start of supper, and they began to eat. "I'm curious," she remarked as she dabbed at her lips with her napkin. "Did I notice you wearing a new pair of gloves?"

Kate nearly choked on a bite of chicken and took a swallow of water. "Yes. They're lovely, aren't they?"

Dolly's eyes narrowed. "A new purchase?"

"Oh, no. Not at all. They were a gift." She swallowed hard, but refused to consider telling Dolly anything less than the truth. "I met Mr. Massey as I was coming home, and he was just returning from Mrs. Spencer's."

"I knew it!" Maggie grinned, her eyes sparkling. "He's trying to court you, and he gave them to you as a token of his affection."

"Most inappropriate," Dolly sniffed. "I thought I made my feelings on the matter perfectly clear."

A shiver of alarm raced up Kate's spine. "Yes. You did, but please don't interpret Mr. Massey's gift as anything more than kindness. He . . . he felt badly about having to cut the glove I had borrowed from you when I had burned my fingers and felt obligated to replace it. I tried to decline—"

"He's such a dear man," Maggie sighed.

"Well-intentioned, but unreliable in the long run. As most men are," Dolly snapped.

She sounded almost bitter.

"It wasn't Mr. Massey's obligation to replace the pair of gloves," she continued. "It was yours, Kate. And they were my gloves, after all. If he intended to make amends, he should have—"

"I've already ordered your gloves from Mrs. Spencer," Kate said firmly. As much as she respected Miss Dolly and appreciated the position that had allowed Kate to forge a new life for herself, there was an occasional streak of selfishness in her mentor that had quietly emerged in the past six weeks.

Yet even as she recognized this minor flaw in Dolly's character, Kate felt a surge of sympathy for the elderly woman. Her resentment of Philip Massey's intentions, even though Kate was sure they had been misconstrued, must stem from a deep and long-ago disappointment with a man who had hurt Dolly so badly that the pain suffered in the past had never healed.

Her heart softened as her own difficult past joined with

Miss Dolly's and bound them together as closely as the bonds of friendship between Kate and Miss Maggie. "I hope you like the gloves I ordered. Mrs. Spencer helped me to select a beautiful dark brown shade, and she assured me the gloves would be ready before I leave for the circuit again. In the meantime, if you'd like to use the new gloves . . ."

"No," Dolly whispered as though struggling to find her voice. "I shall be perfectly content to wait for my own." She set her fork down and sighed. "I'm not feeling very hungry. If you'll both excuse me." She rose without waiting for an answer and left the room, leaving behind a wake of awkward stillness in the kitchen until the strains of a plaintive melody began to float through the air as Dolly took to her pianoforte.

Maggie reached across the table and patted Kate's hand. "Don't you fret about your new gloves. Dolly's just a bit tired today. The heat gets to her. She'll feel better after she plays for a while."

She looked up at the doorway, then winked at Kate. "Now tell me about your students and don't leave out the smallest little piece of gossip."

Laughing softly, Kate recounted a few tidbits of news while they finished supper, ending with a spicy rendering of how Mrs. Bennett had canceled her lesson.

"You've left something out," Maggie challenged, her voice low.

Guilt painted a blush on Kate's cheeks. "The Mullan girls."

"Of course. Dolly never came back from the circuit without some complaint about them. What are they up to now?"

Giggling, Kate could not resist telling Maggie about the girls' first argument while Dolly was still playing in the other room. "Kissing."

Maggie's eyes widened. "Kissing? Oh, those girls are going to make their papa's hair turn white unless he gets them married off soon."

"He's already white and losing a bit on top," Kate admitted as she sampled a dish of custard for dessert.

"The poor man. All alone without a wife. He's got a full plate with those two." Maggie sat back in her chair. "Did they bother you about the Duchess again?"

Kate's heart began to pound. She was torn between telling Maggie about the newspaper article or keeping it to herself, but since Dolly was still at her pianoforte, it seemed harmless enough to mention to Maggie. Of the two sisters, Kate felt closest to Maggie. Sharing the news contained in the article with her would give Kate the opportunity to gauge someone else's reaction to the clipping other than Philip or her own. "Well, actually . . . Wait. I have something to show you."

She paused a moment to get Maggie's assent and retrieved the article from her room. She handed the clipping to Maggie before retaking her seat. "I wasn't going to mention this since Miss Dolly seems to find the girls' fascination with the Ivory Duchess unsettling, so maybe it's best if you don't tell her about it."

"Oh, Dolly and I saw this article. I was wondering if anyone had shown it to you." She handed the article back to Kate who quickly folded it and put it into her pocket. Few of the families on her circuit had a recent newspaper, and even if they had, it was unlikely they would have shared it with her.

"What do you think? About the Ivory Duchess choosing to settle permanently in America?" she asked as her heart began to hammer with anticipation.

"What do I think? Well, I think it's—"

Dolly's voice rang out. "It's totally irrelevant what anyone thinks."

Why hadn't Kate noticed the music had stopped? Startled, she turned around in her seat and found Dolly standing in the doorway between the music room and the kitchen.

With a forbidding glare, she tilted her chin in the air. "I thought you were going to stifle the girls' curiosity about the Ivory Duchess, not encourage it, Kate. And as for your insatiable thirst for gossip, sister dear, I have one suggestion. Try drinking a glass of water. It's far less dangerous than gossip."

Kate met Dolly's gaze with her own. "I meant no harm by bringing up the Ivory Duchess. I . . . I took the article away from Patti and Susan and told them I was distressed by their behavior." Well, it was as close to the truth as she dared to get, and Kate held her breath as she stood her ground. If she was going to live here with Maggie and Dolly for any length of time, she could not let Dolly intimidate her. At the same time, she could not afford to alienate the one woman who held the only key to Kate's security and future. "Patti was very apologetic," she said quietly.

"And Susan merely shrugged her strong-willed shoulders," Dolly added, obviously well-familiar with both girls' temperaments.

"That's why I set Susan to her lesson first. To distract her. To be fair, I think the girls are very talented, and their interest in the Ivory Duchess is more as a source of inspiration than mere idle prattle."

"Perhaps." Dolly's expression softened. "Then you handled the situation well. With time, you may learn to be a good teacher. It all depends on how you intend to spend your life. You have a gift for the pianoforte that you can share with your students, and I'd hate to see you throw all of that away by tarnishing your reputation."

Kate furrowed her brows. "Have I . . . have I done something else . . ."

Dolly shook her head. "Not yet, but if you continue to

give Philip Massey serious thought as part of your future, you may. You've admitted yourself that you've been foolish in affairs of the heart once before, and I think—''

"Pshaw! The girl is young, but she's not a total ninny. Leave her be. Leave them both. be," Maggie urged. "They've only just met, and Kate has a good head on her shoulders. She's not about to give her heart away to the first man who pays her any heed."

"Second."

"What?"

"Second man," Dolly repeated before Kate could squeeze in a word.

"And she's not going to leave us for a good, long while. Are you, Kate?"

Maggie's question opened the door to perhaps an unspoken concern each of the two women had obviously shared with each other, and one look at the uncertainty in Dolly's eyes was enough to unleash the insight Kate had been struggling to gain. Dolly's reticence and Maggie's open friendship were both laced with the same concern: How long would Kate stay?

If they only knew how desperately she needed to stay!

Relief surged through her body like cool lotion spread on fevered flesh, and she smiled. "I would never do anything to put my position at risk." She gulped hard. "Philip Massey is my friend. Nothing more. If it would set your mind at ease, perhaps it might be better if he came here for lessons instead of my traveling to his home."

Dolly blinked several times, but quickly regained her composure. "For a while, I think that might be best. I find it hard to believe Mr. Massey's attentions are based purely on friendship."

"But he'd never compromise our Kate. He's far too honorable," Maggie complained as she started to clear the table. "I'd be delighted to have him come here for I simply enjoy the man's company."

Joining in the task of cleanup, Kate started to wash the dishes, but her mind was not focused on her work or the fact that she would have to tell Philip Massey tomorrow that if he wanted to continue his lessons on the pianoforte, he would have to come to the cottage. Instead, she found herself reacting very much on the defensive as Maggie and Dolly discussed what time Mr. Massey's lessons would be scheduled so they would not interfere with Dolly's students.

Philip's interest in Kate was too premature to qualify as anything more than friendship, but she was certain he would never act less than a gentleman . . . until her lips began to tingle with the memory of the kisses they had shared by the creek.

Was she so naive and inexperienced with men that she could believe it was possible for a man and woman to share friendship and nothing more? Obviously, neither Dolly nor Maggie believed it was possible, but even though they were old enough to be her grandmother, neither had ever been married.

Oh, Gram, I need you!

Gram would know what to do and say to ease Kate's confusion, but Gram was not here. Kate only had Maggie and Dolly and was reluctant to really confide in either of them or to seek their advice on such a sensitive topic.

While Maggie's spells might have precluded courtship and marriage, Dolly had obviously been very attractive in her youth and would have had any number of suitors vying for her hand. One suitor, in particular, must have caught her eye and misled her, stealing her heart with false intentions. Is that why Dolly was so protective, in her own way, of Kate? Was disappointment in love the cause of the flare of bitterness that occasionally rose to the surface?

When the kitchen had been restored to order, Maggie and

Dolly both retired to their rooms, satisfied they had resolved the issue. They had decided to send a note to Philip Massey with the iceman who was making deliveries in the area early in the morning. Kate wandered to the music room and lightly ran her fingers over the keyboard of the pianoforte. How had Philip described her playing?

As caressing.

As a gift of love to her audience.

Tears misted her vision, and she sat down on the bench to play. Immersing herself in her music, she began to see her role as the Ivory Duchess as much more complicated than just a single layer of scandal. If she truly had moved her audiences, if she had inspired just one young woman to discover the joy of music and the satisfaction of learning to play the pianoforte, perhaps she had judged herself and her past too harshly.

As she continued to play, her troubled thoughts began to dissipate. She became one with the instrument beneath her fingertips, flowing into the selection, and losing her identity until she soared above the forces that kept her bound to earth, flying higher still to the planes of another existence— one filled with goodness and truth, gentleness and love.

Her heart swelled with joy, and she dared to believe that one day she would be forever freed from the mistakes of her past. One day, she prayed, she would truly escape into a future filled with the promises of love that had yet to be fulfilled.

Her fingers stroked the keys. In the deepest recesses of her spirit, she knew that just as she had made peace with her pianoforte and her talent, she would one day find a way to reconcile her past with the present. One day, she might find a man who would love her totally and completely. One man—who would steal her heart away and forever bind it with his own.

If that dream would ever come true, she had quite a bit

to resolve in her life, and she knew in that brief moment of self-examination that Dolly and Maggie were right after all. It was very hard, if not impossible, for a man and a woman to share nothing more than friendship.

She had only to look within herself to realize that what she felt for Philip Massey was much, much more than just friendship. She loved him. She had given her heart to him, one small piece at a time, until she had nothing left for herself but a longing that ached to be fulfilled.

Yet, if she ever hoped to be loved in return by a man—truly loved— there was only one thing she could do to be prepared . . . just in case her dream did come true.

She must find a way to get her heart back.

Unless by some miracle, he might grow to love her, too.

Chapter 16

A nother blessed note.

Philip crumpled the paper in his fist and tossed it to the floor. If he had his way, he would keep that woman away from every piece of paper between here and Philadelphia to prevent her from writing another note for the rest of the summer.

This note was a bit more creative than her other ones, but Philip did not believe her excuse for declining to continue his lessons at the country seat for as long as it took to read it. The stupid mule only had to make it from the roadway to the barn yesterday and had no more come up lame than he had been born in a cabbage patch.

He walked across his bedroom and outside to the balcony to brace his hands on the railing. As he scanned the early morning river traffic, he realized he had no other choice but to bend to her request and go to the cottage for his lessons because he had pushed her too hard. Again.

She had seemed pleased with his gift yesterday, and by the time they had started back to the cottage together, he was sure she had recovered from the kisses they had shared. His own recovery took a lot longer. In point of fact, he had spent little time in his bed last night. Every time he closed his eyes, he saw her face and those dazzling hazel eyes, filled with wonder, haunted him. Her lush lips, moist with his kisses, teased him, luring him back into that moment in suspended time when she had reached out and touched his soul and tempted him to believe she was the woman of his dreams.

Damn!

He had been right. The woman was no ordinary sorceress. She rocked his judgment like no one had ever done before, and if for no other reason, he was anxious to end this assignment once and for all before he lost what little skill or common sense he had left.

He raked one hand through his hair and tried to focus on only one goal—finding the cameo brooch and returning her with it to Morrell—which brought him right back to thinking about why she had decided not to come back to the country seat.

The only reason for her abrupt change about where he would take his lessons had to stem from their discussion of the Ivory Duchess. Curiously, it was a discussion which she had initiated in the impetuous way he had come to expect of her.

Although her eyes had filled with panic when he had mentioned having attended one of her performances, she had quickly regained her composure. When he had mentioned the newspaper article he had planted in the newspaper, she had pretended not to have read it with any interest. Judging by the way her hands shook, rattling the reins, and how quickly her words had tumbled out in a breathless rush, he knew differently.

He had to give her credit. Someone less secure might have fled the scene as soon as the article appeared, but she was more astute than she was impetuous. She had interpreted the information in the article exactly as he had hoped she would. Yesterday, he had apparently interrupted her rather spontaneous celebration as she danced by the creek looking like a sea nymph who had taken human form in a brief escape from the confines of the sea, and he knew exactly why she had been so excited. The stubborn, impetuous woman thought she was safe!

It was his pride, or perhaps his growing frustration and determination to be done with this assignment, that had prompted him to invite her to attend the Ivory Duchess' performance with him, but his ploy had boomeranged.

Instead of enjoying the pleasure of seeing her rendered nearly speechless, he found her stammering through one excuse after another yet more unsettling evidence that the woman known as the Ivory Duchess was not the conniving, manipulative liar Morrell had claimed her to be. Philip had no idea how hard he had shaken her until this morning.

Until he had received her note and realized he had jolted her out of her secure little world. He had yet to figure out whether she intended to remain here permanently or simply stay long enough to convince Morrell to give in to her demands before she agreed to return to the stage.

Philip's concern about her motives notwithstanding, her sudden reversal about coming to his country seat gave him the opportunity he needed to gain access to the cottage and learn the exact layout so he could search for the cameo brooch.

He turned away from the balcony and checked his pocket watch. Eleven o'clock. According to her note, she expected him at one which meant he had time to work on Cynthia's necklace and still arrive according to his own schedule— around four o'clock.

He was not coming.

Her heart heavy with disappointment, Kate found no solace in Dolly's pompous assertion she had been right and Mr. Massey had only continued his lessons as a way to lure

Kate into an improper relationship. Maggie's assurances he would probably reconsider and contact Kate in a few days offered no comfort at all. Did their discussion of the Ivory Duchess have anything to do with his decision not to come today? Had her refusal to attend one of the Ivory Duchess' performances hurt his feelings?

When Josie Gordon and her mother arrived early for the girl's three o'clock lesson, Kate finally gave up her vigil at the front window. With Dolly occupied and Maggie in her room, Kate decided to take a walk. She had never gone beyond the rear garden, but the woods surrounding the cottage offered cool refuge and a quiet privacy she would not find in her room. She left a note for Dolly and Maggie on the kitchen table and slipped out the back door.

Bright sunshine, crisp blue sky, and cream puff clouds overhead did little to brighten her mood, and she meandered past the garden with her head bowed and her arms locked behind her back. Thick shadowed woods greeted a kindred spirit, and she wandered aimlessly with only the rustle of trees or the chirping of birds for company.

She had no path to follow, no roadbed to guide her way, just dense stands of oak and chestnut trees hugged by an undergrowth of shrubs and vines, an occasional small clearing, or shallow ravines where streams had once gurgled. A latticed canopy of green blocked the sun and a cool breeze brushed her cheeks as she watched herself take one slow step after another—steps that led nowhere and everywhere until she finally decided to turn back.

She glanced around and realized she had gone so far into the woods she had lost sight of the cottage. She was lost, hopelessly swallowed up by the forest with absolutely no idea how to find her way back home.

A swell of despair tightened in her chest. Blinking back the tears that had been threatening to fall since one o'clock, she took a deep breath and inhaled the sweet scent of mountain laurel that bloomed at the edge of a small ravine.

Her life, at the moment, was not very sweet, and her newfound freedom was nothing more than a maze filled with as many confusing twists and turns as the way back to the cottage. The one person she had hoped would show her the way through the maze that led to the future she longed to claim had abandoned her.

Philip.

Her guide. Her inspiration. Her love.

How would she ever manage to overcome the obstacles that lay before her without him? How could she ever reclaim her heart if she never saw him again?

She would survive. Somehow she would survive.

Just like she had learned to embrace and survive every other heartache and disappointment in her life.

Feeling trapped by her own inadequacies, she looked around her. She had no idea what to do or what to expect if she could not find her way back to the cottage. She certainly would not die out here from exposure. The weather was too balmy, even at night. She would not starve to death. Blueberries and blackberries grew in abundance. There were several hours of daylight left, and since she did not relish spending the night under the stars, there was only one thing left to do: start walking.

She turned around and headed back in the opposite direction. Taking time to note an unusually gnarled tree that had apparently been struck by lightning to use as a base, she walked for nearly twenty minutes. Her confidence grew with every step she took, and she even stopped to gather a handful of tart, but tasty blueberries which she popped into her mouth as she walked—straight back to the gnarled tree.

She stared at the tree in total disbelief. She must have walked in a complete circle! Squaring her shoulders, she tried again, only to wind up right back in the same spot. Thoroughly disgusted with herself, she eyed the ravine with interest sparked by her growing desperation. She did not remember crossing the ravine before, but there did not seem to be any other way to try.

Edging past several laurel bushes, she snagged her skirt on a devil's walking stick. By the time she had extricated herself from the thorn-covered stalk, her patience had been pricked thin, not to mention her skirts. She stomped across the shallow ravine, tripped over a vine that tangled her feet, and plopped straight down on her bottom in a thick bed of plants and banged both elbows in the process.

A god-awful, malodorous stench enveloped her, stung her eyes, and left her gasping for breath. She scrambled to her feet and ran as fast as she could along the ravine, but the smell clung to her like a second skin. Pausing, she brushed broken leaves from her skirts, gagging for air.

Had she frightened a nearby skunk?

Of all the unlucky things to do!

She tilted her face up and away from herself and took heaving breaths of clean-smelling air. Close to tears, she tried to think of something—anything—she could do to get rid of the smell. Removing her gown was *not* an option she even remotely considered for longer than a heartbeat. Given the way her day had progressed so far, she would be likely to take her rest in a bed of poison ivy while her gown aired out.

The smell was just awful!

She wrinkled her nose and glanced around. There was a small clearing over the ravine just ahead where the sun was shining bright. She was obviously alone, and there was literally no chance anyone might see her.

Stepping cautiously, she made her way to the clearing, stopped, and listened carefully to make sure she had not gotten close to a path where someone might pass by.

A path?

She had not seen a single path during the whole miserable escapade.

In short order, she removed her stained skirts and spread them out on a shrub to air after rubbing at the stinky stains with handfuls of sand. Halfheartedly, she slipped out of her bodice and hung it from a low tree branch after using the sand again to clean the sleeves where her elbows had hit the plant.

Standing only in her chemise, the sun kissed her flesh and kept her warm. Since there was nothing left to do but wait, she walked far enough upwind to make her wait bearable and sat down with her legs curled beneath her. Modest even though she felt confident she was alone, she hugged her arms around her waist and the brooch pinned to her chemise pinched the inside of her arm.

She had grown so accustomed to wearing the brooch hidden beneath her bodice, she had almost forgotten its presence. In fact, she had meant to start hiding the brooch in her room or somewhere in the cottage when she was not on the circuit, but had continued to wear the brooch out of habit. Deciding that this misadventure had taught her more than one lesson, she would make it a point to remove the brooch and hide it as soon as she got back.

Still left with the problem of hiding the brooch until the stink left her clothes, she questioned whether trying to air her clothes out at all was even a good idea. All she could do was to hide the brooch by keeping her arm close to her body, but more than her modesty was at stake now. The new life she had created for herself was in grave danger should anyone happen along and catch sight of the brooch and recognize it.

Questioning how long she should leave herself so vulnerable, she looked up at the sky. Judging by the position of the sun, she thought she might have been gone for perhaps two or three hours. By now Dolly and Maggie were probably growing concerned since the note only said Kate would be going for a short walk.

"A short walk, not a disastrous one," she grumbled. Smell or no smell, she had to try to get back to the cottage before . . . The sound of an approaching rider sent her scurrying to her feet. Her heart pounding, she realized that the rider was getting dangerously close and blocked her way back to her clothes.

Hugging her left arm to her side to conceal the brooch, she took several small steps backward and looked in every direction before making a quick charge from the middle of the clearing to the safe cover of the woods. Shivering in the shadow of a beechwood tree, she pressed against the smooth bark to hide and peered around the trunk every few thundering heartbeats to get a glimpse of the person who had intruded on her privacy. As far as she could guess, no one traveled these back woods. Had Dolly and Maggie sent someone to look for her?

Mercy!

She closed her eyes and made a series of solemn promises no saint could ever hope to keep if God would perform a miracle and make her as invisible as the wind. When she opened her eyes, she blinked twice and slammed them shut again.

No miracle. No escape. No reprieve from the most embarrassing moment in her entire life.

Philip Massey was in the middle of the clearing!

Groaning inwardly, she wanted to drop to her knees, dig a tunnel, burrow inside and never come out. Forget the future. She did not have one if he got sight of her brooch before she had a chance to explain why she had lied about her identity. She did not want a future, and at this exact moment, she was willing to exchange one very short life on earth for a pair of wings to fly straight to eternity.

The sound of his laughter pealed through the air. "Having a bit of an adventure today, Miss Danaher?''

Her eyes snapped open. ''How kind of you to notice,'' she spat. ''What are you doing here?''

''Looking for you.''

She peered around the trunk, careful to keep her torso hidden, and glared at him. ''How did you find me?''

He chuckled and sniffed the air. ''You're not serious.''

''I'm not exactly in the mood for witty conversation,'' she retorted.

He urged his prancing horse around and plucked her bodice and skirts from their hanging places. He held them at arm's length and cantered over to her useless hiding spot. ''I assume you'd like to have these back.''

She practically snorted. ''No. I'd rather walk back in my chemise.''

''That might be rather interesting.''

The man had a wicked, perverted sense of humor that snapped her patience. ''What will be interesting, Mr. Massey, is how you intend to explain your unchivalrous behavior to Miss Dolly and Miss Maggie.''

''Unchivalrous? I've just rescued a damsel in distress.'' He wrinkled his nose. ''A rather smelly damsel at the moment, but I'm intrigued. What did you do? Try to pet a skunk? They don't take to people very well . . . in case you think you just stumbled on a grumpy one.''

''I'm not stupid,'' she huffed. ''Just . . . just clumsy.''

Silence.

The cad did not even argue with her!

Neither could she. Not when the truth was so downright embarrassing.

''So you tripped over the skunk.''

''I suppose I did,'' she groaned. ''I . . . I was trying to get back to the cottage, but I couldn't find my way. I . . . I kept walking in circles and lost my temper. I rushed through the ravine, tangled my feet in a clump of vines, fell right into this big patch of plants of some kind."

He laughed. "Skunk cabbage. You fell into skunk cabbage. Pretty awful stuff."

She hung her shoulders. "It certainly is."

Sobering, he dismounted and handed her clothes to her from around the other side of the tree. "Are you hurt?"

She grabbed her clothes, relieved that he had turned his back to her. She clutched them to her chest and tried not to cry. "I'm fine. Just totally embarrassed. I don't suppose you'd consider letting me die of shame and burying me right here so no one else will know what happened."

She heard him stifle a chuckle. "Sorry. I can't do that," he said as he walked a few feet away.

She scrambled into her bodice and stepped into her skirts. "Why not? It seems a reasonable request. You've never told anyone about what Precious did to the barn."

"That's a totally different issue. Even if I did pledge to keep today's misadventure a secret, I doubt it would hold for long. There's no way your clothes will be scent free until you . . . well, until you wash them with something." He paused. "Besides, what would I do for lessons? Miss Dolly made it perfectly clear she wasn't taking any new students."

Lessons?

Her heart began to race. "I wasn't sure you wanted to continue your lessons after getting my note."

"It might be inconvenient, but I've never let that stop me from pursuing anything I put my mind to before. I apologize for being late. I was working on a new piece of jewelry and just lost track of the time. When I finally did arrive, Miss Dolly was growing worried about you, and I offered to make sure you were all right."

She peeked around the tree again. "I'm sure I'll be able to properly thank you if I ever forget how embarrassed I am." She moistened her lips. "Are you sure you don't mind coming to the cottage for your lessons?''

He glanced back at her over his shoulder and frowned, but his eyes were dancing with mirth. ''Not unless you insist we start today. If you don't mind, tomorrow might be better. For both of us.''

She did not blush. She did not cry. And she could not stop the laughter that bubbled out of her throat. Before long, he was laughing with her, and she could not help noticing how handsome he was with the sun bathing him in a golden aura that caught the highlights in his hair. His smile danced from his lips to his eyes, and she knew it would be very hard to find a man as dear as Philip.

She had no right to expect he would ever return the love she felt for him—a love that filled her with such joy—until she had told him the whole truth about herself. But as their laughter faded, she also knew she would be more than foolish to give up this man without a fight—a fight within herself to find the courage to become the woman he deserved.

''Are you ready to start back?''

His question brought her back from dreams to reality. She nodded. ''If you lead the way, I'll just follow from behind.''

When he smiled again, he took her breath away. ''Let's walk together, and I'll show you how to find your way home for next time.''

Together.

Her heart leaped in her chest. If Philip could walk by her side today, as bedraggled and smelly as she was, there was a chance—a beautiful, wonderful chance—he might one day choose to stay by her side for all time and return her deep affection for him with a love that would last forever.

''I can hardly stand the smell myself,'' she admitted, giving him the opportunity to withdraw his offer. ''You don't have to walk with me.''

Chuckling, he held out his arm like he was offering to

squire her to a formal ball. ''I know I don't, but the smell isn't so bad.''

She took his arm. ''You lie so convincingly, I almost believe you mean it.''

As they walked back toward the cottage side-by-side with the horse trailing behind, hope warmed the tight bud of her future which blossomed once again.

Just as he was leading her back to the cottage, he would serve as her guide to a life based on truth. She could face the world with her head held high as long as he was by her side. She prayed with all her being that his feelings for her would deepen and grow from friendship to love.

Her more immediate concern, however, was facing Dolly and Maggie and recounting her rather misadventurous afternoon.

Chapter 17

The following day, Philip appeared precisely at one o'clock, spent half an hour with Kathryn for his lesson, and accepted Miss Maggie's invitation to tea.

Seated on the portico with the three women, he sipped the bitter-tasting motherwort tea Maggie had prepared especially for him.

She beamed at him over the rim of her teacup. "And you say you haven't had a single episode of insomnia since you tried Mrs. Child's remedy?"

He grinned. "Not one, although I haven't resorted to drinking the remedy during the daytime." He wondered how many remedies she had tried to find a cure for her spells. Her sister's expression remained grim, and he sensed her suspicion of him with alarm.

Ever patient and understanding, Kathryn hovered about, pouring fresh tea into the women's cups as soon as they were empty and smiling reassuringly at him.

"I'd like to do more to show my appreciation," he ventured. "Will you all come for dinner? Mrs. Spade is a marvelous cook."

Dolly immediately stiffened in her seat. "We don't socialize and get tangled in a net of social obligations that would be difficult for us to meet. Not with my sister's condition.''

Maggie's beaming smile dipped into a crestfallen frown, and Philip swallowed hard. "I didn't intend to—"

"Whatever your intentions," Dolly huffed, "we must decline. I won't have my sister subjected to public ridicule should she suffer one of her spells—"

"I'd like to accept Mr. Massey's invitation." Maggie set her cup down and turned toward her sister. "As long as no one else would be there. We haven't accepted an invitation to dinner for . . . for years. Please, Dolly?"

"Nelda Spade will be there, and she's anything but an understanding woman. She will not treat you kindly if she sees you slip into one of your trances."

"She's right." Kathryn intervened, obviously startling both women who stared at her openmouthed. "I've spoken to Mrs. Spade at great length, and I agree with Miss Dolly because I've . . . I've seen how poorly she treats you, Mr. Massey."

She paused and gazed at him with such tenderness, he almost forgot to breathe. Was there a woman alive who could be so genuinely concerned and in tune with others' needs?

"I'm not sure why you tolerate her insolence," she continued, "but I'd be very reluctant to expose Miss Maggie to Mrs. Spade's sharp tongue."

Dolly nodded approvingly, and he noted a warmth for Kate in Dolly's eyes he had never seen before. Thwarted in his attempt to get all of the women out of the cottage so he could search for the brooch, he did not have to feign disappointment. Lowering his gaze, he did slump his shoulders for added effect. "I'm sorry. I never meant to put Miss Maggie in a difficult situation. I would never want anyone to suffer on my account. I was hoping . . . well, as you can probably discern for yourselves, there are very few people willing to travel here for a visit. I was hoping perhaps you might consider . . . The house has a glorious view of the river from the porch and cool breezes I thought you might enjoy."

Just when he thought the silence could not be more awkward, Kathryn's voice rang out. "I know a way . . . if it's not too bold of me to offer a suggestion." Immediately the center of attention, she moistened her lips.

He quickly took his cue. "Go on."

She took a deep breath. "I believe Mr. and Mrs. Spade go to Philadelphia to pick up special supplies and have relatives there they like to visit."

"They do."

Her eyes danced with mischief. "Would it be possible . . . I mean, if you could manage without Mrs. Spade, why not suggest they go to Philadelphia and spend the night? They would probably enjoy a night off to visit and that would solve the problem."

"And create another," he moaned. "I couldn't cook a meal for you."

"You wouldn't have to. We'll bring it with us!"

Excitement pulsed through every vein in his body, and he could have kissed her a dozen times. Reluctant to acquiesce too quickly and arouse any suspicion he had an ulterior motive behind his invitation, he shook his head. "I couldn't ask you to do that. I wanted to do something to show my appreciation, not make work for you."

Maggie clapped her hands together. "It's a grand idea, Kate. Why, we'll make it a picnic. I haven't been on a picnic for ever so long. We accept, don't we, Dolly? Kathryn has told us so much about Mr. Massey's grand piano, and I know you'd just love to play it." She blushed and took a side glance at him. "You wouldn't mind if my sister played for you, would you?"

"Maggie! I can't believe your audacity!" Dolly fumed.

He chuckled. "I'd be delighted, and I'd also like to hear Miss Danaher play for me. If you're sure you don't mind."

With Maggie and Kathryn staring at her, Dolly finally relented. "I suppose I'm outnumbered. We accept your invitation."

He furrowed his brow. "It's a little odd having one's dinner guests provide their own meal, but I defer to your willingness to help. Since you insist. There's only one more problem," he added with a smile.

"Problem?" Kathryn cocked her head.

"Never mind. I'll just pick you up. Since the mule came up lame, you obviously can't use the road cart."

Kathryn's eyes widened, and her cheeks flushed with guilt he recognized at once. "Oh. I forgot about Precious. You're . . . you're right. We can't expect her to—"

"If we wait a week or so, I'm sure she'll be fully recovered," Dolly suggested.

She was lying, too, but he was not sure why she had gone along with Kathryn's excuse for not coming to the country seat for his lessons. He plunged ahead anyway. "Why not next Thursday at four? The Spades are already planning to go to Philadelphia that day, and if we wait until then, they wouldn't have any reason to suspect I might be having visitors."

He was lying now, but he would make sure they did go to Philadelphia next Thursday if he had to row them downriver himself.

"I think that would give us all time to get ready," Dolly announced.

More than enough.

While the women's conversation focused on the menu, he was already refining his plan to hide outside the cottage next Thursday, get inside the moment they all left, find the cameo brooch, and get back home before they arrived for their picnic supper.

*   *   *

The next week passed by so quickly, Kate could hardly believe it was already Thursday. She had spent the morning helping Maggie prepare the picnic supper to take to Philip Massey's while Dolly had conducted her regular lessons with Carolbeth Hamilton and Josie Gordon.

Shortly after three o'clock, Dolly and Maggie secured the windows and front door while Kate loaded their feast into the back of the road cart built to normally handle no more than two passengers. They would have to squeeze together to make enough room. Rather than risk wearing the cameo brooch and having either of the women brush up against it, Kate decided to leave the brooch behind. She had found a clever hiding place for the brooch, and as long as the doors and windows were locked, she felt confident the brooch would be safe from being discovered should an intruder invade the cottage.

She checked the mule's harness and bridle before climbing into the cart and onto her seat. While she waited for the sisters to appear, she smoothed her skirts and checked the buttons on her bodice. She was wearing a new gown today, the first one she had sewn since leaving Simon and Helen. After taking Dolly's advice, she had buried her skunk cabbage gown, and both women vowed to drop the subject of Kate's misadventure.

Sweet, dear Maggie had offered Kate several gowns that had once belonged to the woman who had lived with them for years before she died. Decidedly old-fashioned and a bit faded in spots, the gowns were too big and too short for Kate, but with Maggie's permission, she had taken them apart and cut them down to create two new gowns for herself—one of which she wore today.

The pale pink skirts were perhaps a bit too narrow for the day's fashion, but she preferred a slimmer look after wearing the voluminous costume as the Ivory Duchess. The matching bodice had sleeves with a thin lavender stripe from fabric she had rescued from a different gown, and by adding a deep striped hem to the skirts, she ended up with a very suitable costume.

Although the weather was warm, the day was a bit overcast, and she had decided to leave her bonnet at home and used another scrap of striped fabric to weave in her hair as she braided it and hoped he would notice.

She blushed and decided to dwell on something other than the man who had been so charming this past week even Dolly seemed to be beginning to revise her opinion of him Maggie, of course, held firm to her conviction that while his intentions were unclear, they were based on much more than friendship.

Kate prayed she was right.

The minute she heard the back door open, she put on her gloves and picked up the reins.

Dolly locked the back door while Maggie climbed aboard, inching her way closer to Kate. Her eyes were dancing. "I'm so excited. I can't remember the last time I made a social call."

"You'll love the house, and Mr. Massey is right. The river view is magnificent."

Ever ready to take control, Dolly took her seat. "We'll have to be very sure to arrive home well before dark. I don't feel comfortable traveling at night."

Without answering right away, Kate clicked the reins and the road cart crunched across the backyard. "All you have to do is give me a little time to hitch Precious back to the road cart, and we can leave whenever you think best."

"And there's a place in the barn for Precious to rest?"

Swallowing back the urge to tell Dolly that Precious already had made herself more than at home in Mr. Massey's barn, Kate nodded.

"Did you remember to wrap the biscuits in several towels to keep them warm?'' Dolly asked as they turned the corner of the cottage.

Maggie patted Kate's arm and answered for her. ''Just like you suggested.''

''I hope you didn't forget to use the blue crock for the rice pudding or it will be cold by the time we get to dessert.''

Maggie grinned at her sister. ''We didn't forget to do a thing, but if it makes you feel better, you can go right down your list.''

Dolly tilted her chin up and stared straight ahead. ''You needn't belittle my concern for detail, and you'd be the first one to whine when you realize, too late, you'd left something behind.''

As the sisters continued to gently banter back and forth, Kate could not help but wonder why she had been so blessed. She had found a wonderful home, and she still had her pianoforte. Philip Massey, however, was the most amazing part of her new life, and she recalled the first time she had ever seen him and dreaded the idea of spending any time alone with him in his house.

As Precious clopped down the roadway, Kate could not wait to get to the country seat and would have given anything to stay there for the rest of her life . . . if he would have her.

With his horse tethered a good one hundred yards away, Philip watched the three women as they crowded into the road cart. He was not surprised to see Dolly lock the back door, and he had no doubt every window had been bolted shut.

He dug a skeleton key out of his pocket and smiled as the women finally started on their way. Cautious to the extreme, he waited until every creaking sound the road cart made had disappeared before he came out from his hiding place at the rear of the barn.

When he got to the back door, he paused again to listen and make sure the women had not returned for something they might have forgotten. Noting the number of baskets in the back of the road cart, he thought they might have packed enough food to feed every poor soul at the Locust Street Almshouse and doubted either Dolly or Maggie would stop arguing before they got to his estate.

Feeling more confident than he had since starting this assignment, he turned the key in the lock and slipped inside in less than ten seconds. He had already located the three bedrooms during his visits this past week, but had yet to discover which one belonged to Kathryn.

He moved quickly through the house to check the bedrooms at the front first so he would have advance warning they had turned around, although he doubted very much that either of those two rooms belonged to her.

He opened the door to the first room and peered inside. Intrigued, he took a step inside the room. More elegant than the stateliest room he had ever seen, he knew at once this was not Kathryn's room, although it would certainly befit the most discriminating of duchesses. Thick wool carpet in burnished gold matched brocaded wall coverings and a massive canopied bed replete with bedcurtains. He moved through the room quickly and checked an open door. To his surprise, it led to the adjoining bedroom that was almost identically furnished in a complementary deep green color. The bed in this room was not canopied, and several articles of clothing lay draped across the bed.

Teaching the pianoforte certainly paid well, he noted, and quickly left the two rooms which obviously belonged to the Gresham sisters. He made his way back to the kitchen and entered the last bedroom. As sparse as the other two rooms were almost opulent, he knew he had found Kathryn's room. Working methodically, but carefully, he searched every square inch of the room, including the trunk at the foot of the bed.

No brooch.

Remembering an earlier assignment, he checked beneath the windowsill.

No brooch.

Had she found a hiding place elsewhere in the cottage? He could hardly imagine her taking the risk that either Dolly or Maggie would find it. A sound outside the window sent him scurrying to investigate. One quick peek, and he slammed his body out of sight against the wall. Kathryn and the women were back, and she had just parked the road cart outside the kitchen door!

He held his breath, his heart pounding. With no valid excuse for being inside the cottage and no brooch to support his claim that he had been hired to track the Ivory Duchess, he had to either escape or hide. He strained to hear a muted conversation and took a desperate glance out of the window again. Kathryn had gotten out of the road cart and was headed straight for the back door.

With every second as important as his own heartbeat, he charged out of her room, through the kitchen and music room to the front door. Unable to exit through the door and bolt it behind him, he went into the middle bedroom which he thought probably belonged to Maggie. With his ear pressed against the wall he would be able to hear Kate enter her room.

The back door creaked open, and he heard her enter the kitchen. He pressed closer to the wall, but the sound of her footsteps grew dimmer, not louder, and he knew she was heading away from her room.

Trapped in the middle bedroom, he dropped to the floor and inched under the bed on his stomach, cursing himself for being so careless and allowing himself to be cornered.

He heard her enter the adjoining bedroom, and since his head was on the floor at the foot of the bed, he even caught a glimpse of her feet as she entered the room he was in. Her skirts practically brushed against his face when she leaned over the bed.

With his pulse pounding in his ears, he held his breath while she apparently took something off the bed and quickly left the room. He exhaled slowly, very slowly, and remained beneath the bed even after the back door had closed. Just his luck, one of the women would send Kathryn back inside for something else!

He waited until he heard the road cart start to pull away before he let his tense muscles relax and eased out from beneath the bed. Although he might have time to widen his search to other rooms in the cottage, his instincts told him to leave. Now.

He had avoided discovery once today; to continue hunting for the brooch courted disaster should the women come home again and catch him. Discouraged, but only temporarily thwarted, he postponed his search for the brooch for another day and made his way back through the cottage. Careful to make sure the back door was locked again, he hurried the steps that carried him back to his horse, determined to be back at the country seat before the women arrived.

Chapter 18

⁓⁓

Short of a miracle, nothing would turn this social visit with Philip Massey into a success.

Kate pulled in front of the porch steps and brought the road cart to a relieved halt. Still sulking after being not-so-gently reprimanded by her sister for forgetting her shawl, Maggie had suffered a mild spell along the way to the country seat. Dolly had retreated into frozen silence when her suggestion to turn back had been soundly rejected after Kate had reminded her Mr. Massey had gone to a great deal of trouble on their behalf by sending the Spades away for the night.

Precious, ever full of surprises, had nearly overturned the road cart not once but twice. With the day already half-spoiled, Kate could only hope there were no further disasters. She looked up at the porch and saw Philip through a front window. Apparently, he was working on a piece of jewelry. When he looked up momentarily and smiled, she smiled back at him—the miracle who might be able to salvage the day with his good nature and natural charm.

Alighting from the road cart, she helped Maggie and Dolly descend before starting to unload the goodies they had brought for their picnic. Customarily avoiding anything associated with cooking or housework, Dolly immediately took a seat on the porch while her sister helped Kate with the baskets of food.

Philip emerged from the house just as Maggie started up the steps. "Let me help you," he offered as he bounded down the steps and took the baskets from her.

"We're late and it's all my fault," she announced, obviously intending to waylay her sister before she had a chance to blame Maggie herself. "I forgot my shawl, and we had to turn back to get it."

"I'm glad you did. The air is cooler here by the river, even more so as the sun goes down."

Kate followed them up the steps and set her baskets down on the porch next to a small table he had already set for their picnic.

"We're not staying until sundown," Dolly interjected, "but I was afraid Maggie might take a chill without her shawl. You did say the Spades weren't returning until mid-morning tomorrow, didn't you?"

He winked at Kate who had heard Dolly ask him the same question for the past three days when he had come for his lesson.

"At the earliest," he replied, repeating the very same answer he had given her before without any hint of impatience in his voice. "Shall we start? I'm famished. Never do stop to eat when I'm working unless someone reminds me."

"Mr. Massey has an incredible talent," Kate said as she nodded to the two sisters. "He was generous enough to show me some of the gemstones he brought with him. They're absolutely exquisite," she explained when they looked at her askance.

Dolly raised her eyebrows. "I wasn't aware you had spent more time with Mr. Massey than the half hour allocated for his lessons. Was Mrs. Spade—"

"She was quite about," Philip said quickly. "I showed Miss Danaher the gemstones the day I helped her to remove the glove from her injured hand. Since it was rather tedious work, I used the work table I have set up in the other room."

"I'd love to see the gems," Maggie prompted, and Dolly frowned her disapproval.

He took a deep breath before he smiled. "Then I'd be privileged to show all of the jewels to you as well."

"Let's eat first, shall we?" Kate suggested, changing the direction of the conversation to one Dolly could not turn into an inquisition.

Kate heaved a sigh of relief. Dolly was acting a tad too overbearing to suit Kate, although Philip had intervened and had not allowed Dolly to find fault with either of them.

After he excused himself and left to settle Precious into a stall in the barn, with a whispered reminder from Kate to tie the stall door shut as a precaution, she set out the food so everything was ready by the time he rejoined them.

The banquet of food and refreshing glasses of raspberry shrub did much to keep the conversation to more pleasant discussions. When they finished, he insisted on carrying the dishes into the kitchen where he left them, promising to wash and dry them as soon as they left for home. He even helped Kate to put the remaining food back into the baskets and had carried them to the barn to store them in the road cart.

While they waited for him to return, empty-handed, but with an update on the mule for Dolly, Kate looked forward to several pleasant hours before heading home. She felt more relaxed and content than she had in a long time and even more determined to end the charade that prevented her from claiming the man she loved.

Did he love her, too? He must have some feelings for

her, or he never would have kissed her so convincingly by the creek. Could he trust himself to believe she loved him, despite the gossip that laced his reputation, and forgive her for lying about her identity?

Her love for him swelled the courage she had been saving up to tell him the truth, and she wished with all her heart they were alone. She was ready to bare her heart and soul to him, but not with Dolly and Maggie present.

The minute he turned the corner of the house, her heart skipped a beat. Tan and confident, he took her breath away the same way he had done the day they had met. It was more than his powerful physical presence that had joined her trembling heart with his these past few weeks. His attentiveness had turned her initial infatuation into love—a blessed, wonderfully redeeming love she could never hope to find with any other man.

He had scarcely reached the top of the steps when Maggie stood up. "I'd like to see your work now, young man." She turned to her sister before she could protest. "And I'm not being bold. Mr. Massey promised to show us his work, and I'm simply reminding him of his offer."

Chuckling, he went to the front door, held it open, and waved them inside, although Kate sensed he was a bit reluctant. "I'd be delighted, but I want to make sure we have enough time for Miss Dolly to play the grand piano for us. And you, too, Miss Danaher," he whispered as she passed by him.

She let his comment go unanswered, but she had no intention of playing for him. Not today. Not when he had been able to so eloquently describe her performance as the Ivory Duchess. She would feign a swoon if pressured, but she would never play for him . . . until she had been able to tell him that she and the Ivory Duchess were one and the same woman.

*   *   *

Philip followed the women into his workroom and stepped around them to walk over to his worktable. He picked up a velvet tray containing the pair of amethyst earrings and carried it back to them. He watched Kathryn closely. Just like the first time she had seen the gemstones, she was drawn immediately to the amethysts. This time, she did not pick them up; instead, she caressed them with the tip of her finger.

She raised her eyes and met his gaze. "They were beautiful before, but now . . . now you've created a masterpiece."

He laughed and handed her the tray. "Hardly that. The settings aren't as intricate to fashion as you might expect."

Maggie leaned forward and studied the earrings. "I'm impressed, young man. You do truly beautiful work. Where are the others Kate mentioned? Locked in a safe, I hope."

"As a matter of fact, I have them right over here." He pointed to his worktable and nodded. "Shall we?"

Dolly was the first one to reach the table. She surveyed the stones with a sweep of her gaze, cocked her head, and slowly examined each and every stone. She held silent while Maggie and Kate clucked over the display until Maggie turned to him with a worried expression on her face. "Aren't you being careless leaving all these valuable jewels lying here just beneath the window where someone can see them from outside the house?"

He shrugged, although he felt the same stirrings of alarm that had raced through him when Maggie had first asked to see the jewels. "Actually, I—"

"Mr. Massey is a jeweler, Maggie. Not a fool. As it is, I believe they're quite remarkable imitations. Paste, I believe, is the proper term for them."

"Paste?" Kathryn repeated, her eyes wide with hurt and confusion.

His heart plummeted. Astounded that Dolly had correctly

identified the jewels as fake, he had no choice but to admit the truth while attempting to redeem himself in Kathryn's eyes. He should have told her the truth when he first showed her the fake gemstones, but he had been swept away by her excitement and her effusive admiration for his work. He swallowed his pride and swept his hand over the stones. "You have quite an eye, Miss Dolly. Most jewelers would need to examine the stones with an eyepiece before correctly determining the jewels are not genuine."

She stared at him down the length of her nose, no easy task since he was half a foot taller than she was. "Obviously, I'm not an expert on gemstones, but I do have a healthy dose of common sense. If the jewels had been genuine, you would never have left them out in plain view. I recall reading about some members of the European nobility. As they've fallen on hard times, some have had replicas made of heirlooms before they sell the originals. Others have a jeweler discreetly remove and sell the original stones and substitute paste. The owners sell the genuine stones. To keep face. Very important in some circles. Or . . . or so I've read."

He tried to catch Kathryn's expression to gauge her reaction, but she had lowered her head. "You're quite correct," he responded. "We don't have many bluebloods as clients, but it's growing even more common for people with considerable wealth to commission two exact pieces. The one with imitation stones is reserved to be worn in very public places where the danger that the jewels might be stolen is greatest."

He had Dolly's and Maggie's complete attention, but Kathryn still refused to look at him. He was concerned that he had opened a gulf in their relationship, and as he expected, when she looked up at him, she did not try to hide her disappointment.

"You led me to believe the jewels were real. I feel like such a fool."

"I'm sorry. I never meant to deliberately mislead you," he murmured. "My uncle is finishing the jewelry with genuine stones at his emporium while I complete the replicas here. Our clients expect secrecy and insist upon our total discretion. If word should spread, even inadvertently, about a particular piece, the attempt to keep the genuine articles safe would be undermined."

She nodded, but his apology did not lift the slump in her shoulders or bring a smile to her lips. He swallowed hard, surprised by how important it was to him to have her forgive him. "I should have told you the truth. I'm sorry. You were just so excited about reciting what you had read about jewels, I didn't have the heart to tell you the jewels were not genuine. Forgive me."

He thought he saw her attempt a smile this time, but Maggie put her arm around Kate's shoulders and turned her around to face the window so he could not be sure. "I thought they were real, too, so don't be so hard on yourself, Kate. It's become a glorious day outside. The sun is shining again, and look! There are even a few small sailboats on the river. Do you sail, Mr. Massey?" she asked over her shoulder.

"Sail? Yes. As a matter of fact I do. There's a skiff here at the estate, but—"

"Lovely. Why don't you take Kate for a sail while Dolly takes a turn at that grand piano of yours."

"It's growing late," Dolly argued.

"Just a short sail, then," Maggie suggested. "These two young people should have a little time to enjoy themselves without having the two of us watching over them like they're a pair of caged birds."

Before he could voice a polite, but firm decline, he was standing there alone with the one woman who tested his ability to keep his mind focused and his heart safe. If he found that difficult to do when sharing company with the Gresham sisters, he would find it nigh impossible when he and Kathryn shared the afternoon all alone on a small sailing skiff—a decidedly small sailing skiff that would keep her far too close and offer him more temptation than any man could be expected to resist.

Even for Omega.

Chapter 19

Positioned on a small cushion on the bottom of the skiff's narrow hull, Kate used the center seat behind her to support her back. Just overhead, the boom attached to the canvas sail swung from side to side like an inverted pendulum. Seated behind her at the stern, Philip maneuvered the small boat through the stiff wind and strong current that carried them straight downriver.

She gripped her hands on either side of the wooden skiff to keep her balance, but she had nothing except her love for him to anchor the disillusionment that swirled in her mind like the waves dashing against the side of the boat.

He had lied to her about the gemstones and rocked her perception of him as a man of honesty and integrity. Was her love so strong it had blinded her to his true nature? Had he lied to her before about his role in the land scheme? What else had he lied to her about, other than not being repulsed by the smell of skunk cabbage?

Her heart pleaded with her mind to calm down before she judged him unfairly. She understood his need to protect his clients' interests and respected his integrity for placing those interests above her pride. The man she had grown to love was a kind and sensitive man who would never intentionally hurt anyone, especially a very naive and nervous young woman who tried to match his expertise as a jeweler with little tidbits of nonsense about gemstones he had studied and worked with for years.

She *had* been out to impress him with what little she could remember reading about gemstones, and if he had told her the truth—that the jewels she had been admiring were paste—she would have been twice as embarrassed as she had been today.

His lie of omission must have been meant to protect her from her own impetuosity, nothing more, and she tried to forgive him now as completely as though it had never happened. What choice did she have if she expected him to forgive her in return when she told him her real identity—a far bigger lie that was not as unselfish as his had been.

"Do you swim, Miss Danaher?"

She barely heard his shout above the sound of the snapping sail and churning waters, but she immediately tightened her hold on the sides of the boat. Their sail around Petty's Island just south of the country seat had started out rather sedately, but in the past few minutes, the wind had become decidedly stronger and their sojourn on the river a bit rough.

She shook her head to answer him since it was useless to try to voice an answer. The wind would only carry her words in the opposite direction.

"Keep your head down and hang on. There seems to be a bit of rough weather brewing. I'll try to turn us about and get ahead of it."

She dipped her head until her chin touched her chest. Peering over the side of the boat as best she could, she saw the outskirts of the city of Philadelphia at the shoreline. Up ahead, the flag atop the Jayne Building flew above other buildings in the center of the city, and her heart skipped a beat. She had not realized how close they had come to the city where she had made her escape. Were Simon and Helen still at the Morningstar Hotel waiting for her to be found and returned to them? She gulped for air and tried to control the panic that raced through her body.

Waves started crashing over the side of the skiff and drenched her gown with cold water. Overhead, the sun disappeared behind a band of clouds that scudded across the sky faster than she believed naturally possible. The wind shifted direction again and again until she thought they had been caught in the vortex of a powerful wind tunnel.

She heard a sickening snap behind her. The sail suddenly flapped free.

"Damn!"

She lifted her head and turned around instinctively to see what was wrong. The wind shifted again, and suddenly there was pain. Horrendous, blinding pain exploded in the side of her head as the boom smacked her skull. Dazed, she toppled to the side and caught a blurred glimpse of the boom as it swung in a sharp arc to the opposite side of the skiff. She cradled her head in her hands as tears streamed down her face. Breathing hard, she curled into a ball and fought a wave of nausea that swept through her.

"Miss Danaher!"

She did not have the will or the strength to answer him.

The boat rocked ominously to one side before strong arms wrapped around her and pulled her up against him as he curled alongside of her. "Are you all right? Are you conscious? Answer me, woman!"

She let out a sob and nodded as she pressed closer to him. The pain in her head was so atrocious she gave no more thought to their rather scandalous embrace than it took to form the thought and dismiss it.

"We've been hit with a squall," he shouted. "The tiller broke off from the rudder and the mainsheet snapped free. Are you sure you're all right?"

His chest heaved against her body as he struggled to keep them both from being tossed overboard, and she burrowed into his strength. He cradled her in his arms, obviously trying to protect her from being bashed against the sides of the boat that bobbed wildly at the mercy of the elements.

As quickly as the weather had turned deadly, the sun popped out from behind the clouds, the churning wind gentled to a strong breeze, and the swirling river turned more tranquil. She heard the canvas sail flapping uselessly as the skiff drifted along in the current.

"The worst is over," he crooned as he changed to a full sitting position and tucked her beneath his arm. "I've never seen anything build so fast and then evaporate in just minutes. How does your head feel? Are you cut or bleeding?"

She gingerly felt her scalp with trembling fingertips and winced. "No cuts or blood. Just a huge bump." Another wave of nausea threatened to overtake her, and she closed her eyes to combat the confusing double images that greeted her vision. She was sure she was only a bit rattled and did not want to worry him with more complaints. "I'll be good as new in a few minutes."

"You need to see a doctor."

She stiffened, but when she tried to pull away from him, he tightened his hold on her. "Once we drift ashore, I'll get you to Dr. Hunt. He's a friend—"

"In Philadelphia? Why can't we just go back home? Miss Maggie—"

"She isn't a doctor, and since we've lost control of the rudder and the sail, I can't steer the skiff anywhere, let alone upriver against the current." He paused, and she felt his body turn as though he were scanning their surroundings.

He sighed, and his body relaxed. "We're on the far side of the river, and the current is fairly strong. We should be able to get ashore by sundown. I'll get you to Dr. Hunt, let him make sure you're not hurt more seriously than you think you are, and then take you home.''

She wanted to argue with him, but her head throbbed so hard she had trouble finding more than a few words before she forgot what they were. For the second time in her new life, she allowed herself a moment of weakness. Like the day in the barn when she had indulged herself with a fit of crying, she gave herself permission to take a little time to rest before she convinced him she did not need a doctor, especially one in Philadelphia. Just a few moments to rest . . . until the pain in her head went away. She sighed, and her eyelids began to droop. She listened to the steady rhythm of his heartbeat and took a few minutes . . . just a few minutes . . . to close her eyes and rest.

Philip paced the waiting room in the doctor's office, but he was not alone. Like ravenous vultures, guilt and anxiety had stripped and shredded nearly every layer of his flesh and followed on his heels waiting to claim the last ounce before they devoured his soul. Reduced to the essence of his own humanity, he cursed himself for being careless and inept. He had violated the first rule of sailing: watch the sky! He had never even seen the squall coming until it was too late because he had been distracted by the more fascinating view of the woman seated in front of him in the skiff.

When the wind whipped at her skirts giving him a view of her sculpted ankles, he almost let go of the mainsheet to reach out and touch them. The outline of her firm breasts had been heightened as river mist dampened her bodice, and when the wind started to unbraid her hair, she had set her ribbon-bound tresses free.

Fool! He had damn near fallen overboard trying to catch

the homemade ribbon for her when the wind ripped it out of her hands.

He stopped pacing and reached into his pocket, pulled out the damp strand, and studied the tattered pink and lavender striped fabric. How he had wanted to take it out of her hair himself and slide his fingers through hair as dark and rich as a moonless sky!

He crumbled the ribbon in his fist and closed his eyes. If he had not cursed out loud when the tiller snapped and he had lost his hold on the mainsheet, she never would have lifted her head to look around to see what had gone wrong.

He trembled as the sound of the boom striking her head echoed in his mind to remind him it was his fault she had been hurt. The heavy pounding of his heart echoed the same accusation, and he stared at the door to the examining room.

What was taking Mark so long? Was she more seriously injured than he thought or was she in there trying to convince Mark she was less seriously hurt so she could ease Philip's guilt? The second option would not work since Mark Hunt was a close personal friend which only left the first option as a possibility.

He started pacing the room again. If her life was truly in danger, he would never forgive himself if she did not recover.

A chill ran through his body, and he took several deep breaths of air to remain calm and rational. She had slept most of the time it had taken to drift ashore, but he had been able to rouse her fairly easily when they finally reached land at Port Richmond, several miles northeast of Philadelphia where he had eventually managed to hail a coach. She had slept again during the coach ride to Mark's home where he kept his office, and Philip had been relieved when she was almost strong enough to walk into the office on her own.

Unfortunately, Mark had been out on another call, and she had slipped in and out of consciousness several times while they waited for the doctor to return. Each time she had fallen asleep, Philip had found it more difficult to awaken her.

The door to the examining room opened, and he spun around. He searched Mark's face and instantly heaved a question at his friend. "She's going to be all right?"

Mark widened his smile. "A mild concussion. A few bumps and bruises. A day or two of rest is all she needs. Come see for yourself." He ushered Philip into the room and closed the door behind them.

Seated on a chair with a gray wool blanket wrapped around her shoulders, Kathryn looked like a shipwrecked survivor who had washed ashore which was just about the truth of what had happened. Her hair was matted against her scalp, and the bruise along the hairline on the left side of her face looked garish in the brighter light inside the examining room. Her normally dazzling eyes were still clouded with pain, but they brightened as she smiled up at him. "Dr. Hunt says I'm going to be fine. Can we go home now?"

Mark caught Philip's gaze before he shook his head at her. "Not so fast, Miss Danaher. You're not going any farther than necessary to get you into dry clothes and in front of a fire. The brandy you sipped won't last very long to keep you warm."

Her eyes widened with alarm. "I can't stay here all night. We have to get home. Poor Miss Dolly and Miss Maggie must be sick with worry. They're probably convinced we drowned in the river!"

Mark frowned. "As much as I admire your concern for your friends, there's no way you should be traveling to-night, and I'll need to see you again in the morning to make sure your head injury isn't more serious than I believe it is."

She trembled as though fighting against panic. "I can't stay here in the city. I have to go home." She turned and looked up at Philip. "Please, Mr. Massey. Isn't there some way we can—"

"If the doctor says you can't travel, then you can't."

"B-but what about Miss Dolly and Miss Maggie?"

"The telegraph office is closed by now, and even if it weren't, I'm not sure how long the telegram might take to get delivered to the country seat. It's fairly isolated." He checked his pocket watch. "There's still time before the last ferry. Mark, can you send a messenger with a note to the country seat explaining what happened and that Miss Danaher will be under your care until tomorrow and that I'll take her straight back to their cottage?"

"I'll see to it right away. Is there anything else I can do for you tonight?" He yawned and offered a weak smile. "It's been a long day. I'm sorry. If you'll both excuse me, I'll get that note off and be right back. Philip, there are a few things I'll need you to do tonight when you're watching over my patient."

He left the room and Philip thought she might bolt out the door, too. He walked over and put his hands on her shoulders and gently eased her back into the chair. "Not a good idea," he murmured. "I'm not sure if you're steady on your feet yet, and until Mark gets back, I'm not so sure I want to find out. I know you've been through an ordeal today, and I'll get you out of here as soon as I can."

He held his hands in place until he felt her body relax.

Her bottom lip quivered. "Aren't I staying here tonight?"

He chuckled. "Not unless Mark has added another room. At last count, he and Georgina had six children. I doubt there's a spare bed, let alone a room for you."

She glanced around the room. "I could stay right here."

"No. I don't. think so. Mark sees patients at all hours, and you may not be the last one tonight even if he is practically asleep on his feet."

She bowed her head. "Where . . . where will we go? We . . . we aren't married, and it wouldn't be proper to register for a room together. I don't have any money for a room . . ." Her cheeks flamed the color of a burnt sunset, and she closed her eyes as a few tears trickled down her cheeks.

"Since this is all my fault, why don't you let me do the worrying?" he whispered. It pained him to see her so bereft and humbled, and his heart softened to her plight as she tried to wipe away her tears. As often as he had credited her with magical powers, he did not believe for half a heartbeat that she could have conjured up the squall and put them both in danger so she would have to stay in the city where by some quirk of fate Morrell or his wife might see her. He saw her now as she really was—a woman who was just as human as any other—and knew she was not able to travel tonight. "I have apartments over my uncle's jewelry emporium. I'll take you there and since I live alone, no one will ever know we were there."

She nodded. "But we can leave first thing in the morning?"

"As soon as you see Dr. Hunt and he gives his permission for you to travel."

Mark reentered the room carrying an envelope. "Did I just hear my name being taken in vain?"

Philip stepped to her side. "I was just reminding Miss Danaher you'll need to see her again."

Mark handed the envelope to Philip. "Bring her by around nine." Stooping down in front of Kathryn, the doctor put his finger under her chin and tilted her face up to him. "I know you're very tired and all you want to do right now is crawl into a big soft bed and get some sleep. Unfortunately, that's the last thing you can do. You need to stay awake. I've written down some instructions for Philip and some danger signs he's to watch for. I want you to promise to do what he says."

She chewed on her lower lip and pulled the blanket tighter around her shoulders. "Is it all right to bathe? I feel so sticky."

"Just a sponge bath. I don't want you to slip and fall in a tub. Any more questions?"

She squared her shoulders and slipped her hand out from beneath the blanket. "No. Thank you, Dr. Hunt. For everything," she said as she shook his hand. "If . . . if you can have a bill ready for me tomorrow, I'll make arrangements to send payment to you. I might not be able to pay it all at once, but I promise—"

"All I need is your promise to follow my instructions and listen to Philip," he said as he helped her to her feet.

She swayed a bit, and Philip caught her against him. He thanked Mark and quickly led her to the coach. With his arm wrapped around her shoulders and her body pressed close to him as the coach carried them both to his apartments, his heart swelled with an emotion he had long ago dismissed as one he would ever experience: love. Love so profound he could scarcely believe he had been chosen by the fates with such a precious gift.

However impossible it might seem, he knew that only sophistry would deny the surge of protectiveness and tenderness he felt for this woman was founded on mere physical attraction or inspired by guilt for causing her injury.

He loved her, and every beat of his heart echoed that love. He loved her gentleness and her innocence, her impetuousness and her passion for life, and the sheer wonder of the depth of his love for her shook the foundation of his jaded existence.

He hugged her to his side to prove she was not just an illusion his lonely heart had created. She was here. She was real. And he loved her.

Even if he was unworthy to claim her as his own, he was not going to be fool enough to refute his feelings or explain them away. He would simply love her, cherish her, and take her into his heart.

He had no idea how the future might unfold, but for tonight, he would stay by her side and watch over her until he was sure she was completely recovered. Then and only then would he be forced to face a task more daunting than he had ever faced before: loving her enough to let her go.

It was nearly midnight when he finally led her into the parlor in his apartments over the jewelry emporium. With her concerns about propriety apparently still mellowed by the short stiff of brandy Mark had given her, she stood meekly next to the door while he lit a reading lamp to give the room only enough light to chase away the dark. He turned around just in time to catch her trying to stifle a yawn. She gazed at one of the two upholstered chairs set before the fireplace with such longing he could not stop the surge of compassion that filled his heart.

She looked like a bedraggled waif with her hair undone and tangled and a blanket wrapped around her shoulders. Her gown might be salvageable, but her skirts were still damp and hung as limp as a sail waiting for wind. Her face was still very pale except for a flush that painted her cheeks pink, and he prayed she was not starting to fever.

"Let me bring you some warm water and towels so you can freshen up. You'll feet better."

She glanced around the room nervously. "Where will you . . ."

"I'll change in my room while you bathe."

"Here?"

He chuckled as he crossed the room, took her arm, and got her settled into one of the chairs. "Sit right here. I'll be right back."

After setting some water to heat, he gathered up some fresh linens and one of his long-sleeved, flannel shirts for her to wear. He pulled a blanket off the bed in the spare room and carried his bounty back to her. After starting a small fire in the fireplace, he left her alone.

He bathed quickly, changed into dry clothes, and waited an extra twenty minutes before going back to the parlor. He found her huddled under the new blanket with her feet tucked beneath her in the chair. Her eyes were closed and he tapped her shoulder gently. "Miss Danaher?"

She batted her eyes open. "Oh? Mr. Massey. I'm fine now. All I need is a little more rest. I'm not going to slip into a coma and die."

"You're not fine. You have a concussion, and you can't go to sleep. Not until Dr. Hunt checks you again in the morning."

"Then help me to stay awake," she murmured. "Talk to me. I can't bear to just sit here with nothing to do." She smiled up at him. "I haven't even thanked you for saving me and taking care of me, and you haven't even realized what you did today, have you?"

He swallowed hard. "I know I put you at risk by being inattentive to the weather. It's all my fault you were hurt. I'm truly sorry."

She shook her head and reached out to take one of his hands and tugged on it until he stooped down in front of her. "That's not what I mean. You can't predict or control the weather. A squall can form and hit almost without warning, like it did today, yet you acted decisively and with courage. In fact, you were . . . you were quite a hero today, Mr. Massey."

"I'm hardly that," he murmured, finding it difficult to

believe anyone would ever use the word *hero* and his name in the same breath unless trying to give an example of an oxymoron—except for the unique woman who sat before him.

"Oh, but you're wrong, Mr. Massey. You've always been a hero in my eyes, but today you truly *were* my hero," she whispered, her voice tremulous and full of wonder.

He met her gaze and nearly drowned in the adoration that filled her hazel eyes. He had never dreamed he would have a woman gaze at him with such affection or devotion. He gulped hard, knowing that she had once again opened the gates to the deepest yearning of his heart and set it free. He stood up and let go of her hand before he gave in to the urge to hold her in his arms. "I should get something to read to you. I think I can find a newspaper around here somewhere. It's dated, but I'm sure there's some bit of news you'll find interesting."

She shook her head very slowly, and when she moistened her lips with the tip of her tongue, his mouth went dry with longing he could barely control.

He cleared the lump in his throat. "Then some poetry. Do you prefer Shakespeare or Emerson?"

As though emerging from a cocoon, she slipped out of the blanket, touched her feet to the floor, and stood up. Barely a hand's length away from him, she gazed up at him. Her eyes smoldered with a desire that took his breath away. "I believe I should prefer only your company to either Shakespeare or Emerson," she whispered. "Won't you please hold me and kiss me again, Philip?"

Chapter 20

Please. Kiss me, Philip.

*P*lease. Kiss me, Philip.
    Kate caught and held her breath for a moment as she waited for him to kiss her. A lock of his dark hair lay on his forehead, and his gaze was intense and filled with the same longing that tugged at her own heart. His masculine body emanated that aura and powerful combination of strength forged with gentleness that had made him the unique and desirable man who had stolen her heart for all time. The dull ache in her head disappeared, and she listened to the sound of her pounding heart. With his face cast in filtered light from the reading lamp, his features were muted, but ever as handsome as they were to her in the full light of day.

At his back, a gentle fire had taken the chill from the room, but it was the expression in his eyes that warmed her hopes he would not turn away from her. In the depths of his earth brown eyes, she saw him waging an inner battle between desperate yearning, disbelief, and powerful need.

A bevy of questions in her mind created a paralyzing anxiety she could not control. Had the years he had been the subject of gossip and speculation robbed him of any hope that one day a woman would fall in love with him?

Couldn't he see how much she loved him and open his heart to accept her love?

She took one step closer to him and held perfectly still, but she could not let this moment pass without telling him how she felt. "I love you, Philip. I think I've loved you from the first moment we met."

Emboldened by the love in her heart, she had taken the first step to be part of his life, but left the last big step to him. Would he close the small space that separated them now and forever seal the gap that had prevented him from believing he was worthy of her love?

Unless Philip had the courage to do that, she could never hope he would recognize the courage she would need to risk his love by telling him the truth of who she was and forgive her.

Would he take that one step . . . forged in courage and redeemed by love?

Did he have the courage to take that one step . . . from yesterday into tomorrow?

"Kate."

He murmured her name, his voice ragged with emotion as he lifted her into his arms and hugged her against him. His chest heaved as he took deep breaths of air, and when he dipped his head to claim her lips, she wrapped her arms around his neck and held him tight.

"Kate."

When he whispered her name again, his breath fanned her lips and left them tingling. Aching. Begging for the wonder he had given to her before with kisses that had been so powerful they had seemingly shattered the natural order of the universe and created a moment in suspended time so that two hearts, two souls, and two spirits could meet and heal one another.

He pressed his lips to hers. Gently. Tenderly. Sharing the joy and the wonder of a very special love they shared with each fleeting caress, rekindling the memory of the very first kisses they had shared.

When he broke their kiss, her lips trembled. When he began raining kisses across her forehead and along the edge of the bruise at her hairline, the sensations he unleashed rippled pleasure to every pore in her body.

He carried her with him as he settled down in the chair. Cradled on his lap, she held his face between her hands as he continued his tender exploration of her face, sighing when his hand began to massage the back of her neck and his lips pressed against the side of her throat.

A languid warmth seeped through her body, and she melted against him, kissing his forehead even as he continued to bring her flesh alive with every touch of his lips. He loved her! She could taste it on his lips and hear it in the pounding of his heart.

Magic. Pure unadulterated magic was the only explanation Philip had the strength to consider as the source of the power of her touch. With his will to resist her weakened by the amazing gift of love, he could not turn away from her. "Kate," he groaned as he nipped at the sweet flesh along the column of her throat where he felt the vibrations of the soft little purring noises that escaped through her parted lips.

Sweet, luscious lips. They lured him back to kiss her again. Urgent with need, he heightened his assault by delving into the cool refreshment beyond those sweet, warm lips, hungry for more of the magic that only the woman in his arms could unleash. She was no longer his quarry. She was Kate, the woman of his dreams, the very soulmate fate had created for him, and he could no more turn away from her now than stop breathing.

Her magic was so mystical and powerful he gave no thought to her past or the future. Only this moment existed . . . this amazing, miraculous moment . . . when time had given him one more reprieve, one more impossible glimpse of heaven on earth before reality returned. He was not a man who deserved the love she offered to him. He was, after all, Omega, the master of subterfuge, a man so accustomed to deviousness and pretense it was more than just his second nature. It had become instinctive, a facet of his character unlikely to ever change. He was forced to admit his love for her was doomed to wither on the vine of wonder that she loved him too before it had the chance to fully bloom.

Until that happened, he wanted one more kiss. One sweet, everlasting kiss.

He cradled her head in his hands and turned her to give him even greater access to the source of her magic when she winced and cried out in pain. He dropped his hands and pulled her against him. Breathing hard, he realized he had been completely consumed by his own needs and had forgotten about her injury. "I'm sorry. Please don't cry. Forgive me," he crooned as she laid her head against his shoulder.

She snuggled closer and wrapped her arms around his chest. "It's still very sore, but I'm all right now," she murmured, pressing her lips against the flesh just below his ear.

He let out a deep breath and laid his head against the back of the chair. His heart was still pumping furiously, and the powerful drive to satisfy his need to know this woman even more intimately did not die an easy death. Not when she was still on his lap, her firm buttocks pressing against the evidence of his arousal, and her bare legs offering him the most tempting view of her long, slender limbs.

He shifted her in his lap, reached down, pulled the blanket from the floor, and covered her. What kind of man was he to take advantage of a woman who had been hurt? One who was so exhausted he had been quite susceptible to the powerful spell she had cast over him.

He touched a kiss to the top of her head. "I'm sorry. I didn't mean to hurt you. Are you sure you're all right? Would you like something? A glass of brandy? Water?"

She nipped his earlobe with her teeth. "I'm fine."

He sucked in his breath. "You're . . . you're not fine. You've been injured. I can't believe—"

"I'm fine. You've followed Dr. Hunt's instructions to help keep me awake quite nicely."

She kissed his chin, and he gulped down the lump in his throat. He set her back from him and met and captured her gaze. "I read his instructions twice, and I don't recall seeing anything about . . . about squeezing your head or pressing on your injury. Are you sure you're all right?"

"I'm fine." She sighed, closed her eyes, and curled back against his chest.

"Not a good idea," he cautioned as he lifted her away from him again. "I'm supposed to make sure you don't fall asleep, remember?"

She sighed again. "But I'm so tired . . ."

"I know," he murmured as he brushed her hair back from her face.

"I want to go to sleep. Just for a few minutes."

She started to close her eyes again, and he shook her gently. "Don't. Don't think about how tired you are or how much you want to go to sleep. Stay awake. Doctors orders, remember?"

When she opened her eyes and looked at him, he nearly forgot to breathe. A surprising and delightful blend of mischief and desire sparkled in the depths of her eyes. "Then I suppose you have no other choice," she whispered as she pressed her lips to his. "You'll simply have to kiss me again. And again. Then there's something I want to discuss with you. What time did you say Dr. Hunt expected us in the morning?''

Philip ignored the harsh rapping of his heart at the door to his consciousness. It was a wonder his heart was still beating after pounding so hard time and time again during a night that had tested his limits of self-control.

The rapping grew louder and more insistent, and he roused from a deep sleep realizing that the rapping was not the echo of his heartbeat. Someone was knocking at the door.

Caught in the fuzzy haze between sleep and consciousness, he took deep breaths to clear his head when he realized he had been derelict in his duty and had fallen asleep with Kate in his arms. He looked down at her and saw her eyes closed.

How long had they both been asleep? *Was* she asleep, or had she slipped into a coma?

"Philip! It's Mark Hunt. Open the door."

Startled into full wakefulness, he blinked in the bright light of day and covered her with the blanket before he shook her gently and called back to the door over his shoulder. "I'm on my way."

The pounding at the door stopped, and he bent down to stroke the side of her face. "Wake up, Kate. Dr. Hunt is here to see you."

She sighed and curled into the chair.

"Wake up!" he gritted, glancing behind him at the door.

She pulled away from his hand and burrowed beneath the blanket. He lifted her into a sitting position and tucked the blanket around her shoulders. When Mark started pounding on the door again, she opened sleepy eyes and blinked several times. "What . . . what time is it?"

"Time to pay the piper," he quipped, annoyed she had been able to slip past all his defenses and into his heart so easily. He rubbed his chin and shook his head. He needed a sharp razor to shave the stubble from his face, but there was not a blade on the entire planet sharp enough to slice her out of his heart without inflicting a mortal wound on himself that would drain the lifeblood from his body and the very nectar from his soul.

Facing the prospect of his own emotional death, he much preferred one that was quick rather than slow and painful. He forced the tip of a blade of regret into his heart before he drew his next breath. No more magic. No more dreams.

Not after hearing Kate admit she had fallen in love with him and entrusted him with her love—a love he had no right to claim. If he truly loved her, he would have to find the strength to convince her she had given her heart to a man who would break it into so many pieces it would be useless to try to put them back together. She had fallen in love with Philip Massey, completely unaware he was only an illusion. He would have given anything to be the man she thought him to be, but he was far too jaded to believe love alone would change him.

He needed to bring this assignment to an abrupt end which meant he had no choice but to confront her and demand the cameo brooch instead of wasting any more time trying to find it.

He had never expected to win the game he had waged with her, but lose in the process, and until this very moment, he had never known how steep the price would be to make amends for his past mistakes. He had sacrificed his honor, his name, and now he knew he would have to surrender the only thing of value he had left: his heart.

He turned away from her and let Mark into the room with an apology. "Sorry, old friend. I fell asleep. We both did."

Mark raised a brow. "I was on my way to another patient when I decided to stop by to check on Miss Danaher," he explained before he turned and headed straight for his patient.

Philip left them alone together and retired to his room where he shaved with the dull razor he had left behind. His cheeks were still stinging by the time he had changed into yet another set of clothes and walked back into the parlor. He glanced around the room. "Where's Mark?"

Dressed again in her gown, Kathryn twisted her hands in front of her. "He . . . he left a few minutes ago. He said to tell you . . ." She lowered her gaze. "To tell you I was well enough to travel back home as soon as you're ready."

"The sooner the better." He opened the door for her, but she made no move to leave. Short on patience and long on the desire to get back to the country seat and bring an end to this charade, he crossed the room and took her arm. She looked up at him with disappointment swimming in her eyes. "I think we should leave," he urged.

"Could we sit down a moment? There's something I wanted to explain before—"

"There's no need for an explanation. We were both exhausted—"

"But you don't understand—"

"I understand things perfectly. Even more than you can imagine," he added under his breath as he fought to resist the urge to pull her into his arms and hold her close to him for one last time. "Miss Dolly and Miss Maggie won't be able to rest easy until they see you. Once I have you safely back home, there will be plenty of opportunities for us to talk."

"I want to talk to you now," she insisted. "It's important to me."

He tensed. It was hard to deny her anything, but there was no way he was going to give her the opportunity to say words she was bound to regret after he told her he had been hired to find her and the cameo brooch. He struggled to find his voice and kept his tone gentle. "It's important to you? More important than the two women who are waiting to see if you're really all right? Miss Dolly is a strong woman, but Miss Maggie has a fragile state of mind. Have you forgotten it was Miss Maggie who suggested we go for a sail? I imagine she's taken to her bed and buried herself under a heavy blanket of guilt, but if you insist . . ."

He dropped her arm and motioned toward the chairs. "Shall we sit down for this very important talk or should we stand?"

Her eyes flickered with indecision, and her cheeks flushed—with guilt or disappointment? He could not be sure, but in either case, he doubted she would accept his offer. He counted on her to be more concerned about the Gresham sisters than herself, and by the time he drew his next breath, she did not disappoint him.

"You're right. I'm being very selfish. We should leave right away, but . . . but we will be able to talk? Later today?"

"Absolutely," he replied and made a mental note to remind her later that he had kept his promise. He always kept his promises, but as he ushered her from the room, he knew this one would be the hardest he had ever honored.

Whatever her reason for abandoning her career or deceiving him about her identity, she would be far better off returning to Morrell than staying with Philip. He would do whatever he could to see that the trouble between her and her agent were resolved. Then he would make a quick exit and disappear knowing he had condemned himself to hell on earth by falling in love with the Ivory Duchess, certain there was nothing he could ever do to deserve or redeem that love.

Nothing.

Chapter 21

⌒⌒⌒⌒

"Aren't you going to come inside?"

Standing on the roadway that ran in front of the cottage after Philip had helped her to the ground, Kate was surprised when Philip climbed back into the wagon he had rented after a short ferry ride from Philadelphia. During the rest of the short journey home, he had been attentive, but distant. She had assumed, however, that he would at least speak to Miss Dolly and Miss Maggie before he went back to his country seat.

Made more unsteady on her feet by his confusing behavior than the injury to her head, she gripped the side of the wagon for support.

He steadied her by putting his hand on her shoulder. "I think it's better if you have some time alone with them before I make my appearance. Do you have the note Dr. Hunt gave you today?"

She nodded and glanced toward the path that led to the front door before she looked up at him. "Will you stop by this afternoon? You promised we would have some time together to talk."

His gaze narrowed, and a chill went through her heart. "I'll stop by after supper. By then you'll have had a chance to rest and recover a bit more from your ordeal. Are you steady now, or would you like me to walk you to the door?''

She squared her shoulders and stepped back from the wagon. ''I'm fine,'' she insisted, despite being stung by his refusal to stay with her at the cottage. Did he have second thoughts about the night they had spent wrapped in one another's arms? Had she made a fool of herself by declaring her love for him when all he felt for her was physical attraction or worse, mere pity? If he did love her, why hadn't he whispered the words she longed to hear?

''Until later,'' he murmured and clicked the reins to set the wagon into motion.

Her fearful questions only aggravated her dull headache, and she took a deep breath to clear them away as she turned and began walking down the path. The sound of the retreating wagon reminded her that barely two months ago, she had stood by the holly bush near this very path and listened to the sound of the wagon that had first brought her to the cottage.

That day she had been relieved when the sound of creaking wheels had faded, but today, she waited with bated breath hoping that by some chance Philip would turn around and come back to her.

He did not.

Disappointed, she put her hand into her pocket and felt for the note Dr. Hunt had given to her just in case his first one had not been delivered. She shivered, slipping back in time to relive the day she had arrived at the cottage with only Dolly's note and her love for music and the pianoforte to sustain her hopes and dreams.

She shook her head. The notes and chords of each precious day here, including her first, had already been played. She could not go back in time to that first day or any other to recompose the sonata of her life, no matter how much she regretted the dissonant half-truths and outright lies that jeopardized her home with Dolly and Maggie, her position as a teacher, or her love for Philip Massey.

She started down the path, slower than that first day, but with the determination to compose the rest of the music of her life as a sweet melody inspired by courage and truth that would give her the sanctuary she had longed to find here.

One of the greatest lessons she had learned in her short stay here was that sanctuary was only a state of mind, an inner peace she alone could achieve for herself. No one could invade her peace or take it away from her unless she allowed them to do so. For her, there would be no sanctuary and no true peace of mind until she had reconciled her past life with her present one. If the sonata of her life had been awkwardly written thus far, it was nevertheless uniquely her own, and she embraced it.

As she got closer to the cottage, she knew Philip was not the only one who deserved to be told the truth. Two very special women were waiting for her inside this cottage—women who had welcomed her into their home and given her a glimpse of the respectable life she could have. She wanted that life, not just for a few months or years until Simon eventually found her. She would not spend every day of her life listening to rumbling chords of fear or insecurity, and she would no longer jeopardize her love for Philip with deception.

Sanctuary would be hers, but only if she possessed the strength of will to reach out and claim it.

It would take every ounce of her courage to unburden the guilt she had carried for over two months and speak the truth about her real identity. By the time she reached the front door to the cottage, she had also made a very important decision. She would wait until early this evening for Philip to arrive, and when the three people who were the most important in her life were gathered together, she would tell them the truth. Every tiny piece. Every sordid detail. Beginning with her foolish little game with Charlotte Ann Ludfallow, and a painful, but necessary recounting of the day their ruse had been discovered and she had been exiled and placed under the control of the man who had ruined her life: Simon Morrell.

Blinking back tears of joy that her journey from a shameful past to a blessed future was about to begin, she opened the front door and stepped inside.

When Philip arrived back at the country seat, he did not bother to unhitch the horses. He simply pulled up to the back door, set the brake, and brought fresh water and grain to the horses where they stood. He charged into the house and encountered Nelda Spade who was fussing while unpacking a bundle in the kitchen.

She looked up at him, glanced out the window, and scowled. "Horses belong in the barn."

He did not slow his pace as he walked past her and through the kitchen, but he still took notice that the Gresham sisters had been careful to restore the kitchen to order before they had left. "I'm only staying long enough to change and pack."

"Going on a trip, Mr. Massey? Seems like you're doing a lot less relaxing in the country—"

"What I'm doing or not doing," he spat as he ground to a halt, "is no longer your concern. If it ever was. I'm going back to Philadelphia where I intend to spend the rest of the summer. You may close up the house or just a few rooms. I really don't care . . . as long as you do it after I'm gone."

He was as close to complete physical and emotional exhaustion as humanly possible and still be on his feet, but he could not condone being rude to anyone, even a servant who had been as disrespectful as she had been. He raked his hand through his hair. "I'm sorry. I'm tired, hungry, and short on patience. I didn't mean to be cross with you."

She glared at him. "What about your lease? And your lessons with Miss Danaher?"

He exhaled slowly and counted to five. "If you'll recall, I paid the full lease in advance. As for Miss Danaher, I intend to stop by the cottage and speak to her before I leave."

Before we both leave.

"Now if you'll excuse me, I'm going to my room, and I'd like a tray—anything would be fine—so I can eat while I pack."

He turned, left the room, and headed straight to the safe in his workroom. He placed Cynthia's necklace into a large leather traveling case and turned away without bothering to close the safe door. From his worktable, he gathered up the imitation jewels and put them inside the case with the necklace. He packed his lapidary tools which were stacked on his worktable into another case and carried everything with him upstairs and laid them on the bed.

He had changed into more formal attire and filled half a trunk with his clothing when Nelda finally arrived with a tray of food. With his arms full of more clothing, he nodded to the chest of drawers. "Set it down there, and if you would close the door on your way out, I'd appreciate it."

She grunted a nasty comment he did not quite catch, set down the tray, and slammed the door shut behind her.

He dropped the bundle of clothing into the trunk, took a look at the rumpled mess, and sighed. "I really should have made her do my packing," he complained as he surveyed the sorry contents of the trunk.

He shrugged his shoulders, walked over to the tray, picked up a narrow strip of ham, and popped it into his mouth. He was more ravenous than he had realized and interrupted his packing to finish the tray of food. With his hunger satisfied, he was still exhausted. He practically stumbled around the room to check for anything he might have missed.

Content he had not forgotten anything, he put his tool case and the leather case with the jewels into the trunk. Now he was ready to confront Kate and demand the cameo brooch she had taken from her agent. Until he handed them both over to Morrell, he was not going to let either one of them out of his sight.

There were still several hours before he was expected at the cottage. He eyed the bed, but instantly dismissed the idea of a short nap. As much as he needed the rest, he was too keyed up to do more than toss and turn.

There was really nothing else for him to do and no valid reason why he should delay his leave, yet he hesitated. He doubted Kate had even managed to finish recounting the sailing mishap, but even if she had, the Gresham sisters had probably sent her straight to her bed. The very image of her lying abed sent his pulse into double time, but he had no right to ever expect he would be able to fulfill the fantasies that danced through his mind. Deciding the path to honor and valor meant denying the deepest yearnings of his heart, he had to put Kathryn's interests before his own.

Instead of prolonging the inevitable, he picked up the trunk, carried it downstairs, and loaded it into the wagon. With a last look at the house and a sigh of relief that Nelda Spade had not intercepted him, he proceeded straight for the cottage.

Tonight the Ivory Duchess and her cameo brooch would be back where they both belonged—with Simon Morrell—and with the funds Philip had earned as payment for his services, he would see that Bradford received his money. With the last promissory note redeemed, his name and honor would be restored, satisfying, at least, what little conscience he had left. While he doubted he would ever go back to the life he had left behind before he had become Omega, he was absolutely sure he would have to live with the pain of knowing he had given his heart to the one woman on earth he would never claim as his own: The Ivory Duchess.

Kate stepped inside the cottage and immediately froze in place. Instead of finding joy at her return, from behind one of the closed bedroom doors came the sound of a woman weeping and the muted, gentle voice of another woman who was apparently trying to console her.

Her head started pounding, and she pressed her hand to her forehead. Was it Miss Maggie who was crying? Had she suffered another spell, one that had been very severe? Or had the note Dr. Hunt had sent with a messenger never arrived to reassure them Kate and Philip had survived their sailing mishap, leading the sisters to believe Philip and Kate had both drowned in the river?

Chills tingled along the length of her spine, and she stumbled her way to the door that led to Maggie's bedroom. The door was slightly ajar, but she hesitated to barge in. She might frighten both women to death, especially if they believed the worst had happened to her and Philip. The muffled sobs grew louder, and she pushed the door open, hoping the sound of the creaking door might catch their attention and soften the shock of her presence. The scene that greeted her eyes and the words that reached her ears nearly broke her heart.

Maggie was lying prostrate in bed on top of the coverlet, and her sister was seated on the edge of the bed with her hands holding a cloth to her sister's forehead. Eyes already swollen with tears, Maggie was pleading with her sister.

"Why, Dolly? Why did this have to happen? I didn't mean to bring harm to either of those young people. It's all my fault. What am I going to do? I was so fond of Kate . . .''

"Hush," Dolly crooned. "There's nothing we can do to change what's happened, and you must not take the blame for something no one could have foreseen. And until we hear for certain, it's possible they could have survived. Maybe we'll hear something today."

Touched to the core by the depth of their affection for her and their unnecessary grief, Kate could not bear to see either of them suffering for a single moment longer. She stepped into the room and walked straight toward the bed. "Miss Dolly? Miss Maggie? Please don't cry. I'm all right. I've come home."

Dolly practically leaped up from the bed, and Maggie bolted into an upright position. "Kate!" Her face lit with a smile of wonder and disbelief. "Kate! You're here! I was so afraid . . ."

"I'm so sorry to have worried you," Kate whispered. "Didn't you get the note from Dr. Hunt?"

Dolly's smile of relief and surprise faded quickly as her lips pursed into a frown. "Note? No, we never got a note. We waited until long after dark, and when you and Mr. Massey did not come back, we assumed . . . well, we didn't have any choice but to clean up the dishes and leave the estate as quickly as we could since we did not know how early the Spades would be returning."

Bending to put her arms around Maggie, Kate gave her a hug as she reached into her pocket and handed the second note from Dr. Hunt to Dolly. "I'm not sure, but I think Mr. Massey told Dr. Hunt to send the messenger to the country seat instead of the cottage. I'm so sorry. I didn't mean to have you both so worried."

"We're both so glad to have you home safe and sound," Maggie whispered. Her eyes widened when she looked at Kate's face, and she ran her fingers gently down the bruise.

"You've been hurt, poor dear. What happened? Are you truly all right?"

Kate closed her eyes for a moment as Maggie stroked her cheek. "Dr. Hunt assures me I'll be fine with a day or two of rest. The boom struck my head when we were hit with a squall. Mr. Massey . . . oh, Miss Maggie! He was so courageous! He took care of me and brought me home this morning—"

"According to his note, Dr. Hunt says you were under *his* care for the night," Dolly snapped. "You didn't spend time alone with Mr. Massey, did you? Your reputation is at stake here, and if I thought otherwise for one minute, you can be sure that Mr. Massey will be held to the strictest account for his behavior."

"Mr. Massey did nothing more than take me to Dr. Hunt last night and . . . and bring me home this morning. He was a total gentleman," Kate insisted, wondering if spending the night kissing her to keep her awake qualified as gentlemanly or proper behavior, a thought that only rekindled her memory of the discussion the Mullan sisters had had about kissing. She forgave her lie because she did not have any intention of confusing her already complicated relationship with Philip by telling either Dolly or her sister of the night spent in his arms.

"Will you forgive me, Kate? I never meant to put you in harm's way by suggesting Mr. Massey should take you for a sail." Maggie's eyes filled with tears again, and Kate wiped them from her face.

"It's not your fault, unless you conjured up that squall!" Laughing, Kate pressed a kiss to Maggie's forehead. "It was an accident. A freak accident. Please don't think for a moment it was your fault."

"Which is precisely what I was telling you before Kate arrived," Dolly reminded her sister. "I suppose we should try to put this all behind us."

"And get this young lady a good hot bath and something to eat. Are you hungry, Kate?" Maggie asked as she got to her feet and put her arm around Kate's waist.

Overwhelmed with the affection that surrounded her, Kate knew the time had come to tell them both the truth, and if she waited until later when Philip arrived, they might be offended that she had not told them earlier. After all, Kate had been with them for much longer than she had known him, and since they had opened their home as well as their hearts to her, it only seemed fair that she speak to them first.

She took a deep breath as they began to walk from the room. "Actually, I'm not very hungry, but I would like to talk to both of you. Perhaps we could sit together in the parlor where we would all be comfortable."

By the time they had settled themselves in the sitting room, Kate's knees were shaking under her skirts. Her palms grew sweaty, and the dull ache in her head had begun to throb. She thought about Philip—his courage and his honesty—and prayed for courage of her own. With her heart beating fast, she looked both sisters in the eye. "I haven't been totally honest with either of you," she blurted, "but I can no longer live with what I've done. I hope you will forgive me for deceiving you, but until now, I never had the courage to tell you the truth."

She lowered her gaze, unable to bear the thought of seeing their affection for her turn into rejection or loathing. "Kathryn Danaher is not my name. My real name is Baxter. Kathryn Baxter," she blurted before her courage failed her. "Audiences around the world simply know me as the Duchess . . . the Ivory Duchess."

A sharp intake of breath.

A deep sigh.

She tensed, squared her shoulders, and began to lift her gaze, hoping that there was still a little affection for her left in their hearts, affection that would shine in their eyes and forgive her for lying to them. If she had extinguished that affection forever, finding nothing more than scorn staring back at her, she would blame no one but herself.

And she would wonder if the same fate awaited her when she told Philip the truth in just a matter of hours.

Before she managed to raise her gaze high enough to see the women's faces, one soft voice rang out.

"I told you she would tell us as soon as she was ready."

Chapter 22

Searching for some visual sign she had heard Maggie correctly, Kate felt her heart nearly stop beating. She looked frantically from one sister to the other as they sat side by side on the sofa.

Beaming with self-righteousness, Maggie had a huge smile on her face. Apparently not happy about being proven wrong, Dolly had an expression that was skeptical at best. Kate gripped the sides of her chair and gaped at them. "You . . . you knew? You knew who I was? All this time?"

Dolly pursed her lips, and they whitened to match the color of her hair. "Of course we knew. Although you made every effort to convince us otherwise. Once you played for us, I recognized your gift for the pianoforte immediately." Her gaze grew softer than Kate had ever seen before. "You may not have needed to disguise your face, but you could not hide your talent, even though you deliberately stumbled through a selection during your audition."

"But why didn't you challenge me? Why did you let me stay if you knew I was lying to you?" Kate breathed, remembering how hard she had tried to play poorly during the audition. Obviously she had been right to be afraid she had played too well, but were her fears that they might ask her to leave also well-founded?

She held her breath and prayed for their understanding and forgiveness.

Maggie leaned forward in her seat. "We were curious, Kate. I'm sure you have a very good reason for trying to keep your true identity a secret from some people, but Dolly had written to you and told you we both admired your talent. You've been an inspiration to many young women, but why did you decide to abandon your career? Why did you come here and pretend to be looking for a position?"

"Why indeed," Dolly added firmly. "I think we have a right to know the truth and deserve to know if you have actually decided to give up the life you've led to pursue a more respectable one, or are you simply spending time 'in seclusion' as your agent reported to the newspaper?"

Kate drew several shaky breaths and moistened her lips. "My agent wouldn't let me retire and forced me to continue to perform as the Ivory Duchess. I just couldn't bear it any longer so I . . . I ran away," she blurted. "I think he had the article printed because he wanted to frighten me into running away again because he hasn't been able to find me." Her eyes filled with tears of regret for deceiving both women. "I wanted so much to confide in you, but I was so afraid." Her last word was nothing more than a whisper, but she hoped they would hear it with what was most important: their hearts.

"What were you afraid of, dear?" Maggie said softly.

"That you wouldn't believe me," she whispered. "I'm not a duchess, and I've never done any of the things they say I've done. I'm just . . . just so tired of living a lie."

Dolly sat even more erect in her seat. "If you expect us to believe you, then perhaps you'd better start at the beginning. At the very beginning," she emphasized with a haughty tilt to her chin.

"We promise to listen and not judge you, dear. Go on. Tell us everything."

Maggie's encouragement soothed Kate's battered confidence that telling the truth was the right thing to do. In a shaky voice, she told them about Gram, the love for the pianoforte that had given Kate such joy, and the foolish game she had played with Charlotte Ann Ludfallow, recounting all the events that led up to that fateful night so long ago—the night her life changed forever. Pausing, she took a deep breath to fight against the most painful memory of her life. "The Ludfallows hosted a dinner party one night, and they surprised Charlotte Ann by insisting she play for several dozen important guests. Unfortunately, her performance proved to be a total disaster, and her parents were more than embarrassed. They were furious and terribly distressed after they uncovered the game Charlotte Ann and I had been playing. They had invited a theatrical agent and his wife to dinner hoping once he heard Charlotte Ann play the pianoforte, he would agree to develop a career for her as a concert pianist."

"They had a right to be upset," Dolly pronounced.

"But you were only children," Maggie countered in a softer, more understanding tone of voice.

"I was eleven. I should have known better," Kate responded, wishing she could go back and undo that one fateful mistake of agreeing to play Charlotte Ann's game.

"What happened next?" Maggie prompted.

A painful flash of memories pierced her heart. "They fired my gram and told us both to leave. That's when the agent, Simon Morrell, intervened and offered to take me away with him. The Ludfallows agreed to let Gram stay if she would relinquish custody of me to him. When he promised to see that I received the lessons on the pianoforte I so desperately wanted, she relented. We were never permitted to see one another again."

Choking back tears, she closed her eyes and fought to maintain her composure. When her heartbeat slowed down, she chanced a look at Maggie and Dolly. She thought she saw another glimmer of sympathy in Maggie's eyes, but Dolly's gaze did not offer her more than a small token of hope that she was as understanding as her sister.

Kate cleared her throat and quickly detailed her years of isolation and training, her failure to achieve the level of skill necessary to become a concert pianist of world stature, and Simon's decision to introduce her to the stage using the invented persona of the Ivory Duchess.

Dolly instantly grew more alert. "Did Simon Morrell plan your tours in Europe as well as in America?"

Kate nodded. "He also planted rumors about the Ivory Duchess to create interest so patrons would flock to the theaters. His wife designed a special costume so my real identity would remain a secret." She sighed. "The Ivory Duchess and her scandalous background were nothing more than a theatrical ploy designed to make money for Simon."

"Do you really believe your agent invented this . . . this persona out of thin air?"

Dolly's question did not surprise Kate. She had wondered about the same thing for the first few years. "I don't know where or when he first got the idea," she admitted. "All I remember is that Simon and Helen, his wife, were convinced they could make a fortune. Maybe by making the Ivory Duchess so mysterious, they thought they could appeal to audiences all over Europe, and they were right. In each country where I played, people were convinced I was somehow connected to one of their own nobility. I'm . . . I'm not proud of myself for playing that role for Simon. I even tried to escape once before when we had stopped in Vienna, but I never made it past the back door of the hotel."

More memories. More pain. Revealing her past was tantamount to reliving it, but she persevered. "Last May I turned twenty-one, and I expected to leave the stage. I was looking forward to leading a normal, respectable life when I discovered he had arranged for a new concert tour. That's when I ran away, and I've been hiding with you ever since."

She toyed with her hands. "I can only pray you'll forgive me for deceiving both of you, and as much as I want to stay with you . . . I'll understand if you want me to leave."

"Where would you go?" Maggie asked in a quiet voice.

Kate let out a sigh she had been holding in for almost her entire life. "I don't know. As far as I'm concerned, the Ivory Duchess no longer exists, and I will never go back to the stage."

"You shouldn't have to go back," Maggie insisted. She turned to face her sister. "I think we should let Kate remain with us for as long as she wants to stay. What do you think?"

Apparently deep in thought, Dolly did not answer for several long minutes. "I have a few questions to ask before I can decide whether to let her stay." She looked directly at Kate. "Does anyone—a servant or someone who helped you to escape—know where you are?"

"No. No one. I'm absolutely certain because I escaped alone without anyone's help or guidance."

"What do you expect to do if Simon Morrell should find you or sends someone to find you."

Kate stiffened her back. "I'm not going back on stage to play the pianoforte. If he finds me and forces me to go back to the stage, I'll just sit there and simply refuse to play. I should have done that the first time I appeared on stage as the Ivory Duchess."

"How old were you then?" Maggie asked.

"Sixteen."

"Still a mere child," she exclaimed. "The man should be ashamed of himself."

"The man doesn't have a conscience," Dolly sniffed. "I think it's time he got one. While I don't condone what you did, I believe you were very much at his mercy." She turned to her sister. "Kate may stay here with us, and once he's realized she won't be returning, he'll be forced to cancel her concerts. His reputation will be ruined and that should help him to learn that what he's done to her is wrong."

Kate's disbelief evaporated like dew under the strong sun when she saw the determination in Dolly's expression and the smile on Maggie's face. Joy exploded in her spirit like fireworks and as they faded, one by one, a gentle peace settled in her mind. "You'll let me stay? You'll help me to hide?"

"We'll help you," Dolly agreed, "only because you finally came to us and told us the truth."

Maggie rose and helped Kate to her feet. "Now I want you to stop worrying. You'll be safe here with us." She looped her arm with Kate's. "I just knew you had a good reason for not telling us the first day you came to us. Now let's see if we can't fix us all a good strong cup of tea before we get you into a nice hot tub. We'll talk more about this later."

Weak with gratitude, Kate could not stop the tears that flowed down her cheeks. As the three of them passed through to the music room, she glanced at the pianoforte: her friend, her nemesis, and once again, her salvation. All the years she had spent on stage dressed in that elaborate costume to play the pianoforte were truly over. No more guilt. No more veils or cameo brooch.

The brooch! How had she neglected to mention the cameo brooch?

Disappointed in herself, she decided there was still plenty

of time left. She would tell them about the cameo brooch over supper. For now, she simply wanted to share a few quiet moments with Dolly and Maggie before taking a long, hot bath and finding something special to wear tonight for when Philip stopped by.

Philip! She had been so consumed with her emotional confession and overjoyed at being accepted by Dolly and Maggie, she had also forgotten to tell them he was coming. A harrowing thought stole her peace of mind before it had barely settled into place. If Dolly and Maggie had known her real identity all along, it was not a huge stretch of her imagination to assume Philip had known it, too.

The room started to spin. She shivered with cold, teeth-chattering dread as the remnants of their conversation about the Ivory Duchess filtered through her dazed mind.

She owed Philip a tremendous debt of gratitude for giving her the gift of his own valiant example. Without him to guide her way, she would have never had the courage to reveal her past or have the future she had dreamed about for so many years.

Without him, she never would have known the amazing healing power of love. He was her guide, her hero, and her love . . . her one and only true love.

He also very well might be her enemy.

During their night together, he had been tender and loving. It was entirely possible he already knew she was really the Ivory Duchess which might explain his abrupt behavior earlier today. She was almost too weak to breathe as she anticipated seeing him in a matter of hours because only one of several scenarios was bound to unfold if he did not know the truth about her past. If he returned her affection, he might not be able to accept her deception or her past. If he had no strong feelings for her at all, her confession would be a moot issue. On the other hand, it was just as possible he was going to shatter the illusion she had found sanctuary here at all by informing her she had been quite easily tricked because he was the man Simon had hired to find her.

Only a naive woman would dare to think he had fallen in love with her and might have been converted from her enemy into her advocate.

Only a woman hopelessly naive enough to believe in love and to trust in the man who had claimed her heart.

Feeling physically refreshed after a long soak in the tub and looking much more presentable in a fresh gown, Kate stared at her image in the mirror above the washstand. With her hair redone, her bruise was barely noticeable, but her haunted eyes gave away her inner turmoil and confusion. While her heart begged for her to trust Philip, her common sense and survival instinct proved implacable and cast him as her adversary.

She turned away from the mirror, trying not to let fear or doubt destroy her trust in him. As soon as he arrived, she would confront him by telling him her true identity and face the consequences. A broken heart seemed the least price she might have to pay.

She slipped out of her bedroom and walked to the music room while Maggie was in the kitchen starting supper and Dolly was in her room changing.

After removing the metronome and a stack of music books from atop the square pianoforte and setting them on the floor, she lifted the hinged lid to the pianoforte and leaned it back against the wall. She took a quick glance around the room to make sure she was still alone. Holding her skirts with one hand, she stepped up onto the piano bench and leaned across the pianoforte. She held herself steady with one hand while she reached inside with the other to retrieve the cameo brooch she had hidden there.

Once she had the brooch, she slipped it into her pocket,

stepped down from the bench, and worked quickly to put the pianoforte back to order. Now prepared to tell Dolly and Maggie about the brooch and seek their advice on how and when to return the brooch to Simon, she turned to go back into the kitchen to help Maggie.

She had barely stepped in the room when she saw that something was wrong. The table had not been set, and no food had been put out. Maggie stood at the window with her back to the room.

Another spell.

With her heart beginning to beat faster, Kate walked over to Maggie, put her arms around the elderly woman's shoulders, and gazed at her lovingly.

Maggie's dazed expression was so peaceful and happy, Kate almost felt guilty for intruding. Where did Maggie's thoughts go when she had a spell? Someplace far away and long ago, she decided, wondering if Maggie ever remembered what she had been thinking about while she was away. "It's time to fix supper," she whispered, afraid one day Maggie might not want to come back.

Aged eyelids fluttered and creased lips trembled for a moment, but her eyes were clear and focused when Maggie finally looked at Kate. "Oh, dear," she murmured as she glanced at the counter and the empty cookstove. "Supper may be a little late. I'm so sorry. I didn't frighten you, did I?"

Kate gave her a hug. "Not at all. Why don't you let me help you?"

"Dolly's not going to be very pleased. She tried, but she doesn't really understand how hard it is for me. Some days are better than others, but today—"

"Today you've made me very happy," Kate said quickly to distract Maggie from feeling guilty for an affliction she could not control. Dolly had lived under considerable strain for many years. Now forced into retirement, she could not be faulted for occasionally losing patience with her sister.

A knock at the front door interrupted their conversation, and Maggie turned her about. "I presume that might be your young man. Why don't you see?"

"I didn't even tell you he planned to stop by," Kate murmured. She felt the blood drain from her face. "I didn't expect him until after supper. How did you know he was coming?"

Maggie walked her to the door to the music room. "Have you told him the truth about who you are yet?"

Trembling, Kate shook her head. Maggie did not seem to think he already knew. Had Kate let her own paranoia run wild? Had she failed him already by not believing in him?

"Tell him," Maggie urged. "If he loves you as much as you love him, he'll understand why you waited to tell him."

Speechless, Kate could only stare at Maggie who laughed softly and cupped Kate's cheek with her hand. "You're so young and so innocent. I wonder how you ever thought you could hide your feelings or the truth. Go to him. Tell him what you've told us. Believe in the love I've seen in both your faces."

"I do love him. With all my heart," Kate whispered, feeling guilty, but Maggie's faith and trust made her suspicions about Philip constitute betrayal. "I just don't know if love is enough to make up for deceiving him."

"Love is trusting and kind, selfless and forgiving, my dear. Go," Maggie urged with a gentle nudge.

Kate took several steps before she turned around and went back to embrace Maggie.

Maggie's eyes misted with tears. "True love comes but once. Don't let it slip away."

"I won't," Kate promised as she wiped the tears from her own eyes. *Not without a fight.*

The knock sounded again, louder and more insistent.

"He's an anxious man," Maggie noted with a twinkle in her eye. "I don't think he likes to be kept waiting." She surprised Kate with a wink. "See if he would like to sit for a while in the portico. It's more private there."

"But Miss Dolly—"

"Oh, Dolly won't even know he's here until you've had a chance to chat with him."

Kate took a deep breath and felt for the cameo brooch in her pocket as she walked to the door.

Another knock.

She hurried her steps praying that Maggie was right and Philip had arrived early so Kate would have time to speak to him alone and tell him the truth. If not, if someone else was at the door perhaps to inquire about lessons, she did not know if she could bear waiting until after supper to see Philip. She needed to end the unbearable tension that locked her entire spirit in an incredible struggle between faith and despair.

Her hands shook as she unlatched the inside lock and opened the door. Dazzling sunlight nearly blinded her. The man's features were obscured in a haze as her vision fought to adjust to the bright light, but she immediately recognized his silhouette.

Her heart began to pound. Her legs suddenly felt weak. Her mouth went dry, and when she tried to say his name, nothing came out except a croaked whisper.

Chapter 23

"Kate," he whispered, his heart pounding in his chest as he gazed at her face, glowing with awed surprise and the wonder of love that filled her heart as the sun bathed her with its golden warmth.

His throat tightened, and dangerous sensations tingled up his spine. As she gazed back at him with those dazzling hazel eyes, he gripped his hat in one hand and balled his other hand into a fist to keep from reaching out to touch her. "I apologize for coming early, but we need to talk," he said quietly. "Is it possible we might have a few minutes alone?"

She nodded and stepped outside, closing the front door behind her. She looked up at him and took a hesitant step. "We can sit on the portico, if you wouldn't mind. You're dressed very formally."

He stiffened and offered her his arm. "Today is an important day. For both of us," he suggested. The moment she laid her hand in the crook of his elbow, his muscles tensed, and the memory of holding her in his arms last night nearly swept away his resolve to take her back to Philadelphia today and exile himself from any place in her life.

They walked around the outside of the cottage and past

the rear garden without speaking. As they stepped from warm sunshine into the shade of the portico he struggled to find the right words to begin. She was so close he could see the pulse beating in the hollow of her throat, and he swallowed hard. He could almost reach out and touch the powerful and intoxicating love that flowed between them. If he truly loved her, however, he would never be able to admit the depth of his love without losing the edge he needed to successfully convince her that returning to her agent was her only option.

With his heart already heavy with grief, he glanced at her. With one look at her beautiful face and the expectancy in her eyes, he reined in any remaining doubts that he had to bring this assignment to an abrupt end.

They sat down side by side on the portico bench. While he turned and put his hat down next to him, she arranged her skirts and put her hand into one of her pockets. Her trust in him was apparent in the way she rested her shoulder against his, and he knew she had no idea she had offered her trust and her heart to a man who was her nemesis and nothing more than an illusion he had created for his own selfish purposes.

She turned to him and smiled. "I should thank you again for . . . everything."

When he noted the slight bruise along her hairline, his heart lurched in his chest. "I hope you can forgive me for being so inattentive and causing your injury."

"There's nothing to forgive," she gushed. "You couldn't anticipate the squall, and when it hit, you reacted quickly. You're an exceptional man," she whispered. "Courageous and strong and honest."

The lump in his throat made it difficult to breathe, and he coughed it away. "Appearances can be deceiving."

"But not always ill-intentioned." She lowered her gaze for just a moment. "I was hoping to talk to you last night, but there wasn't . . . wasn't enough time. I'm the one who should be asking for your forgiveness because . . . because I haven't been totally honest with you.''

Her lips quivered, triggering the memory of their shared kisses. The thought nearly stole his resolve when he realized he might never kiss her again. Before he could take more than a single breath, she took her hand out of her pocket, opened her hand, and held it out to him as though her entire life hung in the balance. ''Do you recognize this?'' she whispered.

Her hand was shaking, but he did not reach out to steady it. Totally transfixed by the cameo brooch resting in the cradle of her palm, he was rendered speechless by her willingness to show him the very jewel he had been trying to find.

When he looked at her quizzically, she smiled tremulously. ''It's the brooch worn by—''

''The Ivory Duchess,'' he murmured. He lifted the brooch out of her hand and stared at it with profound disbelief for several long, tense moments. ''What are you doing—''

''For the past five years, I've worn this brooch when I've performed on stage as the Ivory Duchess.'' She took a deep breath. ''My name is not Kathryn Danaher. It's really Baxter. Kate Baxter.''

He captured her gaze and held it. Unable to take more than shallow breaths of air or control his pounding heartbeat, he watched her catch her bottom lip in a vain effort to keep it from trembling. Tenderness, fierce and protective, raged through his body, but he hardened his heart against an emotion he had no right to claim. The desire to hold her in his arms one more time nipped at his resolve, but he did not risk touching her for fear he would waver from his decision to take her back to her agent.

''Why are you telling me the truth now?'' he prompted,

stalling for time. He needed to bring his emotions under control long enough to clear away impossible thoughts that raced through his mind and tempted him to believe love could surmount the obstacles that stood between them. He forced himself to remain focused on his mission here today.

"Because I was wrong to mislead you. I'm sorry. So very sorry." Her voice broke, and her eyes clouded with misery.

He stiffened his back and scowled, deliberately trying to convince her he was angry when he was truly in awe of her spirited courage. Nothing less than immediate rejection would ever convince her she had fallen in love with the wrong man, but he had had no idea how painful it would be to be cruel to her. "An apology doesn't seem to be quite enough. Not after all that's happened between us."

Tears welled in her eyes. "I love you, Philip. I can't bear to deceive you any longer. Please. Will you let me tell you why I had to lie about who I was?"

He swallowed another lump in his throat and nodded as he closed his fist around the brooch. "What kind of explanation could you possibly have?"

His harsh tone unleashed an immediate flow of tears, and she brushed them away with hands that shook so hard it took an obvious effort for her to control them. Her distress tugged at his soul.

"I had hoped you might be more understanding. Obviously, I misjudged your . . . your feelings for me," she croaked, her voice laced with pain and sadness instead of the anger he would have preferred.

"Obviously," he snapped, hiding anguish so profound he could feel it pumping through his body.

She flinched, but after only a brief moment of hesitation, she began her tale. With brutal honesty and thorough detail, she recounted the events that had sent her to Morrell ten years ago and ended with her arrival at Dolly and Maggie's home this past spring. When she had finished unraveling every mistruth she had told him to conceal her actual identity and explaining her reasons for running away from her agent, he was physically reeling with clashing emotions that coursed through his body.

Humbled by her courageous confession, he could not deny what his heart urged him to accept as readily as the love he felt for her: every word she had spoken was true.

In one glittering flash of hindsight, he knew that it was his own misguided pride or conceit that had labeled the beguiling innocence he had seen shimmering in her eyes the very first time he had seen her as subterfuge. Her perception of him as a man of courage and honesty, when in truth he was a man of pretense and intrigue, was a bitter irony—one her heart would never be able to forgive.

Nor should she.

Not after what Morrell had done to her. To imagine him creating such a scandalous reputation for this young, innocent woman and actually holding her prisoner fueled an anger that surged through Philip's veins like a firestorm. His perceptions of Morrell as a victimized man burned into ashes, singeing any cynicism he had that she might have painted her situation more desperate than it actually was to convince him she had no other choice than to lie about her identity.

He could not change the kind of man he really was, but he could use his jaded character and gift for artifice to Kate's advantage instead of his own. When he did return her to Morrell, he would have no choice but to agree to demands Philip would make—demands that would have to be met if Morrell ever wanted to see his Ivory Duchess again. Demands that would allow Kate to be recognized for her talent and free her from the scandal that had laced her career and the prison of Morrell's control. Demands that, in the end, would still cost Philip the greatest love he had ever known.

As Omega, he had perfected deception to an art form. He lied effortlessly and manipulated people with ease, but nothing he had ever done before prepared him for the difficult task of forcing Kate to believe that he did not love her.

My hero.

Her words came back to haunt him, and his chest tightened with pain. If he had any hope of convincing her to return to her agent, he had to destroy her image of him and convince her that the man she had fallen in love with was only an illusion.

He forced his voice to be calm and even. "Permit me to indulge in a confession of my own," he suggested, although he gave her no opportunity to argue with him. "Although Philip Massey is my real name and I am a jeweler by trade, I also recover stolen jewelry and occasionally— very occasionally—a runaway. Simon Morrell hired me to find the brooch you stole and bring you back to him as well."

She bolted to her feet and stared at him as she took several steps to the side. Shock. Disbelief. Horror. Each emotion was etched in her face and tremors wracked her body. She seemed to struggle for each breath she managed to take. Huge tears filled her eyes, and disappointment, deeper and more profound than he had ever seen, changed the color of her eyes to dull gray. "No. This can't be happening. No . . . not with you, Philip. Not with you," she cried in a ragged whisper as she swayed on her feet. "I loved you."

He rose and steadied her by putting his hand on her shoulder. When she pulled away from him, he braced himself to be able to put the last nail in the coffin of her love for him. "Perhaps you can share some of your finer moments with all the other men you've claimed to love on our trip back to Philadelphia.''

She paled so quickly, he thought she might faint, and he knew at that very moment that the penance he would pay for his lies and deception was more severe than he had ever envisioned. He watched as the horror of knowing she had made a fateful misjudgment about him ripped through her spirit, and he knew he had succeeded in convincing her that the man she thought epitomized honesty, integrity, and courage, was a fantasy, a total fabrication of her own imagination.

He studied her face and watched as the light of her love for him sputtered out and cast a deep shadow of pain in her eyes. ''You were my hero,'' she whispered. ''I trusted you. I believed in you. How could you betray me?''

His heart trembled. His spirit filled with agony. He deserved anger and outrage, but hearing in her voice such profound pain was far worse a fate, one he richly deserved. Convincing her she had fallen in love with the wrong man was painful, but he had to be sure he had stripped away any remaining remnants of her ill-fated illusion that he deserved her love. ''The same way you could play false with the man who turned you into an international celebrity,'' he countered.

Tears misted her eyes. ''If you have any kindness left in your heart for me at all, I would ask you to reconsider. And please don't share what I've told you with anyone.''

He snorted. ''What about Miss Dolly and Miss Maggie? Don't you think they deserve to know who and what you really are?''

She tilted her chin up. ''I told them this afternoon.''

''And?''

She moistened her lips. ''They believe me, and they've agreed to let me stay with them.''

He shook his head. "For how long? Until you decide to run away again?"

She ignored his question and stared at him.

He pressed her further. "Just what did you expect to gain by showing me the brooch? Did you think I might sell it for you, or simply pawn it?"

"No," she cried, her eyes widening with horror. "I wanted to ask you to help me get it back to my guardian without giving him any clues about where I might be. I'm sure he's already hired someone to find me, but I don't think he's been very successful. That's why he planted that false article in the newspaper—to see if he could flush me out of hiding and follow my trail."

"What an incredible twist of ironic justice," he spat, flinching as though yet another blade of steel pierced his heart when fear dulled the color of her eyes and the blood drained from her face.

"You trusted your story to the wrong man," he said quietly as he stood up, "and you overestimated your power to seduce me into thinking I might want to help you."

Visibly shaken, she swayed on her feet. She bowed her head and took small gulping breaths of air.

Pain sliced through his chest, pain so intense he could scarcely breathe. Agony. Pure, unadulterated agony tore his heart into jagged pieces, and he knew that if he survived this moment in time, he would never again be whole.

She glared at him. "I'd like my brooch back."

She held out her hand, but he shook his head. "The brooch is going back to Morrell, and so are you."

"After what I've told you?" she cried. "Why don't you believe me?" She pushed his hand away and caught him off guard. The brooch sailed through the air and hit the ground.

She moved to retrieve it, but he caught her hands and held her still. "I'll get the brooch, but not before I make sure you understand that there's nothing you can do to dissuade me from completing my assignment.''

She pulled away from him, stumbled her way to the brooch, picked it up out of the dirt, and walked back to place it into his hand. ''Take it. Take it back to Simon. Apparently he lied to me when he told me the money was all gone. He obviously had enough to hire you. He's quite good at lying, but you're even better than he is,'' she managed before her voice broke.

Tears streamed down her face, but she did not wipe them away this time. Defiantly, she seemed to wear them like shimmering badges of honor that mirrored the ignominy of his betrayal. ''I won't bother to ask you to believe me or to remind you again that Simon invented the whole persona of the Ivory Duchess and spread rumors to create scandals that are nothing more than a theatrical stunt designed to line his pockets. You wouldn't recognize the truth if it . . . if it *kissed* you.''

He flinched. Every muscle in his body tensed, and he knew he would never again experience the pain that sliced through his chest and the empty place where his heart used to be.

''Please take the brooch back to him,'' she pleaded. ''Please don't make me go with you. I have a new life now. A respectable life. Please don't force me to go back to Simon.''

She held her breath and waited for him to answer her plea, but he ignored her. Using his sleeve, he wiped the brooch clean. He stared at it for a moment before he stepped out from beneath the shadowed portico into the sunlight. He breathed on the stones and studied them. When he held the brooch up to his cheek, he was more than intrigued. He was utterly and thoroughly confused.

He walked back to her but stayed beyond the portico in the sunshine. Breathing hard, he held the brooch out to her just beyond her reach. "Paste," he said quietly. "You tried to pawn this brooch off to me when it's nothing but paste? Didn't you think I'd be able to tell you had given me a replica?" He shook his head. "I have no idea what you're trying to do, but you have precisely one minute to get the genuine brooch, or you'll live to regret it."

Chapter 24

"Paste? That's ... that's impossible," Kate breathed. "That's the brooch I wore on stage and brought with me." The color drained from her face, and her eyes were as troubled as he had ever seen them.

Dismissing any inkling of thought she might be trying to trick him, Philip recognized the look of total surprise on her face. He had seen her react precisely the same way only yesterday when she learned the gemstones on his worktable were not genuine while he and Dolly discussed the reasons why some people had replicas made of genuine jewelry.

He wanted to believe she had no idea the brooch was fashioned with fake jewels. If he did believe her, then Morrell had lied about more than this woman. He had lied about the value of the brooch.

When first presenting the assignment, Morrell had been adamant that Philip had to find and return the brooch as well as the Ivory Duchess. When he turned down the assignment because of his dislike for getting involved in returning runaways, Morrell had doubled the finder's fee, but only if both the brooch and the woman were returned.

The amount of the new fee meant Philip could redeem his promissory note to Bradford in full—just in time for his September first deadline with funds to spare.

He studied her face more closely and acted instinctively when she swayed on her feet again. He led her back to the bench and sat her down. He remained standing, however, and waited for her to regain her composure. She took several breaths of air before the color fully returned to her cheeks.

"How can you be sure the brooch is made of paste?" she asked as she searched his gaze frantically. "Simon never told me—"

"I'm positive," he said quickly. "I'm a jeweler, remember?"

"Don't you have to test it or something?" she argued. "Don't you need to use one of those special tools or an eyepiece?"

He shook his head. "I've tested it enough already. The larger stones took too long to demist when I breathed on them and felt too warm to the touch to be genuine. Trust me. I've worked with paste long enough to recognize it when I see it."

Her shoulders slumped, her eyes turned dull and clouded, and her expression was pitiful and dejected. "All this time I felt so guilty . . ." In the next heartbeat, her eyes flashed with the dazzling combination of blue and green that had first beguiled him. "How do I know you're telling me the truth? Why . . . why should I believe you?" she whispered. "You lied about so many other things."

"I hardly think you're in a position to complain," he argued. "You haven't exactly been the paragon of truth, now have you? My assignment was a legitimate business arrangement."

She never blinked, and her eyes turned an even bleaker shade of disbelief. "Maybe you're lying to me now. Maybe the stones on the brooch are genuine, but you want me to think they're just paste."

Her eyes flashed with pain so deep he wondered how she could experience such pain without losing a piece of her soul. "Maybe you're only pretending Simon lied to you about the brooch and you're going to sneak back to Philadelphia where you'll take it apart and sell the diamonds. They're worth more than the fee he's paying you, aren't they?"

Shaking, she did not take more than a single breath before getting to her feet. "Are you going to play with me, make me beg you not to tell Simon where I am when all you really want is what you have in your hands?" Looking hurt and victimized, she pleaded with him with her eyes that gave him a glimpse into her heart and soul. Trembling, she shook her head. "It's so hard to sort out the truth. Obviously we're both quite practiced at deception."

"That we are," he said quietly. He dropped his gaze and studied the cameo brooch he held in his hands and knew it held much more significance than being the trademark brooch made infamous by the Ivory Duchess. Whether this particular brooch was genuine or not, he still held his very future in the palm of his hands.

Breathing irregularly, he closed his eyes, envisioning the freedom he had thought awaited him once he delivered the brooch and the Ivory Duchess back to Simon Morrell. Only moments earlier, Philip had almost heard the pages turn and close a difficult chapter in his life since his last promissory note to Bradford had been as good as redeemed. With every debt of honor repaid, his honor would have been restored.

Morrell would never accept this imitation as the one Philip had recovered, and Bradford could not be convinced to extend the deadline for the promissory note unless . . . Was it possible that Morrell had lied about the value of the brooch because it was really the Ivory Duchess he wanted all along, and Philip had refused to accept the assignment until the fee had been doubled? Or was she stalling for time now, hoping to undermine his commitment to return her to Morrell by planting doubt in his mind so he would leave to verify her story, giving her just enough time to run away again?

He could not let that happen.

He would not let that happen.

Not now. Now when he was so close to achieving the goal he had set for himself seven years ago.

"We're going to Philadelphia," he said firmly. "I'll let Morrell deal with you. If you're telling the truth about the brooch, he'll be satisfied because you were what he really wanted all along. If you're not, I'll give him the pleasure of forcing you to tell me where you hid the genuine brooch. Either way I'll still earn my fee."

"And how would you find the brooch? Barge into the cottage and frighten two old women who have shown you nothing but kindness? How cold and heartless you've become." She waved her hand toward the cottage. "Why don't you just do it right now? Go ahead. Force your way inside and scare them half to death while you ransack their home."

He stiffened his back, knowing she would believe he was capable of being so calculating or cruel after the way he had reacted to her courageous confession and pleas for his understanding. She could never know, however, the price he would pay for hurting her. "I would never do anything to upset Miss Dolly or Miss Maggie."

She sighed. "Neither would I. That's the only thing we've agreed upon so far. Perhaps it's one thing we can trust each other to believe."

Her eyes filled with such sincerity and longing, he wanted to trust her with every beat of his heart. She captured his gaze and held it. Fear laced the innocence and goodness gazing back at him and touched his tortured soul. To his amazement, he saw himself mirrored in her eyes as three different men, each battling for dominance, each claiming the right to control his decision.

Omega, the jaded cynic, sneered back at him and mocked him for even considering her tale might ring true. Philip Massey, a man who had been driven by superficial values and disgraced by scandal, shook his head as though the lessons from his own past had been forgotten and self-interest blinded him to the truth of her words.

A third man, one he had thought long condemned to remain buried beneath the scars of his mistakes, emerged from the depths of his soul. An idealist and a dreamer, he had been nourished and strengthened by the presence of this exceptional woman and the gifts she had given to him during the past two months: Acceptance. Trust. Love.

The dreamer alone had kept vigilance over the deepest yearnings of Philip's heart and demanded one last chance to prove himself as the greatest force with Philip's character. He offered Philip a vision of how good life would be if he had the courage to believe her now and to love her enough to put her welfare above his own selfish interests.

He swallowed hard.

The vision was too powerful to relinquish without a fight. He wanted to believe everything she had told him about the brooch. He wanted to hold her in his arms and protect her from Morrell, but he was damned in a hell of his own making—a hell that had lasted for seven long years and seemed destined to imprison him for the rest of his life.

"Please," she whispered. "Won't you please believe me? Everything I've told you is the truth."

Literally at war with himself, he gazed at her as she stood in the shadows.

"Please."

Kathryn's plaintive plea broke through his reverie. Despite his resolve to harden his heart against her and resist her, he could not stop himself. He turned around and gazed into her eyes. A lump lodged in his throat.

He took a deep breath and swallowed hard as the dreamer swept aside the other two facets of Philip's character, but borrowed just enough cynicism and experience to guide him.

Philip put the brooch into his pocket and captured her gaze with his own. "If you are playing me for a fool and think to disappear before I get back, be forewarned. I found you once. I can find you again." He paused, his heart pounding in his chest. "Wherever you go, I will follow. Wherever you hide, I will find you."

She blinked back tears, but she did not flinch at his threat. Her backbone stiffened. "I will be right here with Miss Dolly and Miss Maggie. This is my home now. How soon . . . how long . . ."

"For as long as it takes," he whispered and turned away from her. His steps were heavy, but determined. His will was strong. And his heart kept custody of the impossible dream that the vision of the future he had glimpsed ever so fleetingly was not merely an illusion that would prove him truly the King of All Fools who would reign supreme over the cynic, the idealist, and the dreamer after all.

Chapter 25

Philip mounted the carpeted stairs to Morrell's suite on the fourth floor of the Morningstar Hotel just before eight o'clock that same night. The brooch, thoroughly cleaned and polished now, rested in a new pouch inside his pocket.

He faced the inevitable confrontation with Morrell with no small measure of both trepidation and relief. During the journey from the cottage back to Philadelphia, Philip had had time to reflect on his meeting with Kate and to plan his approach to Morrell. Fully cognizant he was at the threshold of a pivotal moment, one that would alter the course of his life, Philip also recognized other critical events in his past with the wisdom of hindsight.

His decision to remain in Philadelphia and become apprenticed to his uncle instead of moving west with his family was one of them. Getting involved in the land scheme was another, which only led to assuming a second identity as Omega.

This moment in his life, filled with ramifications he had now fully considered, was perhaps the culminating event in a lifelong journey that would render his previous decisions as either designed by fate to set him free or merely another foolish decision that would keep him in a never-ending circle of self-destruction.

In either event, he had no desire to prolong or reevaluate his decision to confront Morrell face-to-face, something he had never done with anyone who had ever hired him as Omega. Since Philip had already violated every other rule on this assignment, it seemed only fitting to break one last tradition and put both his identities on the line.

For Kate. For himself and his own self-respect.

If Kate was lying about the brooch, he could return to the cottage and have her back in Philadelphia by midnight. He could repay Bradford in the morning after delivering Cynthia's necklace and celebrate a long-awaited freedom.

If she was telling the truth, as he suspected, his career as Omega would be over because his real identity would have been revealed. He would have a small portion to pledge against his promissory note, but it would take years to redeem the rest. Long, lonely years, and he would spend every day of those years regretting this decision.

With his mind set on unraveling the strings of deception that wove this assignment into a strong rope that formed a noose around his neck, he paused on the landing and loosened his cravat. He also tried to keep Kate's beguiling nature in mind, superimposing it over the description of the treacherous character of the Ivory Duchess Morrell had given him.

He took a deep breath and resumed his climb up one more flight. Morrell was not expecting him tonight, a factor in Philip's favor. Without time to fabricate a story, if by chance there was one needed, Morrell would not be able to withstand Philip's questioning without ultimately revealing the truth.

A young Irish maid with dark black hair and a lilting accent answered his knock at the suite door, but kept him waiting in the hallway while she checked to see if he could see Morrell. Philip had the urge to charge in and demand to talk to the man but decided that would only alienate him and raise his suspicions there might be something amiss.

Moments later, she returned and led him through a foyer to a large, splendidly furnished sitting room where three people sat together. He tried to decide which one of the two gentlemen was Morrell. Tall and imposing, the dark-haired man rose first and Philip silently congratulated himself for correctly identifying the agent as the maid left and closed the door behind her.

"I'm rather shocked to see you and meet you in person. Simon Morrell," he said in a clipped voice. He extended his hand. "Shall I still call you Omega or—"

"Massey. Philip Massey," he replied, knowing he could never turn back now that he had revealed his identity.

"Massey. Let me introduce you to my wife, Helen, and William Pennington."

Philip nodded to the pale, red-haired woman and noted the array of expensive jewelry displayed on her slender body. "Mrs. Morrell."

Curiosity flashed like lightning through sky blue eyes. "I hope you bring us good news, Mr. Massey."

He clenched his teeth together and glanced at the other man, reluctant to discuss anything about the Ivory Duchess in front of an uninvolved party.

The angular, white-haired gentleman rose and shook Philip's hand. "Good to meet you. I've heard so much about your . . . your work." His words carried a distinct English accent, and his carriage was understated, but aristocratic, a sharp contrast to Morrell's cockney speech and overbearing presence.

Philip cocked a brow. "I thought I had kept my real identity quite separate from my work as Omega."

Dusty blue eyes narrowed under white bridges of brow. "Indeed, you have. I was referring to your reputation as a man who never failed to recover stolen jewelry. I trust you've been successful again?''

The man's reassurance that he only knew Philip as Omega did not slow his rapid heartbeat, and he turned to Morrell for an explanation why Pennington knew about the assignment.

Morrell had taken a seat next to his wife and gestured for Philip to take a chair opposite the settee and next to the Englishman. ''Pennington is an investor,'' he explained.

The older man chuckled. ''His major and only investor, I'm afraid. Without the Duchess, neither one of us can continue to reap the healthy profits she earns for us. Do sit down and tell us your news.''

Maintaining an outward composure, Philip kept his surprise at the open admission of their financial success, a far cry from Kathryn's claims, limited to a question as he sat down. ''You never mentioned an investor when we discussed the assignment.''

The theatrical agent frowned. ''I don't normally divulge every aspect of my business with hirelings unless it's absolutely necessary. Did you find her or didn't you?''

Philip ignored the question, but it did not escape his notice that Morrell asked about the Ivory Duchess first without mentioning the cameo brooch—the very bait he had used to lure Philip into accepting this assignment in the first place. He pulled the pouch from his pocket and held it out to Morrell.

Helen grabbed it first. She removed the cameo brooch, eyed it carefully, and smiled. ''You actually found it!'' she exclaimed. She handed it to her husband who studied it briefly and casually slipped it into his own pocket. ''What about the Duchess?''

''Yes,'' Pennington added. ''Do tell us. Have you found her?''

Again, Philip ignored their questions to keep control of

the conversation. "I think you should look at the brooch again."

Helen's brows furrowed, and Morrell cocked his head.

"Take a closer look at it," Philip urged as his heart began to pound.

Morrell fumbled in his pocket to find the brooch and looked at it before he handed it to his wife who also studied it again. When she looked up at Philip with her eyes full of questions, the grim expression on his face was not feigned. "It's paste. There isn't a genuine stone on the entire brooch, including the woman's silhouette. That's not even carved in ivory."

Morrell's expression remained nonchalant. "Are you sure the brooch is a fake?"

"Don't be a fool. Of course he is. The man's a jeweler," Pennington interjected. He looked at Philip. "I expected Morrell would have told you the brooch wasn't genuine. It was used on stage as part of the Duchess' costume, and it hardly seemed necessary to risk a valuable brooch. Thefts are quite common in the theater."

Philip's chest tightened, and his hands balled into fists. With his muscles tense, dread flowed through his veins. "I don't recover theater costumes, and I don't work under false pretenses, particularly since I told you I don't ordinarily accept assignments involving missing persons."

Morrell's face turned crimson and his features distorted with agitation. "You were hired to find the brooch and bring back the Duchess. It's irrelevant at this point whether or not you were misled about the value of the brooch. You found it, I've accepted it, and now I want to know where she is. Without the Duchess, you don't collect your fee, or have you forgotten the terms of our agreement?"

"I haven't forgotten the terms," Philip snapped. "I just don't appreciate deception." Relief that Kate had been telling the truth was laced with the heartfelt certainty she had been honest about everything else she had told him.

Helen nervously toyed with the brooch, but Pennington remained almost ice calm. "What's important at the moment, Massey, is whether or not you've found our Duchess. I understand your annoyance at being misled, and I apologize on Morrell's behalf. He should have been absolutely forthright about the value of the brooch. Although I've only recently been informed about the Duchess' disappearance, you yourself stated only minutes ago you don't normally accept assignments to search for missing persons. Morrell obviously needed to hire the best, and if that meant being less than candid—"

Philip snorted. "The ends do not always justify the means, and I don't play the pawn for any man. Fee or no fee."

"We all have the same goal, Massey." Pennington sighed. "And that is to see the Ivory Duchess return to the stage where she belongs. You'll have your fee, and we'll be able to see that the concert tour will proceed as arranged."

Pennington's argument was reasonable since he stated the terms Philip had originally agreed to, and the investor had an air of integrity about him that gave added credence to his words as well as his logic.

Morrell, apparently, was not in the mood to be conciliatory. "You have avoided my questions repeatedly, and I'll ask you just once more. Do you have the Duchess or don't you?"

Philip tensed. "I have spoken to her," he admitted, "but I won't reveal her location or any information concerning what she's been doing since her disappearance until you've answered some questions of my own."

Morrell bolted to his feet, his face mottled with splashes of red. "You're not in a position to make demands!"

"Aren't I?" Philip spat as stood up to meet Morrell's

threatening posture with his own. "You lied to me about the brooch. What other lies did you use to convince me to find the Ivory Duchess for you?" Chest heaving, he wanted to strangle the damn agent to get the truth out of him.

"Gentlemen. Please sit down. This whole angry display of male pride is quite unsettling, especially with a lady present. Do take a seat so we can discuss this rationally and civilly."

Morrell plopped back onto the settee, and his wife immediately tried to calm him. Philip glared at both of them, but eventually sat down.

"Now that we're all calm," Pennington began, "suppose we let Mr. Massey ask his questions first." He raised his hand when Morrell opened his mouth to protest. "I'm sure you can mollify Mr. Massey's concerns and get this matter quickly settled. Agreed?"

Helen whispered into her husband's ear before he nodded stiffly.

Philip unclenched his fists. "Agreed." He cleared his throat, but another lump formed to replace the first. The answers he elicited with his questions would be critical, and he swallowed hard again. Knowing he would face no greater moment of truth in his life, he took a deep breath. "I'd like to know how and when you first met Kathryn . . . Kate Baxter."

Outside the cottage, dark had fallen, but Kate's spirit had been shadowed and mired in disappointment from the moment Philip had told her he had been hired by Simon to find her and bring her back.

After she had told Dolly and Maggie what had happened on the portico, Maggie's support and Dolly's smug self-satisfaction at having pegged Philip as a potential disappointment did little to soften the blow of his deceitful betrayal or help to ease the harsh echo of his charges against her.

Bereft and abandoned by her once shining guide and inspiration, she huddled under the blankets on her bed and stared at the small beacon of moonlight that spilled through her bedroom window. The moonlight would quickly disappear once the sun challenged and won control of the heavens in the morning and bathed the world with glorious, warm sunshine. Philip, as the man she had loved, had been as gentle as the moonlight, subtly guiding her way from the past to the present. Even if he had been nothing more than a fancy chimera inspired by her dreams, he had guided her well.

Still, she grieved for the loss of the man she had loved— still loved—and knew there would never be anyone to fill her life with the gentle light of love Philip had given to her.

Drained and nearly broken, her spirit had little fight left, but she was determined not to be defeated. She would not run away again. She had earned her freedom, and she meant to keep it, regardless of whether or not Philip decided to believe Simon instead of her.

If either Philip or Simon came for her, she would simply defy them. There was nothing they could do to her to force her to leave. Unless they stooped so low as to threaten Dolly or Maggie, Kate would have to hold firm in her stand against her agent and her betrayer.

Peace of mind, that elusive inner sanctuary she had struggled to achieve by telling the truth about her past, was an important gift she had earned in her bid for freedom. She did not regret telling Philip the truth, but the sad legacy of her decision was a broken heart, one that would never mend whether Philip eventually accepted her account of the past and forgave her for deceiving him or not.

Too weak to shed another tear, too heartsick to think

about life without Philip by her side, she closed her eyes. Physically exhausted, not fully recovered from her injury during the sailing mishap, and emotionally wrenched by Philip's betrayal and the destruction of her dreams, she hugged the pillow to her chest and sighed.

She would be starting the circuit again in a few days. She needed to rest, to heal, and to gain strength. She needed time to get her clothes packed for the trip, yet all she could think about now was how hard it would be to find a way to live the rest of her life without him.

Unless Philip returned for her and tried to take her back to Simon.

Whether she liked it or not, Philip still held her future in his hands. Despite what he had done to her, he was still the keeper of her heart. She had once thought to reclaim her heart from him and failed. Until she found a way to survive the pain of his deception, she would not be strong enough to fight to get her heart back.

She gave sleep the power to pull her away from her troubles, but she knew she was only fighting the inevitable. When she woke up in the morning, she would still face unbearable heartache. She prayed that with a little sleep, she might be able to face the first of many long days that stretched ahead in her lifetime, and one day she would be able to take part of the blame for destroying any chance she might have had for happiness with him.

Not with the Philip Massey she had discovered today, but the man of character and courage who lay buried beneath the man who had betrayed her. It might take an eternity before she accepted the sad fact that he did not exist, and it was with another small sigh that she knew she still held one small spark of hope he would reappear as the man of her dreams and convince her that today had only been a nightmare.

A soul-shaking, heartbreaking nightmare.

*   *   *

Philip stared at the three people in the room. Morrell fidgeted in his seat while his wife sat stone-faced and silent. With his expression bland and difficult to read, Pennington sat with his hands folded on his lap.

"Is that all you have to say?" Philip asked Morrell, too impatient to wait for an answer. "You don't even bother to deny you kept her a virtual prisoner as a child?"

"I was her guardian. I had every right to make sure she developed her talent!"

Helen spoke up to defend her husband as well as herself. "Kate wanted for nothing. She had the finest teachers—"

"She wanted to see her grandmother, and you wouldn't let her. Not even once," he spat. "What harm would that have done? She'd already lost her mother and father. How much loss did you expect a child to bear?" He turned to Pennington, who had gone pale, and dismissed him as the proper target for his wrath.

Dazed by how coldly Morrell had verified Kate's version of the events that had led to his being named as her guardian and how begrudgingly he had dispelled the public image of the Ivory Duchess as merely a theatrical ploy, Philip pressed forward. "What about the new concert tour, the one you arranged despite her repeated requests to let her retire from the stage?"

Pennington flinched, and Morrell's face flushed crimson again. "I . . . I . . ."

"You were such a fool! I told you to let her take a brief vacation before you forced her back on the concert circuit again. Didn't you learn anything from what happened in Vienna?" Helen hissed. "If you had listened to me and had let her rest longer—"

Pennington sat forward in his seat. "Vienna? What happened in Vienna?"

Helen's eyes burned with disgust. "The girl tried to run

away. Even though we interrupted the tour and let her rest for a few days, she became increasingly uncooperative and more demanding.''

''Like last May when she asked for the funds she had earned over the past five years, and you convinced her they were gone? Funds you used to pay your expenses because the receipts were lower than you wanted?'' Philip's chest heaved with indignation. ''Did you even bother to set her funds aside and just take them from her account, or was it just easier to lie and pretend the funds never existed?''

''How dare you!'' Helen cried. ''We worked very hard to make her a success.''

''Apparently, you did,'' Pennington noted, ''but since I received a sizable return on my investment in the Ivory Duchess, I presumed quite naturally Miss Baxter was also amply rewarded for her work. I'm distressed to think you took advantage of her and even more troubled to think she was unhappy.''

''You expected a profit, and I made sure you received it,'' Morrell protested. ''You were the one who insisted on a new concert tour!''

''That I did.'' Pennington sighed and rubbed his eyes with bony fingers. He nodded to Philip. ''If you would be kind enough to bring the Duchess back, I'm sure we can resolve our . . . our differences. I assure you Miss Baxter will be given every consideration and will be handsomely rewarded. I personally guarantee it.''

Philip braced himself in his seat. Was Pennington the voice of reason in this entire mad episode, or was he merely trying to placate Philip by playing the naive investor who had been misled by his partner? Was he so eager to make additional profits he could overlook what Morrell had done before and not expect him to do it again?

Pennington pursed his lips when Philip did not respond

to the offer. "Your fee, of course, will be paid immediately upon the return of the Ivory Duchess."

"My fee," Philip repeated in a whisper. He was certain Kate would receive little, if any, consideration from Morrell that would be different from what she had gotten from him in the past.

If he had to live the rest of his days knowing he had destroyed any chance to redeem himself with Kate, he could take some solace in knowing he had set her free from the vultures who had feasted on the fruits of her talent.

When he had first met Kate, he had allowed his drive to be free of his own past to jade his thinking and deny what he had seen sparkling in her eyes: her trust, her sweet innocence, and her innate goodness that years of bondage to Morrell had not been able to destroy.

As much as Philip needed to break the chains that kept him manacled to his past, he could not set himself free by sending her back to Morrell or even divulging her whereabouts.

"My hero." He cringed as her words came back to haunt him. He let her words resound in his mind again and again until they became a challenge. He had never seen himself as anything more than an ordinary man, flawed perhaps more than most. He had never believed himself worthy of being called a hero.

Until Kate.

Until gentle, innocent, trusting Kate.

He squared his shoulders. He never wanted to be anyone's hero, but he would be now—for Kate. He exhaled slowly and rose from his seat knowing he would do anything to be able to live up to her expectations of him. He drew his own courage now from her shining example, and his love for her empowered him to stand firm as her protector. "My fee, gentlemen, will not be stained with the knowledge that Miss Baxter does not want to return to the stage under any condition," he informed them firmly. "If you'll excuse me . . ."

He turned to leave when Morrell charged at him with fury blazing in his eyes. "You bastard! You'll tell me where she is right now. You're not fooling anyone. You intend to put her on the stage yourself! So help me, Massey, I'll sue you! You won't get away with this!" Panting like a bull who had charged toward a cow only to ram into a fence, Morrell stopped short when Philip faced him down.

"I don't think so," he spat, determined to be the protector and hero she deserved. "You can't intimidate me like you did a young woman. And if I see one advertisement posted anywhere announcing the return of the Ivory Duchess on a fall tour, I'll make sure the newspapers carry a very interesting follow-up story in the next edition." He paused and welcomed the pounding of his heart as a sign of his commitment to her. "I'm sure there are any number of fans who would like to know the real identity of the Ivory Duchess, and they'll be more than disappointed to learn she's just an ordinary woman of low birth with an extraordinary talent."

And the woman I love.

The pain that sliced through his heart nearly caught his breath and held it, but Philip greeted the pain as a reminder he was still alive.

"You wouldn't dare!" Helen whined as she got up from the settee to join her husband.

"Wouldn't I? Think long and hard before you try to find her and force her back into a life she doesn't want."

"I'll ruin you," Morrell snarled. "I'll destroy your reputation."

Philip laughed out loud. "Now you're really bordering on lunacy. I have no reputation that can be destroyed any more than I've already managed to do on my own."

"You sniveling worm," Morrell hissed. "Do you think

you're the only one I hired to find her?'' When Philip jerked with surprise, Morrell snorted. ''You may not want to cooperate, but I expect at least one of the others will. Rest assured, Massey. I will find her. It's merely a matter of time.''

''Considering my position, won't you please reconsider?''

Pennington's plea was almost pitiful, and Philip glanced over his shoulder at him. ''Why? So you can line your pockets while you're back in England and she's with a man whose word isn't worth the air it takes to give it?''

''I'll personally double your fee. Even triple it.''

Philip shook his head. ''My conscience is not for sale, and neither is Kate.'' He strode from the room and left the suite, slamming the door behind him. As he continued down the hall and three flights of stairs, he knew he might have to spend the rest of his life finding a way to redeem the promissory note Bradford held. He had no regrets save for one: He would never be able to find a way to earn her forgiveness and redeem the love she had once offered to him.

Chapter 26

Kate rose the next morning, dressed quickly, and ate a fast breakfast. She left a note for Dolly and Maggie on the kitchen table and hurried to the barn to hitch Precious to the road cart. If the circuit started on Monday, she needed to get to Mrs. Spencer's to pick up the gloves she had ordered for Dolly.

She had to do something. Wallowing in self-pity for the next three days while she waited for the circuit to begin made as much sense as the dream she had enjoyed last night. Philip was not coming back into her life, and if he did, he only meant to try to force her to go back to Simon.

She also needed time alone, away from the cottage, to decide whether to stay here or start over again somewhere else. Although she had vowed to stand and fight for the new life she had created for herself, she was afraid to involve Dolly and Maggie any more than she had already. Simon was just about the most unscrupulous man she had ever met, although Philip came close, and she knew her agent would not hesitate to use threats against the two sisters to convince Kate to go back to the stage.

She guided the road cart down the drive along the house and onto the gravel roadway that would take her to Haddonfield. The weather was unusually cool for July, and she was glad to have her shawl. Once she picked up Dolly's gloves, she intended to go back to the place along the creek where she had gone to read the newspaper clipping about the Ivory Duchess.

And where Philip had first kissed her.

Shivering in spite of her shawl, she would not let her memories of that fateful day discourage her. She would learn how to forget him, and there was no better place to try to make her plans and sort through her options than the very place where she had given the first piece of her heart to him.

The gravel crunched beneath the wheels of the road cart, and she briefly glanced down at the roadway. Her dream that Philip would be the one man who would be able to see beyond the layers of deception and still accept her now seemed foolish and terribly naive, a romantic fantasy that only deepened her own pain and disappointment.

She did not fight the tears that blurred her vision, and she did not spare herself blame. She had opened her heart to him, and she would have to learn how to stitch the shattered remnants back together. She would never trust another man again because she could not trust her own judgment. Not after being so wrong about Philip.

She clicked the reins and urged Precious into a trot. If she was going to leave and try to start a new life somewhere else, she had little time to spare. She may have been a fool once, but not twice. Before day's end, she would either be committed to staying with Dolly and Maggie or well on her way to somewhere Philip would never find her.

Functioning on nervous energy after a sleepless night, Philip wasted no time getting back into the life he had left behind when he had accepted Morrell's assignment and rented the country seat.

After meeting with his uncle when he opened the jewelry

emporium and agreeing to return to work early the next week, Philip had one of the store clerks wrap Cynthia's necklace. With the package in tow, he had gone straight to Bradford's residence where he had been immediately escorted to a small study.

He paced the room now, anxious to deliver the necklace and convince Bradford that although Philip would be unable to redeem the promissory note by September first, he would begin to make small, regular payments. That would tie up at least the next five years, but with his double identity now exposed, he had no other choice.

"Massey! You don't waste any time, do you?"

Philip looked up to see Bradford approaching him.

A square man with a thick girth, he had a broad smile on his face. "Not that I'm complaining, mind you. It's a great worry off my mind." He shook hands with Philip and gestured to a decanter of sherry on the desk. "If you'd like to celebrate—"

"It's a bit early." Philip declined, his mind awash with confusion. "I promised the necklace in time for your anniversary next week," he said as he extended the package to Bradford. Since he was only a few days early, he was bemused by Bradford's attitude. He did not doubt that Cynthia had been badgering the poor man to death about the necklace and notched up another reason to be glad he had been spared spending the rest of his life married to her.

Bradford laid the package on his desk, opened it, and held the necklace up to the light. The garnets sparkled like tiny red suns, and the pearls glistened like they had been kissed with dew. "Incredible," he murmured before he smiled. "Cynthia will be thrilled. I've got to give you credit, Massey," he said as he reached into a desk drawer. "You kept your word. There were times . . ." He paused to look in the drawer. "Here it is. I drew this up for you last night."

He handed an envelope to Philip who accepted payment for the necklace mired in a haze of total confusion since he had not notified Bradford that the necklace would be delivered today. "I'm rather surprised you have this ready," Philip admitted.

"The messenger said you'd probably be here to take care of this yourself sometime today."

Philip thought he might be losing his grip on reality. "Messenger?"

"The one you sent last night." Bradford laughed and held up his hands. "Don't tell me. You won a wager, but were in an alcoholic stupor. Now that you've sobered, you don't remember a thing."

"Something like that," he quipped as he opened the envelope to make sure it was a bank draft to cover the price of the necklace. He pulled out a piece of paper that looked so familiar, he blinked his eyes, read it twice, and still did not believe his own eyes.

"You needn't look so almighty surprised. What did you expect me to do with the promissory note? Trust it to the post?"

Philip's hand trembled so hard it shook the paper. "It's marked paid," he rasped. "In . . . in full."

"And more than a month early. Like I said, you're a man of your word, and I respect that. If you'll send a bill for the necklace, I'll see that it's taken care of right away."

Nearly speechless, Philip had dreamed about the elation he would feel when he held this redeemed promissory note in his hand. There was no elation. No joy. Suspicion built into dread, and when he finally spoke to Bradford, his voice cracked. "The . . . ah . . . the messenger. Can you describe him to me?"

Bradford poured himself a sherry. "You really were addled, weren't you?"

"The messenger," he repeated, his pulse racing.

With a shrug of his shoulders, Bradford narrowed his eyes. "Slender. Very angular. Maybe sixty, judging by his wrinkles and white hair. Right pleasant chap for a blue-blood. Thought he might even be a friend of your uncle's."

Pennington! Caught between total surprise and bewilderment, Philip felt anger slowly begin to build. He folded the redeemed promissory note and put it back into the envelope which he stored in his pocket. "I appreciate your patience as much as the description you've just given me," he said quietly as he rose, mumbled an excuse about another appointment, and made a hasty retreat.

He managed to get back to the Morningstar Hotel before his anger built into an uncontrollable rage. If Morrell put Pennington up to this trick, Philip could not figure out why. If Pennington acted alone, he could only have one goal: to get Philip to change his mind and bring the Ivory Duchess back to Philadelphia.

Just thinking about Pennington's audacity made Philip's blood boil a little harder. How did Pennington know about the promissory note Bradford held? More importantly, why had Pennington redeemed it? Technically, Philip had no obligation to do anything for Pennington, but was savvy enough to know he expected something in return—like a lady with outrageous hazel eyes and incredible talent?

Ten minutes after he entered the hotel, he was back on the street even more confounded. Morrell and his wife had checked out late last night, and Pennington had never been registered. Dismissing even the remotest chance that Pennington had experienced an attack of conscience for his role as an investor who had allowed a young woman to be victimized, Philip started a systematic check of every major hotel in the city. Failing to find a trace of the man, he sent out several contacts to check boardinghouses, including the one where Kate had hidden when she had made her escape.

No trace of Morrell or Pennington.

By noon, he extended the search to the railroad station and the shipping houses. No luck there either, although he still had yet to hear from one contact. By midafternoon, Philip returned to his apartments over the jewelry emporium exhausted and befuddled.

He climbed the stairs cursing himself for a fool. Morrell had not been bluffing and must have hired others to search for the Ivory Duchess which meant there was only one place Morrell and Pennington could have gone: to the cottage to get Kate.

Philip had lost valuable time trying to find them in the city. If they had discovered where she was living now and had gone to get her, Philip had to hurry if he hoped to reach the cottage before they were able to force her to leave with them.

If she had stayed there.

If she had not decided to make a quick escape and try to disappear again before Philip returned.

He let himself into his apartments with every intention of changing into comfortable traveling clothes, packing a small valise in case he had to go searching for her again, and catching the three o'clock ferry to Camden.

The moment he stepped inside the door, he froze in place and stared at the man seated in a chair in the sitting room.

"I do hope you'll forgive me for intruding. Your uncle was kind enough to let me in. I had hoped to see you early this morning, but you left a bit earlier than I expected."

Every muscle in Philip's body tensed. His lips taut, he fought to remain calm and rational. "Pennington," he drawled, hoping he sounded more in control than he felt. He took the envelope out of his pocket and held it in his outstretched hand. "Would you care to explain this?"

Chuckling softly, the older man's eyes twinkled. "I rather thought that might get your attention."

"Oh, you've got my attention, but you've also got a lot of explaining to do." Philip eased into the room and stood directly in front of the man. "Starting right now. Why did you pay my debt to Bradford? And while you're at it, maybe you'd better tell me how you even found out about it."

"It's a bit of a long story," Pennington suggested. "Perhaps you might want to take a seat."

"Shorten it," Philip spat. "I have no intention of letting you play the decoy while Morrell starts searching for Kate, assuming he's not already on his way to the cottage to force her to return with him."

Pennington's expression, while sober, seemed genuinely saddened. "Morrell and his wife no longer pose any threat to Miss Baxter."

"Since when?"

"They sailed for Liverpool on the early tide," he murmured. "From there, they'll make connections to the Continent where Morrell will most likely be searching for his next celebrity."

Philip found that answer so impossible to believe he dismissed it as a lie since his contacts, save one, had not reported Morrell's departure. He checked his pocket watch. Two-thirty. Only half an hour till the next ferry. "Better make this even shorter. I have an appointment."

"I was rather hoping you might spare me—"

"You're wasting my time."

Pennington sighed, reached inside his waistcoat, and took out a small package which he handed to Philip.

He refused to touch it. "If this is another attempt to bribe me into taking you to Kate Baxter—"

"Take the package and open it, Mr. Massey."

Intrigued, but frustrated to the breaking point, Philip grabbed the package and tore it open. He stared at the contents in total amazement. His hands started to shake, and his heart began to pound. He stepped to the side and dropped into the chair next to Pennington.

His throat went dry, and he looked at the older man, unable to utter a sound. His mind raced with a dozen questions, but he could not pose a single one.

Pennington smiled. "You have information I need. To be more specific, you know where I can find the Duchess. Before you object, you need to hear what I have to say."

Philip could only nod.

He listened carefully as Pennington began to talk, slowly at first, and with great emotion. For the next hour, Philip listened, asked questions, and swung from disbelief to relief and back again so many times he lost count.

By the time Pennington had finished, Philip was convinced that if the white-haired gentleman sitting in the chair next to him was not the greatest storyteller of all time, he was the most inventive as well as the most convincing.

Philip held the proof of Pennington's tale in the palm of his hand.

He moistened his lips and cleared his throat. "What is it you want me to do?" he rasped, and the reply was exactly what he had feared.

"Take me to the Duchess."

Dusk ended another day, but Kate had already made her decision to stay here and had formulated a plan. Her travel valise was packed and ready, and all she had to do now was convince Dolly and Maggie to agree that starting the circuit a few days early was a good idea.

Seated next to Maggie in the music room while Dolly played several short selections after supper, Kate leaned back and closed her eyes. Just over two months had passed since she had first sat in this very chair. Her prayers had been answered that day, and she had been given the position as Dolly's replacement.

The layers of deception that had shrouded her new life were gone now, and the acceptance both women had offered to her filled her with happiness. Heartbreak tempered her joy, yet in the silent depths of her mourning, she heard the whisper of hope; She also listened to her conscience and knew neither she nor Philip deserved all the blame for the misunderstanding between them.

She had not been wrong about Philip.

He was a man of courage and integrity, and she could not fault him for deceiving her. It was not his fault Simon had lied to Philip and misrepresented the facts.

When she had finally found the courage to tell him the truth, it had been too late. She could not blame him for not believing her. If she had been honest with him from the very beginning, she might have been able to convince him she was not lying again.

Her heated charges against him resounded in her mind. He had no motive to try to trick her by telling her the brooch was made of paste. If he intended to double-cross Simon and sell the brooch, he could have simply taken the brooch and left. She would have been overjoyed to have been left behind.

She believed him now and knew the brooch must be made of paste, but Simon had deliberately misrepresented its value to lure Philip into accepting the assignment. Would he use the truth about her background she had told him to challenge Simon? How would Philip know which story about the Ivory Duchess to believe?

He would know because he loved her. The hunger in his kisses, and the longing in his eyes had been real, but he had been hurt too badly to believe her when she had finally been able to tell him the truth. Although she did not ever expect he might be able to forgive her, neither would he betray her and divulge her whereabouts to Simon, unless Philip's need for his fee stood between them.

"Kate, dear? Are you too tired to play for us?"

She smiled before she even opened her eyes. "Of course not, Miss Maggie. What would you like me to play?"

Dolly stood up from her seat on the piano bench and turned around. "Something you usually played during a performance," she suggested as she walked over to join them.

"Für Elise," Maggie whispered, and her eyes began to shimmer. "You played it the first day you came to us, remember?"

Kate glanced from one woman to another as she got to her feet. "I was hoping to ask you if it might be all right to start the circuit a few days early. I'd like to leave in the morning."

Dolly's gaze narrowed. "Are you thinking of running away?"

Kate shook her head. "I told Phil—Mr. Massey I had no intention of leaving my home with you, and I don't. It's just I'd rather keep busy than . . ."

"Are you sure you're feeling well enough? You should probably use the next few days to rest," Maggie suggested.

"Or wait to see if Mr. Massey decides to come back for you and take you back to your agent," Dolly sniffed. "He'll be back. Mark my word. I never trusted that man and with good reason, as it turns out."

Kate blanched. "He won't be back," she whispered, defending him even as her heart began to tremble with the fear that she might be wrong. "If he does return while I'm on the circuit, he'll just have to wait until I get back. If . . . if he threatens you in any way, you can tell him where I'll be and . . . and . . ."

"We can always send for you, Kate," Maggie murmured, her voice gentle. "Won't you play for me now? Later we can talk about your leaving for the circuit in the morning."

Kate walked over to the pianoforte and trailed her fingertips over the ivory and ebony keys as she sat down on the bench. She bowed her head, searched her memory for the right opening notes to begin Beethoven's *Für Elise*, and placed her hands into position.

She closed her eyes and began to play. Slowly. Haltingly. Until the music began to flow once again from her heart to her fingertips. The melancholy that filled her spirit seeped into her interpretation, and she released herself into a realm where gentle music soothed broken spirits and love—ever fragile—could be strengthened and renewed.

Chapter 27

Eventually successful in her bid for Dolly's approval to start the circuit early, Kate waved good-bye to both sisters and urged Precious down the drive past the cottage the very next morning. Cheerful and growing more and more confident that Philip would not return once he discovered she had been telling him the truth, she looked forward to keeping busy for the next two weeks.

With her view of the main roadway obscured by dense summer foliage, she was alert to the danger of the near blind entry. Hearing an approaching wagon, she quickly brought Precious to a halt. Was it Philip? Her heart began to pound, and she caught her breath. She had not even left the grounds, yet she allowed worry to undermine her confidence.

When Abner Spade passed by and nodded pleasantly as he tipped his hat to her, she smiled and sighed with relief. Philip was not going to return. She repeated the mantra over and over in her mind until her pulse returned to normal. How long would it take before her mind accepted what her heart embraced? Would she spend the rest of her life in constant worry that he was not the man she believed him to be?

With a click of the reins, she clamped a lid of determination on her worries and rounded the turn to enter the roadway. Along the next several miles, she met and recognized several local farmers taking produce to Cooper's Creek to be loaded onto barges and transported to Camden and Philadelphia.

With her confidence gaining ground, the sight of a distant coach traveling toward her sent her heart and mind into another battle with one another. She refused to let fear or her imagination take control. She tightened her hold on the reins and straightened her back, hoping the coach would turn at the crossroads just ahead.

It did not.

With considerably less distance between the road cart and the coach now, she stared at the driver as he drew closer. Blurred features sharpened into an image that exploded her confidence and ripped through the fortress of all her defenses. She caught her lower lip with her teeth to keep from crying out his name, but it echoed with every dull beat of her heart.

Philip.

Her first instinct was to turn around, lather Precious into a gallop and escape. Fast. Now. Anywhere! Her second instinct, more rational and controlled, took command. She would not run. She would not try to hide. She would face him courageously without shame or regret. Obviously he had no conscience if he could listen to what she had told him and still come back to force her to return to Simon.

One day Philip might realize he was wrong, but then it would be too late. For either of them. Would he ever know how much she had loved him and how callously he had disregarded her love? She had risked everything—her home, her position, and even her heart—only to lose it all.

Her earlier vow to defy him was admirable, but impossible given the differences between their physical strength, and she had only one advantage as he drew within several feet of the road cart. She had peace of mind. The light of truth shined on her new life, but he would spend all of his days in the shadows of his own deceitful, selfish character. Her only other consolation was they were not near the cottage where Miss Dolly and Maggie would have to witness the final confrontation which would end in ignominy when he forced Kate to go back to Philadelphia with him.

Saving a portion of her strength to defy Simon later, she garnered the rest to remain calm. With a gentle tug on the reins, she halted the road cart, set the brake, and laced her hands together on her lap to keep them from shaking. With the morning sun just over her left shoulder, she turned her head slightly to let her bonnet cut the glare and slightly bowed her head.

When the coach stopped alongside the road cart, she looked up. Philip's gaze captured hers and held it as her heart leaped for joy. The cold, hard mask he had worn was gone, and the gentle, sensitive man who had stolen her heart smiled at her.

"Kate."

He whispered her name so softly his voice caressed her heart, but tears welled in her eyes. Why would he mock her affections for him by pretending to care about her when it was obvious he had come to take her back to Simon? How could he be so cruel?

She blinked back her tears and at least attempted to keep her promise to herself. "I'm not going back with you." Her voice was not as steady as she had intended it to be, but she held her back stiff and her head high. "I have students waiting. If you'll excuse me . . ."

"I can't let you leave on the circuit."

She lowered her gaze and stared straight ahead. When he climbed down from the driver's box, she braced her feet. Did he intend to lift her bodily out of the cart and force her into the coach? She looked around, frantically searching in both directions for a passing rider or wagon.

Her heart sank. The roadway was clear. There was no one to help her. No one to hear her screams of protest. She was completely and utterly alone.

She gripped the reins tighter when he approached her. "I'm not going back," she repeated, refusing to look at him even though he stood right next to the road cart and his shadow fell over her. Her heart pounding, she locked her knees and pressed them together to keep them from knocking.

"I'm so sorry," he murmured. "I wish I could find a way to make you believe me. Or forgive me."

Her throat tightened, and her mouth went dry. Too numb to cry, she doubted she had the strength left to draw her next breath. Disappointment built to such despair her heart truly ached.

Philip—her hero and her inspiration—never truly existed at all. The dream that he existed, even if there was no hope they might one day forgive one another or reconcile their differences, was truly gone. With it, her power to defy him weakened and broke, and she faced the bitter fact that Simon had been right all along.

She could never escape him. She could never have a respectable life and fall in love with a man who would accept her past and love her in spite of it. "I'd like to say good-bye to Miss Dolly and Miss Maggie. Will you grant me that?"

He shook his head. "Not right now. I'd like you to get into the coach."

His voice was low, but firm. She flinched, and her head snapped to the side. Eyes wide, she looked at him as though he were a virtual stranger. "Are you so anxious to collect your fee you would deny me a few minutes to say good-bye? Are you really that coldhearted, or are you simply trying to punish me?''

He stiffened, and his expression hardened. ''I'm not being vindictive. I'm trying to tell you there's someone waiting for you in the coach.''

Had he brought Simon with him? Here? Her head started to throb, and she pressed her fingertips against her forehead. She would never want Simon to go anywhere near Dolly or Maggie and knew she had no choice but to go with him now and hope she would be allowed to write to them later.

She ignored Philip's outstretched hand and climbed out of the road cart on her own. Walking ahead of him, she approached the coach with shaky steps and held perfectly still with her gaze to the ground while Philip opened the coach door for her.

Taking a deep breath, she looked inside the coach. An elderly man with soft blue eyes and dove white hair greeted her gaze with a tremulous smile. He appeared to be old enough to be her grandfather, and his formal attire underscored an authoritative, but kindly presence.

''You're quite an elusive young woman, Miss Baxter. I do apologize for this rather awkward meeting—''

''Do I know you?'' she whispered, frightened only by his clipped English accent. ''Why are you here? What do you want of me?''

Instead of answering her, he mopped his brow. ''Infuriating weather,'' he grumbled. ''Only yesterday it was rather cold and cloudy. Today, it's miserably warm. Won't you please come inside so Philip can get the coach moving and we can get a bit of a breeze while we talk?''

She glanced back at Philip, but his eyes were shuttered and his lips were taut. ''I'll drive to the country seat and bring you back later,'' he promised.

''What about Precious?''

"I'll tie her lead to the back of the coach. She won't have any choice but to follow."

"Please don't be afraid," the man said softly. "I assure you I only want to talk to you. When I'm finished, Philip will see you on your way."

With no other recourse and growing ever more curious, she climbed into the coach and sat down on the red leather seat across from him. It took a few moments for her vision to adjust to the shaded interior, but by the time the coach started to roll, she could see him quite clearly. She removed her gloves, placed them on the seat beside her, and twisted her hands on her lap while she waited for him to begin a conversation.

"I'd like to begin by showing you something," he suggested. He took a small package out of his pocket and handed it to her. Although it appeared to have been opened before and then loosely rewrapped, her fingers trembled too hard to open it and he helped her.

"It's my brooch!"

He laughed nervously. "Not precisely."

She brought the brooch closer to her face and studied it in the light that poured in through the uncurtained coach windows. "It looks like—"

"Like this one?" He placed a second brooch into her hand.

Slightly larger than the first one, the second brooch had fewer diamonds and the woman's silhouette on the cameo was not carved as intricately. "There are two? There are really two of them?"

He pointed to the second brooch. "This one is the replica you wore on stage. The other one was created as a wedding gift nearly thirty-five years ago for my bride." He paused, and his voice dropped to an awed whisper. "She was the sweetest treasure of my life."

Wide-eyed and speechless, she gaped at him. "Are you

telling me that . . . that Simon didn't invent the Ivory Duchess?''

He shook his head and his expression soured. ''Hardly. The man hasn't got the brains.''

''There really was a duchess?''

He nodded. ''Elizabeth.''

''Then . . . then you're a . . . you're a duke!'' she gasped.

''Arthur George Winthrop, Duke of Grengarden,'' he announced as he confiscated both brooches.

''Your . . . your grace,'' she stuttered and instinctively went to curtsy, an impossible notion since she was seated in a coach and did not have enough room to even stand up if she wanted to, let alone curtsy.

If the coach had fallen into a ditch, Kate could not have been more shaken. Or more disoriented and confused. Already reminded of her injury with a dull headache, her head began to pound unmercifully. As it was, the coach was traveling over a rough stretch of roadway, and she was being bounced about. She braced her feet on the floor of the coach and arched her back against the seat to keep her balance.

The coach creaked and squeaked too loudly to permit any conversation, but she had a sinking feeling in the pit of her stomach that this was only a temporary reprieve. The duke would not have suddenly appeared in her life unless he had come to wreak some sort of vengeance against her for besmirching the reputation of his late duchess by performing as the Ivory Duchess.

Had he already confronted Simon? What role did Philip play is this wretched scenario? Why had he agreed to bring the duke to her? What did the duke actually intend to do now that he found her?

The moment the coach quieted and rolled more smoothly, her body stiffened with dread. Her mouth went dry, and she gripped the seat so tightly her hands ached.

When the coach stopped, she looked out the window and saw they had arrived at the house Philip had rented for the summer.

She swallowed the lump in her throat and almost wished Philip had forced her to go back to Simon the day before yesterday. She would have found some way to endure returning to the stage as the Ivory Duchess, but she did not know how she would ever survive the next few hours. Undoubtedly, she would be held accountable for the role she had played in tarnishing the reputation of an innocent woman, but no one could ever hurt her as much as Philip had already done.

While the duke helped Kate out of the coach, Philip took the front steps two at a time. He had barely reached the porch when Nelda Spade opened the front door.

With her hands on her hips, she blocked his entry into the house. "Thought you left for good."

"I'm back."

She snorted and glanced around him. Her eyes snapped with indignation. "With that . . . that beastly animal in tow? And with guests? What's Kate doing here?"

"Important guests. We'll have tea in the parlor," he said firmly. "See if you can't have it ready in ten minutes." He kept walking toward her and repressed a grin when she stepped back to let him into the house.

"I'm not prepared to serve company. I'm busy closing up the house."

"That won't be necessary. In fact," he continued as she took another step backward, "I've changed my mind. Whatever rooms you've closed off, reopen. After you serve tea."

He let his words hang in the air, and she stormed off to the kitchen just as the duke escorted a pale and shaken Kate into the house. Philip tried to catch her gaze, but she kept her eyes lowered to the ground.

He was not sure how much the duke had been able to tell her so far. Judging by her appearance, Philip assumed the duke had already shown her both brooches and clenched his hands into fists to keep himself from reaching out to her; instead, he escorted his guests into the parlor.

The duke, who had hidden his real identity under the name William Pennington from all concerned until he had met with Philip in his apartments, sat down next to Kate on the settee. With no other seat available for himself, he sat down on the piano bench with his back to the instrument. Unprepared for the storm of emotions unleashed by the memories of the time he had spent with Kate sitting before the grand piano, he cursed himself for a total fool.

Again.

When she finally looked up at him, her eyes brimming with tears, his chest tightened. He wanted to demand to see Kate alone, but he was in no position to demand anything. Not from Kate and certainly not from the duke. Not yet.

"Must he . . . must he stay while we talk?"

She directed her question to the duke, but Philip could not steel himself against the pain of her rejection. If he had harbored any hope she might easily or quickly forgive him, they were dashed on craggy reefs of disappointment.

The elderly man steepled his hands on his lap. "Perhaps it might be best if you left us alone."

Philip rose stiffly. "Actually, I have several tasks to attend to." Tempted to argue his authority in his own house, he chose to use this opportunity to his own advantage.

Kate's face had lost what little color she had left, and Philip feared she might swoon. He took a step toward her, but Nelda chose that moment to arrive with the tea. Conversation immediately ceased, and the housekeeper wisely put the tea service on the side table and left the room.

When the duke leaned toward Kate and started to talk, Philip followed Nelda back to the kitchen and decided to start implementing his own plans. "I won't be needing your services for several days," he informed her.

She snorted at him. "Yesterday, you wanted me to close up the house. Ten minutes ago, you barged back in here with guests. Now you want me to—"

"Take a week off. Visit your sister. Do whatever you like, but I expect you and your husband to be gone in an hour."

She tilted her chin. "What about our wages? You failed to pay us two days ago, and you can't expect us to do without when—"

Her mouth dropped open when he took several bills from his wallet and laid them on the table. "There's a month's salary. Consider it a bonus for your inconvenience."

She scooped the money off the table so quickly he was amazed a woman of her girth could move that fast. "We'll be back next Friday."

Mumbling to herself as she made a beeline for the back door, she never even realized he followed her outside and proceeded directly to the stables to get his horse.

The duke may have directed today's events, but Philip had his own plans for tonight—plans with a surprise ending that no one, not even the Duke, could anticipate.

Or stop.

Chapter 28

⌒⌒

With her cheeks still wet with tears, Kate leaned against the back of the settee. She felt battered by the emotional whirlwind that had struck the moment she had seen Philip driving the coach and had continued unabated for the past half hour spent with the duke.

Now that Philip had left, she faced the consequences of her life as the Ivory Duchess totally alone.

Still seated beside her, the duke gently squeezed her hand. "You're shaking," he murmured.

She nodded, too distraught to offer an excuse or beg for his forgiveness for her role in tainting the reputation of his duchess.

"Are you afraid of me?"

She nodded again.

"Oh, my dearest Kate," he whispered. "How I've wronged you, too."

Startled, she looked at him and found his eyes as teary as her own.

He shook his head. "I never knew how unhappy you were. All those years." He stopped to clear his throat. "I owe you a tremendous apology and a debt I can never hope to repay."

Thoroughly confused, Kate could scarcely breathe. "I . . . I don't understand. I thought you came to . . . to punish me for what I've done as the Ivory Duchess."

His eyes widened. "Punish you? Merciful heavens, no! I came to thank you."

The room started to spin, and she closed her eyes for a moment. When she opened them, his face had taken on a pallor of guilt that only added to her confusion.

"Let me tell you about Elizabeth," he began. "We were married for ten years, but to our great heartbreak, we had no children. *No heir.*" His gaze grew distant. "Duty before honor or love," he whispered as he shook his head sadly. "I was raised to worship at the altar of duty and sacrifice. We both were. Elizabeth loved me—perhaps more than I deserved. She persuaded the king to let me set her aside and marry another. God help me, I did."

"You . . . you divorced her?"

He frowned. "The scandal was ugly. Unrelenting. I tried to warn her . . ."

His voice dropped so low Kate could scarcely hear him above the pounding of her heart. She waited for him to regain his composure and held his hand tightly, trying to give some warmth to his cold fingers.

"She went into hiding, but she promised to contact me if she was ever in need. In the meantime, I quickly remarried. James was born within a year, but my new wife, Eleanor, nearly died giving birth. She remained an invalid for the rest of her life. I devoted myself to her and to my son. She died seven years ago, and I've been searching for Elizabeth every day since. I never stopped loving her. My duchess. My Ivory Duchess."

Kate's throat constricted as his eyes filled with incredible pain for the years he had lost. Since she had unwittingly helped to keep alive the scandal associated with their divorce, she could not understand how her role in his search for his duchess merited anything less than his scorn, not his gratitude.

He looked at her and smiled as he took the genuine brooch out of his pocket to stare at it a few moments before he closed his fingers around it. "The first two years of my search turned up no trace of her. I was desperate enough to try anything. That's when I heard about Morrell who was just about ready to launch your career. He'd been renting a small estate from a friend of mine who overheard you practicing. Quite by mistake, I might add, but he was very impressed by your gift for the pianoforte. He said he was reminded of Elizabeth. She played beautifully, too, which gave me the idea of a new way to search for her."

"Was that in Avon?" she asked, trying to sort through the half-dozen isolated locations Simon had used during her training.

"A bit farther south. Out of concern for my son, I couldn't risk approaching Morrell as the Duke of Grengarden so I kept my real identity a secret. I used the name William Pennington and approached Morrell as a private investor. I was the one who created and orchestrated your entire career as the Ivory Duchess hoping the notoriety would lead me to Elizabeth." He opened his hand and looked at the cameo brooch. "It's her likeness, you know."

Kate shook her head, and she braced herself on the settee to keep from floating into a reality far too incredible to believe. The past five years of her life suddenly took on a whole different perspective—one that left her mind scrambling for more answers.

"I never knew how unhappy you were or how badly Morrell treated you. He assured me you were willing to cooperate, especially since the funds you earned would be more than enough to allow you ultimately to settle into a comfortable retirement." He withdrew his hand from her clasp, took an envelope out of his vest pocket, and laid it on her lap. "Please forgive me and allow me to make up for what Morrell and his wife have done to you."

She stared at the envelope. "My earnings?"

"And a bit more to help ease my conscience," he admitted. "I insisted that Morrell get you to agree to another concert tour. I simply couldn't give up hope that you'd help me just a little longer to find Elizabeth."

Kate swallowed hard, unsure if she could deny him if he asked her to go back to the stage. "Do you still want me to perform?"

This time his smile was full and radiant. "That won't be necessary," he said quickly. "Thanks to you, I've found my Elizabeth."

Relief swept through her body and left her weak and breathless. "You found her?"

"I have. She sent me a package containing her brooch along with a letter which miraculously survived a rather stormy crossing. The brooch arrived intact, as you can see, but the letter had been saturated and most of her words horribly blurred beyond legibility." He laughed softly. "It seemed rather cruel that after all this time, when she finally tried to contact me, I couldn't read most of what she wrote, and I had no idea where she was."

Kate gripped the arm of the settee. "But you said you found her."

"I know where to find her," he corrected. "The few words I could read mentioned you and Philip Massey. Since the ship sailed from Philadelphia, I came directly to the city where I found Morrell and did a little investigating on my own."

"As William Pennington?"

He nodded. "Fortunately, I happened to be with Morrell when Philip arrived."

Her heart sank. "Philip told you and Simon where to find me," she said in a wooden voice.

"Simon and Helen gave Philip quite a hard time of it, but he was a true warrior defending his own. He never wavered. Never faltered. He absolutely refused to tell us where to find you. Even when I offered to triple his fee."

"He didn't?" she gushed, her faith in Philip ultimately rewarded.

The duke chuckled. "Poor Morrell. Even Helen couldn't console him. Naturally, I had to withdraw my support for your next tour, and I made sure they both sailed on the next ship to Europe before I contacted Philip and convinced him to let me meet with you."

"What would you have done if he had accepted your first offer?" she asked.

The duke shrugged his shoulders. "I would have paid it, of course. My goal was to find you and tell you the truth. At any price."

A blush warmed her cheeks, and she was too overcome with emotion to know what to say.

"Your young man is not easily convinced or dissuaded," the duke added.

She lowered her gaze and stared at her lap. "No, he's not." In her hands, she clutched an envelope containing a bank draft representing her earnings for the past five years. In her mind, she stored the duke's tale of two star-crossed lovers, separated by social traditions that placed duty before love or sacred marriage vows.

In her heart, she treasured the man who had made it possible for her to finally learn the real truth behind her life as the Ivory Duchess: Philip.

Again, her hero.

Once more, her inspiration.

Always, her love.

A cynical man would have taken her back to Simon by force, if necessary, collected the fee, and walked away. A dreamer would have turned away from her and saved his heart for a woman more perfect.

Philip was both cynic and dreamer. A man of strong conscience. A careful man. A quiet man, yet courageous and loyal. He had protected her from Simon at great personal cost. He had freed her from the shame of her past by bringing the duke to see her. And in the end, he had proven himself a most uncommon hero for a most imperfect woman, and she loved him with all her heart.

She had judged Philip too quickly again today, but her love for him trembled and grew stronger than ever before. They had both been victims of circumstance and pawns of fate. Tossed together, they had both made mistakes that erected tremendous obstacles for them to overcome.

She thought about the duke and the still-mysterious Duchess of Grengarden who had lost irreplaceable years together. Were she and Philip destined to do the same? Would they be able to resolve their misunderstandings now . . . or ever?

Experience was a difficult, but worthy taskmaster. Escape from her life on stage had once seemed impossible, but learning to be patient and prudent, she had achieved her goal. Creating a new life for herself had also been hard and rife with costly errors in judgment, but she had learned important lessons in her difficult journey from the past to the present—lessons that would guide her past the most difficult obstacle of all: reclaiming Philip's affection.

"One obstacle at a time," she whispered.

"What did you say?"

Startled that the duke had heard her, she leaned forward on the settee. "Oh . . . just that you had so many obstacles to overcome to find your duchess," she murmured as she glanced at him sitting next to her.

"And I could never have done it without you, my dear. Or Philip."

The duke stood up and paced around the room, startling her back from her reverie. "Where do you suppose Philip is hiding himself? I'm very anxious to leave." He glanced out the window and frowned. "Now that we've reached an understanding, I really wanted to be on my way to see Elizabeth."

She rose, laid her envelope on the settee, and glanced out the window. "The coach is still here, and so is my road cart. Philip must be around here somewhere." She walked across the hall to Philip's workroom, found it empty, and met the duke at the door to the drawing room. "Let me talk to Mrs. Spade," Kate suggested. "She'll know where he is."

Hurrying to the kitchen, she was surprised the housekeeper was not there. Assuming Mrs. Spade had gone back to her cottage, Kate dismissed the impropriety of going to the private rooms upstairs. She used the servants' staircase to make her way to the second floor. She walked past a series of closed doors to the room at the end of the hall. With its door wide-open, she could see through the room to a balcony and the magnificent view of the river.

Certain that she had found his room, she slowed her steps. She entered the room, and her heart sank. The room was empty. More than empty, she decided with a closer look. Barren and devoid of any personal items, the room was in the process of being closed. A sheet covered a chaise lounge and chest of drawers, and a pile of cleaning rags and a bucket of stale water sat by the door.

Philip was gone, and apparently, he was not coming back.

Clinging to the barest thread of hope he had simply decided to settle back into his apartments in the city now that he had finished his assignment for Simon and the duke, she rejoined the duke downstairs in the drawing room. "He's not here," she said, her voice shaking as much as her belief that Philip wanted to reconcile the differences between them. Since the duke had left little to chance so far, she prayed he might ease the worry that tugged at her heart. "Do you have any idea where he might have gone?"

"Haven't a clue," he responded.

His answer dashed her hopes that Philip had confided his plans to the duke. "He's probably just gone for a ride," she suggested, knowing he could not leave for good without returning his mount, which belonged to the estate. Since she faced their possible reconciliation today as a daunting event, he no doubt harbored the same trepidation as she did and needed time away from the country seat to gather his thoughts.

If the duke would agree to take the coach himself and leave now, Philip and Kate would be able to have time alone when he returned. "If you're anxious to leave now, you could always take the coach," she prompted. "I'm sure Philip wouldn't mind."

He practically blanched. "My dear, I've never driven a coach in my life. Never had the desire or the need."

"Neither have I." She giggled as an idea popped into her head. "I can take you. In the road cart. It's a bit bumpy, and you'll get rather dusty, but if you're truly anxious to be on your way . . ."

His eyes began to twinkle. "You haven't even asked where I'd like to go."

"Well, I . . . I thought you'd want to go back to Philadelphia. I can take you to the ferry in Camden and still be back in time to—"

"To see Philip?"

She nodded and twisted her skirts with her hand.

He sighed. "I've waited all these years to find Elizabeth, I suppose a little longer shouldn't matter. Perhaps I should wait."

"I'd rather see Philip alone," she gushed, mustering her

resolve to see that the duke left now. "I can leave Philip a note telling him . . . asking him to wait for me to get back so we can talk. I'll take you to the ferry in the road cart."

He avoided her gaze. "Actually, I should tell you a bit more about my plans before we leave." He paused, lost in his own thoughts, before he continued. "Why don't you write that note to Philip after all? I can finish my story along the way."

Relieved and unabashedly curious to hear the rest of the duke's tale, she quickly secured paper and pen from the lady's writing desk and wrote a brief note asking Philip to wait for her here at the country seat. She placed it on the grand piano and put the envelope containing her bank draft in the lady's desk for safekeeping.

She led the duke outside to the road cart, stopped to get her gloves out of the coach where she had left them, and unhitched Precious from the coach ring. She checked the sky. From the position of the sun, she thought it to be around noon. She climbed into her seat in the road cart, hoping to be back by two o'clock.

"Don't worry. You'll be back before long," the duke said, apparently trying to ease her frown into a smile.

She had no sooner driven the road cart to the rear of the house when she encountered Nelda Spade and her husband aboard a wagon.

"Hope you locked the doors behind you," the housekeeper snapped. "We won't be back for a week. Mr. Massey already hightailed it out of here like he was riding the tail wind of a hurricane. Looks like you're the last to leave."

Chills raced up and down Kate's spine, and she yanked hard on the reins. "He's . . . he's gone?"

"And good riddance to him. Never met a man like him before and don't expect I will again. 'Close the house. Open the house. Close the house,' " she mimicked. "Man can't decide what to do from one minute to the next.''

Refusing to believe that Philip would leave without saying good-bye to her or without meeting his responsibility to the duke, Kate shook her head. ''He must be coming back, if only to return the horse.''

''I doubt it.''

Abner Spade rarely, if ever, spoke up in front of his wife, and Kate stared at him. Half the size of the woman he had married, he was equally dour. ''Went to the barn to get the wagon and saw him just before he left. Heard him mumbling something to himself about letting the duke fend for himself because Massey had his own plans.''

The duke put one of his arms around her shoulders when she began to tremble. ''Did Mr. Massey say what those plans might be?''

Abner shook his head. ''Didn't say. Didn't ask. The man barely acknowledged my presence.''

''Typical,'' his wife spewed. ''In the space of a few days, the man's turned into a bear. I'm glad he's gone.'' She nodded to her husband and they pulled away.

Gulping back tears, Kate could scarcely breathe. Philip was not coming back. Not for her. Not for the duke.

The older man hugged her close as she dissolved into tears. ''I'm so sorry,'' he whispered. ''So very sorry. I really thought you two might be able to work your way through your differences.''

So had she, but apparently Philip had no intention of ever seeing her again. When her tears were spent, she dried her cheeks with her gloved hands. She held them in front of her and sighed. As long as she had the gloves he had given to her, she would have something left to remind her how foolish she had been to think she and Philip would ever be together.

Other than her broken heart.

She took a deep breath. If there was no happy ending

for her and Philip, at least she could continue to play a role that would help to reunite the duke with his long-lost duchess. Kate had years to grieve for the mistakes she had made with Philip, and helping the duke now might keep her from dissolving into tears again.

She started to drive away, but he laid his hand on top of hers. "Do you want to go back and retrieve your note or lock the doors?"

She shook her head. She could never go back into that house. Not now. Maybe never. "I just want to leave," she whispered. "Let Philip worry about locking the doors."

"Then suppose I tell you the rest of my story while you drive."

Glad to have her mind occupied with happier thoughts, she smiled. "I must admit I'm rather curious to know more about your duchess and where she's waiting for you. I hope I'm not too presumptuous, your grace."

He grinned as though he had a secret he was bursting to tell. "I have a bit of another surprise for you, but first, you would be helping my cause if you simply addressed me as Mr. Winthrop."

Thoroughly caught off guard, she glanced sideways at him. "Mr. Winthrop?"

He chuckled, but when the road cart veered sharply to the right, he paled. "If I'm ever to see her again, you'd better keep your eyes on the road."

Startled, she quickly steered Precious away from the tempting foliage along the side of the roadway. "I'm sorry. You just shocked me. I thought—"

"I intend to ask Elizabeth to marry me again, but I have no intention of taking her back to England. The scandal would be twice as unbearable this time. She's suffered enough. We both have," he murmured. "I spoke to my son before I left. My affairs are quite in order, and he's more than capable of handling his responsibilities. If I'm to stay here, I won't have any need for my title. Arthur Winthrop will be sufficient.''

As he continued to speak about his plans for the life he hoped to make with Elizabeth, Kate kept her eyes on the road, but her mind reeled with absolute disbelief. The longer he spoke, the tighter her grip on the reins. The events of her life, especially the past two months, unraveled. Again.

By the time he finished, he had identified his duchess in a tale so impossible to believe, she needed to brace her feet against the floorboard until her toes ached to reassure herself she was awake and not dreaming.

''Are you sure? There's no possibility you've made a mistake?''

''Certainly not,'' he huffed.

Too numb to think or feel, she continued to drive the road cart, and when they neared the cottage grounds, she began to tremble. With her hands shaking, she took another deep breath and slowed the road cart to take a quick glance down the walking path that led to the front door of the cottage.

When he placed his hand atop hers, she sighed and brought Precious to a halt.

The road cart creaked as the duke stepped to the ground, but he never looked back. He brushed the dust from his waistcoat and strode straight to the front door of the cottage—a sanctuary that had proved to be a safe haven to another young woman many years ago, Elizabeth, the Duchess of Grengarden, and her devoted sister, Rosamunde.

The melody of *Für Elise* began to play in Kate's mind, and she now understood why that selection had been used to open her performances. ''For Elizabeth.'' She murmured the English translation and bowed her head, letting the notes to the selection that began every one of her performances ease the pain in her heart.

Chapter 29

B efore the duke was halfway down the front path to the cottage, Kate urged Precious into a trot and drove away. Blinded by her tears, she could not let her curiosity about whether Dolly or Maggie was Elizabeth, the Duchess of Grengarden, intrude on a reunion that should be very private. She tried not to let the sisters' own deception dampen her warm affection for them. They had taken her into their home, more of a sanctuary than Kate could ever have imagined, and she could only feel tremendous grief for having been the source of their concern when she had arrived on their doorstep.

Like the day she had wandered through the woods and gotten lost, she drove anywhere and everywhere and gave Precious her own head. Kate had no direction. No anchor for her thoughts other than total and irrevocable confusion. In less than twenty-four hours, her life had been turned upside down and inside out until she was so disconcerted she could scarcely separate reality from fantasy or truth from mistruth.

Had everyone she had met lied about their identities in some way or another?

Arthur Winthrop, the Duke of Grengarden, was also Wil-

liam Pennington, the man who had hired Simon and Helen
to carry out a plan to find the only woman the duke had
ever loved when all his previous attempts had ended in
failure.

Simon and Helen were not the master manipulators Kate
had thought them to be, although they had tailored the
duke's plans to suit their own greed. She could only be
consoled that they were on their way to Europe with no
idea how they themselves had been used.

Miss Dolly and Miss Maggie, by all appearances two
very ordinary women of middling means, had been born to
wealth and position in England. Elizabeth, Duchess of
Grengarden, had been forced into hiding by a devastating
scandal she endured for the sake of her beloved. Her sister,
Lady Rosamunde of Sheldonshire, in mourning for her betrothed who had been killed in India, had her own reputation tainted by her sister's scandal and had fled with her
sister.

Wearied by trying to sort through her thoughts and
heated by the harsh sun, she pulled to the shaded side of
the roadway. She set the brake and let Precious nibble at
the foliage to her heart's content. After removing her bonnet and gloves, Kate freshened her damp hair with shaking
fingers and wiped the tears from her face as a whole host
of questions began to pummel their way to the surface of
her confusion.

Why had Dolly written to the Ivory Duchess instead of
trying to contact the duke? Had Dolly been trying to see
the performer to ask her to stop for fear the scandal the
Ivory Duchess' tours evoked might reopen the scandal that
had driven her from England and the man she loved? Or
was Kate wrong? Was Dolly only trying to protect her sister, the real duchess?

Too many questions.

Too few answers.

Kate's head began to spin. Now that the duke had found his duchess, Dolly and Maggie would have no need for Kate. She would have to return later for her belongings before she left to make a new life for herself, and she hoped they would be able to talk together before she left.

She shook her head and closed her swollen eyes to rest them. She had no right to judge anyone harshly. She had had more aliases than any of them. Baxter was not even her real name since her mother had had no idea which man had fathered the child she carried. She had simply borrowed the name from an itinerant merchant shortly before Kate was born, and her mother drew her last breath. The Ivory Duchess was the name she had merely borrowed herself and truly belonged to the courageous woman who had stepped willingly into a scandalous divorce to allow her beloved to marry someone who could give him an heir.

Danaher, Kate had hoped, would be a new name that would carry her into a new life that had exploded into a replica of the past with more lies, more deception, and more pain.

Content to think of herself as simply Kate, she opened her eyes and realized she was not far from the country seat.

Philip. He was a man who also had more than one identity. He was a complex man shaped by sharp contradictions. She pulled her thoughts away from memories that evoked so much pain her heart surely ached. He had made his break with her quickly and cleanly, and it was patently obvious he had no place for her in his life.

It was time to stop bemoaning the past or dissecting the present. The future was hers to control, and the duke had given her the means to start over.

The bank draft!

She had left it at the country seat. Anxious to bring an end to the most painful day of her new life, she put on her gloves, clicked the reins, and started to drive toward the estate.

Sniffling back tears, she knew she had only one friend left who would go with her to her new life: her pianoforte.

Wherever she settled, whatever she chose to do with the rest of her life, the pianoforte would always be there waiting to soothe her troubles as it had done so many times in the past. She hoped the pianoforte would be able to heal the greatest hurt of all—a broken heart.

Philip knew something was wrong the minute he tore through the back door to the country seat. It was too quiet. Eerily still.

He strode toward the drawing room, hoping to catch the sound of a voice. A cry. Anything that would reassure him that Kate and the duke were still discussing the events that had led to the most amazing twenty-four hours of his life.

His heart pounding after a long ride to make arrangements for the surprise he planned, he slowed his pace and entered the drawing room with his worst fears confirmed the moment he glanced around the room.

Kate was gone.

So was the duke, which made no sense at all once Philip took a quick glance through the window. The coach he had rented for the duke was still out front, but the road cart was gone.

"Kate." His voice cracked as he whispered her name. He clenched his hands into fists, furious that the duke had broken his promise and allowed her to leave before Philip got back.

Since the duke had also disappeared, Philip could reach only one conclusion: Kate had listened to what the duke had to say and decided to go back to the cottage. She did not want to see Philip or give him a chance to beg for her forgiveness.

They were probably with Dolly and Maggie celebrating the duke and duchess' reunion, leaving Philip alone to ponder the depths of his loss and suffer the consequences because he had betrayed Kate's trust and had not loved her enough to set her free after she had told him the truth about her past.

He swallowed hard and turned away from the window. Out of the corner of his eye, he spied the note lying atop the grand piano. Another damn note? She could not even wait for him to come back and tell him to his face that he had destroyed the love she had pledged to him?

He walked over to the grand piano. His hands trembling, he reached out and picked up the note. She had scrawled his name on the outside: Mr. Massey.

What tiny spark of hope he still had that she might accept his apologies instantly sputtered and died. She had gone right back to the stiff formality that she had insisted upon the very first day she had come to begin his instruction on the pianoforte.

He trailed the back of his hand along the onyx and mother-of-pearl keys and closed his eyes. He saw her again in his mind's eye just as she had looked that day. Flustered and nervous, she had nearly leaped out of her skin when he touched her hand and took the valise from her. The sparkling innocence and instant attraction that had filled her eyes had not been feigned. They were real—so real his chest tightened with the pain of his loss.

She had given him so many opportunities to question what Morrell had told him about the Ivory Duchess. Her gentleness with Maggie, her dedication to her students on the circuit, her open admiration for him when he had seen nothing but pity or rejection in the eyes of every other woman who learned of his past. She had placed herself as a buffer between him and a housekeeper who was more cruel than she was unsympathetic.

My hero.

Her words still echoed in his mind, and he still trembled when he heard them. His lips tingled with the memory of the kisses they had shared, and his arms ached to hold her again.

He stared at the note in his hands, unwilling to read her parting words—words that would be etched into his memory along with every other sound and sight, feeling and taste they had every shared.

He had nothing to console him but his memories. Even repayment of his final debt of honor was now tainted, and the prospect of facing a future without her swept through his disappointment and built into anger.

He was not going to let her go.

Not this way.

Not without a fight.

Leaving a note to avoid confronting him was so infuriatingly typical, he wondered why she did not do the same thing when she wanted to tell him about her past. He crumpled the note and tossed it across the room. It was his own fault she had chosen to leave him a note instead of waiting to see him.

He had not exactly been receptive the one and only time she did try to talk to him, and he could not blame her for taking the easier way out.

"Never again," he said out loud as he made up his mind to ride to the cottage and demand to see her. This time when they talked, he would listen and so would she.

He was halfway to the barn before he realized his horse was still lathered from a mad ride to get back to see Kate. He paused and turned toward the river. Rather than pace in the barn while the horse got her wind, his time would be better spent in quiet contemplation as he tried to plan a way to win her back.

He had to go back to the house again anyway to retrieve

Kate's note before Nelda Spade returned, found it, and used it to fuel another piece of malicious gossip. He scowled. He also had to wait for his surprise to arrive, a humbling prospect since there had been an unexpected change in plans. He trudged back to the house. When he walked into the drawing room, he glanced at the grand piano again. The instrument had inspired his first meeting with Kate. He closed his eyes and his breathing grew shallow.

Once before, the fates had given him a rare gift and held still the hands of time so that two very lonely, wounded souls could meet and heal, if only for an instant. He should have used that gift wisely; instead, he had discarded it. He doubted if the fates would ever consider an even greater gift and turn back the hands of time, erase the lies and deceptions, harsh words and foolish actions.

His chest constricted with pain. Kate had been the greatest gift of all—one that truly came along only once in a man's lifetime and would give him the opportunity to become the man he wanted to be.

He did not allow the sound of wheels crunching on the gravel at the front of the house to dispel his impossible dream that the fates were as forgiving of a fool as they were fickle. He walked to the front door and opened it, pretending he did not have to send away the wagon full of people who were several hours early, but were destined to be turned away disappointed.

When he stepped out onto the porch, he glanced at the drive and blinked his eyes. Unable to slow the hammering of his heart, he did not question the bewildering guiles of fate.

Chapter 30

〰〰

"Philip."

Kate whispered his name as she reached out and clutched the side of the road cart to keep her balance. He was standing on the shadowed porch right outside the front door, just like the first day they had met. Too stunned to say another word, she held perfectly still for fear he was only an illusion created by her spirit's deepest yearnings. Her heart pounded in her chest. Tears welled in her eyes, and she began to tremble as disbelief transformed itself into joy that turned her dreams into a fantasy-come-true.

He gazed at her, hesitated only briefly, and crossed the porch to descend the steps. Bright sunlight danced in shimmering highlights in his earth brown hair, and the longing in his dark eyes set her heartbeat into a familiar, erratic rhythm that only Philip could inspire. He stopped at the bottom of the steps, and she knew that he was no illusion.

He was here. He was real. And he stole her breath away with his very presence.

She blinked away the tears of regret that misted her vision and mirrored the emotion that shimmered in the depths of the dark eyes gazing back at her. With all the layers of deception that had marked their time together, it was not surprising they had caused one another tremendous pain and anguish.

But they had also found love, and she wished with all her heart she and Philip could redeem the love that had miraculously blossomed between them. Was it too late or too foolish to believe that love could overcome the greatest obstacles and the deepest hurts?

She knew that time, once spent, continued to flow forward, never backward, and neither one of them could change what had happened in the past few months. Time, however, was not unforgiving or rigidly cast. For the strong of heart, each day offered new opportunities, not to change the past, but to direct the future.

"Miss Danaher?"

His voice was both gentle and strong, and his question triggered the memory of the day they had met and without logic, rhyme, or reason, she felt herself being literally swept back in time. As though truly reliving the past and being given a blessed opportunity to change it, she spoke before the magic of the moment slipped away. "Mr . . . Mr. Massey?"

He walked toward her, and she instinctively reached out with one hand to grip the valise she had packed for the circuit. His smile was more tentative than the one he had flashed that first day, but her heart still skipped a beat. Had he felt it, too? That mystical aura that surrounded them?

"And you're Miss Danaher, I presume. I've been expecting you . . . for my lesson." He laid his hand on top of hers to take the valise, replaying the moment he had tried to help her. Her arm dimpled with gooseflesh, and her heart filled with hope. "Let me help you inside," he whispered, his eyes turning even darker with emotions that were as poignant as her own.

She gazed down at his beautifully sculpted hand. She had once thought his hands worthy of a concert pianist, but all she could remember now was how his hands felt when he cradled her face or held her in his arms.

She turned her hand upside down and entwined her fingers with his as though she could keep them both back in time for just a little longer. "My name is Kate," she murmured. "Just Kate." She took a deep breath and tried not to choke on the tears that constricted her throat and ran down her face.

The rest of her words stumbled out in a cracking voice. "I don't want to mislead you. Danaher is not my real name. Neither is Baxter. I've spent the past five years on stage as the Ivory Duchess, but I've . . . I've run away. I took my brooch with me even though it doesn't belong to me because . . . because I want to live a more respectable life as a teacher of the pianoforte. If . . . if you want to hire someone else, I'll . . . I'll understand. I just don't want to lie anymore, especially to you. Not ever to you."

His eyes filled with a longing that caressed her very soul, and he tightened his grip on her hand. "My name is Philip. Philip Massey. I'm a jeweler by trade and a fool by my own design. I lead a double life because I made a terrible mistake seven years ago and got involved in a land scheme that failed. As Omega, I've accepted an assignment to find the brooch you stole and return you to your agent because I need the funds to repay one last person who trusted me." He paused to take a deep breath. "I hired you under false pretenses because I thought . . ."

His voice faded away, and her heart began to pound so hard and so fast she thought it would explode. Taking advantage of the momentary silence, she dared to continue as she might have done that first day. "Simon Morrell lied to you about who and what I am. If you would be willing to listen to me, I can tell you the truth. If you could help me to return the brooch without revealing where I am . . ." She choked back more tears. "Please. I don't ever want to go back."

He let go of her hand, but in the next heartbeat, he had come around the road cart and stood before her. "I believe you," he whispered. "Please don't be afraid. I'll just have to find another way to repay my debt. I'll return the brooch for you, and you won't ever have to go back."

His gaze burned brighter and deeper than she had ever seen it before. She cradled his cheek with her hand, and he kissed her palm, sending impossibly outrageous sensations racing through her entire body. "Do you think it could have been different if we had been honest with one another from the very beginning?" she asked as he continued to rain kisses across the back of her hand.

He stopped and paused ever so briefly before he raised his gaze to meet hers. "No. I don't think so. I have to admit I never would have believed you."

She sighed. "I never would have had the courage to tell you the truth."

They had reached an impasse, and the silence that curtained each of their thoughts from the other was thick with tension that tugged at her heartstrings. If she had the courage to see opportunity in the depths of her pain, she might hear a new melody—a quick-tempoed, whimsical caprice that would change the sonata of her life into a concerto she could compose not with her talent, but with her love for this man.

She moistened her lips, unwilling to let go of her dream that they would somehow find a way to forgive one another. "I'm sorry. For not trusting you, even today, when . . ."

He reached out and cradled her face with both his hands. Sorrow churned in his eyes. "Facing what happened between us will never be easy," he murmured. "But we can come to terms with our mistakes and learn from them. We can't really change the past, but the future . . ." He paused and caressed her with his gaze. "I can't erase the harsh words I've said or the things I've done, but I want you to know that I'll regret them for the rest of my life. Please, Kate. I want you to give me another chance. Give *us* another chance."

She put her fist to her mouth, too overcome to do more than cry as another avalanche of tears poured straight from her heart to stream silently down her cheeks.

"Let me spend the rest of my life showing you how much I treasure you," he pleaded. "I love you. I need you. Take as long as you need to make up your mind. I'll wait for you. I'll come to you wherever you go and do whatever it takes to convince you that I love you more than life itself. Can you give me some hope that one day you'll be able to forgive me?"

She trembled, unable to do more than nod her head. In the next heartbeat, he had pulled her into his arms and pressed her against his chest. She buried her face in the column of his throat and clung to him. He held her tight, crooning words of love that soothed her. She felt his heart beating as hard and as fast as her own, and she let his strength and his resolve wrap around her trembling body. Once her tears were spent and her fears washed away, she wiped her cheeks and gazed up at him.

"I still can't believe you actually came back," he whispered. "I thought you had left for good."

She attempted to smile. "Didn't you get my note? I left it for you on the piano."

He shook his head. "I couldn't make myself read it because I couldn't bear the thought you weren't coming back, let alone see it written by your hand."

She locked her hands behind his neck and gazed into his eyes. "Do you mean it? Do you really think we can start over?"

He smiled and kissed the tip of her nose. "I love you,

Kate. Just tell me when you're ready to start over—''

"Now," she whispered, nearly dazed by the powerful emotions that coursed through her body. "I love you, Philip. I always will."

His grin was wolfish, his eyes full of devilment. He kissed her hard and then again. Tingling from head to toe and back again, she was giddy with joy. "Mr. Massey! How very improperly you're behaving!" she teased, hoping her cheeks were not flaming as red as they felt.

"You have no idea how very improper I intend to be, Miss . . . Miss . . . ''

"Kate. Just call me Kate." She squealed as he picked her up, carried her into the house, and strode up the stairs to his room. He set her down on her feet, shoved the bucket and pile of rags into the hall, and closed the door.

He turned to face her, but his expression had sobered. "We've both made mistakes. We've both learned lessons the hard way. We almost lost each other. We can't let that happen again."

She nodded, glanced nervously at the bed, and smiled. "I never . . . I mean . . . I suppose I'll need a few lessons before . . .''

He flashed a smile that would have outshined the brightest star and closed the distance between them before she could draw her next breath. "Lesson number one," he growled as he stole a quick kiss and pulled her into his arms, "never leave this man a note." He nibbled at her lower lip with the edge of his teeth. "I detest notes."

"Agreed," she moaned as he slipped his hand up along her spine and teased the side of her breasts with the pads of his thumbs.

When she wrapped her arms around his neck, he lifted them away long enough to unpin her hair and run his fingers along the edge of her bruise.

She closed her eyes and leaned toward him, but he held

her away from him. When her eyes snapped open and she tried to voice her protest, he silenced her with another kiss. "More lessons," he teased and slowly peeled off each of her gloves and kissed every square inch of flesh on her arms till they were pulsing. "Never wear your gloves when you kiss a man or—"

She slid her hand inside his shirt and caressed his chest and felt another wave of delicious sensations as her fingers brushed against the mat of curls beneath them. "Hmm. Definitely an advantage."

He groaned and pulled her against him. Hard. "No more lessons. You're far too apt a pupil," he confessed as he devoured her lips in a kiss that left her trembling.

Philip gazed down at the glorious woman who stood before him and knew that the ghosts of the past had already slipped away forever, but not before each had left behind an irreplaceable gift. Kate Baxter, the orphaned, bastard child, had grown up and bequeathed her innocence. The Ivory Duchess had removed her veils and taken her final bow before donating her talent. Kathryn Danaher, the prim and proper pianoforte teacher, had probably blushed before skittering away, but not before leaving behind twin gifts of trust and faith.

His heart bursting with love, Philip at long last held her fast—this very special woman simply called Kate.

"Kate," he groaned. More beautiful in spirit than he had ever imagined her to be, he paused, unwilling to taint this amazing woman with anything from his own past.

He exiled the jaded Omega away, far away, but kept some of his realism. Older and wiser, Philip cut the chains that had bound him to his past, but kept wisdom born in experience to guide him in the years ahead. To the dreamer in his heart, he made a vow to love without reservation, without fear, and with total commitment before carrying her to the bed and laying her beside him.

No more teasing words were spoken, or regrets given. With two hearts beating as one, they celebrated their commitment to one another by sharing the gift of physical pleasure. Each kiss they shared was poignant and new. Each caress an adventure in mutual pleasure. Each touch, healing and sensitive, and each cry of delight a rhapsody of love that belonged only to them. A spiritual baptism blessed their physical union, cleansed away the stains of the past, and promised a lifetime of mutual devotion.

Kate stirred beneath the covers, but dared not open her eyes for fear she would discover she had only been dreaming. She snuggled closer to Philip, and he pressed a kiss to the tip of her nose.

"Sleepy? Or waking up for more?"

She blushed, and as the heat traveled over her body, she knew he had left no pore of her flesh unattended during their lovemaking. She peeked one eye open, saw the clothing that littered the floor, and slammed her eye shut. "I'm thinking," she mumbled as he slid his hand around her waist.

"Mmmmm . . . about this?" he moaned as he nibbled on her earlobe.

"No." She giggled and tilted her head back to look at him. "About you. About me. About . . ."

She paused, listened hard, and froze in place at the unmistakable sound of a wagon drawing up along the front drive. She swallowed her surprise and looked at him frantically. "Aren't Nelda and her husband supposed to be away for a week? Were you expecting someone?"

His eyes widened with alarm before he dissolved into a deep chuckle. "I forgot."

"You *forgot?*" She scrambled out of bed and started to get dressed. "You . . . you invited someone and we . . . I mean, I . . ."

She fumbled with the ribbons on her chemise, but he reached out, caught her hands, and pulled her back into bed. "Don't worry. I'll handle everything," he said calmly as he tucked the covers around her shoulders. "Just don't take too much time getting dressed."

He kissed her next question into oblivion and was practically dressed himself by the time she floated back to earth. He straightened his cravat, sat down on the bed, and took her hand. "Before I go downstairs, I suppose I should ask you something."

She nodded and glanced nervously at the double windows. He tilted her face around and gazed at her. "For a woman whose had more names in the space of twenty-odd years—"

"Twenty-one," she said absently as she put her hand to his lips. She was surprised by how soft his lips were now when she touched them when only minutes ago . . .

When he frowned, she dropped her hand.

"I thought perhaps you might agree to one name you can keep for a while. For the sake of introductions. I rather like the sound of Kate Massey. Do you?"

Her eyes widened. "You're asking me to—"

"Marry me, Kate. Right now, or . . ." His eyes started to twinkle. "I can always ask Reverand Mullan to come back another time, but Patti and Susan will be sorely disappointed."

"You invited the minister? And his daughters? They're here? Now? How did you ever . . . How could you be sure?"

He grinned. "I wasn't. Just determined. And hopeful. While you were talking with the duke, I went to see Reverend Mullan and convinced him to make an exception and marry us tonight. I asked Mrs. Spencer and her husband, too. I'm sure she wouldn't mind helping the blushing bride to get dressed."

She pulled the covers over her head.

"Aren't you going to ask about Miss Dolly and Miss Maggie?"

She tossed the covers back. "You couldn't have invited them. Didn't the duke tell you—"

"He's coming, too," he quipped as he got to the door. "Wouldn't be surprised if he's getting married today. Maybe we'll just make it a double wedding."

She scrambled out of bed and tried to block him from opening the door. "Did he tell you which one of the sisters is his duchess?"

He nodded. "Haven't you figured it out?"

"It's Miss Dolly, isn't it?"

He grinned again.

"It's Miss Maggie?"

There was another knock at the door. When she turned to the side, he slipped past her. "Why don't you get dressed and come downstairs to see for yourself?"

"Philip Massey, you get back here right now," she whispered as loudly as she dared as he strode down the hall. "I haven't said yes!"

He paused midstride, turned around, and swept her into his arms before she could take her next breath. "Will you please marry me, Kate? Will you?"

She smiled through her tears. "Yes, I'll marry you."

He grinned again, pressed a quick kiss to her forehead, and set her back before he disappeared down the hall.

Speechless, she turned back into the room and got dressed as fast as she could. There was only one reason to hurry, and her heart pounded with the very thought she was only minutes away from becoming Mrs. Philip Massey.

She fixed her hair and replaced a few pins she found on the floor and met Mrs. Spencer at the top of the stairs.

"My dear! I thought Mr. Massey said you might need some help, but I can see you're quite ready. Terribly romantic man, isn't he," she droned as Kate preceded her downstairs where Philip was waiting for her.

He escorted her into the drawing room where the rest of the guests had gathered. Her heart racing, she embraced Miss Dolly and Miss Maggie and the duke who stood between them, silencing their worried expressions with a smile and a whispered, "Later."

Unwilling to wait a moment longer to become Philip's wife and take her new name, she stood with him in front of the minister. The Mullan twins, their eyes glazed with thoughts of romance that weddings typically evoked, stood to the side. Their father, with Mr. and Mrs. Spencer standing ready to act as witnesses, nodded, and Kate glanced up at the man by her side as soft music began to fill the room.

Philip leaned down and whispered the name of the duchess into her ear. She smiled but saved her most dazzling smile for when the minister pronounced Philip and Kate man and wife.

Philip turned her to face him. When he kissed her, she closed her eyes, but not before she caught a glimpse of the couple who had stepped forward to be married next.

"I love you, Mrs. Massey," he whispered as he tightened his arm around her waist.

The sound of her new name brought tears to her eyes. She gazed up at him and knew that she would carry his name with joy and with pride for the rest of her life—a life filled with truth, honor, and most of all, love. "You are the light of my life," she whispered back, knowing that all of her dreams had finally come true. "Only you, Philip. Forever you."

When he kissed her again, she heard the Mullan girls stifle a giggle as the next wedding ceremony began and another couple renewed their pledge to love one another as husband and wife. The duke's voice was low and firm, but his duchess spoke just above a whisper.

"I, Elizabeth Magnolia, pledge to thee, Arthur George . . ."

Kate held Philip's hand and watched with amazement as a beaming Maggie exchanged vows with her beloved duke. At that moment, Kate knew precisely where Maggie had gone each time she had suffered one of her spells. She had traveled back in time to be with the man who had claimed her heart all these years.

With a deep sigh of contentment, Kate melted into her husband's embrace, and understood, at long last, that she would always be loved and find haven in the sweetest sanctuary of all—love that was trusting and kind, selfless and forgiving.

With Philip.

Her hero. Her inspiration. Her love.

For years John Logan had searched for the infant daughter his wife had taken from him. The trail leads to Autumn Welles, an artist who paints tinware for a living and who is posing as the mother of his child. John knows that Autumn's world is built on the shifting sands of deceit and he plans to use all means necessary to reclaim his child.

Luring her into a tangled web, John leads them across three states, from Connecticut to Ohio, bound to each other by a marriage that is supposed to be a charade. But as the awakening fires begin to touch their souls, they find in each other a love born in secrets and deception, and a love that may not survive the changing seasons of their hearts.

The Fire in ❦ Autumn ❦

Delia Parr

THE FIRE IN AUTUMN
Delia Parr
_____ 95690-8 $5.50 U.S./$6.50 CAN.